A PASSION TOO LONG DENIED

John reached up and caught her hand. Sarah could feel the heat zip up her arm. When he turned her hand over and kissed her palm, she thought she might have forgotten how to breathe.

"I don't want you to get hurt, Sarah."

She nodded, her head feeling heavy on her neck.

John kissed her wrist and her arm jerked in response. A smile drifted across his lips. He moved his mouth up her arm, and when he licked the soft spot at her elbow, she felt the answering tug deep inside.

"This is crazy," he murmured, looking up at her.

"Yes," she whispered.

"Just once," he said.

"Just once what?"

He rose up, pulled her close, and wrapped her arms around his neck. "Just once this." He bent his head and kissed her . . .

STAY WITH ME

BEVERLY LONG

BERKLEY SENSATION, NEW YORK

THE BERKLEY PUBLISHING GROUP
Published by the Penguin Group
Penguin Group (USA) Inc.
375 Hudson Street, New York, New York 10014, USA
Penguin Group (Canada), 10 Alcorn Avenue, Toronto, Ontario M4V 3B2, Canada
(a division of Pearson Penguin Canada Inc.)
Penguin Books Ltd., 80 Strand, London WC2R 0RL, England
Penguin Group Ireland, 25 St. Stephen's Green, Dublin 2, Ireland (a division of Penguin Books Ltd.)
Penguin Group (Australia), 250 Camberwell Road, Camberwell, Victoria 3124, Australia
(a division of Pearson Australia Group Pty. Ltd.)
Penguin Books India Pvt. Ltd., 11 Community Centre, Panchsheel Park, New Delhi—110 017, India
Penguin Group (NZ), Cnr. Airborne and Rosedale Roads, Albany, Auckland 1310, New Zealand
(a division of Pearson New Zealand Ltd.)
Penguin Books (South Africa) (Pty.) Ltd., 24 Sturdee Avenue, Rosebank, Johannesburg 2196, South
Africa

Penguin Books Ltd., Registered Offices: 80 Strand, London WC2R 0RL, England

This is a work of fiction. Names, characters, places, and incidents either are the product of the author's imagination or are used fictitiously, and any resemblance to actual persons, living or dead, business establishments, events, or locales is entirely coincidental.

STAY WITH ME

A Berkley Sensation Book / published by arrangement with the author

PRINTING HISTORY
Berkley Sensation edition / January 2005

Copyright © 2005 by Beverly Long.
Cover art by Franco Accornero.
Cover design by George Long.
Hand lettering by Ron Zinn.
Interior text design by Kristin del Rosario.

ISBN: 0-425-20062-0

BERKLEY® SENSATION
Berkley Sensation Books are published by The Berkley Publishing Group,
a division of Penguin Group (USA) Inc.,
375 Hudson Street, New York, New York 10014.
BERKLEY SENSATION and the "B" design
are trademarks belonging to Penguin Group (USA) Inc.

PRINTED IN THE UNITED STATES OF AMERICA

10 9 8 7 6 5 4 3 2 1

For Kate and Brynn—
may your own dreams come true someday

ONE

California, Present Day

"YOU can't just quit."

Sarah Jane Tremont smiled at Melody, the woman who had been both her friend and her coworker for the last six years. She walked across the small office and grabbed her diplomas and professional license off the wall. "Actually, I can," Sarah said, dropping the frames into the cardboard box, not caring when they scraped together.

With more care, she removed the remaining frame. She'd picked up the old black-and-white photo last year while walking through an antiques mall. Just a simple nine-by-seven print, it had stopped her in her tracks. It was a picture of a woman sitting on a log, facing a campfire. Her back was to the camera, her long skirt touching the ground, her hair ribbons dancing in the wind. The photographer had captured the sun just as it slipped behind the mountains in the distance.

What had captured Sarah's attention had been the man.

He stood off to the woman's side, just a foot or so back. He had one leg propped on a tree stump and his lanky frame was bent over as he rested an elbow on his thigh. He watched the woman as she watched the fire.

The photographer had chosen an angle that offered just a hint of the man's profile, just a peek at a strong chin. He wore a cowboy hat and a long coat. Sarah reached out and traced the man, letting her finger run down the length of his body. A tingle started in the tip of her finger and traveled across her hand, causing the hair on her arm to rise.

She yanked her hand back and rubbed her still-tingling fingers together. They felt almost hot. She raised her hand toward her face and sniffed her fingers. She could smell the campfire, the burning evergreens.

"What the heck are you doing?" Melody asked.

Dreaming. "Nothing," Sarah denied. Before she lost her nerve, she reached for the picture, careful to touch just the frame. She lifted it off the wall and gently laid it on top of the rest of her things.

She pulled the small nails out of their holes and dropped them into the garbage. "Who knows?" Sarah said, waving a hand toward the faded wall. "Maybe this will be a good excuse for them to paint the office."

"I don't care about paint," Melody said, her eyes filling with tears. "I care about you. I don't understand why you have to leave."

That was easy. "Because I can't stay," she said. She stood next to the door, her half-full box propped on her hip, and took one last look around the small, windowless office. For the next months, as long as it took, she'd do what she could for the Lopez family. When that was over, she'd didn't have a clue what she'd do. She only knew that she couldn't come back here.

These kids and their families deserved better—certainly more—but she had nothing else to give. She was empty.

Melody brushed a tear off her cheek with an impatient swipe. "For God's sake, you're a social worker, Sarah, not a miracle worker."

That was too bad, because Rosa Lopez and her sweet eight-year-old son had needed a miracle.

"I'll call you," Sarah said as she wrapped one arm around her friend's shoulder and pulled her close. "Maybe not right away. But I will."

When Sarah left the four-story brick school, she heard the click of the metal security door as it closed behind her. Without looking back, she walked across the deserted cement lot, stepping over the wide cracks. Two basketball hoops, looking forlorn with their torn netting and scratched poles, swayed in the brisk spring wind. A slide, more rust than metal, stood off to one end.

During the day, kids played in the front and staff parked in the back two rows, separated from the busy street by a wire fence that did little to protect the children from the local drug dealers but caught every piece of garbage that blew around the gray streets.

When she got to her car, she threw her box and purse in the trunk. As she eased her six-year-old Toyota into traffic and headed west, she saw Mr. Ramirez flip the sign on his front door. During the day, he sold gas and magazines to the teachers and candy and soda to the children. At night, he pulled the grates over his windows and got, as the saying went, the hell out of Dodge.

Except this wasn't Dodge. It was Salt Flats, the poorest suburb of Los Angeles. Sixty percent of the population earned under what the government defined as the poverty level. In actuality, almost everybody in Salt Flats lived in poverty. If it weren't for the drug dealers and the hookers, there would have been no real commerce.

Twenty-five minutes later, Sarah took her exit, just like every other night, but at the last minute, she turned left, heading for the ocean. There was no need to go home, to her tiny apartment with its white walls and beige carpet. There were no files to read, no case reports to dictate, or telephone calls to return.

Well, that was mostly true. An hour ago the harried school secretary had jammed a note in her hand with a name and a number she didn't recognize. Sarah had slipped it in her pocket. She supposed the least she could do was call from the beach and let this person know that she wasn't going to be able to help.

She was done helping.

She needed time to breathe, to think, to find her center again. She'd sit in the sun, jog in the park, maybe even take up the piano again. She'd missed the music, the sense of peace playing gave her.

When she got to the beach, she pulled into the empty parking lot, grateful that it was really too cool to be there. She didn't feel like sharing space with anybody else tonight. Shifting in her seat, she kicked off her shoes, then reached under her long silk skirt to yank off her pantyhose. It had felt odd to have a dress on at work. Her standard uniform was slacks and a blouse, something that could survive milk carton missiles in the cafeteria, gum on chairs, and vomit from nervous kids.

She'd dressed up for the potluck, the going-away party that Melody had insisted upon. The symbolism of the event hadn't been lost on her. She'd dressed the way she might for her own funeral, and the well-wishers had milled around, staring at her, talking in low tones, not really sure what to say. What *was* the right thing to say to someone who was giving up?

All she'd ever wanted was to make a difference. But it was too late for that. She wasn't going to get her wish.

Sarah opened her car door and, at the last minute, slipped out of her conservative suit jacket. She'd freeze in her sleeveless blouse but she wanted to feel the harsh spray of the cold water on her skin. She grabbed her cell phone and put it and her keys in her pocket.

Sarah loved the beach, especially at night when the tide rolled in, each wave more aggressive than the last, leaving jumbles of seaweed and all kinds of other treasures in its swift retreat. She could spend hours looking across the water, searching for the exact point where the dark blue sea met the purple sky, and the two became one, a perfect welcome mat for the moon.

Tonight's sky had streaks of pink and lavender, and a splash of red where the sun barely kissed the horizon as it slipped away. It would be dark soon. She strolled along the deserted beach, stopping every so often to examine a pretty shell or an unusual piece of wood. When she slipped one of the shells into her pocket, her fingers brushed the message slip. Before the light faded completely, she needed to return the call.

She'd dialed the first three numbers when she saw the footprints. They started thirty feet in front of her. She watched as the bubbles of the gurgling tide swept over the prints, and she waited for them to disappear.

But they didn't.

She dialed the remaining four numbers and took another few steps. A wave washed first against her calves, then flowed over the footprints. Their perfection remained undiminished.

The phone rang three times before a man answered. "This is Sarah Jane Tremont," she said as she put one bare foot inside the first print. It stretched inches beyond her toes. "I'm returning your call."

"Thank you," he said, then paused, as if he was trying to remember why he'd called. "Oh, yeah. Here's the file. I'm a customer service representative for Dynasty Insurance. You had called a couple of weeks ago about a policy that Rosa Lopez purchased last year."

She'd called about twenty times. She wondered which

time he was referring to. She took another step and thought she might be crazy. It almost seemed like the footprint fit better. "Yes."

"I'm not sure how to tell you this, but I think we made a mistake. We . . ."

Sarah listened and walked and realized that this was the miracle that Rosa Lopez had been waiting for. When the call ended, she snapped her cell phone shut, stunned by the turn of events.

It took her a minute to realize that the footprints had become a perfect fit.

A sizzle started in her toes, jumped over the arch of her foot, streaked up her leg, and lodged itself in the middle of her chest. She felt as if she'd stuck a knife in the toaster. She wanted to move, to fling herself forward, to hurl herself back, to protect herself, but she couldn't.

A jagged spear of lightning split the now-dark sky and thunder roared. Wind, so strong it pushed her to her knees, came from behind. Sand whirled around her, biting into her skin. She squeezed her eyes shut and cupped her hands over her ears. The ground shook, sending her sprawling facedown in the sand.

Her cell phone flew. "No," she cried. She had to call Rosa Lopez. Now.

Then she heard it. The noise. A hundred times louder than the thunder, a hundred times more frightening. She opened her eyes. A wall of water swept across the ocean, heading right toward her. Sarah screamed as the first spray hit her face.

SHE woke up flat on her back. Every bone in her body ached, her head throbbed, her eyes felt glued shut, and her tongue seemed too big for her mouth. She licked her dry lips and tasted salt.

She'd undoubtedly drowned. She was dead. Done. Finished. The fat lady had sung.

She wiggled her fingers and her toes. Everything moved. She patted her arms, her cheeks. Everything felt pretty solid. So much for all that stuff about ashes to ashes, dust to dust.

She pried one eye open, then the other. Rolling to her side, she got to her knees, and then stood up. She felt a little light-headed, the way she did when she skipped both breakfast and lunch.

In the moonlight, the trees, their branches full, cast long shadows. She saw mountains in the distance. Stars, brighter than any she'd ever seen, sparkled in the sky. Grass, a whole field of it, tall enough to reach her waist, swayed in the soft breeze. It smelled sweet, like spring flowers.

It had to be Heaven.

She jumped when she heard a noise behind her. Whirling around, she saw two yellow eyes, ground level, staring at her. She screamed, the sound echoing in the quiet night. The startled squirrel ran up the trunk of the nearest tree.

Just seeing the animal made her feel a little better. She'd always hoped her fat old cat who'd died last year had made it to Heaven. If a squirrel got in, Tiny was a sure thing.

She looked to her left, then to her right. A narrow dirt road stretched as far as the eye could see in both directions. Hoping for a bit of divine inspiration, she looked up and studied the sky.

She tried to pick out the brightest star. That had, after all, worked out okay for the Wise Men. She patted the pockets of her still-damp skirt. Fresh out of frankincense or gold. Oh, well.

She turned to the right and began walking down the dirt road, wincing when she stepped on a sharp rock. She got another hundred yards before a second rock sliced into her other foot. She stood first on one foot, then the other, probing the cuts with her fingers.

When had she had her last tetanus booster?

She laughed, feeling giddy. What did it matter?

She squatted down, rubbed her hands across the grass, attempting to wipe the blood off. She managed to smear it up past both wrists. She resisted the urge to use the edge of her skirt. It might have to last her through eternity. Now she really regretted that she hadn't worn her practical slacks and blouse. "I hope you've got some extra bathrobes, God." She spoke quietly as she continued down the path. "Some of those white thick ones, the kind they have in expensive hotels."

She took a few more steps. "I always figured Heaven would have pizza and hot chocolate and red licorice." Another six steps. "Not that I'm complaining, God. I'm sure there's more than this." She didn't want the Big Guy to think poorly of her. After all, she'd handled this death thing pretty well so far. No sense letting Him down now.

She walked another ten minutes, each step a bit more painful than the last. She had almost decided to give up and let God or whoever come and find her, when she reached the top of the hill and spied a log cabin, another half mile down the road. A wooden barn, three times as big as the cabin, stood a hundred yards to the right.

She hobbled as fast as her sore feet allowed, slowing when she got close enough to see better. No porch light beckoned. No sidewalk led up to the front door. Just more dirt. "I'm assuming there's more, God," she whispered. "That I'm going to walk through that door and find Paradise. Eternal peace."

For the first time, she felt fear. What if she was doomed to live an eternity of unending dirt roads and bloody feet? The biggest fear of all hit her, almost taking her breath away. What if this wasn't Heaven? What if it was something else? She didn't even want to say the name.

"Here's the deal, God. I know I gave up. That doesn't make me a bad person. I know I could have—"

A dog's angry bark interrupted her. That scared her. In Heaven, all the dogs would be gentle Labradors. In the other place, they'd be pit bulls.

She wanted to run, but to where? Heart pounding, hands clammy, she edged closer to the door. She raised her hand to knock, but before she got the chance, the door swung open. A man—a big, terrifyingly menacing man with a gun slung over one shoulder—stood there. He held a lantern in one hand. The light played over his strong features, his broad forehead, straight nose, and whiskered chin.

He extended his arm, raising the lantern to get a good look at her. He didn't say a word; he just glared at her, his eyes filled with hostility. She opened her mouth but no words came out. She wanted to run but her legs refused to obey.

"That's enough, Morton," he said, turning his head slightly. The barking stopped.

The devil and his dog, Morton.

He turned back toward her. He set the lantern down, shrugged one powerful shoulder, and lowered his gun, placing it next to the door. Then he looked at her again. "What the hell are you doing here?" he asked. "I thought you said you were never coming back."

JOHN barely kept her head from hitting the floor. She'd dropped like a stone. But once he held her in his arms, he didn't have any notion of what to do with her. Then he saw the blood on her hands and feet, and he knew he had to help her.

"Damn, Morton," he said to the dog. "She's hurt."

The big dog whined in response and ran nervous circles around John's legs. "Get out of the way," he scolded the dog as he carried the woman to the bed in the far corner of the room. With as much care as he could, he placed her on top of the worn blanket, then took a step back. She looked small and pale and so very still. Reaching forward, he held his hand in front of her lips. Delicate breaths warmed his fingers.

"It's okay, boy," he said, patting the dog's head, knowing he wasn't reassuring the animal so much as himself. What had brought this woman to his door in the middle of the night wearing nothing but her shift? Trying to ignore her barely covered breasts, her small waist, and the sweet flare of her hips, he concentrated on her face.

She looked thinner than he remembered. She'd cut her hair, too. Now it just brushed her shoulders. He remembered the hours she'd spent in front of the mirror, crimping her long hair with the hot iron. Then she'd laid out her powders and her paints and weighed down her face with a layer of oil. Tonight her skin, still pale, looked bare. He ran a thumb across her cheek. Just skin. He could see the faint shadow of freckles on her nose. Somehow, it made her look younger. Innocent.

"Deceitful witch," he muttered. This woman was no innocent. She probably hadn't been born innocent.

He held the lantern above her head and moved it down the length of her body, looking for injuries. When he got to her feet and saw fresh blood oozing from both, he quickly set the lantern down on the table next to the bed. He walked across the room, grabbed a clean cloth from the cupboard, and wet it with water from the pitcher he kept on the table. He returned to the end of the bed and picked up one foot. The warmth and softness of her skin shocked him.

"Conniving gold digger," he reminded himself.

He wiped first one foot, then the other. One of the cuts worried him. Grabbing another clean cloth from the cupboard, he doubled it over once, and then again. Pressing the edges of the cut skin together, he wrapped the cloth around her foot, tying it in a knot on top.

He got his third cloth, the last clean one he had, wet it, and wiped off her hands. She sighed, a soft sweet sound.

He flicked his eyes to her face. Her pale pink lips parted and he could see just the tip of her tongue.

"Manipulative, spoiled, rude," he said, kneading his forehead with his fingers. Damn, his head hurt. "Come on," he said. "You're not the fainting type." He put his hand on her shoulder and shook her gently. She didn't stir.

Making yet another trip to his cupboards, he reached for his vinegar bottle. After pouring a generous amount into a cup, he brought it back to the bed and held it under her nose. She sniffed, coughed, and turned her head to avoid the smell.

"Good girl," he urged. "Now open your damn eyes or I swear, I'll dunk your head in a pail of this stuff."

Her dark lashes fluttered against her pale skin. She opened her eyes, startling him. He'd never noticed before just how blue they were.

He watched as she looked first at him, then from one corner of the room to the other, then at Morton, who sat at the end of the bed, growling. Her gaze settled back on him. Big and round, her eyes filled her face. She looked scared to death.

He didn't remember her ever looking scared. Belligerent. Sullen. All that and more. But never scared.

"Sarah, you're okay," he assured her.

If anything, she looked even more frightened.

"Did someone hurt you?" he asked, struggling to get the words out. No woman deserved to be mistreated. Not even this one.

She shook her head.

"Tell me what happened," he demanded.

She cowered against the bed, causing the narrow strap of her shift to slip a couple inches lower on her bare shoulder. He worked hard to keep his eyes on her face.

"Never mind," he said. "We'll talk about it later. Would you like some water?"

She nodded.

On his way to get the cup, he opened the door for Morton. When the dog didn't look inclined to move, John whistled. The dog whined one more time, gave Sarah a quick look, and then left, but not before brushing his big body up against John's legs. John shut the door and walked over to the shelf above his stove, picked up his extra cup, and filled it with water from the pitcher. He went back to the bed and held it out to her.

Their fingers met around the metal cup. His large tanned ones seemed twice the size of her small white ones. He saw the scar across the first joint of his ring finger, an old reminder of Peter's clumsiness with a fishing hook.

Peter. His brother. Younger than John by just a year. The two of them had been inseparable. The only thing that had ever come between them had been a woman. This woman.

He let go of the cup. She caught it but not before a little water sloshed over the edge. The water stain spread across the pale blue of her shift. He backed up, needing to put some distance between them.

She might look soft and sweet, but this woman had killed his brother.

Maybe she hadn't pushed him down the silver mine shaft with her own hands, but if not for her incessant wanting, her need for things, her inability ever to be satisfied, Peter wouldn't have been compelled to take the risk that had cost him his life.

"How was Cheyenne?" he asked. That's where she'd been headed six months ago, just three weeks after his brother's death. He'd come home, after working a backbreaking ten hours clearing trees, and her bags had been packed.

His mother, who had moved in after Peter's funeral, had been sitting at the table. Sarah stood by the window. She hadn't even bothered to say hello when he'd entered the room.

"I'm leaving," she'd said. "I kept my promise. I stuck

around long enough to know I'm not with child. Proof positive came today. Thank the sweet Lord."

He still remembered how cold her words had sounded. He'd understood the sadness in his mother's eyes. It wasn't Sarah's leaving that pained her. She wouldn't miss her daughter-in-law. It was that she'd lost her last hope. There'd be no grandchild to rock in her arms. No chance to hold Peter's child tight against her breast.

"I'll be on tomorrow's stage," Sarah had said. "I need you to get my bags to town. Is the wagon fixed?"

He'd nodded. It didn't matter. He'd drag her damn cases on his back, the full three miles, to get the evil out of his house. He wanted her at the other end of the earth. Cheyenne, a three-day stage ride south, would have to do.

"I'd like my money," she'd said, holding out her hand.

He'd walked back to the barn, dug the money out of its hiding place, and returned to his house. He'd thrown the packet on the table. She'd picked it up, counted it, and put it into her valise.

"Sarah, you don't have to go," his mother had said. "You're my son's wife. There's a place for you here."

"I was your son's wife," she'd responded. "Now I'm a rich widow. I'm leaving and I'm never coming back."

But she had. Tonight of all nights. Had Peter lived, he'd have been thirty-one today. "You're not welcome here," John said. "I'm not as charitable as my mother."

"Mother?" she whispered.

She looked confused, almost forlorn.

"You're on the next stage," he said. "I'll put you on it myself."

"Stage?" She took another small sip of water.

"You're not my responsibility," he said.

She nodded, never taking her big blue eyes off him. "I thought I was dead."

He stood up and grabbed his hat off the hook. "I couldn't be so lucky," he muttered, not wanting to admit how her words shook him. He hated her, sure. But he didn't want her dead.

She didn't respond at all, just blinked her big eyes a couple times. And then a tear slid down one pale cheek.

What kind of man made a woman cry? He turned away, unwilling to watch the results of his own surliness. He got to the door before she spoke.

"Thank you for helping me," she said, looking at her bandaged foot.

He didn't want her gratitude. He wanted her gone. "Forget it. Just get better so you can get the hell out of my life."

TWO

❧

SHE wasn't dead. Instead the storm had tossed her right into a stranger's bed. A stranger who had called her Sarah as if he knew her, and couldn't wait to get rid of her.

She swung her legs to the side. Mindful of her bandaged foot, she eased out of bed, walked over to the window, and pulled back the thin cotton curtain. Early dawn had pushed the dark night aside, bathing the land in a soft purple hue. She watched the man and his big black dog walk toward the weathered, unpainted barn. When he opened the big door and disappeared inside, she let out a deep breath.

He knew her name. How creepy was that? She must have talked in her sleep. As a child, she'd done that. She hadn't believed it until the night her father had turned on a tape recorder. She'd hoped she'd outgrown it.

Now, it had caused her to be at a serious information disadvantage. She knew nothing about him. She looked at her clean hands and feet. He hadn't been exactly friendly, but then again he hadn't given her any real reason to be afraid.

Then why couldn't she shake the feeling this man was trouble? He acted like he'd met her before. He'd said something about a stage. Maybe he had trouble separating fact from fiction and he'd confused her with some actress.

She walked over to the shelf, the one he'd pulled the extra cup from. She picked up a small mirror and held it in front of her face. She looked for a moment, studied the reflection, then put the mirror down. She counted to ten and picked it up again. Same thick blond, absolutely straight, shoulder-length hair. Same blue eyes. Same small scar running through her left eyebrow. She checked her teeth. Nothing new.

Sarah Jane Tremont looked like she did every other morning. She'd dropped out of the clouds and landed flat on her back on some country road, but other than that, nothing much had changed. Now she just needed to find her way home. After all, how far could it be? Was it possible the storm had carried her miles? Could a person survive that?

She had. Looking around, she noted the old black stove, like one she'd seen in history books, in one corner of the room. Where was the refrigerator? Surely, in this day and age, even the most rural houses had refrigerators.

A small table stood against the far wall. On it was a book of some sort, with a piece of paper sticking out. She walked over and pulled out the paper. It looked like an invoice. Flour, salt, sugar, and coffee. The man had made a grocery run. He'd stocked up on the basics.

She looked a little closer. He'd bought a barrel of flour. Who the heck bought flour in a barrel? Was there a bakery out back she hadn't seen?

She ran her finger down the list. He'd bought eight pounds of coffee for a dollar. What? She looked again. The last time she'd bought coffee, it had been over five dollars a pound.

Hooper's Mercantile. The name, like the purchases, was handwritten. She focused on the date at the top of the invoice. April 16, 1888. She grabbed the book and flipped through it. Entries recorded the weather, crops planted, livestock bought and sold. She flipped to the last page. Halfway down the page, she saw the last entry. It, too, was dated April 16, 1888.

She picked up the invoice again. She'd been too stunned by the date to take much notice of the signature. Now she ran her fingers across the large, slanted writing. John Beckett. She opened the ledger once again, this time to the first page. *Property of John Beckett, Cedarbrook, Wyoming Territory.*

The guy had to be a history nut. She flipped the invoice over. The paper looked new, the ink fresh. She sniffed the ledger. It didn't smell old.

She jumped when she heard the rattle of the doorknob. She stuffed the invoice back inside the book and pushed it toward the middle of the table. The man, carrying a bucket of water in one hand and a basket of eggs in the other, opened the door.

He didn't say a word or even look at her when he entered. Setting the basket and the bucket on top of the stove, he took off his cowboy hat and hung it on a nail by the door. He bent down and scooped up a handful of wood from the box next to the stove. Using a small hook, he pulled out a burner and shoved the wood inside before striking a match and throwing it on the pile. He replaced the burner. Each movement was efficient, no wasted action.

In the morning light, he looked less devilish and more handsome. He did not, however, look any smaller. His shoulders still looked incredibly wide and she could see muscles in his back ripple as he worked. From her vantage point, she noted he also had one great butt. All nice and firm. Heck, he had a better butt than she did.

He turned toward her and she jerked her glance away. "I thought you might be hungry," he said. "Still like your eggs fried?"

She preferred scrambled but she didn't want to debate it. "Yes," she said.

"You want some coffee?" he asked.

Maybe it was Heaven. "Flavored?" she asked.

He frowned at her. "I hope so. It better taste like coffee. Or Hooper's owes me a refund."

"Hooper's?" *As in Hooper's Mercantile?*

He looked at her more closely. "Are you sure you didn't bump your head?"

"I don't think so."

He didn't look convinced. "Alice Hooper still talks about you. I don't know why. You barely ever gave the poor woman the time of day. Even so, on Tuesday, when I went to town, I heard her talking to another customer. She said Cedarbrook lost all its style the day you left."

On Tuesday, when I went to town.

April 16, 1888.

Cedarbrook lost all its style the day you left.

I thought you said you weren't coming back.

Her heart slammed against her chest and her knees started to buckle. "What . . . what day is it?" she asked.

He frowned at her. "It's Thursday."

She shook her head. "What's the date?"

"The eighteenth of April."

"The year?" she demanded.

"It's 1888. What the hell's wrong with you, Sarah?"

She put her hand over her mouth, afraid she might throw up. Like pieces of a puzzle, the log walls, the bare wood floor, the old stove, and the long-handled, lethal-looking razor next to the mirror all slipped into place, making a clear picture.

"Sarah? Damn it, don't you faint on me again." The man

dropped the spoon he held and crossed the room in five strides.

She held up her hand, stopping him. "I'm fine," she lied. "Just hungry. Breakfast would be good."

"You're sure?"

She was sure, all right. Sure she was in a heck of a jam. *Property of John Beckett, Cedarbrook, Wyoming Territory. April 1888.* No, she hadn't gone to Hell. But she'd come close.

Time travel. The very idea of it seemed beyond comprehension. But the reality of her situation was all too tangible. She could touch it, smell it, and see it. Things like this didn't happen to Sarah Jane Tremont. She went to work, she came home, had some dinner in front of the television, and then went to bed so it could start all over the next day.

She watched him while he cooked. He cracked the eggs with one hand and deftly turned them in the pan. He took a sharp knife and cut big slices off a loaf of bread before grabbing two plates and some silverware off the shelf.

He had on a plain tan shirt. Almost like a long-sleeved T-shirt only it had three or four buttons at the neckline. He'd tucked it into darker tan pants held up by blue suspenders. He wore a bright red bandanna around his neck. His boots, scuffed and scratched, added another inch to his already tall frame. He had thick brown hair, almost touching his shoulders. She guessed he might be around thirty. No middle-age spread here.

A man's man. A sexy, handsome, rough-and-tumble, get-the-hell-out-of-my-way type of guy. Who was he? He acted like he'd known her well. She couldn't accept that. He wasn't the type of man she'd forget. She might have gone back in time, but she refused to accept that she'd lived here once before. This had to be her first pass through.

She tried in vain to remember her sophomore year of American history. Had Wyoming even been a state in 1888?

Evidently not, she realized as her mind jumped into gear and started to work once again. The invoice said Wyoming Territory. Good grief. She wasn't even in a state. Hadn't the Oregon Trail cut through Wyoming? Were the Indians friendly in 1888?

What she didn't know far outweighed what she did know. Not that it mattered. She really only needed to know two things. How far was California, and what was the best way to get there? She needed to get back to her beach and walk along the shore and, somehow, find the door back to her own world.

"When's the next stage?" she asked.

He set her plate on the table. "Next week. Stage still goes on Wednesday mornings, just like before."

She couldn't stay here another six days. She didn't want to stay another six hours. "Then I need to find another way. I need to get back," she said.

He pulled his chair out from the table, sat down, and folded his arms across his chest. "At last, we agree on something. Where you going this time?"

She walked to the table and took the chair opposite him. She took a small bite of bread, chewed it to death, and wondered what she could tell him. He wouldn't believe that she'd stumbled across a set of footprints on the beach and been blown back more than a century. She barely believed it. She swallowed, hoping the bread wouldn't stick in her throat. "Look, John," she said, trying out his name, "it's hard for me to explain."

He shrugged, looking a little bored. He pointed to her plate. "You going to eat those eggs or just look at them?"

She stabbed her fork into one. Yellow yolk spread across the plate. She ignored it and took a bite. She'd eat to keep up her strength. She had a long trip ahead of her. If the stage didn't go for a week, she'd find another way.

"You wouldn't happen to have a horse I could borrow?"

He laughed but he didn't sound amused. "Sure. Take my

horse. Why not? Six months ago you took most of my money."

She hadn't taken his money. It hurt to be accused of something and not be able to defend herself.

"What happened?" he asked, pushing his chair back so suddenly that the front legs came off the wood floor. "Did you run out? Is that what brought you back?"

She shook her head. He looked mad, dangerously mad.

"Listen here, sweetheart. You're not getting another dollar from me. My brother never should have married you."

His brother. One more piece of the puzzle started to slide into place. Perhaps she'd walked out on his brother. She felt oddly disappointed until she remembered that it hadn't been her, her marriage, or her leaving. Six months ago, she'd been slogging through case files and counseling sessions.

"I don't want anything from you," she assured him.

"That's hard to believe. Why else would you show up at my doorstep? How the hell did you get here anyway?"

She'd like an answer to that one as well. "I walked," she said. At least she had the last mile or so.

"What happened to your clothes?"

Her clothes? She looked down at her wrinkled silk camisole and skirt. Her Jones of New York had seen better days. She doubted that was what he meant anyway. She was probably dressed pretty scantily for the day. "They got wet."

"Wet? They wouldn't dry?"

She needed to be more careful. "They got wet when I waded into the river. After they caught on fire. I was . . . cooking. On a campfire."

He looked at her like she'd lost her mind. It didn't matter. She didn't need to convince him of her sanity. She just needed a horse.

"If you could just reconsider letting me borrow a horse," she said, "then I could be out of your hair today."

He shook his head. "I can't afford to lose another horse. All I've got left is mine, mother's mare, and a bullheaded colt I'm breaking in. You'll have to stay here until Wednesday."

"No," she argued. "I can't." What if the window, the door, the crack in time, shut before she could get to California? "You don't understand," she said.

"I understand, all right. You come back here, all pitiful, hoping you could talk my mother out of another pile of money. But it's just me. Hell of a mess, isn't it, Sarah?"

He had no idea. "Your mother?" she asked.

"She moved to town just weeks after you left. She needed to be around folks, not stuck out here on the ranch. Peter's death hit her hard. Harder than it hit his wife, obviously."

Peter, the husband she'd never met, had died. The man had lost his brother. "I'm sorry," she said.

"Sorry she's not around? I'll bet you are." He looked at her with such disgust that she felt dirty. "Don't be getting any crazy ideas about going to town to see her. You'll keep your little backside here until Wednesday morning, and then I'll personally see to it that you get on that stage. She doesn't need any more heartache from you."

"I don't want to cause anybody any heartache," Sarah protested. "Can you at least loan me a pair of shoes so that I can walk to town?"

"No. I just told you why."

She wouldn't know his mother if the woman stood next to her. "Fine," she said, trying hard to hold on to her temper. "I'll walk in the opposite direction."

"I suppose you've forgotten that the closest town in that direction is a day's ride? That's a three-day walk."

She didn't care. She had to do something. Any action seemed better than no action. "I like to walk," she said.

"Your feet are in no shape for a walk like that."

"So, I'm stuck here," she said, not even trying to keep the disappointment out of her voice.

"Yeah. And there's nobody unhappier about that than me."

Debatable. She tried to think of other options but the dog's barking interrupted her. John walked over to the window. "Hell," he said, and rubbed his hand across his face, as if trying to rub away the last twelve hours of his life. "Stay back. I don't want Fred to see you."

"Fred?"

He sighed, loud enough that it was easy to hear. "Were we all that easy to forget, Sarah?"

She ignored his question. Instead, she peeked around his shoulder and saw a giant of a man get off his horse and stoop to pet the dog, who had stopped barking and now lay on his back, his four legs pointed at the sun, his tail wagging. "At least one of us is happy," she muttered.

"I'm not the one who just decided to drop in."

She'd dropped in all right. "Why can't he see me?"

"Fred Goodie gossips with the church ladies every Sunday."

John didn't sound angry. More like half-amused. Fred didn't look like a man who'd have a lot in common with church ladies. He looked as if he might like to hang around with other giants, maybe lift some small trees, or for a real workout, shot-put some boulders. "Why does he do that?"

"He's hungry for some good cooking. He and the children eat Sunday dinner at a different house every week. When your father-in-law is the preacher, things like that get arranged."

She probably should have known Fred had children. She decided to go for broke. "So his oldest is about ten now?"

"Not hardly," John said. "She can't be a day past eight. And the twins were just five last month."

"Still as pretty as ever?"

"Don't let Thomas hear you call him pretty. The girls are real beauties though. Spittin' image of their momma."

"Mrs. Goodie doesn't go to dinner with them?"

He shook his head. "She got the fever."

The fever? Yikes. She wished she'd packed a few antibiotics for the trip. "How is she?"

"Franny died four months ago."

She could hear the genuine sadness in his voice. He grabbed his hat off the nail by the door. "I'll be right back," he said. "Stay here. I mean it."

He didn't wait for a reply. He opened the door and walked outside, intercepting Fred a good twenty yards from the house. Sarah peeked around the edge of the curtain. Somehow he'd managed to turn Fred, and now the giant's back faced the cabin. It gave John a straight shot at the door.

He acted as if she might make a run for it. Unless an express bus back to the future waited at the corner, that didn't seem like an option. Of course, John didn't know that. He thought she'd returned home to fleece his unsuspecting mother out of her retirement money. Sarah Number One must have been a real piece of work. Not that that was any of her concern. Her issue was finding a way back, but first she needed to find a way past the formidable John Beckett, who, at this very moment, seemed determined to keep her separated from the rest of the living world. The men had moved over to Fred's horse, a huge beast of an animal, and Fred had his saddlebag open, his head down, as he looked for something.

Even to Sarah's inexperienced eye, the saddlebags seemed to be bulging. Fred, it appeared, had packed for some kind of trip. What if he was headed west? What if, at this very moment, the two men discussed such a trip? Would John think to tell his friend that Sarah would appreciate a lift?

She hadn't had the chance to tell him that California loomed as her final destination. Sarah debated all of five more seconds, then pushed open the front door.

She walked with purpose, as much as one could with a bandaged foot, her head held high, her shoulders squared.

At least until the moment the two men saw her. She'd expected John's reaction. Rage. Even though it hurt her, she'd prepared for that. But Fred surprised her. The big man who looked like he ate small, uncooked animals for breakfast stood still for a few seconds, his broad mouth hanging open. Then, with each step she took, he took an equal step backward. As if he were prepared to walk forever to keep distance between them.

"Christ Almighty," Fred said, his voice loud in the quiet morning. "How the hell did she get here? And why doesn't she have a dress on?"

Oh boy, did she have a story for him. He wouldn't be able to get away fast enough.

Sarah looked at John, waiting for him to explain. He, however, had his lips locked together, as if afraid of what might come out if given half a chance.

"I had a bit of bad luck," Sarah said. Let them make of that what they would. She didn't feel inclined to say more. She remembered just enough history to know that crazy people, or at least those perceived to be crazy, had faced all kinds of inhumane treatment over the years. She didn't want these men to add two and two and come up with the answer that she was one fry short of a Big Deal Meal.

Fred ran his long, thick fingers through his red hair, making it even wilder. He looked from Sarah to John, then back to Sarah. She smiled at him. He frowned at her and looked at John. "Say something, man," Fred instructed. "Don't just stand there and pretend she's not there."

"Go back inside, Sarah," John said, not looking at her. "It's not proper for you to be out here dressed in such a manner. I know you probably don't care about things like that, but I do."

That stung a bit. "I'm sorry to interrupt," Sarah said. "I couldn't help wondering if Mr. Goodie is headed west. I'm interested in getting to California."

"California?" Both men spoke at the same time, their voices vibrating over the quiet land. The dog barked, too, as if he couldn't quite believe it either.

"Yes. I . . . I have a friend there. I thought maybe I could ride along."

"I ain't going to California, Mrs. Beckett," Fred said.

Sarah was so disappointed that it took her a moment to realize that Fred had spoken to her. *Mrs. Beckett.* She didn't want him calling her that. "Sarah is fine," she said. "There's no need for formality. After all, we're friends."

Both John and Fred looked surprised. She realized too late that Sarah One probably didn't have a lot of friends. "If you're not going all the way, maybe I could catch a ride partway."

"Fred is only going to town," John said. "He'll be home tomorrow. He can't leave his children alone longer than that."

"I've got to find me a woman," Fred added.

That was certainly blunt. Sarah could feel the heat rush to her face.

"Not like that," John said, frowning at her. "He needs someone to watch his children so he can get his spring planting done. He had an old Indian woman helping out but she ran out yesterday, leaving him high and dry."

"Isn't there anyone else who can watch the children?"

"My father-in-law would," Fred said, "but he's got his ministry, and anyway, he doesn't get around too fast anymore. Not fast enough to keep up. Missy's as ornery as a wild goat."

"Missy?"

"The deaf one," he said, no doubt thinking Sarah rude for not remembering his children.

Deaf.

Sarah's heart constricted. She wondered how much was known about deafness in 1888 Wyoming. Was the poor little girl locked in her own quiet world, battling to be heard?

"I better get going," Fred said. "I'm going to try old Mrs. Warner first. She's a sour thing but she doesn't have any kin of her own to look after."

"Who is with your children now?" Sarah asked.

"Nobody. That's why I can't be dawdling here. Helen will do the best she can but she's only eight. Barely fair to her to have to be responsible for both her brother and sister."

Eight. Just like Miguel. Both of them with responsibilities no eight-year-old should bear. "Maybe I could help out for a couple days," Sarah said.

"What?" Again, both men spoke at the same time. They were starting to sound like a regular chorus.

"I'm taking the next stage out of here," Sarah said, "but since that doesn't go for another six days, I might as well make myself useful. Then maybe you won't have to settle for sour Mrs. Warner." She smiled at Fred, choosing to ignore John.

"I don't know," Fred said, shaking his head. "I guess I never expected you to—"

"Volunteer to help." John finished his friend's sentence. "What's going on here, Sarah?"

She realized her mistake. Mindful that she needed to be careful, she said, "I'm assuming you paid the Indian woman something. I'd expect the same. Maybe even a bit more since I'm getting you out of a jam."

John stopped stroking his chin. "It always comes down to the money, doesn't it, Sarah?"

Right. Like anybody interested in money picked social work as a career. "A woman has needs," she said, thinking she sounded positively Victorian.

He didn't respond, choosing to turn toward Fred. "You might want to take her up on it," he said. "You don't have a lot of choices right now."

Gee, thanks. Sarah wished he stood close enough to kick.

"I don't know." Fred shifted from foot to foot, his big frame swaying dangerously from side to side.

Great. Snubbed by a desperate man. What he didn't know was that she was pretty desperate herself. "Look, I could ride back with you now. You could be in your fields by midmorning. I just need to be back to town by next Wednesday to catch the stage."

"You can't stay at his house at night," John said. "It wouldn't be proper."

God save her from narrow-minded idiots. "I need a place to stay. What's the difference if I stay here or at Fred's house?"

"I'm your brother-in-law," John hissed. "Fred is a widower. People might start to talk. Especially when they find out it's you. I wouldn't want his children hurt by that."

Now she wouldn't be content just to kick him. She wanted to rub his snooty nose in the dirt. She looked at Fred but he'd suddenly developed an interest in his worn boots.

"I won't compromise your friend," she said.

"You'd have to put some clothes on," Fred said, looking up. His face was almost as red as his hair.

"I'm a little short on clothes right now," Sarah tried to explain. "Maybe I could borrow a shirt, John?"

He snorted. "About all I got left is the one on my back."

What had Sarah One done to put that chip on John's shoulder?

Fred reached into his saddlebag, digging deep. "Here," he said. "I packed an extra shirt. You might as well wear it."

Sarah unrolled the bundle he handed to her. She held it up. "Perfect," she said, and slipped it over her head. She pushed her arms through and pulled the material down over her hips. It came almost to her knees. She knew she looked like she'd stepped into a brown sack. "I'm ready," she said, looking from Fred to John.

"John?" Fred questioned, clearly not sure what to do.

"Take her," John said. "Just don't say I didn't warn you." He turned on his heel and walked toward the barn.

That did it. She'd make him eat the damn dirt.

THREE

FRED smelled a bit like violets. She hadn't expected that. He'd waited until John had walked into the barn before getting back on his horse. Then he'd offered her one of his huge hands and literally swung her off the ground. His big frame left little room in the saddle so she'd ended up with her bottom just resting on a tiny bit of space in front of the saddle horn. Fred held the reins, each strong arms extended, with her back balanced against his right forearm and her legs, bent at the knees, thrown over his left forearm.

She'd simply closed her eyes, hoping that the horse would have the good manners to step over her in the likely event that Fred dropped her. But he hadn't. And now fifteen minutes later, all thoughts of violets gone, she stood in front of his house, and three red-haired children, all barefoot, all with dirty faces, one with fresh blood on his knee, stared at her.

"This is Helen, Thomas, and Missy," Fred said.

"Hello." Sarah smiled at them. "I'm Sarah."

"Mrs. Beckett is going to take care of you," Fred explained.

The oldest girl put her hands on her narrow hips. "We don't need somebody else to take care of us. I can do it."

"Helen," Fred said, "don't be rude."

"Miss Suzanne has prettier dresses," Helen said, her pointed chin stuck out in defiance.

"Be quiet," Fred admonished his daughter.

"Who is Miss Suzanne?" Thomas asked.

Neither Fred nor his oldest daughter seemed inclined to answer. They simply stared at each other.

"What did you do to your knee, Thomas?" Sarah asked the boy, hoping to break the silence.

"Fell off the roof of the privy," he said.

"Great. You do that often?" she asked, thinking it could be a long six days. She moved a step closer to the children and squatted down in front of the youngest girl. "You must be Missy. M. I. S. S. Y." She signed the girl's name as she spoke each letter. Then did it a second time.

She reached for the little girl's hand, but Missy jerked it back. Then slowly, with infinite care, the child spelled her own name, fumbling a little on the Y. When she finished, she looked absolutely triumphant. Her eyes were big and a wide grin almost split her face.

Sarah thought her own face probably matched. "She signs! Do all of you?"

"No," Fred said, his voice more subdued than before. "Franny had gotten a book and she was teaching her before she . . ." He stopped and ran a big hand over the top of Thomas's head. "Anyway," he said, his voice husky, "where'd you learn to talk to the deaf, Sarah?"

Her mother had been deaf. It had never stopped them from having wonderful conversations. Even now, with both her parents dead for more than five years, she missed them terribly. "I picked it up a while back. Do you mind if I teach Missy and the other children a few words while I'm here?"

"I guess not. Does John know you can do this?"

"No. If you don't mind," she said, turning back toward the big man, "let's keep it our little secret."

Fred snorted. "Seems like all I do lately."

"Pardon me?" Sarah said.

"Never mind." Fred waved off her comment. "It's not your concern. I've got to get out to my fields. Are you settled here?"

Given that *settled* was likely a relative term, Sarah nodded. She didn't have a clue what to do next. But the look of hope in Missy's eyes made it impossible to think she could walk away. "We'll be fine," Sarah assured both Fred and herself. "Don't worry about a thing."

TEN hours later, when Fred finally returned to the house, Sarah sat on the floor, Missy asleep in her arms. "How was your day?" she whispered.

"I got fifteen acres planted," he said. "I gained a whole day by not having to go to town. Thank you for being here."

"We had fun." Mostly. Hauling Thomas out of the stream had been a bit nerve-racking and her fingers and hands ached from teaching words, but all in all, she felt better than she had in many, many days.

Fred bent down, picked up his small daughter, and laid her on the bed in the far corner of the room, next to her already asleep brother and sister. "Did you and Helen get along okay?" Fred asked, looking a bit nervous.

"Fine. She'll come around."

Fred nodded. "Did she tell you about Miss Suzanne?"

Sarah was fascinated. The man could turn red in seconds. "No. I didn't ask, either."

"I appreciate that," he said. "It's a difficult situation."

"You don't need to explain anything to me."

"It . . . it would be helpful if you didn't mention it to John."

"Okay."

"That's it?" He looked surprised. "No questions? No threats now that you know I've got a secret?"

She stood up, stretched her arms over her head, hoping to work the kinks out of her back. "Fred, trust me on this. I've got bigger things to worry about. Besides, you said you wouldn't say anything to John about me being able to talk to the deaf. This makes us even."

He cocked his head and looked at her. "You seem different, Sarah. What happened since you left here six months ago?"

She could tell him the truth but she really didn't want to have to scoop his huge body up off the floor. "It's a really long story and I think I better be getting back."

He opened up the door of the cabin and motioned her out. "Fair enough. I'll see you home."

Home. Oh, if only he could.

JOHN didn't generally believe in luck. But it did seem like damn bad circumstances that Sarah had darkened his door once again. Why the woman hadn't been able to keep herself inside, out of Fred's sight, was beyond understanding.

No, she'd paraded out of the house, wearing her undergarments, and proceeded to ask Fred to take her to California. John had thought his poor neighbor might have a fit. When she'd volunteered to take care of the children, John had thought his own heart might stop. In the six months that Sarah had lived in his house, he'd never once heard her volunteer for extra work.

As if it were yesterday, he could remember the night that Peter had brought Sarah, his wife of two days, back to Cedarbrook. Hardly seemed like it could be almost a year ago now. She'd barely said two words. He'd given her the benefit of the doubt, thinking she might be shy.

Sarah had met Peter on the train between Cheyenne and

Douglas. Five days later, she'd been Mrs. Peter Beckett. Two weeks after that, Peter had been damn miserable.

The house was too small, the furniture too old. Sarah's complaints started there but didn't stop. Cedarbrook bored her. Hooper's didn't have any dresses she liked. Peter hadn't told her she'd be stuck out in the middle of nowhere.

His brother had done the best he could to excuse her behavior. John had wanted to kick his ass then for being such a fool. Instead, he'd moved his stuff out to the barn, saying the newlyweds needed privacy, knowing he needed space away from the sharp-tongued bitch.

He'd managed to avoid her most days but Peter had insisted that he join them for the night meal. Sarah had treated him like a stranger in his own house. If she'd had her way, he'd have starved like a stray dog.

He'd kept coming back for Peter. Had to. He'd been watching out for Peter since the year he turned ten and Peter turned nine. The year their pa got killed by a bear.

Each night at dinner the food and the company got worse. He'd hated seeing the strained look on his brother's face, the drag of his step. They'd barely got the fall crops put to bed when Peter told him Sarah wanted to spend the winter in town. John had celebrated the news. He'd hoped, like a fool, the pair could work it out. That the marriage would survive.

He'd never dreamed that Peter wouldn't return. He'd blamed Sarah then. He blamed her now.

He'd half expected that Sarah wouldn't last the day at Fred's house. He'd watched the children a time or two in those first days after Franny's death. They'd practically run him ragged. And little Missy, pretty as a picture, had spent hours kicking the wall. By the end of the day, he'd been ready to stick his fist through it.

Confident that Sarah would come running back, John had taken the time to ride home at noon. He'd stayed an hour, a full fifty minutes longer than it had taken him to eat a sandwich and fill up his canteen with fresh water. He'd ridden back out to plant his fields, even madder at Sarah. She'd made him waste almost a good hour of daylight.

When he'd dragged his weary body home at suppertime, only to find the house still empty, he'd begun to get worried. Not about Sarah. No. He was more concerned that Fred, who had a big heart, hadn't suddenly developed a soft head, and decided to take her somewhere. He knew, better than most, that a sweet word and a gentle nudge from Sarah could push a strong man to his knees. Once she got him there, she'd poke and prod until she ran him into the ground.

He was saddling his horse, getting ready to ride over to Fred's place, when they arrived. As on the night before, the full moon made it easy enough for him to see them as they approached. Sarah rode Franny's horse. She sat ramrod straight in the saddle.

"Evening, John," Fred called out. "You just getting in?"

John nodded, not willing to admit that he'd been worried. He looked at Sarah, who seemed glued to the saddle. She acted like she'd never ridden a horse before. He extended a hand. She looked at it, at the horse, then in one swift motion she dropped the reins, grabbed his hand, and vaulted off the horse. She wobbled when her feet hit the ground.

"Everything go okay?" John asked. She looked down-right pale.

"I appreciate your help, Sarah," Fred said.

"It was nothing," she said, sounding almost embarrassed. "They're great kids."

"You'll be ready at six tomorrow?" Fred asked.

"Absolutely." Sarah gave her horse an awkward pat on the head. She reached up to grab the small bundle that Fred handed to her. "Thanks for the clothes."

She'd obviously helped herself to Franny's things and had replaced Fred's shirt with a brown skirt and a long-sleeved blouse. Even with the waistband rolled a couple times, the skirt still dragged in the dirt. John wasn't surprised. Franny had been at least five inches taller than

Sarah. He imagined that it bothered the hell out of her to be dressed so poorly.

Fred tipped his hat. "Thank you, Sarah. For everything. I couldn't have managed without you." He gathered up the reins and turned his horse toward home. "Night, John. I'll see you tomorrow."

John ground the toe of his boot in the dirt as he watched his friend ride away. What had gotten into Fred? The man had never been able to stand Sarah. Not after she'd insulted his Franny. When he'd heard the news of her departure, Fred had smiled and pumped John's hand in a bone-crushing shake.

This morning, when he'd accepted Sarah's suggestion that she watch his children, John had understood the man's desperation. The spring had been wet, too wet to plant up until just a few days ago. Given there were no guarantees that another two weeks of rain weren't just around the corner, neither he nor Fred could afford to think of anything else.

John had expected the man to be grateful. He hadn't expected the man to act genuinely friendly, as if he was actually looking forward to seeing Sarah in the morning. He'd think twice about that, if he'd had the benefit of John's experiences.

Some women might wake up sweet, but not Sarah. She woke up ornery. A mere month after exchanging vows, his brother had started sneaking out early in the morning, letting his ill-mannered wife sleep. When Fred had suggested six, John had almost laughed. He had wanted to tell Fred, to keep the man from making a wasted trip for her, but the blissful look on the man's face had stopped him. Let the idiot find out for himself. Then he wouldn't have to worry that Sarah might somehow trick his best friend the way she'd tricked his brother.

John watched Fred until the man crested the hill, expecting Sarah to start complaining about her horrible day.

When she remained silent, he looked at her. She was literally swaying, her eyes half-closed, almost asleep on her feet.

"You should be in bed," he said.

"I need to use the privy first."

He nodded and watched her walk away, one hand holding up her skirt to keep from tripping on it. He waited a minute before stomping off to get his bucket. He'd drawn water from the well, returned to the cabin, and filled the bowl before she opened the front door. "I thought you might want to wash up a bit," he said, handing her a clean towel.

She looked surprised, then pleased. "Thank you," she said, smiling at him. For the first time, he noticed that she had a shallow little dimple on the left side of her mouth.

"It's nothing," he said, backing out of the house.

"Where should I sleep?" she asked before he could get away.

"Right there." John motioned to the bed in the far corner.

"But that's your bed."

She looked so sincere for a moment that he was tempted to believe it. "You didn't have any problem kicking me out of it before," he said, making sure she could hear the disgust in his voice. "What's different now?"

"I . . ." She stopped. "I guess nothing is different."

"That's right, Sarah. Don't forget to turn down the lamp. I'd appreciate it if you didn't burn down my house."

When he got to the barn, he slammed the door for good measure. He heard the nervous shuffle of horses behind him and knew he'd startled the stock. "Get used to it," he said. "It's just you and me for the next six nights."

John pulled several bales of straw together before he realized he'd left his blanket inside. "Damn it," he said. "Damn her." He left the barn, more quietly than he'd entered, mindful that once the horses got good and awake, they'd keep him up for hours. He'd walked halfway back to the house when a flash of movement in front of the window had him stopping in his tracks. Sarah stood facing the window, naked from the waist up. With the lantern shining behind her, the thin white cotton curtains offered little protection.

He watched her reach out a long arm, dip her cloth in the water, and rub it across her breasts. My God, the woman had beautiful breasts. Firm and full. She took one hand, lifted up her hair, and with her free hand, wiped the back of her neck. The movement caused her perfect breasts to pull even higher, to reach out, to beckon to him.

He let himself watch for a minute more before forcing himself to turn away. Disgusted with his own weakness, he stared up at the sky, not even seeing the stars.

What kind of man lusted after his brother's wife?

SARAH woke up slowly, stretching the muscles in her back, her legs. Her bed felt soft and warm and she didn't want to leave it. She reached her arm out, her fingers searching for the annoying alarm clock, intending to stop its incessant pounding. Nothing. She opened her eyes and reality pushed away the sweetness of her dreams.

Her little apartment, her clothes, her refrigerator, her running water—they were all more than a hundred years away. She'd slept in John Beckett's bed. And if she wasn't mistaken, he stood outside the door, about to break it open with his bare fist.

"Hang on," she yelled, swinging her legs over the side of the bed. Good grief, what time was it? She lifted up the edge of the curtain as she hurried past the window. The sun remained half-hidden by the horizon.

She whipped open the door, and John, his fist raised to pound, practically fell through it. She stepped back.

"Good morning," she said. She smiled when she saw a piece of straw sticking out of his hair.

He frowned at her and then looked down at her foot. She'd unwrapped the makeshift bandage the night before, thinking some air might help the cut heal. "It's better," she said. "Thanks."

He had on the same clothes he'd worn the night before. The fabric of the shirt stretched across his broad chest, his flat stomach. His pants clung to his lean hips.

She resisted the urge to snap one of his suspenders. "Were you out there a long time?" she asked.

"Long enough," he said, not looking at her.

"Sorry," she said, feeling awkward. She'd taken the poor man's bed. He had a right to feel put out. "You should have come in. There's no lock," she reminded him. She realized that little tidbit late last night, after he'd left her. She'd washed up quickly, grateful for the clean water. Out of habit, she'd walked over to lock the door only to discover there was no lock, no deadbolt, not even a flimsy chain like the ones you'd find in motel rooms.

For all of ten seconds, she'd contemplated pulling up the chair and wedging it underneath the door handle. She'd dismissed the idea, knowing it would offer little protection, but would send a very clear message to John that she didn't trust him.

She didn't want to do that. While not overly friendly, the man had been a true gentleman. She'd been flat on her back in his bed. He'd had the perfect opportunity to take advantage of her, but he hadn't. Instead, he'd taken care of her and she didn't want to repay his kindness by acting like a scared virgin waiting for him to jump her bones.

Not that being a scared virgin would require any acting.

It probably wasn't in her best interest for him to know that. After all, he thought she'd been married to his brother. She felt fairly confident that Sarah One hadn't left her husband's bed untouched. Not if the man had had much in common with his brother.

"You don't have to knock. I mean," she stammered over her words, "it's not like I sleep naked or anything."

He stared at the plain white nightgown she'd borrowed from Fred's house. It buttoned up to her throat and almost dragged on the ground. Still, the way his eyes raked over her, she suddenly felt like she was wearing a sheer negligee.

"Just answer the damn door the next time," he said.

"No problem." She held up her hands. "Have you had your coffee yet, John?" she asked, hoping he'd get the idea that it was too early to fight.

"Fred will be here in fifteen minutes," he said, turning toward the door. "You better get dressed."

Sarah walked around him and peeked out the door. She took a deep breath, holding the fresh morning air in her lungs. "What a beautiful morning," she said.

"I don't remember you being all that fond of mornings," John said.

She could hear the curiosity in his voice and wanted to kick herself. Sarah One must have been a late riser. "True," she said, without turning around. "I meant in comparison to how cool some of the mornings have been."

"It's spring, Sarah. You know it doesn't warm up here until June." He walked past, careful not to brush up against her. He went out the door and headed toward the barn. Morton, running full speed around the corner of the barn, met him halfway. She heard his sharp whistle and the dog fell into step next to him. John bent over and rubbed his hand across the big dog's head.

The man had nice hands. As terrified as she'd been after realizing that she'd somehow slipped through a crack in time, she'd been coherent enough to catalog a number of things about John Beckett. Nice hands. Sexy walk. Shiny, thick hair. And a mean attitude that wouldn't quit.

His dead brother's wife wasn't welcome and he didn't intend to pretend otherwise.

She tried not to let it bother her as she quickly slipped her nightgown over her head. She grabbed a skirt out of the bag she'd gotten from Fred. When she pulled it on, she realized that more than three inches rested on the ground.

What she wouldn't do for a Saturday morning trip to the mall. She pulled her skirt down, stepped out of it, and walked over to the shelf near the stove. She grabbed a knife. She might be stuck in no-man's-land for another five days but she didn't intend to trip over her skirt the entire time.

With very little patience and even less finesse, she cut a wide strip of fabric off the bottom. She held the skirt up, surveying the damage. She never had been able to cut along the line. However, since only three hungry, dirty kids would see her, she didn't intend to worry about it. She grabbed a blouse from the pile and barely had it buttoned before John was back pounding on the door.

"Fred is here. Are you ready?"

She ran her fingers through her hair and slipped her feet into the shoes she'd worn home from Fred's. They were too big but better than nothing. "I'll be right out," she said.

When she opened up the door, both men turned to stare at her. Fred smiled and John had his usual stern look.

"What did you do to that skirt?" he asked.

"I cut it. With your knife," she said.

He frowned at her.

"It's no problem, John," Fred said. "It's not like Franny would mind. Hell, she'd probably be flattered. To think, Sarah Beckett is wearing her clothes."

"I suppose . . ." John narrowed his eyes at Sarah. "If you were staying longer, maybe you could get Hooper's store to special order you something."

His tone said it all. There wasn't a chance in hell that he'd let her stay long enough. He couldn't wait for her to leave.

Well, that made two of them. She walked over to her

horse, patted the animal on its head, and then turned toward John. "I don't think that's necessary. We've agreed that I'm leaving in five days."

"That's right, you are." John placed his hands on his hips. "I'm going to put you on that stage myself."

FOUR

SARAH had almost made friends with her horse by the time she and Fred reached his house. On the ride over, she concentrated on relaxing one muscle at a time. The hardest had been her hands. She'd watched Fred guide his horse, his massive paws barely holding the reins. She'd had to concentrate fiercely on each finger but had managed to ride the last five hundred yards with the reins just resting in her sweaty palms.

She had hiked up her skirt so that she could slide off the saddle in one motion. It hadn't been smooth or pretty but she had done it on her own. Now she stood next to her horse, rubbing her hand down its velvet nose. "Thanks, sweet thing," she murmured. "Not as convenient as a cab, but you'll do."

"What's that, Sarah?" Fred asked.

For a big man, he moved quietly. "Nothing. Just making small talk with my horse."

Fred pressed his lips together. "I imagine Thunder is glad to have a woman on her back again. Franny loved to ride."

Thunder. Fred's big brute of an animal was named Light-ning. Thunder and Lightning. What nature had seen fit to put together, disease had ripped apart. "I'm sorry about your wife," Sarah said. She didn't need to have known Franny to mourn her loss. Especially not when three children had been left motherless.

Fred cleared his throat. "Thank you," he said. "I miss her. It's the strangest thing. Sometimes, I'll ride in at night and I'll forget. I think that I'm going to go inside my house and she'll be standing there, making dinner, the children gathered around her."

He turned slightly and she could no longer see his face. There was no need. She could hear the tears in his voice.

"I open the door and it hits me. She's gone and my house is empty. Even when the children are there, it still seems empty, like there's a piece missing. She was only twenty-six."

Sarah swallowed hard. Two years younger than she.

She wasn't ready to die. Young people shouldn't die. She thought of poor Miguel Lopez. Of how his mother suf-fered at the thought of losing her child. "It's a terrible thing when someone young dies," Sarah said. "These last months must have been horrible for you."

He turned and faced her, not bothering to wipe away the tears that slid down his cheeks. "I don't deserve your sympa-thy. Everybody thinks I'm strong but I'm not. I'm weak."

His voice held a desperation that touched her. She sup-posed she could give him the standard lecture on the stages of grief but didn't think that was something Sarah One would spout at the drop of a hat. "Everybody handles things differently, Fred. Grief is a personal emotion."

"Is that why you went away so quickly after Peter's death? Was that how you handled your grief?"

It was an ugly question but his tone made it clear he meant no harm. He was curious. "I just knew it was time to go."

"Peter's death hit John hard," Fred said. "You know being older by a year ain't much, but John took his responsibilities as head of the family seriously. I think he blamed himself."

Blamed himself? Oh Lord, had Peter killed himself? Had Sarah One been such a shrew of a wife that her husband had felt compelled to make a final escape? "Why does he feel that way?" she asked, hoping the question wouldn't seem too odd. She wanted to know. She wanted to understand why John hated her so.

"I don't know for sure. He doesn't really talk about it. John was happy about the two of you moving to town. I think he thought the marriage would have a chance if he wasn't around so much. But he never expected that Peter would take such a risk."

A risk? Peter hadn't killed himself. No, he'd done something and the end result had been his death. Had Sarah One been there? She couldn't very well ask that question, could she? By John's attitude, she had to assume she'd played a role, that she'd either done something to cause it or hadn't done enough to prevent it.

"I know John ain't crazy about having you back," Fred continued on, with the blunt honesty she had come to know and love, "but I sure as hell am glad. It's a big relief not having to worry about—"

With a slam, his worries tumbled out the front door. Thomas didn't have on a shirt. Helen had traces of tears on her cheeks, and Missy, sweet silent Missy, had her fingers flying. "Hello," she signed. "My name is Missy."

Sarah laughed, squatted, and hugged the little girl. It felt good to know that she'd made a difference in the little girl's life, kind of like when she'd helped a child at school and had known that she'd given him or her a foothold, something to perch on. "Hello, Missy," she signed back. "How are you?" She reached over and ruffled Thomas's hair. She smiled at Helen.

"I didn't think you'd come back," Helen said, not bothering to smile in return.

Hoped was more like it. "I promised your father."

"Promises don't mean all that much," Helen said.

Sarah saw the pure misery in the child's eyes and knew a story lurked behind her defiant attitude. The slump of Fred's shoulders, however, told her now wasn't the time or place to unravel the mystery.

"How about we go inside," Sarah said, "and let your father get into the field?"

"I want to go fishing," Thomas declared.

Visions of yesterday's near drowning came back in a hurry. "Maybe later," Sarah said.

"Pleeeease." Thomas drew the word out. Missy tugged on her skirt, looking confused. Thomas saw it and fell on the ground, flapping his arms and legs, with one finger stuck down his throat, in imitation of a hook. Missy smiled, a big wide grin. She, too, fell to the ground, flopping around like a fish.

Helen, for once acting like the little girl she was, laughed and pretended to reel Thomas in by pulling on his hair. Sarah was wise enough to know when she was beaten. "Fine, we'll fish. But I'm not cleaning them."

IN the end, none of them cleaned fish. The four rainbow trout stayed in the bucket, forgotten, when the hot, tired, and sunburned group returned home and found an empty buggy, drawn by a single white and gray speckled horse. They walked inside and saw a young woman sitting at the head of the kitchen table.

"Hello," Sarah said, shifting the still-sleeping Missy in her arms. The woman stared at Sarah and then at each of the three grubby children.

Sarah glanced at Helen. The little girl seemed surprised but not frightened. Thomas just looked curious. Had Sarah

One known this woman? She smiled at the visitor, hoping to get a clue.

The woman, her silk dress rustling, stood. She stared somewhere over Sarah's shoulder. "I'm sorry. I didn't mean to intrude," she said.

The woman had absolutely gorgeous hair. Dark brown with just a hint of auburn, it hung almost to her waist, in gentle waves. Her peaches-and-cream complexion made Sarah want to reach up and cover the freckles on her own nose.

"You're not intruding." Sarah walked over to the children's bed and carefully laid Missy on it. She straightened up, rubbing her back. "We've been fishing."

"I . . . I was worried about the children." The woman busied herself with brushing invisible lint off her dress. She picked up her small beaded purse from the table. "I've got to be going." She took two steps toward the door before stopping. She finally made eye contact with Sarah, looking quite miserable. "Would you be so kind," she asked, her voice unsteady, "as to tell Fred that Suzanne stopped by."

Suzanne. It had to be the mysterious Miss Suzanne of the pretty dresses. The woman who could make Fred blush and stammer. Sarah took a chance. "My name is Sarah. I'm in town for a couple days. Fred needed someone to watch the children and I needed a couple extra dollars."

"You're staying just a few days?"

"That's right," she answered. "Just until the next stage passes through."

Suzanne looked around the cabin, her eyes settling on the empty bed directly across the room from where Sarah had put Missy. One of Fred's huge shirts lay on top of the pillow. "I don't see your bags."

Sarah pulled out a chair and sat down. "I'm not staying here."

Suzanne smiled. It was a slightly lopsided grin that made her look very young. "That's wonderful," she said.

With a self-conscious gesture, she pushed her hair behind her ear.

Sarah looked at Helen and Thomas, who still hung close to the door. "Why don't the two of you go outside and play. I want an opportunity to get to know Suzanne."

Thomas nodded and left without a word. Helen looked from Suzanne to Sarah, frowning at both of them.

Suzanne smiled at the girl, clearly trying to win her over. "Helen, it's nice to see you again."

"I don't know why either of you have to be here," Helen said, her hands on her hips. "We were doing fine on our own."

It didn't take a genius to see that Helen wanted to be the woman of the house. Sarah turned her back to the little girl, winking at Suzanne. "Of course you were, Helen. In fact, your father told me he couldn't have managed these last months without your help."

"Did he really say that?" she asked, her voice a mixture of hope and suspicion.

Sarah turned and gave the girl her full attention. "Yes. You've done a wonderful job with your sister and brother. You should be very proud."

"I can't cook like Ma." With her chin in the air, Helen tossed the words out like a challenge.

"Your mother had years of practice," Sarah said.

"I can't sew as good as Ma."

Sarah nodded. "I imagine not."

"Ma promised she was going to teach me but . . ."

Silence hung in the air. Sarah's heart broke for the little girl. *But she died before she had the chance.* Just like little Miguel would die before he'd finished his work. She searched for the right words. "I'm sure—"

"I'm not much of a seamstress either," Suzanne interrupted, her voice soft. "And I haven't ever done much in the way of cooking. But I know a woman in town who can do both. Problem is, she can't read."

"I'm a good reader. Pa is always saying so."

Suzanne walked over to Helen. "You don't suppose you'd be willing to spend a couple hours helping her learn to read? Maybe she'd be willing to share some cooking and sewing secrets with you."

Helen's eyes lit up. "I'll ask my pa."

"You do that. If he says it's fine, then I'll make the arrangements." Suzanne patted the girl's shoulder. "You go on outside now. Who knows what Thomas is in to?"

"Ma used to say that trouble followed Thomas around."

"Your mother was a very wise woman," Suzanne said.

"And pretty, too," Helen added.

"Pretty, too," Suzanne agreed.

"Not as pretty as you," Helen said as she opened the door. Halfway down the steps, she turned. "You're beautiful."

Sarah waited until Helen got out of hearing range before turning to Suzanne. "That was brilliant. She loves books."

"I know. Her father told me."

"Oh. Are you and Fred friends?"

"We're . . ." Suzanne looked around the room as if the answer were written on the walls. "We're sort of friendly. Look, I really do have to be going." She reached for her purse but Sarah grabbed it first.

"Please stay," she said. "I like you, and right now, I could use a friend."

Suzanne shook her head. "It's not in your best interest to be friends with me."

"I don't understand."

"You're not from around here, are you?"

Sarah waved her hand. "I used to live here but it's been a while."

Playing with her earlobe, Suzanne looked at Sarah. "I came to Cedarbrook about two months ago."

Wonderful. She wouldn't have known the dastardly Sarah One. "Do you live in town?" Sarah asked.

Suzanne nodded, looking frustrated. "I live above the saloon."

Those silly puzzle pieces started to line up their irregular edges. Low self-esteem. A room over the saloon.

"Fred was one of my first . . . acquaintances."

Click. Corner piece just slid home. Sarah didn't have to wonder any longer about that pained look in Fred's eyes earlier when he'd confessed his weakness.

"I gather his father-in-law doesn't know," Sarah said.

Suzanne looked alarmed. "That would be horrible for Fred."

So that's the way it was. She didn't care about her own reputation but she didn't want Fred's to be maligned. "Just how long did it take before you knew Fred wasn't just another acquaintance?" Sarah asked.

Suzanne blushed, her fair skin turning a bright pink. "The second time," she whispered. "He brought me a flower. Nobody had ever done that before."

"He'll be sorry he missed you. He's in the field."

"I heard that Missy scared off the Indian woman."

For a world without e-mail or cell phones, word sure did travel fast. "When did you hear that?"

"Last night, at the saloon. The woman must have run right from here to the next place east, the Wainrights'. Homer Wainright sent her away, much to the dismay of his wife, who spends all her time raising their seven children."

"Bad for Mrs. Wainright but good for Fred. Maybe he can convince the woman to come back here," Sarah said.

"I don't think so. She told Mrs. Wainright she had a vision that the same evil spirit who took Missy's hearing and voice is coming back. Anyone in the house is at risk."

A couple of days ago Sarah would have scoffed at the idea of evil spirits. Funny how a little time travel expanded the belief system. "What do you think about that?" she asked.

"I think it's nonsense."

Sarah relaxed, grateful for Suzanne's easy dismissal. She hadn't just found a friend; she'd found a voice of reason.

"I really do have to be getting back to town." Suzanne smiled at Sarah. "I have to work tonight."

Sarah resisted the urge to ask her to reconsider, knowing that her modern-day indignity over Suzanne's chosen profession didn't align all that well with the cold reality of 1888. "It was a pleasure to meet you," she said. "Please come back."

Suzanne's cheeks turned even pinker. "I'll try. I'm a bit embarrassed, though. I was too busy hating you for being here. I think I missed why you said you were only going to be here for a couple days."

The urge for self-protection smothered out the urge to confide. "John Beckett is my brother-in-law. I'm just here for a short visit."

"Oh." Suzanne's eyes got even bigger. "You're *that* Sarah?"

"I guess you've heard of me."

Suzanne ran her tongue over her teeth. "You're different than I would have expected. Nicer."

"I'm mellowing in my old age."

"Your brother-in-law is a very handsome man. He has all that wonderful hair and those muscles."

Suzanne knew John. Oh, my.

He probably went to the saloon. Of course, he would. What else did single men have to do in Wyoming? He probably played cards and had a couple beers with the guys. Maybe he'd even made a trip or two up the old saloon stairs himself.

Sarah felt sick. "Is he one of your acquaintances, too?"

Suzanne chuckled. "Not mine. He's Fred's best friend."

"I suppose that would be awkward."

"Even if I was interested, he wouldn't be. Most every girl there has tried one time or another. He always smiles that sexy little smile and refuses right politely, like they'd offered him a piece of peach pie but he was too full for dessert."

You had to like a man who watched his calorie intake.

"I'll make sure Fred knows you stopped by."

"Thanks. And," Suzanne hesitated, "could you let him know that I hope he can make it on Sunday."

"Sunday? Fred and his father-in-law are having lunch with you?"

"After lunch," Suzanne added, clearly understanding Sarah's confusion. "The children love getting to spend a couple hours with Grandpa."

"Where does dear old dad think Fred is spending his afternoons?"

"Playing cards. He never says much to Fred about it. By the way, where are you headed when you leave here?"

"California."

"That's a long way," Suzanne said. "You going to catch the train in Cheyenne?"

"Train? Please, please, do not be teasing me. There really is a train? I thought I'd have to take a stage the whole way."

Suzanne frowned at her. "Of course there's a train. Just where have you been living the last ten years?"

"Under a rock, obviously," Sarah teased, hoping the woman wouldn't probe. A train meant that she'd be back in California before she had hoped.

"It would be nice if you could stay around," Suzanne said. "I've enjoyed today."

Sarah nodded. "Me, too. But there are people waiting for me in California. I can't stay." Not that she wanted to. She wanted to be back to the land of running water and flush toilets.

"But you've barely had any time to spend with your brother-in-law."

"Trust me on this one. He'll help me pack," Sarah said,

trying to lighten the mood. It hurt that John Beckett hadn't given her a chance. He'd taken one look at her and her fate had been sealed. He hadn't bothered to look deeper.

"I hope to see you before you go," Suzanne said.

"Definitely. I'll stop by the saloon."

FRED, who seemed barely able to drag his tired body into the house, perked up when he heard about Suzanne's visit. He had his mouth full of a ham sandwich that Sarah had made for him. He took a big swig of water to wash it down.

"What did she have to say?" he asked.

"She was worried about the children."

"Anything else?"

"She said she looked forward to seeing you on Sunday."

Fred smiled and folded his big arms across his chest. "What else?"

"That's about it."

Fred looked over his shoulder. Missy slept while Thomas and Helen played dominoes at the corner table. He leaned forward. "Do you think she likes me?"

Good grief. She'd time-traveled back to seventh grade. "We didn't have time to pass notes."

"What?"

"Never mind. Why don't you ask her yourself?"

He looked shocked. "I can't do that. I barely know her."

Right. They'd been too busy screwing to get properly introduced. "I guess there's knowing and then there's *knowing*. By the way, she smells like violets, too."

"I don't smell like violets."

She nodded.

He looked horrified, then a ghost of a smile crossed his lips. "She's got this lotion," he said. "She gave me some one day. When I use a little, it reminds me of her."

Sarah took a deep breath. She didn't know if she wanted

to smack Fred upside the head or hug him silly. "Take my advice. On Sunday, spend a couple minutes talking. She's nice."

"I know that," he snapped. "It's just . . . difficult. I've got the children to consider. It would kill Pastor Dan."

"Pastor Dan?"

"My father-in-law. He's a good man. And John wouldn't like this at all."

"What's John got to do with this?"

"He's my best friend. I'd trust him with my life. I've known him for fourteen years and this is the only secret I've ever kept from him."

"You don't think he'd approve? What right does he have to judge you or your life?"

"It's not a matter of approving and he's certainly not the type to make judgments about anybody else's life. He knows that I loved Franny. He wouldn't doubt that. However, I suspect he'd think I'm not honoring her memory by sneaking up the saloon stairs on Sunday afternoons. I don't think it's what he'd do. He'd be stronger. He'd want me to be stronger. I just don't want to disappoint him."

"Maybe he'd understand if he knew that you cared for Suzanne, that she wasn't just any woman who lived above the saloon."

He looked surprised. "I didn't say I cared for her."

"Trust me, you did." Sarah winked at him.

Fred stared at her for a long minute before a smile crossed his weathered face. "I'm in a hell of a mess, aren't I?"

Sarah nodded. "It's a bit of a pickle."

Fred snorted. "Come on. I need to get you home. John's probably pacing a rut outside his front door."

FIVE

JOHN wasn't, but his horse, still saddled, was.

"I'm worried," Fred said after a quick search didn't turn up his friend.

"What's wrong?" Sarah asked.

"I don't know. My guess is that John's hurt."

Hurt? "Maybe his horse just ran away. Maybe he got off and forgot to tie it to a tree."

Fred shook his head. "John's horses are ground tied, same as mine. You just let their reins go to the ground and the horse stays put."

"How did this horse end up here, then?"

"I'm not sure. John has only been working with this colt for a week or so. My guess is something scared him and he took off. Horses always head back to the barn."

"So John's walking home?"

"Maybe. I doubt it. John's got a real way with horses. Even if the horse got scared, if John had been able, he'd have calmed him down. There's another thing. Morton isn't here. My guess is he stayed with John."

She hadn't even thought about the dog. "What do we do?"

"I'll go look for him. He said he had fence to fix up in the north pasture. I'll go there first. I'll take his horse with me so he'll have something to ride home."

"It's dark. How will you find him?"

"When I get close, I'll fire a couple shots. If he's able, he'll respond the same way."

If he's able. Yikes. "How badly do you think he's hurt?"

Fred shook his head. "Bad enough that he couldn't get on a horse. I've seen John bale hay with a sprained arm, brand cattle with broken ribs, and ride a horse all day and not bother to tell the rest of us he'd snapped his collarbone. He's a tough son of a bitch."

"I'm going, too," Sarah said, putting her foot back up in the stirrup.

"No," Fred said. "You'll slow me down and there's no telling what I'm going to find."

"But—"

At that exact moment, the howl of a coyote echoed from the hills. Sarah wrapped her arms around her middle. "What exactly might have scared the horse?" she asked.

Fred shrugged. "Mountain lion. Bear. Rattlesnake."

"Go," Sarah said. "Find him and bring him home."

CALL 911. Since she'd been a toddler, that's what she'd been trained to do in an emergency. Now what was she supposed to do?

Fumbling with the wick on the lantern, Sarah cursed the good old days. When she finally managed to get the lantern lit, she set it down on the table next to the stove. Think. You have to think, she lectured herself.

She'd read *Little House on the Prairie* a hundred times as a girl. What would Ma Ingalls have done?

She'd have comforted the children.

No need. Skip to step two.

She'd have boiled water.

Perfect. Something to do. Sarah filled her arms with kindling from next to the stove. She lifted the burner plate and dropped the wood inside. In less than a minute, she had a fire started. Then she grabbed the biggest pot from the shelf. Carrying that in one hand and the lantern in the other, she went outside to get water.

She was halfway back from the pump when she heard the gunshots—just two sharp taps. She stopped, her breath coming in short gasps from lugging the heavy pot. Less than five seconds went by and she heard two more taps, fainter, as if they'd come from farther away.

John Beckett had answered. He was alive. Sarah tightened her grip on the pot handle and hurried into the house. She lifted the big pot onto the stove.

Now what? Bandages.

Oh, what she wouldn't do for a Wal-Mart.

She opened the cupboard and looked for towels. Empty. Looking around, she weighed her options. The cotton curtains on the windows certainly weren't sterile. The sheets on the bed would be better. But then what would he sleep on? Next to the bed sat the bag she'd brought home from Fred's house the night before.

Flipping over the canvas flap, she quickly pulled out the entire contents. She sorted through the clothes, pulling out two white petticoats.

She checked the water. Getting warm. She added some more wood to the fire.

She grabbed the knife from the shelf and, within minutes, had carved up both garments into strips of cloth. She laid them on the table next to the bed. Then she walked around the cabin and gathered all three lanterns and placed them next to the bed.

Hot water. Bandages. Light. She started to feel a little better, as if she might not be a complete idiot after all. She sat down on the bed and tried to remember how to do CPR. Was it fifteen breaths and two thumps or two breaths and fifteen thumps?

Either way, she realized with a sick feeling, it didn't matter. If he wasn't breathing at this stage of the game, no amount of thumping on his chest would make it happen.

She did not want John to be dead. Yes, he'd been judgmental, sarcastic, and a bit of a prude. But he'd also given her shelter and cared for her when she'd had literally nowhere to go.

Now, she had nothing to do but wait. It made her feel helpless. More of what she'd been feeling for the last month. Since the day she'd first met Miguel Lopez.

Sarah pulled out a chair and sat at the old wood table, her elbows braced on the scratched surface, her chin resting on her folded hands. She'd never forget that day. She'd gotten a call from one of the second grade teachers, who was concerned about a child. The boy had missed many days of school owing to illness, and on the days he did come to class, he was agitated, almost frantic to catch up. He was disrupting the class.

It had taken Sarah two weeks and four sessions to learn the truth. And if she'd lost her heart on that first day that she'd sat across from the solemn boy with the dark eyes and flyaway hair, she'd felt it break the day he finally confessed his greatest fear.

Miguel Lopez was dying and he knew it. But that wasn't what he was scared of.

His family had come from Mexico. Just the year before, his mother had brought Miguel and his two younger sisters to the United States. When Miguel had started school, Rosa Lopez had told her son to make her proud, to learn to read and write English. That once he had learned, he could teach her.

Miguel was worried that he was going to die before he got the chance.

Later that evening, when she'd gone to his home and talked with Rosa Lopez, she'd realized that even when things are bad, they can get worse. Not only was Miguel Lopez going to die young, he was going to die alone.

At first Sarah hadn't understood. Rosa had explained that Miguel's doctors had arranged for him to go to a children's hospital north of Los Angeles. Sarah had tried to tell Rosa that Miguel would receive excellent care. Then Rosa had explained that she didn't drive, that she could perhaps find the occasional ride or take the long bus trip but that would mean leaving her young daughters with strangers.

When Rosa had told her that the doctors had said that Miguel could be cared for at home with special equipment and special nurses, Sarah had realized how important that was. Miguel would have time with his mother, time to teach, time to know that he'd made her proud. Rosa would keep her family together. Then Rosa had told her, in her halting English, that there had been a man who'd come to her house and sold her the insurance for her family. He'd told her it would pay for someone to come to her home to take care of her family. However, now the company was telling her that they would not pay for home care; they would pay only if he was in a hospital.

Sarah had been sure that she could help. She'd contacted the company, speaking to everyone from the claims examiner to the vice president. They'd all told her the same thing. *No. To set up care in the home would be more expensive and the policy that Rosa Lopez had purchased didn't cover it*. She'd understood perfectly what they hadn't said. They weren't interested in paying for anything they didn't have to. She'd reasoned, she'd debated, she'd argued, and then finally begged—and she'd gotten nowhere.

She'd been sure that she had failed until she'd returned that man's call. But she'd never gotten a chance to tell Rosa. She'd been whisked off the beach and tumbled back in time. She had to find a way back. Before it was too—

Morton's bark interrupted her thoughts. "Late," she finished, her voice a whisper in the quiet cabin. "Please, God. Don't let us be too late tonight." She grabbed the lantern, opened the door, and watched the two horses walk slowly back into the yard. Morton trotted alongside John's horse.

At first she thought one horse was riderless, but when they got another thirty feet closer, she could see John sitting in the saddle, bent over the saddle horn, so that he was almost lying on the horse. Fred had both sets of reins in his hand as he led John's horse.

"How bad is he hurt?" she asked, not able to move off the porch.

"Sliced his head open and he's got a hell of a lump. Might have cracked it."

Didn't people die from fractured skulls? "Cracked it?" she repeated, her voice small in the big, dark night. "Are you sure?"

"Hell no, I'm not sure. All I know is he was conscious when I found him. He's been floating in and out most of the way here."

Concussion. Brain damage. Coma. They'd just been words before. "Let me help you get him inside." She hurried toward the horse but stopped when John lifted his head a couple inches.

"Hi," she said. She wanted to weep but didn't think he'd like it or appreciate it. "I'll bet you've got one heck of a headache."

"I've felt better," he admitted. "You won't want to come too close," he said, his voice rough.

"He smells a bit ripe," Fred said.

He did. He smelled like vomit and sweat and blood. She swallowed hard and took three more steps and raised the lantern to get a better look. Blood covered the left side of his head and neck. His hair, all that beautiful hair, now lay limp and dark, plastered to his skull.

Sarah pressed her lips together tight, afraid she might

get sick, too. Fred got off his horse and moved to her side. He cupped her elbow with his hand. "He needs you, Sarah."

She nodded and took a deep breath. "John, you should be inside. Can you walk?"

No response but she watched as he slowly pulled both feet out of the stirrups.

"Good," she said. "If you can just slide down, Fred will take one side and I'll take the other."

"Too heavy for you," he said.

"I'll just be there for balance," she said. "You can lean on Fred."

He slowly slid sideways in the saddle, and somehow, she and Fred managed to catch him before he hit the ground. Fred, who stood a good six inches taller than John and more than a foot taller than Sarah, bent over and looped one of John's arms over his neck. Sarah reached for John's other arm and flung it over her own shoulder. Together, they managed to get him into the house. They were six feet from the bed when Sarah realized they were literally dragging him. He had passed out again.

They dumped him on the bed as gently as possible. Sarah took a quick step back, sucking in gulps of air.

"Heavy son of a bitch, ain't he?" Fred said, trying to smile, awkwardly patting his friend's leg.

He was. Six feet of pure muscle. "We need a doctor," Sarah said.

"Doc Mosley died two months ago," Fred said. "Nobody new has come yet."

Sarah whirled toward him. "No," she said. "You are not freakin' going to tell me there's no doctor."

Fred shrugged.

Sarah paced in front of the bed. "What kind of godforsaken place is this? No water, no telephones, no doctors. What's wrong with you people?"

Fred frowned at her. "Sarah?"

Sarah rubbed the palm of her hand across her mouth.

"Never mind," she said. "Just never mind. Now what? If there's no doctor, what do we do?"

"We do the same thing we'd do if there was a doctor. We wait. If he's lucky, he'll wake up with a hell of a headache. If he's not, well then, we'll deal with that, too."

Damn him for being so cold. Damn John Beckett for cracking his fool head open. Damn them all. "Okay," she said, walking over to the stove. "We wait. But in the meantime, I'm going to get him cleaned up."

"I'll help you," Fred said, taking off his coat.

Sarah shook her head. "No. You need to get home. Your children are by themselves. I can take care of this."

"He's my best friend," Fred said.

"And he's my family," Sarah lied. "You go now. Come back in the morning. We'll be fine." As she said it, she prayed it would be true.

"You're sure? It could be a long night."

"Positive. Don't worry about me. I can wait with the best of them," she said, standing on tiptoe to brush a kiss across Fred's cheek. "My middle name is Patience."

The big man looked a bit startled and then he smiled. "I like you, Sarah," he said. "You're a strange one, but I like you."

"I like you, Fred. Thank you for knowing what it meant when you saw his horse. Thank you for going to get him and bringing him home. If he . . ." She swallowed and started over. "When he wakes tomorrow, he'll have you to thank for it."

Fred moved to stand close to the bed. He placed his hand on John's shoulder and squeezed gently. "I'll see you tomorrow, John." He turned toward Sarah. "Good luck," he said.

She needed a miracle but she wouldn't turn her nose up at luck.

After Fred left, Sarah dipped enough boiling water out of the pan to fill two bowls. Leaving them to cool, she picked a square tin container off the shelf and opened it.

She had to look through three more before she found what looked like barley. She dumped a generous portion into the still-boiling pot. She didn't intend to waste the water. He'd be hungry when he woke up.

She stuck a finger into one of the bowls. Too hot still. She took the pitcher of water from the table and added just a bit. She needed hot water to get the dried blood off but she didn't want to burn him.

She sat next to him on the bed and set the bowl on the night table. She examined him, wondering where she should start. Afraid to look at his head, she concentrated on his face. He had dirt and blood on one cheek. She dipped her cloth into the bowl, wrung in out, and carefully dabbed at the dirt. When she got the grime off, she could see several scratches, as if he might have been tossed into the sagebrush.

She dipped her cloth again and moved down to his neck. Gently, she wiped off the blood that had dripped down the side of his head. When she ran her cloth across the strong ridge of his collarbone, he groaned.

It scared her so that she jerked back, jarring the bed. He grunted and opened his eyes.

"Hello," she said, a bit out of breath. "How do you feel?"

He closed his eyes. "Fine," he said.

"Right. Just stay still," she instructed.

"Trust me on this, Sarah. I'm not going anywhere," he said, his voice sounding strained.

"You've got a head injury," she said.

"Goddamn horse," he said.

She laughed, feeling absolute relief. If he knew what had happened, he couldn't be hurt too badly.

"Did your horse throw you?"

"Yes," he said, as if he couldn't quite believe it. "I haven't been thrown off a horse since I was fourteen."

"Why today?"

"Rattler came across the path."

"Rattler?" She swallowed hard. "As in rattlesnake?"

"One and the same. We'd have been fine but he had just shed his skin."

"I don't understand," Sarah said.

"Rattlers are blind for about twenty-four hours after they shed their skin. Most days they'll see a horse or a man and get the hell out of the way. But when they go blind, they'll strike at anything."

"Your poor horse," Sarah said.

John frowned at her. "It may be a couple days before I can work up much sympathy for the animal."

"He came home. That's how we knew something was wrong."

"That may save him."

Sarah laughed. "At least Morton stayed by your side."

"That's why he gets to live in the house. Where's Fred?" he asked.

"I sent him home to his children. He'll be back in the morning."

"What time is it?" John opened his eyes and tried to turn his head to the window. He groaned with the effort.

"It's probably about eleven," she said.

"At night?"

"Yes."

John scratched the sheet with his fingertips, as if he'd suddenly realized where he was. "Just give me a minute and I'll go out to the barn."

"You idiot," she said, thinking she might beat him if he wasn't already half-dead. "You're barely conscious. You're not going anywhere."

"No," he said. "I don't want to take your bed." He pulled his elbows back and tried to sit up. He got his head about three inches off the pillow. Every speck of color left his face and he closed his eyes.

"Lie down," Sarah ordered, scared that he'd slip away from her again. "Fine. You can sleep in the barn," she lied. "Just rest first."

He didn't respond but he did lower himself back onto the bed. She breathed a sigh of relief.

"I've got some water here," she said. "I'm going to wipe the blood off your head."

"You shouldn't have to do that," he protested.

"I don't mind. I'll be as gentle as I can. You've got a big bump and a pretty deep cut."

She wiped away the blood, getting as much as she could from his hair, being careful to avoid the edges of the cut. When she wrung out her rag, the water in the bowl turned a dark pink. She picked up a new rag and dipped it into the remaining fresh bowl. She dabbed around the edges of the cut, trying not to pull the reddened skin. It looked so deep. She felt helpless.

"You need stitches," she said. "You really do and I can't help you. I can't even do a stupid hem. Scalp is way out of my league."

"It will heal," he said, dismissing her concerns. "I've had worse. I'm just tired."

"You should stay awake," she said. "In case you have a concussion."

"No concussion," he said, closing his eyes. "Just tired."

She closed her own eyes, unwilling to let the tears escape. Did he know the seriousness of his injury? Did he realize that he might lapse into a coma and never wake up? That at this very minute, his skull could be pressing into his brain, causing internal bleeding that would ultimately cause his death?

Just weeks earlier, a ten-year-old from her school had been riding a bike without a helmet and had sailed over her handlebars. She'd died two hours later from a compressed skull fracture. Her parents had both been at work. They hadn't even gotten to say goodbye.

She placed her hand on his chest. It rose and fell, with each steady breath. She leaned forward until her lips were just inches from his ear. "You are going to wake up," she whispered. "You're going to wake up and smile and insult me and do whatever else comes naturally to you. I'm leaving in five days, and by God, you better be there for me to say goodbye to."

She got up, picked up both bowls, opened the front door, and threw the bloody water out into the yard. She needed fresh. Regretting that she'd been so quick to make soup, she picked up an empty pail, grabbed the lantern, and walked outside to the pump. She hurried, not liking the night sounds, the crickets, the yelp of a prairie dog, or the occasional call of a coyote.

She filled the bucket and quickly returned to the cabin. She checked her patient first. Still sleeping. She pulled two canning jars of what appeared to be cooked beef off the shelf, and added them to the simmering barley.

"Way to multitask," she said, feeling a bit loopy. "Cook. Clean. Care for others. No problem. All without a day planner or a task list. If I had a phone, I could check my voice mails. If I had my computer, I could check my e-mails. I could do them both at the same time. I can do anything. I'm Superwoman."

She sat down hard on the wooden chair, the impact reverberating up her spine. "You need to shut up, Sarah," she said. "You're losing it."

With the back of her hand, she wiped the sweat off her forehead. Pulling at the collar of her blouse, she tried to free her neck of the moist material. She wanted to open a window but knew the bugs would be attracted to the light from the lantern.

"Screens," she said, adding them to her things-to-be-thankful-for list, right behind indoor toilets and transportation with four wheels instead of four legs. "I will never again underestimate the value of a good screen."

She unbuttoned her blouse and shrugged it off, leaving just the sleeveless silk shirt she'd arrived in. The day before, as she'd hunted through Franny's clothes, she'd looked for a bra but hadn't found anything remotely close. Her shirt had a built-in bra but it wasn't like she was going to be able to wear it for the next five days.

She'd found underwear. Sort of. They were like pantaloons, coming down practically to her knees. No way, she'd decided. She would wash out her panties every night or she'd go without.

She reached both hands into the bucket, cupped a handful of water, and splashed it on her cheeks and forehead. She took a second handful and cooled off the back of her neck, enjoying the feel of the water sliding down her skin.

She yearned for a nice cool shower with raspberry shampoo and a really good hair conditioner. But what she wanted and what she was going to have to settle for were two very different things. She poured herself a cup of water, took a big drink, and walked back to the bed.

She felt bad that she'd let John drift off before she got to remove his shirt. He had to be uncomfortable and the smell was getting worse.

"You've got vomit on your shirt," she said quietly, hoping that he'd wake up.

No response.

"It's pretty gross."

She might as well have been talking to the wall. She put her cup of water down on the nightstand, reached for him, and undid the first button.

Her fingertips brushed against the hollow of his throat. His skin was very warm.

Second button. His chest was so tanned it almost seemed bronzed.

Third button. She peeled both edges back far enough that she could see his nipples. Small and pink and almost flat. She reached for her water and took another big gulp. How could she still be so thirsty?

Fourth button. The man had stomach muscles to die for.

Fifth and last button. She followed the faint line of hair from midbelly until it disappeared, captured by his belt.

Oh my God, it was hot in the cabin.

Unable to resist, she ran her fingers lightly down the center of his chest. He smiled, a soft, sexy smile.

She brushed her hand across his nipple. He groaned and arched his back.

She had, undoubtedly, reached the height of desperation.

She picked up her cup, dipped her finger into the water, and ever so lightly, swirled the wet tip around the edge of his belly button, then traced the thin line of hair until it disappeared into his pants.

He raised his hips, in a motion as old as time itself.

The heat lodged itself between her legs.

It didn't help that the buttons on his pants seemed about to burst.

She reached her hand out, wanting to feel him, to know him. She wanted—

Morton barked, a shrill slice into the quiet night. Sarah jerked back so abruptly that she spilled her water on John's bare stomach.

His eyes flew open. "What the hell?" he said, wiping his hand across his absolutely perfect abs.

She stood there, her mouth hanging open.

"Sarah?" John looked around, as if he expected danger to leap from the corner. What he didn't know was that she posed the only threat. My God, what had she been thinking?

"What's going on?" he asked.

She couldn't do a thing but stare at his bulging buttons.

He looked down, his eyes widened, then he glanced up again. "I guess I should be relieved," he said. "Looks like everything still works."

Oh baby, did it. "No problem," she said. "I unbuttoned your shirt. You probably got cold."

"This," he said, looking embarrassed, "is not what happens when a man gets cold."

She could feel the heat rise from her toes all the way to the top of her head. "Don't worry about it," she said, dismissing his concern. "It's no big deal." Liar. He had a big, big deal happening. "I'm going outside. I need some more water." While she was there, she'd stick her head under the pump for a few seconds and try to cool down her raging hormones. "I'll be right back."

"It's too dark out. You might trip. I'll get it," he said, trying to sit up.

She shook her head. "I'll be fine. I've already made one trip. Your shirt needs to be soaked or the blood will never come out."

He looked at his shirt and wrinkled his nose. "I appreciate your help, Sarah."

"It's nothing. Really. You'd do the same for me. Actually," she said, pointing to her foot, "you have done the same. I'll be right back."

"Okay," John said, closing his eyes. He listened to her move around the cabin and kept his eyes shut until he heard the door slam. Then he carefully opened one, then the other. He looked down at his crotch.

He was still painfully erect. He shifted a bit on the bed, trying to make it look a little less obvious. How the hell had this happened? Christ, he'd never lost control like that. Not even when tempted by the women at the saloon or the women at the store or at the bank who managed to brush up against him.

After the damn horse had thrown him and left him, he'd managed to drag himself to some shade. Lucky for him, he'd had his canteen hooked on his belt. Otherwise, he'd probably have died of thirst. He'd drifted in and out all day, always waking up drenched in sweat. More than once, when the pain had lulled him back to sleep, he'd dreamed about her breasts. About the shape, the fullness, the absolute perfection. He'd imagined her nipples. She was so blond and fair skinned. Would they be a pale pink, a beautiful apricot, or a lush rose? Would she cry out when he sucked them? Would she scream in pleasure when he rolled them with his fingertips?

He'd injured his brain. Either that or he'd been without a woman for too long. After all, it had been over six months since he'd had one underneath him, so long that he'd almost forgotten the taste and feel of soft flesh. That had to be the only excuse. Sarah had lived in his house for months and he'd never once been attracted to her. Hell, he hadn't even liked her. Now, she'd been back a day and this was happening.

She seemed different. Sweeter. Funnier.

But she'd been his brother's wife. If nothing else, that made her off-limits.

She'd no doubt been nice to Peter at one time, too. No telling how many men she'd been nice to since she'd left Cedarbrook six months ago. No telling how many she'd let in her bed. The Sarah he knew wasn't above selling her body. She'd be subtler than the girls at the saloon, but before some unsuspecting fool knew it, he'd have stopped thinking with his head and started thinking with his cock.

He didn't intend for her to make a fool of him that way.

SIX

JOHN awoke to an empty cabin. He struggled to sit up, wincing when the slight movement caused the room to spin. He looked toward the window. The breeze coming in blew so strong that the white cotton curtain stood at a forty-five-degree angle. The sun was already well above the horizon.

Sucking in a deep breath, he swung his legs over the side of the bed. Now the room didn't just spin, it whirled, causing him to shut his eyes and hold on to his empty stomach. "Christ," he said. "I'm going to kill him."

Just then, the door opened and Fred stepped inside. He took off his cowboy hat and walked toward the bed. He smiled at John. "Morning. Nice to see you're still with us."

John knew he owed this man his life. Another couple hours and the coyotes would have had him for dinner. "Thanks for coming to get me," he said.

"So I guess it's not me."

John frowned at him.

Fred shrugged. "Window's open," he explained. "Who you going to kill?"

"Not who. What. I'm going to kill that damn horse."

Fred shook his head. "You don't have it in you to hurt an animal."

"Things are different now," John said, shifting slightly so that he could lean his head back against the bed frame. "I've got a hole in my head."

"Just a small slice. Barely a dent."

"Dent? Good Lord, man. Go back up there in the daylight and you'll see. I left most of my brains scattered on those rocks." Which, he decided, might explain why he'd totally stopped thinking the night before. Why he had, for some reason known only to a vindictive and poor-humored God, been able to think about only one thing. No, take that back. Two things. Two absolutely perfect breasts. The two things he vowed never to think about again.

"Where's my sister-in-law?" John asked.

"In the barn."

"She slept in the barn?" When Sarah had returned to the cabin with clean water, he'd somehow managed not to make a fool of himself when she'd helped him take off his shirt. He'd washed himself up and slipped into a clean shirt. Then he'd closed his eyes for just a second.

"I don't think she slept much," Fred said. "You got clean laundry hanging on the line."

She'd done laundry in the middle of the night?

"She's got the eggs gathered and is just finishing up with the second cow."

"She's milking?" John couldn't keep the surprise out of his voice.

"Yeah. She's damned untidy about it, though." Fred shook his head in bewilderment. "Between the floor and her dress, I'll bet you lost half a bucket. Kept talking to the cows."

He couldn't help himself. "What was she saying?"

Fred grinned. "She was apologizing. Something about squeezing and groping."

"She lived here for months and I don't think she ever even went into the barn."

"Well, that explains it," Fred said. "How you feeling?"

"Like someone swung an ax at me, knocked me down, and left the blade in my head."

"You're going to have to take it easy for a few days."

"I put off fixing fence to get my crops in. I can't put it off any longer. I don't want my cattle getting out."

"I'll do it," Fred said.

"You can't. You've got your own work to do." John pushed himself out of bed and managed to get in a standing position. That is, if a person bent over, hanging on to the corner post of the bed, could be counted as standing. "See, I'm fine."

At that exact moment, the door swung open. Sarah came in, carrying a basket of eggs and a pail of milk. "What are you doing?" she asked, hurriedly setting the items on the table. She rushed over to the bed, wrapped an arm around his middle, and gently pushed him back onto the bed.

She smelled like fresh milk and sweet alfalfa.

She turned toward Fred and pointed an accusing finger at him. "Why are you just standing there? Did you intend to let him fall over?"

"He's the most bullheaded person I've ever met," Fred said, not at all embarrassed. "Said he could go out and fix fence today. I figured he'd come to his senses if he stood up and fell over before he got to the door."

"Men," Sarah said, looking disgusted. "I just don't get it."

"Get what?" Fred asked.

"You're supposed to be his friend."

"I am. I wanted him to fall here where I'd have a chance of catching him rather than off some cliff in the high country. Now maybe he'll listen to me and let me finish fixing his fence."

"Quit talking about me like I'm not here," John growled. "I'm not dead yet."

Sarah shook her head and rubbed her temples. She turned toward Fred. "Where are the children?"

"At home. Helen and Thomas were up when I left. No doubt Missy's out and about by now. I told Helen I'd be back later, that I needed to help John."

"You should have brought them with you. I can babysit here just as well as at your house."

"You've got your hands full already, Sarah," Fred said.

"That's me," John said, crossing his arms over his chest. "I'm a handful."

Sarah frowned at him and turned back to Fred. "The clean laundry needs to come in. I've still got the towels to wash. I can take care of that—the children will help. Then you can spend the morning here fixing fence and still have time to do some of your own work."

"You've got to be exhausted," Fred said. "Did you sleep at all last night?"

"Sure," Sarah said, turning her back toward the men. She lifted a stove burner and stuffed some kindling inside.

"You're a bad liar," Fred said. "Maybe the worst I've ever seen. Isn't she a horrible liar, John?"

"I don't know," John said, wondering how this woman had managed to upset his life in just two short days. It had to stop. "Maybe she's lied about so many things, she doesn't even know what the truth is anymore."

He tried to ignore the startled little hiss that escaped from Sarah.

Damn her. How dare she look so hurt? This woman had lied to his brother many times over. "Don't you remember, Sarah? Don't you remember lying to Peter about wanting to live on a ranch, wanting to help him, wanting to have his children?"

Sarah's back looked as if she had a steel rod running up it. She didn't say anything.

"Don't you remember telling him that his dreams had become your dreams?"

With deliberate motions, Sarah picked up two eggs from the basket, cracked them against the counter, and dumped them into an empty bowl. She grabbed a fork from the shelf and started stirring.

No one said a word. Finally, Fred spoke. "John, I know you probably got a hell of a headache, but there ain't no reason to be mean."

"This is none of your business," John said.

"It's not important," Sarah said. "Look, I'm going to make myself some eggs. Would either of you like some?"

Damn her. He didn't want eggs. He wanted her to fight back, to show her true self, so that he could stop thinking crazy thoughts.

"What's that in the pot?" Fred asked, motioning to the stove.

"Beef and barley soup," she said, keeping her back to him.

"Soup?" John asked. "Where did we get soup?"

"I made it last night."

She'd made soup? What else had she done? Washed down the walls? Shod some horses?

"You need to stop doing things," he said. He did not want to be beholden to her.

She whirled toward him, her mouth in a tight line. "I was worried about you," she said. "I wanted to help."

"I don't need or want your help."

"I wouldn't worry about me offering a whole lot more," she said. She set the bowl of raw eggs down and walked out the door.

It made him all the madder when she calmly shut it.

"You're an ass," Fred said, his voice heavy with disappointment.

He was. But it was her fault.

"She's done nothing but be helpful since she got here two days ago. You know it probably wasn't easy for her to see you that way last night but she held up better than most men I know would have," Fred said.

"I didn't ask her to."

"No, you didn't have to. That's the point."

"Well, she's gone now," John said.

Fred walked over to the window and looked out. "She didn't go far," he said.

"What do you mean?"

"She's hauling up water. Probably for the laundry."

"She doesn't even have a hat on."

"Nope."

"She didn't eat her breakfast. She should eat something before working in the sun."

"Probably," Fred agreed.

The two men stared at each other, neither showing any expression.

"You want her," Fred said, his eyes widening. "You want her and it's killing you."

"It's odd that you're the one talking crazy when I'm the one with a hole in my head."

"No. I don't know how to explain it. She seems prettier now. And a whole lot more womanly. A man would be crazy not to want her."

"I don't even like her."

"Try telling that to your cock."

John laughed, glad that he still could. He couldn't think of a bigger mess. He wanted Sarah flat on her back with her legs spread.

"What are you going to do about her?" Fred asked.

John shook his head. "Not one thing. She'll be gone in four days."

"A lot can happen in four days," Fred said.

"Absolutely nothing is going to happen. We'll keep out of each other's way and then she'll get on the stage and I'll never see her again. A month from now, I won't even re-member that she'd been here."

"You'll remember."

He would. As hard as he might try, he thought he might never forget. "Here's what you and I both need to remem-ber. We need to remember what an absolute bitch she was."

"People change."

"Do they? Do they ever really change or are they just good at pretending, hoping you'll see what they want you to see?"

"I've seen her with my children. I don't think she was pretending. I saw her last night. She cared, John. She cared about you."

"It's not possible." He lay back in bed, exhausted over just the small exchange. He hated being ill, being less than ready to handle whatever might come his way.

"I've known you a long time," Fred said, "and I've never known you to be deliberately unkind. I don't think Peter would have wanted you to be cruel to his wife."

"I don't want to talk about Peter," John said.

"Too bad. I don't think Peter would have wanted the two people he cared about most hating each other."

Yeah, but would he have wanted them sleeping together either? "She shouldn't have come back," John said.

"Maybe not. But she did. She's been a big help to me, and if you weren't so stubborn, you'd admit that she helped you, too. John, for God's sake, she's going to be gone in just a couple days. Can't you be decent to her for that amount of time? Can't you just forget about the past and see what might happen?"

John shut his eyes, not wanting to see the disgust that he could hear in his friend's voice.

"Peter's dead and it's her fault."

Fred didn't say anything for a long moment. "John," he said, more quietly than usual. "Did you ever think it might have been Peter's fault? Or maybe nobody's fault at all?

Silver mines collapse. It wasn't the first time and it won't be the last."

John sat up in bed, his eyes now wide open. "Peter would never have gone into that mine if he hadn't been desperate for money. She made him desperate."

"I don't know," Fred said. "Maybe at one time, it would have been easy to believe that. But lately, I've come to realize that we all make choices. Some of them are good choices and some probably bad. But we make them. Circumstances or other people may force us to look at alternatives, but in the end, it's each one of us who makes the choice. Each one of us has to take responsibility for the decision."

"She pushed him," John said, unwilling to accept that Sarah's hands were not stained with Peter's blood.

"Or maybe," Fred said as he opened the door, "he chose to be pushed."

"I'M sorry, Sarah," Fred said. He squatted down next to her.

She turned the wash bucket's handle, wringing out the wet towel. It had taken her fifteen minutes the night before just to figure out how to feed the clothes through the contraption. She really missed the push buttons on her big-load washer. "*You* haven't done anything to apologize for."

"John's a good man." Fred ran his hands through his red hair. "He misses Peter. Maybe more than even I realized."

She thought about how empty her life had been after her parents had died. "It's hard to lose family," she said.

"You feel powerless. When Franny died, I was furious with God. What kind of God took a woman away from her three little children?"

"I suppose your father-in-law wasn't too crazy about that?"

Fred chuckled. "No. Over and over again, he kept telling

me that God works in mysterious ways. I almost hated him for it."

"What changed your mind?"

"I realized he was just trying to convince himself. He couldn't admit it, but his faith had been shaken. Ultimately, I think he came to terms with her death."

"How about you? Are you still angry?"

"Sure. Some. But I've got the children to worry about. I need to take care of them. That's what Franny would have wanted and expected. They give my life purpose. But John, he doesn't have anybody to give him purpose."

"What about his mother?"

"He's been taking care of her since he was a boy. When Peter died, that didn't change. John doesn't have what he needs. He needs a reason to get beyond his grief, his anger."

"If that's true," Sarah said, "I hope he finds it soon. He's going to be an angry old man before he realizes it."

"He'll come around. He just needs a little more time."

"For his sake," Sarah said, "I hope time flies."

"It always does," Fred said, smiling at Sarah. He stood up. "He'll work his way out of this. He just needs to fumble around a bit first."

"His fumbling is hard on my self-esteem," Sarah said, trying to make light of John's comments. She didn't want Fred to know how much it hurt. As odd as it seemed, she'd felt some kind of connection to John since the minute he'd swung open that heavy door, his gun slung over his shoulder, his hair wild around that incredible face.

Last night, when she'd touched him, when she'd run her fingers across his hot skin, she'd felt the power, as if an electric current connected his chest to her fingertips. She'd wanted desperately to kiss him. She regretted her cowardice, regretted that she'd be back in her own time and never have known the softness of his lips.

"Self-esteem?" Fred shook his head. "Sometimes you

say the strangest things. Anyway, I've got to get out and get that fence fixed."

"Fred." Sarah stood up quickly, almost upsetting her bucket. She laid her hand on Fred's thick arm. "John won't let me help him. Will you at least let me help you? Go home and get the children. Bring them back here. I can watch them and keep track of how John's doing as well. That way you can get the fence fixed and still get some of your own planting done. If it gets too late tonight, just leave the children here with me. You can come get them tomorrow."

"Are you sure?"

"Yes. John needs rest. I think he probably has a slight concussion. I'll keep the children outside with me."

WHEN John woke up for the second time that day and heard the sweet laughter of children, he thought he might be delirious. He sat up in bed and looked around, relaxing only when he realized where he was and how he'd gotten there. He still wasn't happy about being stuck in bed like some invalid but at least he hadn't lost his senses. Then he heard the children again, their high-pitched voices floating through the open window.

He edged out of bed and stood still until he got the dizziness under control. When he walked over to the window, he saw all three of Fred's children playing jump rope, with Missy and Thomas swinging the rope and Helen, singing a little song, jumping high, her bare feet barely touching the ground between swings. Morton lay just off to the side, his front paws stretched out, his head resting on them, like he didn't have a care in the world. Like it was perfectly natural to have three children playing in the yard.

For a brief moment, John allowed himself to think about how good it would be to see his own children playing games. He'd always kind of figured it would happen but now, with no real prospects around, and him working eighteen-hour days trying to build up his cattle herd and keep his ranch running, he'd about given up hope. He didn't have the time to find a wife nor the energy to handle one. A wife would turn his life upside down. Even more so than Sarah had these last two days.

Where the hell was she, anyway?

And as simply as that, she appeared, poking her head out of the barn door, as if he'd conjured her up, through some kind of magic. "I'm ready for you," she yelled to the children.

"Five more minutes," Helen yelled back, her voice coming out in breathless spurts.

Sarah smiled. "No. Playtime's over. I need your help."

Help?

Thomas stopped turning his end of the rope and Helen stopped jumping. Missy, looking puzzled, pulled on Helen's bare arm. Helen pointed toward the barn where Sarah stood, waving them toward her. Missy dropped her end of the rope and took off toward the barn, like a hungry cat going for fresh milk. Morton got up, stretched, and went after her. Thomas and Helen followed. John watched until they all disappeared inside the barn.

Just what was Sarah up to?

John took a few cautious steps. Besides having a hell of a headache, being a mite off-balance, and fearing he might get stomach-sick at any moment, he felt all right. Moving slowly, he pulled his boots on and tucked his shirt into his pants. He grabbed his hat from the hook and put it on, pulling the brim low to protect his eyes from the bright sun. He walked outside and headed for the privy. First things first.

Minutes later, he opened the barn door. The children, their small arms full of clean straw, were in one horse stall. Sarah, her back to him, scooped manure out of the next one.

"What the hell is going on?" he asked, his voice echoing in the empty barn.

She whirled around, hitting the blade of her shovel on

the side of the stall. "Ouch," she said as she absorbed the shock in her arms and shoulders. "You scared me," she said, placing one hand over her heart.

"Sorry," he said. Lord, she was a mess. Her hair stuck to her neck, she had dirt on her face, and she'd torn the sleeve of her blouse.

"Should you be up?" she said.

"Never mind what I should be doing," he said, wanting to talk about anything but his health. "What do you think you're doing?"

Thomas spoke up before Sarah had a chance to answer. "We're cleaning up after the horses, Uncle John. Sarah said it would be a nice surprise for you."

"The chicken coop is next," Helen said. "That smells even worse than the barn." She pinched her nose with her fingers. Missy watched her sister for a second then pinched her own nose.

"Doesn't smell as bad as you do," Thomas said to Helen, baiting her as only a five-year-old brother could.

"At least I take a bath once a week," Helen answered, her small nose in the air.

"Baths are for girls," Thomas said, clearly not impressed.

Sarah laughed. "We're all going to need baths after this. Girls and boys alike."

"You don't have to do this," John said, trying hard to identify the emotions coursing through him. It had been a long time since someone had done something to surprise him. He had never expected it from Sarah. He wanted to just appreciate the moment but he couldn't help wondering what the hell she was up to. What could Sarah possibly hope to gain?

"I know," she said. "We wanted to help. All of us did. The children felt bad that you'd been injured."

"My pa thinks you must have a hard head," Thomas said.

John smiled at the boy. "He's right. Where's your pa now?"

"Back at our place," Helen answered. "We're spending the night here."

"I hope you don't mind," Sarah said.

"No, that's fine." Maybe better than fine. With three children in the house, perhaps he wouldn't be tempted to touch Sarah, to invite her into his bed. To do something that immensely stupid.

"As soon as we're done here, I'll get the children cleaned up and we can eat dinner."

"I'll finish this," he said.

"Absolutely not. A couple scoops and you'll probably fall flat on your face in this stuff. Go back inside."

He hated that she was right.

"Just go," she urged. "Get some rest."

He went, cursing his own weakness. But he didn't go back to bed. Instead, he built a roaring fire in the stove, and after making four trips back and forth between the pump and the house, he had a big kettle of water boiling. By the time he dumped the last bucket, he shook with fatigue. He lay down on the bed, grateful that he'd made it that far.

It was all worth it when Sarah and the children came back into the house. "Hot water," she exclaimed. "You crazy man. What were you thinking?"

He'd been thinking that he wanted to do something nice for her, to make up for the nasty things he'd said before. "I know what that chicken coop smells like on a sunny day."

Sarah laughed. "And you didn't want to have dinner with four people who smelled just like it. Well, we're grateful."

In a matter of minutes, she'd hauled in four more buckets of cold water and dumped those in the tin tub. Then she added enough of the boiling water to make a nice warm bath. "Helen, you're first. Missy and Thomas, you go outside and give your sister some privacy."

"I'll go outside, too," John said.

She shook her head. "John, you're pale as a ghost. You really shouldn't have hauled the water. Maybe," she hesitated, "if you could just roll over and face the wall."

Unless she intended to take a bath with her clothes on, that meant she'd be less than ten feet away from him, completely naked.

"That won't be a problem for you, will it?" she asked, obviously worried about him hurting his head.

"No. No problem," he said, hoping she couldn't hear the panic in his voice. He rolled over and shut his eyes. It wouldn't do for her to have any idea what his problem was.

The children obeyed without question. Like clockwork, he listened while first Helen then each of the twins got bathed. Sarah efficiently got them dressed in the extra clothes they'd brought from home and spent a few minutes combing each child's hair. After that, Sarah pitched the dirty water out the door and made two more trips out to the pump to get enough water to fill the tub again. Then, he heard her add the still-boiling water from the stove.

"You guys go out and play," she said, speaking quietly. "Don't get dirty," she warned. "I'm going to get cleaned up and then we'll eat."

He heard the door shut, followed by the faint voices of the children outside. He listened to her take a few steps toward the bed. "John?" He didn't respond, just concentrated on breathing deeply, in and out. She lingered for another long minute. Finally, convinced that he was asleep, she walked back toward the tub.

Next came the rustle of clothing hitting the floor and the gentle lapping of the water on the side of the tub as she lowered herself into the water. When he heard her sigh, he got instantly hard.

Christ, he was a sick bastard. Ever since he'd rolled over, he'd been fantasizing about her body. Having seen her breasts, he'd spent the last fifteen minutes imagining the rest. Slender. Pale skin. A sweet blond triangle of hair. Slim hips. Round bottom. Long legs. Just the right length to wrap around him when he filled her.

John thought he might just spill his seed inside his trousers.

He was concentrating so hard on keeping silent that he didn't hear the sound of a horse's hooves until they were almost at his front door. Suddenly the children squealed, and Fred's voice boomed in response.

Sarah jumped out of the tub. John listened to the sounds of her briskly drying herself off. He heard the flap of Franny's canvas bag flip open and then the rustle of clothing as Sarah slipped something over her head.

Then Fred was knocking and walking in the door. When Sarah didn't scream in protest or Fred didn't crow in admiration, John assumed that Sarah had somehow managed to get adequately covered.

But he knew that there was no way she'd had any time to pull on undergarments. She was naked under her dress. That knowledge did nothing to diminish the wanting that consumed him.

"Hello, Sarah," Fred said.

"Hi." She sounded a bit breathless. "I didn't expect you."

"I know. I got done early and thought I'd come get the children. I know you didn't get any sleep last night. I didn't want them waking up in the middle of the night, getting scared because they were in a strange place without me, and then keeping you up all night again."

"Fred Goodie, you're a nice man," Sarah said.

John heard Fred shuffle his feet in embarrassment. John decided to wake up and save his best friend before he did something stupid like confess his undying love for Sarah. John rolled over and stretched, managing to throw one leg over the other, hopefully hiding his need. He opened his eyes and blinked them several times.

"Fred?" he asked, trying to look appropriately confused. "What time is it?"

"Almost dinnertime," Sarah said. "Will you at least stay and eat with us?"

Fred shook his head. "I've got to get back. I got a mare about to give birth. She might need some help."

"Well, at least let me send some soup home with you," she said. "I've just got to go down to the creek and get it."

"The creek?" Both John and Fred spoke at the same time.

Sarah looked from one to the other. "Yes. I didn't want it to spoil. To keep it cold, I put it in jars and then placed the jars in the stream. That water is practically freezing."

"Why didn't you just put it in the root cellar?" John asked.

"I . . . I guess I wasn't thinking," Sarah said.

"You had a lot on your mind," Fred said, obviously trying to make her feel better.

"Yes. That's it," Sarah said. "I'll just go get it now." She left, almost running for the door.

"That's odd," Fred said, pulling out a chair from the table. "Children told me that the four of them cleaned out the horse stalls and the chicken coop."

John nodded.

"She gets a lot done in a short amount of time," Fred stated. "Doesn't waste time talking about it. Just gets to it."

"You're starting to sound like you're almost sweet on her," John said, giving his friend a hard look. "Don't tell me she's fooled you."

"I ain't fooled about nothing," Fred said. "I ain't trying to hide a log in my pants either. By the way, I've seen you wake up before. Haven't ever seen all that blinking and stretching, though. Must have been one hell of a dream."

John's sexual frustration, his disgust that he wanted Sarah in the worst way even though he knew the kind of woman she was, coupled with his hatred for being hurt and confined to a bed, proved to be too much. "Don't be fooled by her," he said harshly. "She married my brother, and six months later, she walked away with everything that he'd ever worked for, his life savings. She did nothing to earn that money. She's nothing but a lying thief. She can't be trusted."

SARAH lugged the three jars of soup back to the cabin, cursing her foolishness all the way. Root cellar. Of course, the man had a root cellar. She'd probably stumbled past it and hadn't even realized it. Sarah One would have known about the root cellar. Too bad Sarah One hadn't left a note, some quick directions, a few hot tips.

She just hoped the two men had forgotten about the stream thing and had moved on to other fascinating topics. When she got a little closer to the cabin, she could see Thomas sitting in the dirt in front of the cabin. He had traces of tears on his tanned cheeks.

She set the soup down and took the spot next to him. "What's wrong, Thomas? Won't the girls play with you?"

He shook his head.

"Come on. You can tell me. Aren't we friends? You can tell a friend anything."

"Pa and Uncle John yelled at each other. I sat right here and heard everything."

Oh. "Honey, sometimes when adults talk about things that are important to them, it might sound like yelling but it's really just loud conversation. Nothing to worry about."

"Uncle John said that you were a lying thief and that you couldn't be dusted."

Lying thief. Sarah swallowed. "Dusted?"

He nodded.

"Could it have been trusted?"

"Yep, that's it. A lying thief who can't be trusted."

Sarah blinked, hoping she wouldn't cry in front of the child. She felt sick. She'd lost everything and had found nothing. Nothing but a man who couldn't see his way around the past.

She absolutely would not stay here until Wednesday. She wouldn't stay another minute. She'd go to Fred's house.

No. She couldn't do that. Fred would be torn between her and John. Not to mention that Suzanne would assume the worst. She didn't want to cause that kind of trouble for Fred.

She'd go to town. Surely there had to be a hotel. She'd sleep in the damn lobby if they didn't have a bed. Anything to get away from John.

She hugged Thomas. "Go find your sisters. I want to have a word with your pa and Uncle John."

"You're not mad?"

"Not at you," she said.

"At Uncle John and Pa?"

"No. Not even them. Some things aren't worth being mad about."

She stood up, took a deep breath, and walked into the cabin. "Where's the soup?" Fred asked.

"Outside." She grabbed Franny's bag, stuffed back in the clothes she'd pulled out earlier, and walked to the door. "I am neither a liar nor a thief. I'm not a fool either. So I don't intend to stay where I'm not wanted."

Neither John nor Fred made eye contact with her.

"Fred, would it be possible for Missy and Thomas to double up on one horse? Then I could borrow the extra horse and ride to town."

"You can't ride to town," John said. "It's going to be dark soon."

"I'm leaving tonight. I'm either riding or walking. I don't really care which."

"Sarah," John said, looking uncomfortable. "I'm sorry you overheard us."

She didn't correct him. There was no sense incriminating Thomas. "But you're not sorry you said it. After all, it's what you believe."

She could see the muscles in John's jaw working. "Where are you going to stay?" he asked.

"Not your business or your worry," she said.

She turned toward Fred. "Am I walking or riding?"

Fred looked at John. Sarah didn't know if he sought instruction or permission. When John gave him a slight nod of response, she thought it might have been the latter.

"Riding," Fred said. "The children and I'll go with you and make sure you get to the hotel. I expect they'll have rooms."

"I'll be outside."

"Sarah?" John spoke just as her hand touched the door handle.

"Yes," she said, irritated with herself that she still hoped he'd apologize. She turned to look at him.

He stared at her. Then he took a deep breath and let it out. He rubbed his hand over his jaw. "Good luck."

"Yeah. You, too. Goodbye, John."

SEVEN

LIGHT, laughter, music, and an occasional cowboy spilled out of the saloon that stood directly across from the hotel. Young men, their arms around pretty girls, strode along the wooden sidewalk. Three men, all smoking, apparently offering expert advice, stood around a wagon, watching as a fourth man fixed a broken wheel.

She appreciated the chance to sit and observe, to soak up the sounds of civilization. The children had begged to get down while their father checked on a room but she'd convinced them to stay on their horses. She knew firsthand how fast they could scatter and she didn't want to chase them around Cedarbrook.

When Fred emerged from the hotel, she relaxed when she saw his smile. "There's room at the inn?" she asked.

"Yes. You're all set. I told them you'd need a room through next Wednesday morning."

"How much?" she asked, fearing that the ten dollars Fred had given her for babysitting wouldn't go far.

"Price is two dollars a night plus an extra fifty cents if you want a bath."

She did the math. Four nights with two baths would be nine dollars. Great. Maybe she didn't need to eat after all.

"Don't worry," Fred said. "John gave me twenty dollars to give to you. That will cover food, your stage to Cheyenne, and a train ticket to California."

"He really does want me out of his hair," Sarah said, hoping the hurt didn't show. "If I'd stalled a bit, who knows how high the price might have gone."

Fred shook his head, looking troubled. "I can't explain my friend. He's a good man, Sarah. I know it might not seem like that to you."

"I don't want his money," she said.

Fred shrugged. "I don't think you've got much choice. If it makes you feel any better, when you get to where you're going, send it back to him."

Now, that would be quite the trick. "Right," she said. "I'll do that." One more reason for John to think she was a money-grubbing tramp.

"We better get going," Fred said. "Missy and Thomas look like they're about to fall asleep."

Sarah kissed each of the children. "Goodbye," she said. She signed the word for Missy. When the little girl signed back *I love you,* Sarah felt a little piece of her heart break off. She might get back to California but she wouldn't go whole.

"I'll see you before you go," Fred said, his voice gruff with emotion. "I'm sorry things didn't work out with you and John."

Sarah kissed his cheek and then backed away from the horses. "Good night," she said and walked into the hotel. The lobby had polished wooden floors, woven rugs, and a wide staircase leading up to the second floor. Wall lanterns, one every four feet or so, cast a soft glow throughout the room.

An old man, so short that he could barely see over the solid wood check-in counter, glared at her. "Surprised to see you back in town, Mrs. Beckett."

Oh, joy. Another Sarah One fan. Just what she needed. "I'm just here for a few days."

"Figured as much. We lit the lamp in your room," he said, making it sound like it was more than she deserved. He handed her a key. "It's number seven, first door to the right at the top of the stairs. I'll send Freedom along with some water for the basin. You know where the privy is."

"Exactly where was that again?" Sarah asked.

"At the end of the hallway."

"Inside?"

He frowned at her and pointed his nose in the air. "We've had an inside privy for over a year. You're not feeling poorly, are you? Fred Goodie didn't say anything about you being sick. I can't have anybody getting sick. Doc Mosley—"

"Died two months ago," Sarah finished. "Don't worry, I'm perfectly healthy. Just a little tired." She picked up the key. As she climbed the stairs, she wondered how much of a stir she'd cause if she went over to the saloon for a drink. She desperately wanted alcohol. She figured a couple shots of something would adequately numb her mind, her heart, her soul.

"I'd like a whiskey," she said softly, practicing. "Whiskey, please," she tried again. "Make it a double," she said, "with a clean glass."

"It's the clean glass that will pose the problem."

Sarah stopped so suddenly that the man behind her almost knocked her over.

"I'm sorry," he said. "Was that a private conversation?"

The man wore a black suit with a vest and a black cowboy hat. He had a thin face, an even thinner mustache, and pale skin. He stared at her and she had a sudden urge to pull up the neckline of her blouse.

"I didn't mean to scare you," he said.

"You didn't," she denied, wanting to wipe the smirk off his skinny lips.

"Allow me to introduce myself. I'm Mitchell Dority."

Great. This guy would have to be the first man who didn't have a track record with Sarah One.

"I'm Sarah Jane," she said, deciding that was all he needed to know. She might be temporarily misplaced in the nineteenth century but she had plenty of twenty-first-century street smarts.

Something about the man gave her the creeps. He looked too slick. He looked too confident, like the idiots who stood on the corner, practically on school grounds, and sold joints to third graders. Like it was their God-given right to do whatever they wanted, regardless of who got hurt.

"Are you here with your husband?" he asked, looking at her bare fingers.

"My husband is dead," Sarah said. She needed to stick to the story.

"My sympathies," he said.

She smiled, her face feeling tight. "Well, it was a pleasure to meet you, Mr. Dority."

He tipped his hat. "The pleasure's all mine. Perhaps we'll see each other again."

Not if she locked herself in her room until Wednesday. "Perhaps." She walked at a sedate pace up the rest of the stairs, aware that he still stood on the steps. When she got to the top, she turned and looked at him. She did not intend to advertise her room location.

He smiled, an oily sneer, tipped his hat again, and turned. When he walked away, she thought she heard him whistling.

She had a sudden urge to take a shower. She found her room and unlocked the door. When she got inside, she turned the door lock and slipped the cheap hook into place, locking herself in for the night. The oil lamp gave off just enough light that she could see her home-away-from-home for the next four nights. A narrow bed took up most of the space, leaving just enough room for a chair and a squatty, three-drawer chest. A blue-and-white pitcher and a matching bowl sat on top of the chest. She walked over to the window. Her room overlooked the street. She saw that the man with the wagon trouble had solved his problem. He and his consultants had gone home for the night.

She jumped when she heard a sudden knock. Surely, Slick had not come back. She walked closer to the door, wishing for a peephole.

"Ma'am," the voice on the other side said. "Freedom has some water here for your basin in case you'd be wantin' to wash up."

She unhooked the door and opened it. A thin black man, maybe in his mid-twenties, wearing a white shirt and pants, stood outside the door. He looked weighed down by his jug of water.

"Come in," she said, "let me help you with that."

"No, ma'am," he said, shaking his head. "Freedom don't need no help."

He tipped up the jug and poured, filling the pretty blue basin with fresh water. He had a towel draped over his shoulder. He pulled it off, shook it like one might a napkin in a fancy restaurant, and laid it next to the bowl. "You tell me if Freedom can get you anything else. Good night, ma'am."

"Thank you," she said. "You have a very unusual name."

Freedom, king of third person, smiled back. He didn't have any front teeth. "My momma had Freedom the year Mr. Lincoln said it had to stop. That we didn't have to be slaves no more."

Dorothy, this really isn't Kansas. "Does your mother work here also?"

He shook his head. "Freedom's momma is in heaven. She's an angel." He nodded his head toward her. "If you need anything else, you just let Freedom know."

"Actually, I've got a question about the privy."

Freedom's chest puffed up. "We got the only inside flusher in this town. Freedom keeps the tank filled up. Buckets and buckets of water, every day."

"Be still my heart. You've really got toilets that flush?"

"Yes, ma'am. Just pull on the chain."

Okay, maybe John being totally pissed, no pun intended, was a blessing. "Thank you," she said. "For everything. You have no idea how happy you've made me."

"Freedom is much obliged."

She watched the man amble off down the hall, the now empty jug swinging at the end of his long arm. Sarah stuck a finger in the water, hoping it might be warm. It wasn't but it really didn't matter. She quickly washed her face and hands, shed her dress and shoes, pulled back the thin blanket on the bed, and laid her weary body down on the cotton sheets.

Four nights. Four more nights and she'd be on her way home. Yawning, she turned on her side. She might just sleep until she boarded the stage on Wednesday morning.

SARAH woke up when she heard the woman screaming. She jerked up in bed, unable to see a thing in the dark room. The woman screamed again and something heavy hit the floor.

She sprang out of bed and ran toward the door. She fumbled with the hook and the handle but managed to get it open. The door to the next room stood ajar an inch or so. Sarah pushed it open just in time to see Slick backhand a small, dark-haired woman.

Suzanne.

Sarah screamed. Slick turned toward her, his thin face tight with fury. He had his shirt off and his pants were unbuttoned. "Mind your own damn business." He strode toward the door and pushed it, trying to shut her out. Sarah put all her weight against the door, knowing that if he got the door shut, Suzanne was as good as dead.

"Help!" Sarah screamed, wedging her shoulder against the door.

"Shut up," Slick snarled.

Sarah could feel her feet giving way. "Fire!" she yelled. "Fire!"

A door farther down the hall opened.

"Fire!" Sarah cried, out of breath from pushing on the door. "Help me."

Two men crossed the hallway. When Slick saw them, he suddenly stepped back, causing Sarah to plunge through the doorway. The two men followed her in. Slick had backed off to the corner of the room. He stood straight, his arms folded over his bare chest. A table lantern burned, casting eerie shadows.

Sarah looked at Suzanne, who'd managed to pull herself up into a sitting position. She had blood running out of her nose, her lips were cut and bruised, and one eye was almost swollen shut. Her blouse had been ripped from her shoulder to her waist and Sarah could see more marks on her pale breasts.

Most startling of all, one side of her hair, her beautiful hair, had been chopped off. What was left stuck straight out from her head, not more than two inches long. Sarah looked at the bed. Hunks of hair lay on the pillow with a sharp knife on top of the pile.

"Oh, sweetie," Sarah said, kneeling next to Suzanne and wrapping her arms around her shivering frame. "You're going to be fine. Just fine."

Suzanne started to cry.

Sarah looked at Slick and the two men who stood somewhat helplessly in the middle of the room. "Don't just stand there," she yelled at them. "Grab him. Get the sheriff."

"Boys, you know better than that," Slick said. "This is between me and the whore."

Suzanne, her face buried in Sarah's chest, shook so violently that Sarah could barely keep her upright. Slick grabbed his shirt off the floor and edged toward the door. He stopped, took two steps back, reaching for the knife that still lay in the bed.

"You stay right there, mister."

Freedom stood in the doorway, a long-handled mop resting on his shoulder, like a big club. His dark hands looked stark against the white handle. "Freedom knows how to use this mop," he warned.

Slick laughed and picked up his knife with his left hand. "What are you going to do? Clean me to death? Get the hell out of my way, you fool."

Slick walked toward Freedom. When he got close enough, he stuck his right arm out, hitting Freedom in the chest with the heel of his palm. With several swift pushes, he moved the small black man out of the doorway and back into the stair railing. Sarah watched as Freedom struggled to maintain his balance, the heavy mop pulling him over the edge. With no alternative, Freedom let go of the mop and it fell to the first floor, clattering on the wood.

Slick laughed and slipped his knife into his belt. With both hands, he grabbed the front of Freedom's shirt, yanking him off the ground. Freedom's legs dangled and he looked like a rag doll. Then Slick slowly lowered him.

Sarah started to breathe again.

Slick pulled his right fist back and swung it into Freedom's face. The man crumpled.

"You bastard," Sarah yelled and tried to get up. Suzanne, with amazing strength, held her back. "Let him go," Suzanne whispered. "He'll kill us both."

Slick turned and tipped his hat at the two men, who still stood in the middle of the room. Then he turned to the two women. He pointed a finger at Suzanne. "We're not done. I didn't get my money's worth. And you"—he stared at Sarah—"better learn to keep out of things that don't concern you. I don't like people who interfere."

Then he turned and walked out of the room. Sarah could

hear the heels of his boots on the wooden steps. In seconds, she heard the front door close.

This time, when she pulled away from Suzanne, the woman let her go. Sarah ran to Freedom's side. She placed her hand on the man's cheek. The man blinked his brown eyes several times. "Freedom hates that mean man," he said.

"Oh, Freedom," Sarah cried and helped him stand up. With her hand cupped around his elbow, she led him back into the room, to the chair in the corner. Once she got him seated, she whirled toward the two men. "How could you have stood there and watched that happen?"

The one man stared at the floor. The other shrugged his shoulders. "I ain't gonna mess with Mitch Dority. Not for the sake of some whore and a little darkie."

Sarah thought she might explode. "You make me sick."

The man who'd been silent looked up. "Like Dority said. People shouldn't get involved in things that don't concern them."

"Get out," Sarah ordered. "Now."

The two men shuffled out. Sarah shut the door and hooked it, separating the three of them from the rest of the world. She looked at Suzanne. The woman still sat on the floor next to the bed, curled into a ball, her arms wrapped around her legs. She had her head bent and her bare shoulders jerked.

"Freedom," Sarah said, not having any other option. "Do you feel up to going to get the manager? And the sheriff, too? Can you do that?"

He nodded.

"No," Suzanne cried, looking up. Her face was wet with tears. "No sheriff."

Sarah took a step toward her. "Suzanne," she said softly. "What that man did is wrong. He needs to be punished."

"You don't understand. Sheriff Armstrong is gone for the next month. He left his deputy in charge. That man won't do anything. He and Dority drink together all the time. They're friends."

Sarah rubbed a hand over her face. She couldn't remember ever being so weary. "Do you mean to tell me that there's no one who can help us?"

Suzanne shook her head. "The deputy will make it impossible for me to stay in Cedarbrook. I don't have any money or anywhere else to go."

"I've got twenty dollars," Sarah said. "Take it."

"It's not enough."

"There has to be someone who can help you."

Suzanne shook her head. Sarah looked at Freedom. He sat quietly on the chair, not disputing anything Suzanne had said, as if he, too, accepted that people like Suzanne and him didn't deserve protection from those obliged to give it.

"Fred," Sarah said. "Fred would help you."

"No," Suzanne said, fresh tears rolling down her face. "I could never ask him. Oh my God, I don't want him to even know. He can't see me." She rubbed a hand over her shorn hair.

Indecision tore at Sarah's soul.

"Freedom, do you know who John Beckett is?"

Freedom nodded.

"Do you know where he lives?"

Another nod. "Mr. Beckett pays Freedom for helping when branding time comes."

"Go get him. I need him."

WITHIN the hour, Sarah had Suzanne cleaned up and tucked into Sarah's bed. Sarah sat on the floor next to the bed, her back leaning against the wall. She stared out the window, waiting for dawn. She'd tried to sleep, but every time she'd closed her eyes, she could see Dority hitting Suzanne.

When she heard the quick knock, she jumped up and ran to open the door. John stood there, still pale like he'd been the last time she'd been him, but nevertheless looking capable and solid. She felt like she couldn't be strong one more minute. Her own tears, the ones she'd kept at bay while she'd soothed Suzanne, filled her eyes.

"Hey," he said, pulling her toward him. "You're going to be fine."

She realized it was the same assurance she'd given Suzanne. She hoped like hell that she and John were both right.

"I know," she sniffled, unwilling to pull away. She buried her face in his shirt and he wrapped his strong arms around her. When he rocked her back and forth, his big hand petting her back like one might a new kitten, she snuggled closer, feeling warm for the first time in hours.

He stopped rocking, his hand stilled. He moved just slightly and she could feel him pressed against her.

She spread her legs, just a fraction of an inch.

He groaned and, with both hands, cupped her bottom, pulling her even closer. She thought she might just die from the pure pleasure of it. He was hard and thick and she desperately wanted—

"Freedom got the horses taken care of, Mr. Beckett."

John jerked away from Sarah, his face red. He looked everywhere but at her. "Thank you, Freedom," he said, his voice sounding hoarse. "You've been a big help."

Freedom stood in the doorway, his hat in his hand, looking at the two of them. "Freedom guesses you two know each other."

Sarah could feel the heat start in her toes and skyrocket right to the tip of her head. "Yes. We're . . . sort of family," she said.

Evidently incest ran in Freedom's family because he didn't look concerned.

"How is she?" John asked.

"She's been sleeping for about a half hour. She's going to be black and blue with bruises but I don't think there's any permanent damage. Do you know Suzanne?"

He nodded. "I've seen her at the saloon. Pretty lady." John walked closer to the bed, where Suzanne lay flat on her back. "What happened to her hair?" he asked, sounding shocked.

"He chopped it off. Just got the one side."

"That bastard."

She could hear the hatred in his voice. "Do you know Mitchell Dority?" she asked.

"He swings through town every once in a while. I've never heard of him doing something like this. He spends most of his time cheating the Indians."

"Indians?"

"Yes. Sells them alcohol at a huge profit. Goes right on the reservation, like he's got every right to be there."

"He's a friend of the deputy's. Suzanne said they drink together."

"I don't know if he's a friend or not. Deputy Lewis would drink with just about anybody who'd buy. I imagine he's a little afraid of him. Dority is good with his gun."

"Yeah, well, his knife work could use a little improvement."

John nodded. "I'll be back in a few minutes. I'll get you both something to eat on my way back."

"Where are you going?"

"To see the deputy."

"I don't understand. If he's afraid of Dority, what good will that do?"

"I want him to understand a few things."

"What?"

John shrugged.

"I need to know what's going on," Sarah said, feeling like she'd lost control. "Tell me. Please."

John didn't say anything for several seconds. Then he

nodded. "It's simple. I'm going to make sure Deputy Lewis knows that if he won't arrest Dority, he better at least keep him out of Cedarbrook. I don't want there to be any misunderstanding. If Dority comes within a mile of you or Suzanne, he'll have me to deal with."

She almost started to cry again. Finally, someone who had the guts to do something, to help them.

"Thank you," she said. "I didn't know who else to turn to."

"You did the right thing." He looked at her and she knew, by the sudden look of longing that crossed his face, that he, too, remembered how it had felt to be plastered up against her.

"John?"

He shook his head slightly, as if trying to clear his thoughts. "You were my brother's wife," he said. "He'd have wanted me to help you."

"Is that why?" she asked, unable to help herself. She ignored Freedom, who still stood by the door. "Is that the only reason, John?"

"That's the only reason it can be."

She felt the strength leave her body. "So we're going to ignore what happened earlier between the two of us? When you held me? I should just forget it?"

"Yes, damn it. We're both going to forget it. That's the only thing we can do."

EIGHT

ROUSTING Frank Lewis's butt out of bed made John feel a little better. He made a perfunctory knock on the jail door, waited mere seconds, and then walked in. The deputy, sacked out in one of the two empty cells, opened his right eye.

"What's this all about, John?" Lewis asked, rubbing his hand over his face.

The man smelled like he'd taken a dip in a beer keg. Had probably tied one on last night and decided it was in the best interest of his thirty-year marriage that he pretend prisoners required his presence at the jail.

"Mitchell Dority made a mistake last night."

"What?" Lewis sat up on the cot, holding his stomach as if he thought it might try to get away. "Christ. I need coffee. I feel like shit."

"I'll bet you do," John said. "Maybe instead of having your head inside a beer glass, you should have been watching your town."

"What are you talking about?"

"Mitchell Dority beat the hell out of one of the saloon girls last night."

The deputy's face, already pale, turned a bit green. Probably the thought of having to arrest Dority wouldn't have set well even on a settled stomach.

The man stood up and walked, with short, awkward steps, to his desk. He lowered himself down on the edge of it, as if he wasn't too sure how long he could remain standing. "How do you know that?"

"He wasn't too quiet about it. Sarah, my sister-in-law, had the room next door. She broke it up."

"Sarah's back?" The deputy drew his bushy eyebrows together.

"Yes. Just passing through." He tried to sound casual, as if it didn't matter. But damn her, she'd managed to get under his skin. Every time he expected her to revert back to her spoiled and selfish ways, she surprised him with her decency.

If she hadn't been Sarah, he might have liked her. Even though she was Sarah, he wanted to bed her. That knowledge had kept him up the better part of last night. He couldn't figure it out. When Sarah had been married to Peter, he'd never once coveted his brother's wife. Hell, one morning he'd walked in, she'd been stark naked, her back to the door, and he hadn't even felt a glimmer of lust. She'd screamed, he'd apologized, and then he went on about his business.

Now, he thought, if he saw Sarah naked, he'd start to heave and pant and beg like a needy dog.

She'd always been a beautiful woman. But her bitterness and her greed had overshadowed it, stopping him cold. Now, she seemed so much nicer. He couldn't figure it out.

When Freedom had knocked on his door, he'd been half-awake and half-convinced that he'd conjured up Sarah with his thoughts. Freedom's halting explanation of what happened had sent painful spikes of rage and fear through him. He couldn't abide a man who beat up on weaker men, and violence toward a woman was unthinkable.

He'd gotten enough information from Freedom to realize that Sarah had escaped unharmed. However, he knew the kind of man that Dority was, and he knew Dority's anger at being stopped by a woman and a black man wouldn't go unanswered. Thank God she would be on the Wednesday stage. But that still left three days for Dority to strike again.

That's what had brought him to the deputy. He wished like hell that Sheriff Armstrong hadn't been called back East. But the man's mother had died. You couldn't blame him for going home, even if it did leave the citizens of Cedarbrook in the hands of Deputy Lewis. The man had been deputy for at least twenty years. He probably had only a few more in him. Sheriff Armstrong no doubt hoped the man would retire sooner.

John didn't care whether the man planned to retire next week. In the meantime, he expected him to act like a deputy.

"Where's Dority now?" asked Lewis.

"Gone."

The deputy's red, weathered face relaxed. "I see."

"Aren't you going to inquire about the girl?"

"Which one was she?" the deputy muttered, looking longingly at the coffeepot that sat on the cold stove.

"Suzanne."

"The pretty one?"

John nodded. "Yeah, although she's not looking all that pretty right now. The man's a cowardly bastard."

"Well, if I run across Dority, I'll question him about the incident."

"Would that be before you have a beer with him or after?"

"You hold on," the deputy admonished. "You got no right to be accusing me of not doing my job."

"I'm not accusing you of anything," John said, his voice purposely agreeable. "I'm just telling you that I'm going to be watching you and I'm going to be watching out for what's mine. If Dority comes near Sarah, he'll deal with me."

"I don't recall you being all that fond of Sarah. I remember some talk at the time she left that you were glad she was gone. Your ma is friendly with my wife. Seems to me that Sarah didn't do all that well by you or your kin."

"That's none of your business," John said, hating it that people had been gossiping about his family.

"Just saying that maybe she's not worth you getting all excited about this."

John badly wanted to slam his fist into the old man's mouth but didn't, knowing that he could kill the man with one good hit. "You just do your job," John said, "and keep your opinions to yourself."

GOING to see Deputy Lewis had convinced John of one thing. He needed to talk to his mother. Now.

Ever since Sarah had announced her plans to go to town, John had dreaded telling his mother about her return. He had no choice. He couldn't take the chance that Sarah would hunt down his mother, although she didn't seem inclined to, or that, by some twist of fate, Sarah and his mother would bump into each other at Hooper's Mercantile or the dressmaker's.

He'd planned to ride to town this morning, after church hours, hoping his mother would have a full weekly dose of Christian spirit. His grace period had shortened considerably. It wouldn't take Deputy Lewis long to get to his wife and even less time for Lana Lewis to get to his mother.

He walked toward the little white house on the edge of town, smiling when he saw the yellow daffodils and some other purple flower that he couldn't name. His mother had always loved flowers. Before knocking on the door, he pulled out his pocket watch.

Just before five. It would be day soon.

Given his mother's propensity to rise early, he hoped she might already be out of bed. Even so, she wouldn't be expecting company at this hour. He couldn't just walk in. His mother's house, unlike most of the houses in Cedarbrook, had locks on both the front and the back doors. He'd installed them himself.

He knocked and, within seconds, saw the slight movement of the lace curtains on the window to his left. He shifted, giving her an opportunity to see him. He heard a lock click and the door flew open. She reached out and pulled him inside, her still-strong grip tight around his forearm. "What happened?" she said, giving him a thorough once-over.

He rushed to reassure her. "Nothing's wrong," he lied, knowing that nothing would ever be right again. How could it be? He wasn't happy Sarah had come back and he wouldn't be happy when she left. It was a hell of a mess.

He smiled at his mother and sniffed the air. "Is that coffee?"

She nodded and assessed him through narrowed eyes. "It is. And if you want a cup, you'll tell me in the next three seconds why you're knocking at my door at five o'clock."

He draped an arm around her shoulder. "I will, I promise. But please have pity on a desperate man. I've been up for hours and I've had no coffee."

She waited until they were both seated at the small kitchen table with steaming cups of coffee before prompting him again. "How are things at the ranch?"

"Fine."

"Fred and his children?"

"Good."

She paused. "I'm out of ideas."

John shook his head. "This is one you probably wouldn't guess." He took a deep breath. "Sarah's back."

A bit of coffee sloshed out of his mother's cup. Deliberately she lowered her hand and set the cup in the saucer, with an audible clink. "What does she want?"

"I don't know," John admitted. "At first, I thought she came back for more money. But now I'm not sure. It's strange, Ma, really strange. She showed up at the cabin, her feet bare and cut up. She seemed almost dazed."

"How did she get there?"

"Said she walked."

"From Cheyenne?"

He shrugged. "She's not saying much more than that. She seems anxious to get back to Cheyenne and plans to go on the next stage. She's been helping Fred with his children."

"She's been helping? With the children?"

John laughed. "And not complaining once."

"Is she trying to trap Fred?"

"I worried about that," John said. "Then I had a bit of bad luck with a horse and she helped me, too."

"You were hurt?"

"No. Banged up my head a little, that's all. Anyway, Sarah took care of the animals and well, hell, she made me soup." His mother might as well know it all.

John thought he'd never see what happened next. His mother, at barely five o'clock in the morning, calmly got up from her kitchen table, walked to the corner cupboard, pulled out a whiskey bottle, returned to the table, and dumped a liberal amount in her coffee cup. "Where is she now?" she asked.

"At the hotel."

"Right down the street?" She picked up her cup and took a big drink.

"She ran into a spot of trouble last night. She broke up a fight between a man and one of the saloon girls. Probably saved the girl's life."

"Did she get hurt?"

"No. Scared." He did not want his mother to know that

she'd literally melted in his arms. Or that he'd hardened like a stone. She'd drink the whole bottle of whiskey and be at the saloon begging for more.

"I went to see Deputy Lewis."

"Oh. I imagine his Lana can't wait to tell me. I'm surprised she didn't beat you to the door."

"I've got longer legs," John said.

His mother laughed. "She's going back to Cheyenne on the Wednesday stage?"

"Yes."

She picked up her cup and drained it. "It's nothing to worry about. After all, what can happen in three days?"

ON his way back to the hotel, John stopped by Brickstone's café. Rosie, her hands rough from work, paused, her pencil still, when he ordered four breakfasts to be packed up. She didn't say a word and, after a few seconds, finished taking down his order. He knew there was little need to explain. He'd seen Rosie Brickstone and Lana Lewis together on more than one occasion. The two would have their heads huddled together before long. Everybody would know that Sarah Beckett had come back to town. Everybody would be watching, waiting, hoping for the fireworks.

He wanted to tell the whole bunch of them to go to hell. They hadn't felt Sarah's body shake, the terror, the absolute gut-wrenching fear, making her weak. They hadn't seen the despair in her pretty eyes. He had. He didn't think he'd forget it for some time.

When he got back to the hotel, he saw that Deputy Lewis had beat him. The man had probably hoped to get statements from Suzanne, Sarah, and Freedom before John came back.

Suzanne sat up in bed, Freedom stood against one wall, and Sarah paced around the room, talking while she walked. When she saw him, she missed a step. He smiled at her. She didn't smile back.

She resumed her pacing. "I don't understand why you can't go after him," she said. "How can you let this go unpunished?"

"I ain't letting it go unpunished and I wish people would stop saying that," Deputy Lewis said, standing in the middle of the room.

He'd washed his face but he didn't smell a whole lot better.

"I'm the only law in town," Deputy Lewis said, his voice filled with self-importance. "I can't just up and take off after some man who could be halfway across the state. I'll send a wire out. That's the best I can do."

John had his doubts that any wire would get sent. Sarah didn't look very satisfied, either.

"So people, other lawmen, will know to be looking for him?"

"Were you listening? That's what I just said, isn't it?"

Sarah frowned at the man and then ran her tongue over her teeth. John felt the answering tug deep in his gut and wondered how his body could turn on him so.

Sarah looked first at Suzanne, then at Freedom, and finally at John. He prayed the need didn't show on his face. When Sarah turned toward Deputy Lewis, John relaxed.

"Do you have all the information you need from us?" she asked. "I think Suzanne is tired."

Deputy Lewis shuffled his feet and turned toward Suzanne. "She ain't the only one. By the way, has anybody told Thomas about your injuries?"

Suzanne shook her head.

"Thomas?" Sarah asked.

"Thomas Jefferson," Deputy Lewis answered.

For a quick moment, Sarah looked like she might be sick. She stopped pacing and put her hand over her mouth.

"Thomas Jefferson bought the saloon three months ago," John said. "He'll be expecting Suzanne tonight."

"Of course." Sarah laughed, somewhat oddly, John

thought. "That Thomas Jefferson. I certainly didn't think it was Thomas Jefferson, the third president of the United States."

"President Jefferson had himself a whole bunch of slaves," Freedom said. "Freedom's momma said Mr. Jefferson could be Freedom's granddaddy."

Sarah nodded, as if she believed that wild-ass tale.

Deputy Lewis shook his head at both of them.

Wonderful. More stories for John's mother.

"Deputy Lewis," John said, "if you're done, I think we should conclude. Nobody has had much sleep."

"I'll be in touch," Deputy Lewis promised.

Now that John didn't doubt. Lewis's wife would want the latest updates.

JOHN and Freedom ate their breakfast standing up. Suzanne and Sarah, huddled together, sat on the bed, soft murmurs between the two of them. Suzanne ate only a couple bites before waving Freedom over to take her plate. The man, ever gracious, offered to split it with John. When John declined, Freedom couldn't keep his smile hidden. John understood that when a man didn't get to eat in the morning more than once or twice a week, having two breakfasts in one day was just pure indulgence.

When Sarah put her plate aside, John was pleased to see that she'd eaten the majority of her food. She seemed more delicate than he remembered. Everything from her wrists to her ribs to her ankles seemed smaller. Not for the first time, he wondered what hard times Sarah had fallen upon in the last six months. Was that what had changed her?

He saw Suzanne's eyelids flutter shut, and sure enough, in just minutes, she was asleep. He motioned for Sarah to join him in the hall. Freedom excused himself as well, saying it was time to report to work.

"She didn't eat much," John said. He leaned against the

wall, one foot braced up against it. Two feet away, Sarah sat on the top step, her long skirt spread out around her.

"Can you blame her? She said a couple of her teeth are loose."

"If Mitchell Dority walked in here right now, he'd leave without any of his teeth."

Sarah nodded. "I want to kill him," she said.

John jerked away from the wall. She'd said it without emotion, without fear. "You stay away from Mitchell Dority," he warned. "You can't handle him."

She shrugged.

"Until that stage gets here on Wednesday, you better come back to the ranch."

"That's not a good idea," she said.

He had his own reasons for knowing that. He'd spend the next three days hard, his buttons about to burst. For her safety, however, he'd endure it. "Why?"

"We're like oil and water."

"What?"

"We don't mix well."

"You don't have a choice," he said.

She snorted, a very unladylike snort. "There are more than a few things I don't have much choice about right now. But where I spend the next three nights is purely up to me."

How the hell could he protect her if she didn't come home? "Be sensible, Sarah. Dority could come back."

"I know. That's why I need to stay with Suzanne. She's in no shape to protect herself."

"That's the craziest thing I've heard today," John said.

"The day's early," Sarah said. She stood up and dusted off her backside. Her sweet, round bottom. "Go home, John. It's not that I don't appreciate the offer. I do. And even more so, I really appreciate you coming this morning. I'm not sure I could have handled it without you."

He really wanted to pound a fist against something or

somebody. "Fine. Both you and Suzanne can come back to the ranch." His mother was going to love this.

"She won't go."

"How do you know?"

"I already suggested something very similar. She has a . . . a friend who lives on a ranch outside of town. She won't even discuss it. She refuses to involve anyone else. Something about not wanting others to have to pay for her stupidity."

He frowned at her.

"Her words. Look, I think she just needs some rest."

"I don't like the idea of the two of you here by yourself."

"We're not by ourselves. Freedom lives here at the hotel. He'll keep an eye out for Dority. If the snake comes back, I think you've made it clear to Deputy Lewis that he better not choose to look the other way. I imagine"—she wrinkled up her pretty nose—"if I need him, I can find him in the saloon."

"That man is a disgrace," John said.

"It makes it easier to understand why people take the law into their own hands."

"Hopefully Sheriff Armstrong will be back soon. He's a good man."

"Hopefully," she said, "Dority is long gone and I won't need any help."

John thought about Suzanne's bruises and her broken nose. He looked at Sarah's pretty face, her delicate features. Fear gripped him, making it hard to breathe. "Promise me," he said, "that you won't try to deal with Dority on your own. Promise me," he insisted.

He relaxed when she nodded. However, when she walked over and brushed her sweet lips across his cheek, suddenly there wasn't a thing relaxed on his body. He forced his arms to remain at his side.

"Thank you, John Beckett," she said. She reached her

hand up and brushed his hair back from his face. He made the mistake of breathing and her sweet scent filled his lungs. Even after all the ugliness of the past hour, she smelled like the flowers in his mother's garden.

"Fred was right," she said. "You're a good man. I'm sorry I ever doubted it. Good night."

She turned and walked back inside the room. John, feeling old and empty and weak in the knees, stood at the top of the stairs. She was wrong. He wasn't a good man. A good man did not want to throw his sister-in-law in bed and bury himself deep inside her. Good men didn't have those thoughts, let alone the burning need in their bodies.

"SARAH, wake up. Sarah."

Sarah stretched, wishing she'd had the sense to sleep lying on the floor rather than sitting up in the chair next to the bed.

"What time is it?" Sarah asked, blinking her eyes. Lord, she was tired.

"It's a little after nine," Suzanne said. "You've been asleep for a couple hours. Church starts at ten and Fred comes early so that the children can help their grandfather get ready. Sometimes I watch from my window and wave to him." Suzanne's eyes clouded with unshed tears. "I don't want him to see me like this. Promise me, Sarah. Promise me that you'll keep him away."

Unless she could suddenly bench-press three hundred pounds, Sarah didn't know how to guarantee that. She would do her best. She understood Suzanne's reluctance. The woman's nose was swollen to almost twice its normal size, she had two black eyes, her lips were cut and bruised, and with her hair chopped off on one side, she looked lopsided.

"I don't have time now," Sarah said, "but when I get back, we'll fix your hair."

Now the tears spilled down Suzanne's cheeks. "I know it's vain," she said, "but I loved my hair."

Sarah rubbed a hand over her own blond, absolutely straight, shoulder-length bob. What wasn't to love about thick, shiny, naturally wavy, auburn hair? In the twenty-first century, women spent a fortune to have hair like that.

"You still have beautiful hair," Sarah said. "It's just different."

"When Fred and I were together," Suzanne said, a deep blush spreading across her face, "he used to wind it around his . . . his manhood."

Oh, boy. Fred had a hair thing. That was way more information than she needed. She wanted to laugh but couldn't, not when Suzanne looked so miserable. "Don't worry," Sarah said, as if she actually had experience to back up her theory, "he'll be just as happy with a can of whipped cream."

"What?"

"Never mind," Sarah said, thinking that a twenty-eight-year-old virgin had absolutely no business even talking about sex, let alone giving instruction on the fine mechanics of it. "Look, I better get going. I'll bring you back some soup."

"I'm not really very hungry," Suzanne said.

"You need to eat."

"I will," Suzanne answered, closing her eyes. "Tomorrow, I'll eat."

Sarah quietly left the room and walked down the stairs. She waved to Freedom, who was cleaning the lobby windows.

"Miss Sarah," Freedom acknowledged her. "Freedom wonders how Miss Suzanne is."

"She's sleeping. I'm going outside for a while. Can you keep an eye on the room?"

"Freedom will keep two eyes on Miss Suzanne."

"Perfect." Sarah walked outside, blinking at the bright spring sunshine. While it almost blinded her, it didn't seem to give off much heat. The crisp April air blew right through her thin cotton blouse. She wrapped her arms around herself, thinking once again of how much she missed the warm heat of southern California.

She sat down on the bench in front of the hotel. The street seemed quieter, no doubt due to the fact that the saloon hadn't opened for the day. Each person that did walk by, whether on their way into the hotel or on their way past, made no effort to hide their interest. She didn't know if they knew Sarah One or whether they just thought it odd that a lone woman sat in front of the hotel. Either way, she ignored them all, keeping her eyes focused on the narrow dirt road that led through town.

However, when one woman stopped directly in front of her, Sarah felt compelled to say something. "Hello." She smiled at the woman.

"Hello," the woman replied. When she didn't move on, Sarah got nervous. Playing Sarah One was tough enough when there was someone around to take the lead from. Now, she was completely on her own.

"Nice day," Sarah said. If in doubt, she thought, talk about the weather.

"It's been an early spring," the woman replied.

"It's good to have a break from the rain," Sarah said, remembering what John had said about wet fields.

"Yes, it's good."

Sarah looked around the woman, down the long stretch of dirt road, wishing Fred would suddenly materialize. Small talk had never been her strong suit.

The woman sat down on the bench, so close that her wide skirt brushed against Sarah's. "That's it, Sarah? After all this time, we're going to talk about the weather?"

Uh-oh. Trouble ahead. "Of course not," Sarah said. "How have you been?"

"As well as could be expected."

"Right." Not much of a clue. Sarah stood up. She'd just

walk a bit, maybe meet Fred outside of town. "I'll see you around," she said.

"I doubt that," the woman answered. "John said you're leaving on Wednesday's stage."

"John?"

"Yes. He stopped by early this morning. He didn't want me to find out by chance that you'd come back. He's a good son."

Sarah took a closer look. Now that the woman had identified the connection, Sarah could see where John got his broad forehead and his chocolate brown eyes. Mrs. Beckett, who had raised two boys into men and had survived the death of both her husband and one of those precious sons, was still a very attractive woman, although the scowl didn't do much for her.

Pain blossomed deep inside Sarah. John had felt it necessary to cushion the blow, to protect his mother from the ugly eventuality of meeting up with her.

Sarah One, she reminded herself. Not you.

It didn't matter. She'd hoped John would be able to see that she wasn't a threat to his mother, regardless of what had transpired in the past. Just more proof that he would never be able to see her as anything other than his awful sister-in-law.

"I never expected to see you again," Mrs. Beckett said.

"Yes, well, I wasn't exactly expecting to be here either," Sarah said, wishing she'd had more than two hours of sleep. Her brain felt fuzzy, as if she'd had too many glasses of wine.

"John said you've been caring for Fred Goodie's children."

"Great kids," Sarah said.

"I loved Franny Goodie like a daughter. I loved her the way I wanted to love you."

That was certainly clear enough. Not sure how to respond, Sarah lowered her gaze and tried to keep her eyes focused on Franny Goodie's ugly button-up shoes.

"I don't know why you're here," Mrs. Beckett continued. "All I can say is that you better be on that stage come Wednesday. I won't sit back and let you hurt people I care about. Not again."

"I don't have any intention of hurting anyone," Sarah said.

"Maybe not. But somehow, you always manage to." Mrs. Beckett stood up, casting a shadow over her. "You fooled me once. I won't let it happen again."

Sarah waited until she felt the full warmth of the sun before lifting her head. Mrs. Beckett, her head held high, her shoulders back, walked with purpose, obviously trying to put as much distance as quickly as possible between the two of them. Wow. John's worry about protecting his mother seemed a bit unfounded. Give that woman a whip and a chair and she could tame lions.

"Father, there's Sarah."

Sarah turned, just in time to see Fred pull up sharply on his horse. Thomas waved at her. She got up off the bench and walked over to the group. She signed hello to Missy and gave all three kids a quick hug. When she got to Fred, she had a tough time keeping a smile on her face.

"What's wrong, Sarah?" Fred got off his horse with one smooth movement. He reached out and caught both her shoulders. "Did something happen?"

"Can I speak to you privately?"

Fred nodded. He looked at Helen. "Take your brother and sister up to the church. I'll be there in a few minutes."

Sarah waited until they'd ridden a safe distance away before speaking again. "I have some news about Suzanne."

Fred's ears turned pink. "She left town," he said, his voice heavy with disappointment.

Sarah shook her head. "No. She's had a bit of bad luck."

Fred looked over at the saloon, his eyes on Suzanne's second-story window.

"She's not there," Sarah said. "She got beat up last night."

When Fred's face turned absolutely white, Sarah added, "She's okay."

"Where is she?"

"At the hotel. With me."

"How bad?"

He deserved to know. It might help him later. "He broke her nose and loosened some teeth. She's bruised up pretty bad and she's got some cuts and welts on her breasts where he whipped her with a belt. He cut her hair."

"Her hair?" Fred's face went from white to bright red. "Why the hell would he do that?"

Sarah shrugged.

Fred rubbed a big hand over his jaw. "Who was the son of a bitch that did it?"

"Mitchell Dority."

"Where is he? Where the hell is he?"

"He's gone. He left last night." She could see frustration and fear and some emotion she couldn't quite identify cross Fred's face.

Fred looked down the main street of Cedarbrook, all the way to the end where the white church, with its high steeple, sat on a small hill. His children were just getting off their horses. "I'll stop by," he said, his voice cracking, "after dinner. Around two."

Sarah shook her head. "I don't think that's a good idea."

"I'll be there," he said, looking very determined.

Oh boy. She really regretted not having used the free weights at the gym. "I'm sorry, Fred. She doesn't want company."

"I'm not company. We're . . . I . . ."

"Fred," she said, keeping her tone gentle because she knew the words would be harsh and ugly. "She specifically mentioned you. She doesn't want to see you."

He stood there, his mouth hanging open. He shook his head, like he didn't believe her. "Damn it, Sarah. I . . . I care for that woman."

He looked so miserable that her heart ached for him.

He rubbed his forehead and dug the toe of his boot into the soft dirt. "She doesn't deserve this," he said. "She's a good woman."

"She's a strong woman, too. She's got an inner strength. I can see it. I'm sure she'll bounce back."

Fred looked up at the windows of the hotel. "If she needs anything, I mean anything, will you tell me?"

"I will. I promise. I think she's going to be fine. Really I do. She just needs a few days."

NINE

IT took Sarah less than twenty-four hours to realize that everything wouldn't be fine. In fact, if she had to pin a label to it, she'd say everything pretty much sucked.

Suzanne had gotten out of bed only to use the privy at the end of the hall and had eaten less than five bites of every meal that Freedom had brought to her. She'd sat up dutifully while Sarah cut the still-long side of her hair. It had been a quiet, intense half hour while Sarah did her best to repair Dority's damage. In the end, she'd been pretty satisfied with the soft curls and wisps that framed Suzanne's face.

Suzanne had thanked her, lain back down, and closed her eyes. She'd never even looked in the mirror.

"Suzanne," Sarah said. "It's a beautiful spring day. Let's take a walk. It would do us both good."

Suzanne shook her head. "I'm a little tired. You go ahead."

Sarah had been put off long enough. "You've been sleeping since yesterday morning. You need fresh air."

"I don't want people seeing me like this."

"Fine. No town walking. We'll head out to the country."

"No." Suzanne rolled over in bed and pulled the blanket up to her chin. "I'm really tired."

Frustrated and scared that she might not be able to shake Suzanne out of her malaise, Sarah quietly left the room and walked down the stairs, ignoring the disapproving look from the man behind the desk. She stepped outside and gulped in fresh air. That simple action calmed her until she heard a noise. She turned around. The desk clerk had left his hole and now stood behind her. He had his arms crossed over his chest and he tapped one foot.

"Things like this don't happen in this hotel. At least not until you and your friend came to stay."

Sarah flexed her fingers. If she couldn't beat the crap out of Dority, then maybe slugging this guy would have to do.

"I don't know what women like that expect."

Sarah took a step toward him.

"Over the years, Mr. Dority has spent a lot of money here."

She pulled back her arm.

"Miss Sarah!"

Sarah whirled to see Freedom. He held a plate in each hand. She lowered her arm.

Freedom smiled at her. "Freedom got you and Miss Suzanne some lunch. Mr. Brickstone paid for it. When I was sweeping out his store, I told him about poor Miss Suzanne. He looked right concerned."

"Mr. Brickstone?"

The desk clerk stopped tapping his foot. He frowned at her. "Myron and Rosie Brickstone own the café. They've owned it for years."

"He gave me a dollar," Freedom said, "and told me to make sure that Miss Suzanne had something to eat. He seemed very concerned about Miss Suzanne."

Sarah wondered exactly how many men in Cedarbrook would have reason to look concerned about Suzanne and her unexpected hiatus.

"Freedom had enough to buy both of you a good lunch and a stick of candy for Freedom. Freedom thinks Mr. Brickstone is a kind and generous man."

Sarah suspected Mrs. Brickstone had no idea about the depths of her husband's giving.

"You people make me sick," said the desk clerk. He turned around and walked back into the hotel.

"Freedom wants to know why it is that you was about to hit Mr. Turnip?"

Mr. Turnip? That didn't excuse the chip on the little man's shoulder but it did make it a bit easier to understand. "I wasn't going to hit him," she lied. "I was waving good-bye. I'm going for a walk. You can have my lunch."

She took off, barely keeping her pace at a fast walk. She yearned for her beach, where she could throw off her shoes and run on the hard wet sand, pounding out her frustrations. Instead she took long, deliberate steps on the wooden sidewalk, covering ground as fast as she could.

When she had walked the entire length of the town and had reached the church at the top of the hill, she stopped and looked up to the sky. White, puffy clouds dotted the pale blue canvas. As beautiful as California had been, she didn't recall ever seeing the sky so clear and clean.

"Pollution," she said. "That's one thing 1888 has going for it. No pollution."

She sat down on the sloping green grass of the church-yard. "No traffic jams. No AIDS epidemic. No terrorism."

The good old days. Simpler times.

Perhaps simpler. Certainly not easier. There wasn't a darn thing easy about lugging water from the well and having to wait thirty minutes for it to heat up before taking a bath in an ugly, cold tin tub. She missed her coffeepot with its timer and she undoubtedly would miss tampons in another two weeks' time.

Maybe, maybe not. She might be back in her time before she ever had to worry about such mundane things. That's what she'd come to talk to God about.

She got up, dusted off her skirt, and walked into the small white church. She saw two rows of pews, six deep to a side. In the front of the church, there was a piano and a small podium.

She slipped into one of the empty pews and bent her head over her folded hands.

Dear God. Can you hear me?

The walls didn't shake and the floor didn't tremble. Still, she'd always assumed God had a subtle streak so she continued.

It's me. Sarah Jane Tremont. Your living time-travel experiment.

She looked around the church. The sun shining through the stained glass windows caught a few dust motes irreverently dancing around. *Sorry, I don't mean to sound ungrateful. I mean, I'm glad I didn't drown. It's just that I'm feeling a bit uneasy. I'm worried about me.*

She looked up and waited for the lightning to strike. *I've got two issues. Wait, make that three. I've got a thing for John Beckett. Sexy, too sweet for his own good, too obtuse for belief, and too much for me to handle, John Beckett. He can't see me for me. All he knows is the hatred he carries for Sarah One.*

She scooted forward, reached out her hand to the pew in front of her, and ran her finger down the fine wood grain. *He's solid, God. Like this pew. But I'm fluff. Here but not really here. Present but not accounted for.*

She picked up the red hymnal and held it tight against her breasts. *I'm worried about Suzanne. I want to shake her, but she's so close to the edge, I'm afraid she'll crumble, wobble*

*off her wall, and I won't be able to put Humpty-Dumpty
back together again.*

She stood up and started to pace around the small church.
*So problem number one is John and problem number two is
Suzanne. My being here is problem number three. I need to
go back to my own time. If I don't, who is going to help
Miguel Lopez?*

She stood behind the small podium and looked out at the
empty church. She hadn't come to God to have him make
the choice for her. She'd already made it. *Guess what, God.
Listen close because I can barely believe what I'm going to
say. I don't think I can get on that stage on Wednesday.
Who's going to take care of Suzanne? Who's going to make
sure she eats and takes a bath and goes outside and starts
living again?*

She walked over to the piano and ran her fingers lightly
across the keys. The soft sounds flowed through the empty
room. She pulled out the wooden bench and sat down. Lovingly, she began to play, relishing the feel of the hard ivory
keys. Eight years of piano lessons kicked in, as if they'd
ended last week instead of ten years ago. She played her favorite John Lennon song, "Imagine." When she finished,
she closed her eyes and bowed her head, grateful that her
music hadn't been stripped away.

"That's a beautiful song."

Sarah jerked her head around to the left. A man, probably close to sixty, his small frame leaning heavily on a
cane, stood in the doorway.

"I don't believe I've ever heard it before," he said, smiling at her.

"It's a little piece I picked up in Cheyenne," she said.
Forgive me, John.

"I heard you were back in town," he said. "My grandchildren went on and on about you."

Pastor Dan. Fred's father-in-law. "Great kids."

He beamed. "You'll get no argument from me on that. By the way, I had no idea you were such an accomplished pianist."

Wasn't that sweet? "I'm a little rusty."

"Not nearly as rusty as Mrs. Hammerstein and she's played every Sunday for the last three years."

"You won't tell her I touched her piano, will you?"

He shrugged and swung his body into the last pew. "She moved four weeks ago. She's sorely missed. Church just isn't quite the same without music."

"Just like a bad horror movie," she said.

He looked at her oddly.

She waved her hand. "Never mind."

"Fred tells me you're leaving on the next stage."

Sarah nodded. "That was the plan."

"Was?"

He might be old and skinny but his hearing had held up. "Yes. I'm staying another week. My friend needs me."

"Your friend?"

His tone said it all. She didn't have any friends.

"She works at the saloon." At. Over. She didn't feel the need to be specific.

"Ahhh. Miss Suzanne?"

This had the makings of a good nighttime drama. The Two P's. The Preacher and the Prostitute. "You know her?"

"Not well. She's been to church a few times."

"Bet that went over big with the rest of the parishioners."

Pastor Dan laughed. "Not during regular services. She comes during the week, when no one else is here. I suspect she prefers to pray in private."

Good thing he didn't suspect Miss Suzanne was praying about his son-in-law. "She didn't deserve to get beat up."

"Certainly not. I hope they arrest Mr. Dority. He's a disgrace."

She had a few other names for Dority but didn't particularly want to shock Pastor Dan, who looked like a strong wind might blow him over. She got up from the piano. As she stood, she ran her hands one last time over the keys.

"I've got a proposition for you," Pastor Dan said.

Sarah tilted her chin down.

Pastor Dan laughed. "Not that kind of proposition. Is there any possibility that I could persuade you to play for services this Sunday? You could play any songs you like."

She hadn't played for an audience since her last recital. "I couldn't. Really. It's been too long."

"It sounded wonderful to me."

She felt like she was disappointing God. A skinny God. "There's no one else in town who plays the piano?"

"No. The saloon has a piano but the woman that normally plays there broke her hand last week."

Sarah rubbed her fingers together. They itched to get access to those beautiful ivory keys.

"I could pay you a little something from the collection basket. It's just that there's not much left. We have so many families in need."

She shook her head. She wouldn't accept the church's money, even to keep up Sarah One's soiled reputation. "No, that's not necessary. I'd be happy to help."

Pastor Dan stuck out his arm and smiled, showing a row of yellowed teeth. "Welcome to my flock, Sarah."

Yes, well. She hoped his flock didn't mind that he'd invited in a wolf in sheep's clothing.

WHEN Sarah walked into the hotel, she saw John Beckett sitting on the top step of the stairs. He jumped up, as if he'd committed some crime.

"What are you doing here?" Sarah asked, thinking how wonderful it was to see him again.

He glanced around, as if he might be looking for answers in the corners. He adjusted his hat, then rubbed his hands across his thighs.

Wait a minute. She was the one with sweaty palms.

"Stage leaves day after tomorrow," he said. "I wanted to see . . . see that you didn't need anything before you go."

"That's nice of you."

He looked even more uncomfortable, as if he sure as hell didn't want to be caught doing anything nice. "How's Suzanne feeling?" he asked.

"I don't know. Physically, she's better. Her eyes are still black and blue but the swelling on her face has gone away and her lip looks a lot better."

"But?"

"But I think her hurt isn't just physical. It's like Dority took his stupid knife and sliced into her spirit."

"What do you mean?"

"I know it's crazy, but it's almost like she thinks she deserved it, that she's the kind of woman who should get beat up and tossed around."

"No woman deserves that," John said, looking mad.

"I know that and I thought she knew that. But now I'm not so sure. She won't eat. She won't go outside."

"Maybe she's just embarrassed about her black eyes. Once those heal, everything will be fine."

"I don't think so. She doesn't even know what her eyes look like. She won't look in a mirror."

John rubbed a hand over his chin. "How's she feel about your leaving?"

"She hasn't said much."

He did the hand wipe thing again. "I guess I could look in on her after you're gone. I mean, someone's got to do it."

He just couldn't help being a nice guy. "That's very thoughtful of you," she said. "Here's the thing, though. I'm not going on Wednesday."

"What?"

"I can't go. Not when Suzanne is like this. She doesn't

have anybody. People in this town aren't going to care if she withers away in her bed. I can't leave her right now."

With short, jerky steps, John started to pace around the hallway. "You said you had to leave on Wednesday."

"I did. I do. Look, it's difficult to explain. There's someone in another place that needs information that I have."

He stopped pacing and looked at her. "What information?"

She shrugged. "I can't say."

He frowned at her.

"It's nothing about you or your family. I promise."

He stared at her for a long moment. Then he smiled. "I believe you."

Until he said the words, she hadn't realized how important it was to her. "Thank you," she whispered.

"Are you going to stay here at the hotel?"

"Yes."

He reached into his pocket and pulled out some bills. "You'll need more money."

She shook her head. "No, I can't take anything else from you."

His face turned red. "Look, Sarah, I said some things before about you coming back to take more from me and my family. I shouldn't have said that. I don't want you to go without. Peter wouldn't have wanted that."

Sarah's stomach rolled. Everything John did, he did for Peter, certainly not for her. It was wishful thinking to hope that he could look beyond the past. He couldn't forget that she'd been his brother's wife. She needed to start remembering the same thing.

"I saw my mother-in-law this morning."

A muscle in the side of John's jaw jerked. "And?"

"We had a nice chat. I got the impression she couldn't wait for Wednesday. She's going to be disappointed when she learns I'm not on that stage."

"I'll talk to her. I don't want her to be surprised."

"Well, if it's surprises you're trying to avoid, you might want to let her know that I've agreed to play the piano for Pastor Dan's services on Sunday."

John cocked his head to one side. "You don't play the piano," he said.

She shrugged. "Actually, I do. Fairly well, too."

"You never mentioned it," he said, his tone accusing.

"I never had the chance," she said.

He put his hands on his hips, almost rocking back on the heels of his boots. "You know, Sarah. There are times when I don't feel like I know you at all."

Sarah could feel her heart rate speed up. This was it. He'd given her the perfect opportunity. *Hey, there's a reason for that. You're not going to believe this but I haven't even been born yet.*

Sure, that would work. Even if he didn't run screaming into the street, it didn't matter. In a week, she'd be gone, back to her own time.

"I'm full of surprises," she said, unable to keep the bitterness out of her voice. She was tired. For days she'd been the lead actress in a drama. The lights were bright, the crowd unforgiving, and the lines seemed to be fading off the page. She didn't know what to do or say next. She couldn't tell the truth, but every lie she told tore at her soul.

"Look, John," she said. "I think you should go. It's pretty clear that you and I don't have a lot in common."

She could hear his short hiss of breath.

"If you need me," he said, "send Freedom. I'll come. You know I will."

He would. Strong, dependable, responsible. A damn Boy Scout. Except she didn't want him to tie a knot or lead her out of the woods. She wanted him to open his arms and hold her, to rock her against his hard body, to claim her as his own. But he wouldn't. Because Boy Scouts were loyal. He couldn't be anything but loyal to his brother's memory.

WHEN Pastor Dan had mentioned that the saloon was minus one piano player, Sarah had taken that tidbit, added in the cold reality of her empty purse, balanced that off with the need to pay for a hotel room for another week, and before she knew it, she'd bellied up to the bar, asking for work.

"Are you Thomas Jefferson?" she asked the big man standing behind the bar. He had a bald head, a red face, and a clean white apron wrapped around his protruding middle.

"Yes, ma'am."

She almost asked to fill out an application. Just in time, she remembered to smile pretty and act sweet. "I'm Sarah Beckett. It's a pleasure to meet you."

"John Beckett's sister-in-law?"

He said it without malice, as if he was simply trying to put the pieces together.

"Yes."

"You're the one helping Suzanne?"

"Yes."

"How is she?"

"She's getting better," Sarah said, not wanting to share her concerns with a stranger.

"I like her." Thomas Jefferson wiped the bar with a cloth. "If I'd have known that she planned to go off with Dority, I'd have set her straight. I watch out for my girls. Not like some places."

A conscientious pimp. Sarah wanted to be mad but realized that she couldn't hold it against the man. After all, he provided a desired service to his customers.

"I heard you recently lost your piano player. I'd like to have the spot, if it's still available."

"John know you're asking about this?"

"Yes," she lied.

"He don't mind?"

"He knows I love to play."

"Saloon starts to fill up about seven o'clock, right after the dinner hour," Thomas said. "You'll need to play
until midnight. You get a break every hour. Ten minutes.
No going upstairs with any men. Not until your shift is
over."

"No problem."

"Your whiskey is free. Pay is three dollars a night. You
can put a tip jar out. Half goes to you, half to the house."

"Fair enough. Any special requests?"

"Yeah. Make 'em dance."

She pointed at the man sleeping at the far end of the bar,
his head cradled over his folded arms. "I hope your expec-
tations aren't too high."

"Don't worry about him. He's new in town. Don't expect
he'll stay around too long. Said his name was George."

"You don't care if he sleeps here?"

"He said he don't sleep much at night anymore. I think
he might be a little crazy. I caught him talking to the empty
stool next to him yesterday, just like there was somebody
sitting there. But he's had money to spend on whiskey and
cards. That's good enough for me."

Commerce. Greed. Not everything had changed from
the good old days. "When do I start?"

"Tonight." Thomas pulled out his pocket watch. "You've
got three hours. I hope you're not planning to wear that."

Sarah looked down at Franny Goodie's dull brown skirt
and tan blouse. She'd been so busy the last few days, she'd
almost forgotten how hideous she looked. She needed an
outfit with some color, some spark, some appeal. She certainly didn't have any money to purchase anything. That
left one option. "Susanne's letting me borrow some things.
Can you unlock her door?"

A half hour later, Sarah walked back to the hotel. She

climbed the steps, her arms full of gowns. She knocked on the door with her foot. "Suzanne, open the door."

She waited, and finally, the door slowly opened. Sarah walked in, past her friend. If anything, Suzanne looked worse. She'd been crying, making her swollen nose even redder. Her hair, her pretty short hair, stood up on end. Her lip had started to bleed again.

"Thanks for letting me in," Sarah said, trying hard to hide her concern. "These dresses weigh a ton."

Suzanne walked back to the bed, slipped underneath the covers, and turned so that her back faced Sarah.

"I should have asked first," Sarah said, "but I thought you might be sleeping. I had Thomas unlock your room."

"I don't want to get dressed."

"Not for you," Sarah said. "Although I think you definitely need to get dressed by tomorrow. These are for me. I got a job at the saloon."

"A job?" Suzanne rolled over and looked at Sarah. She had her bloody, cracked lips pressed together. "You're taking my place? How could you?"

"Oh, no. Not that kind of job. I'm going to play the piano. Maybe sing a few songs. That's it."

Suzanne didn't look convinced. "You're leaving on Wednesday."

"I was. I've decided to stick around for another week."

"Why?"

To kick your butt. To make you start living again. "It's been months since I've been back to Cedarbrook. There are friends I want to catch up with. I haven't had the chance."

"Oh."

Sarah relaxed. Suzanne looked like she bought it. Hook, line, and sinker. Thank goodness Suzanne hadn't met the real Sarah. She'd know that Sarah One wouldn't have any friends anxious to pick up where they'd left off. "Since I'll be around, I thought I'd pick up a couple extra dollars."

"Playing piano?"

Sarah nodded. "Strictly downstairs work."

Suzanne chuckled and Sarah had a glimpse of the woman she'd met at Fred's house. The woman she'd been before her spirit had been beaten out of her.

"I probably should have stuck with downstairs work," Suzanne said.

"It's never too late."

Suzanne shook her head. "Sometimes it is. Sometimes the hole we dig for ourselves is so deep, we can't crawl out of it."

"I suppose," Sarah said, inspecting the hem of one dress. She didn't want to look too vested in the conversation. "When the hole is that deep, those are the times we need a helping hand."

Suzanne shook her head. "It's not that easy. People may reach out but sometimes, no matter how much you want it, no matter how hard you try to hold on, you slip back. You can't get out of the hole. It's too deep. You're too far down."

"Then somebody needs to get a ladder. A tall one."

Suzanne didn't say anything. Finally, she shrugged and rolled over, once again giving Sarah her back. "Problem is," she said, her voice flat, "that when you put a ladder in soft dirt, it sinks. Then you've got nothing. Just like before."

Sarah, discouraged but not ready to give up, picked up her dresses. She'd find a rock in that hole, something sturdy to balance her ladder on.

And then, she'd find a way to make Suzanne take her hand and together they'd climb out, one rung at a time.

TEN

WHEN Sarah started playing the piano at seven, she entertained an audience of nine, including Thomas Jefferson and two tables of four men each. Thomas poured her a whiskey and looked surprised when she asked for a big glass of water on the side. Seven of the eight remaining men ignored her. She preferred that over the lone man who looked up and stared at her, his face turning red, his eyes blinking furiously.

Another Sarah One hater? Sarah understood the feeling. She pretty much hated Sarah One, too. Not knowing what else to do, Sarah ignored him and kept her eyes on her sheet music. She started off with "Buffalo Gals" and "Jimmy Crack Corn" but soon tired of that. Before her first set ended, she'd drifted into her Billy Joel favorites.

"You're pretty good." Thomas filled up her water glass.

"Thanks. Kind of a quiet crowd tonight?"

"It's early yet. The music will draw them in."

"Nobody seems to be paying much attention," she said.

"Toby's lost eight hands since you started playing. I think you've got his attention."

Toby. The staring man had a name. "Is he a regular?"

"He's been here the last three nights. His wife went to Denver to see her sister."

Sarah stretched her back, leaning from side to side. "Just between you and me, I'm not expecting a big tip from him."

Thomas laughed. "You might be wrong. Last night he drank himself silly. Money practically fell out of his pockets. A dog licking his boots could have gotten a tip."

"I'll remember that. Let me know if you've got any requests." She walked back to the piano and sat down, angling her bench so that she couldn't see Toby.

At nine when she took her next break, a few empty stools at the bar remained but all the tables had filled up. Most of the men played cards, although two tables played some kind of dice game. She felt like she'd crashed a nineteenth-century fraternity party. Everybody had a drink and most had a bottle at the table. Whenever the saloon door swung open, the men would look up, judge the newcomer, and he'd be invited to join a table or relegated to a more solitary spot at the bar.

In the middle of Sarah's third set, the door swung open and the noisy bar quieted immediately. She lost her place in the middle of "Oh! Susannah." George, the man she'd been warned about, stood in the doorway. He didn't speak to anyone and no one spoke to him. He took his seat at the end of the bar.

Thomas poured a whiskey and set the bottle in front of him. George shoved some coins across the scratched wooden bar. Sarah launched into "New York, New York" and watched him over the top of the piano. He looked like a tired thirty. While his tanned skin had just a few lines, the dark circles under his eyes and his scruffy beard aged him. He had to be over six feet and two hundred pounds, but his clothes still seemed too big, as if he'd borrowed them from an older brother.

When Sarah ended her song, she stood up. She needed a bathroom, thanks to the two glasses of water she'd drunk after setting the whiskey aside. Sadly, she remembered Freedom's comment about the hotel having the only inside bathroom. "Thomas, where's the privy?" she asked.

"Out back, across the alley."

"Thanks."

"Unless you can see in the dark, you better take a lantern," Thomas instructed.

"Right." Just one more reason why she needed to get back to her own time. Bathrooms with lights.

She walked out of the saloon and around the corner. Three hundred feet away, she could see the small white building. With her free hand, she picked up the edge of Suzanne's green dress, not wanting to drag it through the dirt. When she got within twenty feet, the smell almost overwhelmed her. Taking breaths as shallow as possible, she opened the door, did what she needed to do, and got the heck out of there.

She'd crossed the alley when Toby stepped out of the shadows. Sarah swung her lantern in front of her, wanting him to keep his distance.

"I've missed you, Sarah," he said, weaving from side to side. "It's been a long time, you little bitch." She could smell the whiskey on him, as if he'd taken a bath in the stuff.

Great. Not only had Toby known Sarah One, he had a bone to pick with her. "I need to get back inside," she said, trying to step around him. "Thomas is expecting me."

He moved, faster than she'd expected given the amount of alcohol in his system, blocking her path again. He leaned toward her. "What are you going to do? Sneak out of town again. With my money?"

Yikes. "I'm not sneaking anywhere. I have a job to do."

"You spread your legs like a common whore," he said, "and you think you've got the right to act like a lady?"

Could it get much worse? Sarah One had been his lover? "Get out of my way," she said.

"You said everything would be fine once you got the money from your dead husband's mother. You said we'd go away together."

"You're drunk," she said.

"You're damn right I'm drunk. You left me with nothing, Sarah. How was I supposed to explain the missing money to my wife? Did you think she wouldn't notice? Did you think she wouldn't know that I'd been a fool for a woman?"

Sarah thought she might throw up. "Get out of my way."

He shoved her, hard enough that she stumbled back. "You're going to pay," he said. "I'm going to—"

"Get your Goddamn hands off of her."

Distracted, Toby whirled around. Sarah used the seconds wisely, running around him.

John stood twenty feet away, his gun pointed at Toby's chest. "Sarah, get behind me," he said, never taking his eyes off Toby.

"Stay the hell out of my business," Toby said.

John shook his head. "You're in my business. Now, Sarah, do what I told you."

She did, placing herself two feet behind him.

"You bastard," Toby yelled, running full speed toward them. Sarah stepped back. John stuck his forearm out, catching Toby right at the larynx. The man dropped to the ground, gagging and coughing.

"Oh, jeez," Sarah said, holding up the lantern.

"He's fine," John said, dismissing the man. "He'll catch his breath." He turned to look at her. "Are you hurt?"

Sarah lowered the lantern. She'd seen the concern in John's beautiful brown eyes. It made her yearn for things that could never be. "I'm fine. Why are you here?"

"I'm not sure," he said.

"I don't understand."

"That makes two of us. I stopped by the hotel. Freedom said you were at the saloon. When I asked Thomas if he'd seen you, he looked surprised and said you'd made a trip outside." He took a step closer. She moved the lantern in front of her, as if the light might save her.

"What the Hell is going on, Sarah? What are you doing in the saloon at night? It's not safe."

Sarah dug her toe in the dirt. "I got a job at the saloon," she said.

"What?"

He'd barked the word, so intense that she had to fight the instinct to flee.

"Not that kind of job. Man, what is it with you and Suzanne? There are other kinds of work."

"Sarah." His tone said it all. He wanted to know what was going on.

"I told you I'm playing the piano at church. Well, church isn't the only place in need of a piano player. Thomas Jefferson hired me to entertain his customers."

"Entertain?"

His voice thundered down the quiet alley. "Could we move along?" she asked. She pointed at Toby, who lay on the ground. "I don't really want him to be part of the conversation."

John gripped her arm and practically dragged her to the end of the alley. "You've got three seconds," he said. He didn't remove his hand from her arm. She could feel his heat, his energy, his solid strength. His steel will.

"Before you do what?" she baited him.

"You don't even want to know," he said. "Talk."

"At four o'clock this afternoon, I asked Thomas Jefferson for a job. He said yes. I started playing at seven. Right now, Thomas is probably pacing behind the bar, cursing me because I'm late getting back from my break."

"You little fool," John said. "Don't you know the kind of

men who spend their nights at the saloon? These are men with nothing to lose. These are men like Toby Ryan."

"Everyone," she said, "with the exception of Toby, has been polite. They haven't even said two words to me."

"What did you do that made Toby follow you into the alley?"

He obviously hadn't heard much of the exchange. Otherwise, he'd know exactly what Toby had thought. "He has me mixed up with somebody else," she said. "Look, I appreciate what you did. You got me out of a tough spot. But you can go home now. If he recovers . . ." She smiled at him, trying to ease his worry. "I don't think he's going to bother me again."

John shook his head, as if he couldn't believe his ears. "Let's go," he said. "You're going to go back to the saloon and tell Thomas Jefferson that you've had a change of heart. That you're no longer interested in *entertaining* his customers."

She shook his hand off. He reached for her again and she took a step back. "I'm not going to do that," she said.

He ran his hands through his hair. "Look, Sarah. Be reasonable. Do you know what might have happened tonight if I hadn't come along?"

"Yes." The damage Dority had inflicted upon Suzanne haunted Sarah's dreams. She knew all too well what would have happened to Suzanne if she hadn't intervened. She'd never again underestimate the power of a man to physically abuse a woman. "I need to be smarter. To drink less water."

"What?" He reached for her lantern and grabbed it out of her hand. He held it up, searching her face. "What are you talking about?"

"No more late-night trips to the privy. If I'd stayed at the saloon, I'd have been fine."

He frowned at her. "It's not that simple, Sarah."

"Maybe not. All I know is that I made a commitment to Thomas and I'm going to keep it."

"I'll talk to him," John said.

"No."

He lifted his chin.

"Please don't," she said, softening her tone. "I know you're trying to help. I do. And I appreciate it. Maybe more than you'll ever know. But I need to do this."

She heard him sigh. "Fine."

"Just fine. That's it?"

"Fine, I'll walk you back. To the saloon."

She started to breathe again. They walked down the dark alley. When they passed Toby, they saw that he'd pulled himself up into a sitting position and was leaning against the wall. He had his eyes closed. John, placing himself between her and the drunk man, kicked at the toe of Toby's boot.

"Do we understand each other, Toby?" John asked, his voice hard.

Toby opened his eyes. He looked at John, then at Sarah. He made a show of bravery but Sarah could see the fear in his eyes. She understood it. Having John Beckett tower over you would scare most men. "You're welcome to her," Toby said.

"Good."

Sarah pulled on John's arm.

"Take the bitch—"

John reeled away, reached down, grabbed Toby by the shirt, and hauled him up. He held him, suspended inches off the ground, his back flat against the wall.

"What did you say?" John asked.

Sarah could see the muscles bulging in John's arm. They matched the veins in Toby's face. He kicked his feet in the air, like a cartoon character.

"Let me down!" Toby squawked.

"Apologize to the lady," John said.

Toby shook his head.

John raised him another three inches and shoved him

back against the wall, causing his head to bounce off the wood with a dull thud.

"Apologize," John instructed.

"I'm sorry," Toby said, his voice shrill. "I didn't mean to offend."

John let go and Toby dropped to the ground. He crumpled into a pile.

"Don't come near her," John said. "If you do, you'll have me to deal with."

John didn't wait for an answer. He grabbed Sarah's hand and pulled her away. "Damn, I'm thirsty," he said.

She stopped walking. "Oh, no. You're not going into the saloon, are you?"

"A man has the right to get a drink."

"You're not thirsty," she said.

"You don't know everything."

She knew that John Beckett made her heart race and her chest feel tight and that she had very non-sister-in-law-like thoughts about him. "Toby isn't going to bother me," she said. "He's not that stupid."

"I agree. I don't think you have to worry about him anymore. He got the message."

"So, there's no need for you to spend valuable time in the saloon."

"It's my time," he said.

"Don't bother me," she warned.

"You won't even know I'm there."

Right.

JOHN walked her home at midnight. True to his word, he hadn't spoken to her the whole night. He'd taken his seat at the bar, had some conversation with Thomas, and pretty much ignored her.

But he hadn't really. She'd seen his body tense up when one of the card players had stopped by the piano and slipped some coins in her tip jar. When George had slid off his stool and come within several feet of the piano, John had been half off his own stool.

Not knowing what else to do, Sarah had smiled at the serious man and he'd moved along. She hadn't missed the frown on John's face.

"You must be tired," she said as they crossed the street.

"Yes."

"How's the planting coming along?"

"Fine."

They walked the remaining thirty feet in silence. When Sarah opened the hotel door, she turned to John. "Thanks again," she said. "For helping me with Toby."

"I'll walk you to your room," he said.

Sarah shrugged. They walked up the stairs. John took the key from Sarah and walked toward her room. She shook her head and pointed at Suzanne's door.

He unlocked the door and stepped back, letting her enter first. "Come on in," she whispered, looking over her shoulder. "She's asleep."

He silently followed her into the room. He stopped a foot from the bed and looked down at Suzanne. She was curled into a ball, a pillow clenched in her arms. John sank down in the chair. "That bastard Dority should be whipped and then hung for this."

"Yes."

John turned to Sarah. "It could be you," he said, his voice hoarse. "Somebody could do this to you."

Knowing better but not able to stop herself, she brushed the back of her hand across his cheek. "I know. I'm not stupid or foolish nor nearly as trusting as Suzanne."

He reached up and caught her hand. She could feel the heat zip up her arm. When he turned her hand over and kissed her palm, she thought she might have forgotten how to breathe.

"I don't want you to get hurt, Sarah."

She nodded, her head feeling heavy on her neck.

John kissed her wrist and her arm jerked in response. A smile drifted across his lips. He moved his mouth up her arm, and when he licked the soft spot at her elbow, she felt the answering tug deep inside.

"This is crazy," he murmured, looking up at her.

"Yes," she whispered.

"Just once," he said.

"Just once what?"

He rose up, pulled her close, and wrapped her arms around his neck. "Just once this." He bent his head and kissed her. Gently at first. Then harder, his tongue stroking into her mouth. Her legs started to shake and he pulled her even closer, his hands low on her spine.

When he finally stopped kissing her, he rested his chin against the top of her head.

"Oh, my," she said. Now her legs were jelly. She clung to him.

"Are you all right?" he asked.

"I think so," she said. She felt warm and cold, weak and strong, brave and cowardly. She was a mess.

"I shouldn't have done that," he said.

That hurt. It didn't matter that he was right. Not for the reason he thought, but for a thousand other reasons. Most of which had something to do with the fact that she'd hadn't been born yet.

"I'm glad you did," she said, wanting him to know that the kiss had meant something to her.

He lifted his chin and stepped away from her. Sarah's arms dropped to her sides. They'd been full of him and now they were empty, useless.

"I'm your brother-in-law," he said.

She had to ask. "Are you reminding yourself or me?"

He ran his fingers through his hair. "I don't know," he said, his whispered voice sounding tortured. "I honestly don't know."

It should not be his burden to bear alone. "I don't think we should kiss again," she said.

He nodded and stepped away. "You're right."

She hated that. "Good night, John."

"I'll walk you to your room."

"I'm in my room."

"Your room's next door," he said.

"My room was next door. I decided to sleep in here with Suzanne."

He looked at Suzanne. She wasn't large but she took up most of the single bed. "Where?"

"I've got some blankets. I sleep on the floor."

He pulled back, looking shocked. "You can't sleep on a wooden floor."

"It's fine. Stop worrying about me. I didn't want Suzanne to be alone and I thought I could save some money by staying with her. It's just until next week's stage."

"Sarah," he said, looking angry. "I never should have said what I did about you coming back to take money from my family. I have more than enough money so that you don't have to sleep on the floor."

"I don't want your money."

"I don't want you sleeping on the floor."

She sighed. "John, it's midnight. I'm tired. You're tired. Let's not fight about this. I'll get another room tomorrow. If they have one."

"You tell Morton Turnip that he better find you a room."

"Turnip's first name is Morton?"

"Yes."

"Your dog is named Morton."

"Yes."

She rubbed her hand across her face, so tired that she felt giddy. "You named your dog after Turnip?"

"Hell, no."

She laughed. John looked stricken.

"Trust me on this," she said, lowering her voice even

more when she saw Suzanne stretch in the bed. "I've only known two Mortons in my entire life. Turnip and your dog. It can't be a coincidence."

John shook his head.

"Now that I think about it," Sarah said, warming up to the subject, "both of them have treated me like they wanted to take a bite out of my . . ."

"Your?" John prompted.

"My bottom," she said, sticking her nose in the air.

He laughed, a deep rumble. Suzanne turned over. Sarah put her hand over John's mouth.

He stilled.

She could feel his warm breath pushing against her hand.

"Good night, John Beckett," she whispered.

He took a step back, away from her hand. She felt the loss of heat immediately. "Good night, sweet Sarah."

SARAH wasn't feeling sweet at three in the morning when light but consistent tapping on her door awakened her. She lay absolutely still, listening for a moment. Yes. Someone was outside the door.

Dority? The fear raced through her. No, he wouldn't knock. He'd barge in like he had every right. Sarah quietly got up, wincing when her back, sore from the wooden floor, didn't want to cooperate. Maybe it was Freedom?

"Yes," she said.

The tapping stopped. "Sarah?"

"Fred?" she whispered back.

"Yes. Open the door."

She moved the chair that she'd wedged up under the doorknob, then unhooked the latch and opened the door. Fred's large shape, barely a shadow in the dark hallway, loomed in front of her. "What are you doing here?" she whispered, pulling him into the room.

"I had to see her. I couldn't wait any longer."

She could hear the pain in his rough voice. "Hang on," she said, trying hard to cover her own emotion. Maybe Suzanne wasn't all alone in this? "Let me light a lamp."

Sarah felt her way over to the table. It took her two tries before the match caught. When she got the lamp lit and held it up, she turned back to Fred. He stood in the same spot, his hat in his hand. He stared at Suzanne. She lay on her side, still curled around a pillow, her back to him.

"How is she?" he asked.

Sarah smiled at him. How could such a big man look like such a little boy? "Come here," she whispered. "Take a look for yourself."

He lumbered around the end of the bed, making the small room seem even smaller. He stood next to Sarah and stared at Suzanne. His hands clenched the brim of his cowboy hat so tightly that she knew it would never look the same.

Then ever so gently he eased his big body down onto the edge of the bed. Suzanne, still asleep, rolled over onto her back, throwing one arm over her head.

Sarah heard his quick intake of breath. She held her lamp a little higher, letting the light dance over Suzanne's battered face. He'd come to see it; he'd had to know. She wouldn't try to keep him from it.

She watched as he took the first two fingers of his right hand, raised them to his lips and kissed them, then brushed them across Suzanne's black and blue eyes, her bruised cheeks, and her cut lips. Opening his hand, he ran the palm of it over her short hair. Sarah literally could see the bed shake when he shuddered.

"I'm going to kill him," he said, so softly that Sarah almost didn't hear him.

"Let the law handle it," she answered.

"I'll handle it," he said, forgetting to whisper.

Suzanne's eyes flew open. She looked frightened and tried to press herself back against the mattress.

"It's just Fred," he said, his voice soft.

"Oh." Suzanne pulled both arms from under the covers and clapped her hands on top of her head, obviously trying to cover her short hair.

"There's no need for that," he said, gently pulling both arms back down.

Tears welled up in Suzanne's eyes. "But you loved my hair. You used to . . ."

Fred glanced up at Sarah, his face red. "I know what I used to do," he said, his voice still soft, nonthreatening. He looked back at Suzanne and slowly raised his hand to her hair. With just the tips of his fingers, he caressed several strands. "And I liked it. Very much. But it doesn't matter. None of that matters. All I care about is that you're alive."

Now the tears ran down Suzanne's battered face. Sarah felt her own tears threaten. When Fred reached forward, gathered Suzanne's body in his arms, and rocked her, back and forth, back and forth, Sarah swallowed hard. She set her lamp down on the bedside table, walked around the end of the bed, and grabbed her blankets off the floor. "I'll just be outside," she said. "Take your time."

Neither Fred nor Suzanne answered. Sarah opened the door and walked out into the dark hallway. She reached out for the wall and felt her way over to the stairs. She wrapped the blanket around her, sat down on the third step from the top, and twisted her body around so that she could rest her folded arms on the top step.

All in all, it was the most comfortable position she'd slept in for two nights. She didn't wake up until Fred lowered his body next to hers. The wood floor groaned under his weight.

"Thank you, Sarah," he said.

"No problem." When she stretched her body, she discovered new aches and pains. "I thought you might appreciate some privacy."

He nodded. "I don't mean just for that. I want to thank you for being here. For helping her."

"You love her, don't you?"

He nodded. "I think I do. I just don't know what to do about it. If it were just me, it would be easy. But I got the children and Franny's pa to think about."

She smiled at him. "I'm sure the children would adjust, and Pastor Dan seems like a pretty tolerant man."

Fred looked miserable. "People in this town know what she is. They won't let her forget. I can take it and she can probably take it. But I don't want people whispering behind my children's backs. I don't want them shunned. I don't want Pastor Dan run out of town, separated from his grandchildren, by a hoard of angry church members."

Sarah slipped her arms under his and wrapped them around his broad back. She hugged the big man. "It's always so darn complicated," she said.

They heard the click of the front door. Sarah and Fred looked up just as Morton Turnip walked in the door, lantern in hand. He saw them on the steps and frowned at them. He took another eight steps toward them.

"What's going on here?" he asked. "What are you doing, Fred Goodie?"

Sarah felt Fred's big body tense. Not knowing what else to do, she lifted her face up and brushed her lips across his. "I'll see you tomorrow, darling."

When she saw the pure relief in his eyes, she knew she'd done the right thing. She stood up, wrapping the blanket around her with a flourish. "I think I'll get some sleep now."

"Well, well," she heard Turnip say as she reached her door. "Fred Goodie, you surprise me. I'd have thought you had more sense than to get mixed up with that little bitch."

It was the second time in less than eight hours that she'd been called a bitch.

"Shut your mouth, Turnip," Fred said. "Or I'll shut it for you."

Turnip laughed.

Sarah knew it would be all over town by breakfast time. No doubt Turnip would embellish the story. It didn't matter. In less than a week, she'd leave. Fred would endure the whispers and the sly looks. They'd chuckle about how poor Fred got suckered in by the evil Sarah Beckett.

Still, it was better than the alternative. Better to be fooled by a bitch than in love with the town whore.

ELEVEN

WHEN Suzanne got up on Tuesday morning and washed her face and brushed her hair, Sarah thought they might have turned the corner. "How are you?" she asked.

"Better," Suzanne said. She sank down on the bed, pulling at the neckline of her cotton nightgown. "I can't believe Fred came to see me."

"He likes you."

"He's a wonderful man. He loves his children so much."

"You're gushing. That's sweet."

"I'm not gushing. It's hard on him being alone."

"I imagine it is. Kids that age can be a handful. He's big enough though that when they act up, he probably just picks them up, throws them in a sack, and shakes them up."

"Oh no," Suzanne protested. "He's never mean."

"I know," Sarah tried to clarify. "I meant—"

"You'd think he would be," Suzanne interrupted. "Most big men are. They can hurt you really bad. You know, in bed."

"Oh." Ouch. Sarah squeezed her legs together. "That makes sense."

"Sometimes," Suzanne said, "when a man takes off his trousers and you see him, you know it's going to hurt. You just have to shut your eyes and do whatever you can to make sure it gets over as fast as possible. When I saw Fred, I almost ran out of the room. But he'd paid his two dollars so I lay back on the bed and spread my legs."

"You don't have to tell me this," Sarah said.

"I have to tell someone. I can't tell anybody else."

Great. "I'm listening."

"I closed my eyes and kept waiting for him to rip me apart. But he just sat next to me on the bed and he asked me what he should do. No man's ever asked me what he should do before."

Sarah nodded.

"I didn't know what to say. I was so surprised that I told him he should kiss me. I never kiss my customers. That's the one thing I won't do."

Kind of like Julia Roberts in *Pretty Woman*. "Did he kiss you?"

"Yes. For a very long time. Then he left."

Sarah narrowed her eyes at Suzanne. "Before he . . . ?"

"Yes. He buttoned his trousers back up and left."

"What did you do?"

"I told him to take his two dollars back."

"Did he?"

"He just shook his head. I didn't think I'd ever see him again. But two nights later, he showed up with two more dollars. I wasn't a bit scared this time."

"Did he . . . ?" Sarah waved her hand.

Suzanne nodded, a wide grin spreading across her face. "Did he ever. Twice."

"Okay. Too much information." She reached over and patted her friend's hand. It was good to see Suzanne smile again. "You two are a good match."

Suzanne's smiled faded. "We don't match at all. He's a good man and a devoted father. I'm a two-dollar saloon girl."

Sarah didn't think she had the time or the energy to dance around the issue. "You are," she said. "You've probably slept with most of the men in this town."

"Yes," Suzanne whispered.

"Did you enjoy it?"

"I don't have to enjoy it. I . . . I'm good at it. It's probably hard for you to understand."

She didn't understand. Nor did she judge. "Try me," she said.

Suzanne slid her legs over the side of the bed. She got up and paced around the small room. "I grew up in Lone Tree, Iowa. We were poor, really poor. My ma got sick after she had my little sister. My pa worked hard but we had to raise ourselves. I sold myself to my first man when I was thirteen."

Sarah wrapped her arm around Suzanne's shoulder, stilling her. "That must have been horrible."

Suzanne shook her off and resumed her pacing. "Not as bad as being hungry. I did it again the next week and then the week after that. I'm only twenty-four years old and I can't even remember how many men have paid for me. All I know is that I haven't been hungry since then. I make enough to support myself and to send a few dollars back to my sister. She still lives in Lone Tree. She's got three babies now and she needs all the help she can get."

"How long do you think you can do this? How long before your body wears out?"

Suzanne shrugged. "I don't think about the future."

"Maybe you should," Sarah said.

"I don't think so. If I think too hard about it, it just makes me sad."

Sarah didn't doubt that. Just hearing about it depressed the hell out of her. "I want breakfast. Let's go."

Suzanne shook her head. "Not yet. Just one more day. That's all I need."

Maybe they hadn't quite rounded the corner yet. "I won't take no for an answer tomorrow," Sarah said.

"I'll be ready by tomorrow. I promise."

Tomorrow was Wednesday. Stage Day. Was it possible that she could still make it? Could she be on her way back to her life by noon tomorrow?

She might have seen John for the last time. She might not have a chance to say goodbye. After all, he thought she was staying for another week. He didn't have any reason to come to town tonight.

She tried to ignore the pain in her heart, to pass it off as hunger. Sadly, she realized, that's exactly what it was. She hungered for John Beckett. For his lips, his arms, his strength, his soul. She would leave a starved woman and in days they'd be centuries apart.

She hoped. Right?

After all, there was no guarantee that she'd make it back to her own time. She might get to California, walk along her beach, and nothing. The only thing that would be different was that she'd be in 1888 California rather than 1888 Wyoming Territory.

Would she come back? Would she take the train in the opposite direction and once again knock on John Beckett's door? Would she tell him the truth this time? Would it matter?

She couldn't even contemplate the other alternatives. What if she got to her beach, stepped in some footprints, and was whisked farther back in time? Knowing her luck, she'd land on some ship sailing to the New World and everybody would have scurvy. The possibilities, ones that once she would have thought unfathomable, now loomed all too real.

There was something else too real to ignore. She'd come all this way and she'd leave with just the memory of

John's kisses. She yearned for more. She wanted to feel his warm, naked body up against hers. She wanted to wrap her hands around him, to hold him. She wanted to press herself against him and make love to him all night.

What she wanted didn't really matter.

"Sarah?"

She grabbed her shawl and wrapped it around her shoulders. "Yes."

"Where were you? You looked like you were about a hundred miles away."

Not really. Could have been a set of sweaty sheets just down the hall. "I'm going to get breakfast," Sarah said.

She walked out of the hotel and lost her appetite. Mrs. Beckett stood there, arms crossed over her chest. "Why, Sarah. I hear you've been busy."

"Good morning, Mrs. Beckett," Sarah said, trying to step around the woman.

Mrs. Beckett tapped her foot. "That's it? Just good morning?"

"How are you, ma'am?"

"I'm rested. Something I imagine you are not. It's hard to be when you're entertaining men in your room at night."

Bless Turnip and his big mouth. "I have to be going."

"On your way to the saloon? To your job? It's not enough to ruin poor Fred Goodie's life? Perhaps there are a few happily married men whose marriages you can destroy by noon? Shouldn't be difficult for a woman with your talents."

Sarah desperately wanted to tell her the truth. She didn't want Mrs. Beckett thinking those terrible things about her. But she wouldn't do that to Fred or to Suzanne. They had to stay in this town. She'd be leaving in days.

"You make me sick," Mrs. Beckett said. "I can't believe I ever thought you could be a part of my family. I can't believe how hard I tried."

Sarah bit her lip. "I guess it must be gratifying to have been right all along," she said.

As if she'd been slapped, John's mother jerked her whole body back. Sarah used the opportunity to slide past her.

"Stay away from my son," the woman called after her.

Sarah didn't bother to turn around; she just kept walking, her stride long, her pace measured. When she got to the restaurant, she grabbed the handle of the door and winced when she saw that her hand shook. She walked through the doorway, keeping the palms of both hands firmly planted against her skirt. Three tables had customers. To a person, each one put down their fork and stared at her.

A woman in a gray dress covered by a long white apron with the name *Rosie* embroidered on it walked by her so fast that she chilled the air. When she made a return sweep, Sarah reached out an arm. "I'd like to place an order," she said.

"For you or for that friend of yours, the whore?"

Sarah clamped down on the impulse to punch the woman. "What did you just say?"

"You heard me. We don't like people who poke their noses where they don't belong. She deserved whatever she got."

Sarah couldn't breathe. How could someone think that? How could one woman think that about another woman?

The woman stuck her arm out and pushed against Sarah's shoulder, sending her a step backward. "Nothing to say? Too busy thinking about Fred Goodie?"

She'd had it. These people had pushed her over the edge. She leaned forward, her face just inches from the other woman's. "You are a stupid cow. And you're ugly, too."

The woman turned as white as her apron. "Why, you . . ."

"Bitch. I think the word you're looking for is *bitch*." She turned, walked out the door, and kept walking toward the church. She might as well face Pastor Dan now. He'd no doubt heard the gossip about her and Fred. Somebody would have made sure of that.

When she got to the church, she walked past it, instead going to the small house next to it. She knocked on the door. Within seconds, Pastor Dan opened it, a Bible in his hand.

"Good morning," she said.

He smiled at her. "Come in, Sarah."

She hadn't expected that. "It might be better if I stay here."

He shook his head. "Nonsense. I've just made a fresh pot of coffee and one of the ladies brought me rolls this morning. We'll enjoy them together."

Was it possible that the lady had brought only rolls or had she served up a full plate of gossip as well? Sarah sat down on the worn couch and waited while Pastor Dan filled two cups of coffee and put the fresh rolls on a plate. Her mouth watered as he carried them toward her. Maybe everything would be better once she had coffee.

He handed her a cup. "I understand Fred came to see you last night," he said.

She bobbled the cup, spilling some coffee on her skirt. Pastor Dan smiled and handed her a cloth napkin. He sat down across from her. "Three church women have been to see me this morning. One brought a chicken for my lunch and the other a ham that will last me a week. My son-in-law should get out more. I'd never have to cook again."

He didn't sound mad; he didn't sound happy. Just very matter-of-fact.

"Pastor Dan," she said, "this is awkward for me. I just came to tell you that I won't be there on Sunday."

"That disappoints me," he said. "I expect I'll have the biggest congregation I've seen in months. I thought I might make a special appeal for the church to get a new roof."

"I don't understand," Sarah said, taking a sip of her coffee. She really, really needed caffeine. All the brain cells hadn't started to fire yet.

"I know why my son-in-law was at the hotel last night."

"You do?" she asked, her voice squeaking a little.

"Yes."

She waited. He took a big bite of his roll. "Do you want to tell me why?" she asked.

He patted his mouth with a cloth napkin. "You were there. I don't think I need to tell you."

This wasn't working. "Pastor Dan, I'm confused. You're not angry?"

"No."

"You don't believe the women who came here this morning?"

"I choose to believe that they came without malice. I forgive them for their lack of knowledge."

"I don't have the technique to tiptoe through this mine-field, Pastor Dan. Do you think that Fred and I are . . . ?"

"Having relations?"

"Yes," she said.

"No."

Sarah got it. The coffee, the sugar from the rolls, it all kicked in. Pastor Dan knew exactly who Fred had been visiting last night. "How long have you known?" she asked.

"For several weeks." Pastor Dan stood up, walked over to the coffeepot, and refilled both their cups. "I am a man of God, Sarah, and every day I pray for the wisdom and the courage to carry out the will of God. I pray for my grand-children, that they will live in a world of peace. I pray the prayers of grandfathers from centuries past."

And centuries forward. When would there be a time when people didn't have to pray for peace?

"I married when I was twenty-five. I loved my wife a great deal. We were blessed with sweet children and spent thirty-three years together. When Margaret died, I missed her dreadfully. I missed her smile, I missed her humor, and I missed her in my bed."

"Oh."

Pastor Dan smiled. "Even a man of God has needs and wants. I am an old man, but I remember. Fred is still a young man, and his needs and wants are those of a young man."

"He doesn't think you know."

"Fred is struggling," Pastor Dan said. "He wants to believe that his body is disloyal to Franny but that his heart is not. That makes him feel better."

"You don't want him to feel better."

"I want him to be very happy and to continue to raise my grandchildren. As importantly, I want him to come to terms with Franny's death and with the realization that he lives on."

"It's almost like he's punishing himself," Sarah said. "Like he's to blame for her death."

"Yes. I imagine you understand his pain better than most. After all, it wasn't all that long ago that you lost your own spouse."

"That's true." Oh, boy. She was really going to Hell now.

"At least Fred had the chance to say goodbye. It must have been horrible for you when you got the news of the silver mine collapse. Then that long wait only to find that Peter's body would never be recovered."

So that's how it had happened? The information helped her understand the pain she'd heard in John's voice when he had talked about Peter. He'd have wanted to bring his brother's body home, to bury him on the ranch. He'd have wanted to dig the grave and mark it with a sturdy cross. He'd have wanted to handle things. He'd have craved closure.

Pastor Dan had found closure. He wanted the same for his son-in-law. "If it's any consolation," she said, "I think Fred really likes Suzanne."

"I imagine he loves her. I think nothing less would make him lie to me, to his children, and to his best friend, John."

"You're okay with all this? I mean, she is a prostitute."

"Yes, but I don't think she will be for long. Regardless of what Fred does, Suzanne is on the cusp of making a life-changing decision. God will lead her. God will protect her."

Sarah leaned back against the couch cushions. She shook her head at Pastor Dan. "Suzanne's doing better. I might be able to make tomorrow's stage. If I don't for some reason and I'm still here on Sunday, I'll play the piano."

"That's all I can ask."

"I'm not sure it's in your best interest."

"I think it will be an excellent opportunity to preach about the vice of judging others."

Sarah stood up, walked over, and gently hugged the old man. "Thank you," she said. "I didn't realize until just now how important it was that someone understand."

"Hold your head up high, Sarah. You've done nothing wrong."

"I called Rosie Brickstone an ugly cow."

He shrugged. "If the hoof fits. Sarah, you've been misjudged. Our Savior Jesus was often in that same predicament."

She held up a hand. "Trust me on this. I'm no one's savior."

He walked her to the door. "I didn't think you were. However, I did hear that you play the piano like an angel. I'm looking forward to Sunday more than ever."

"Who told you that?"

"I had another visitor this morning. He didn't bring me any food but he carried wisdom in his empty hands."

"Who?"

Pastor Dan shook his head. "I don't think he'd want you to know."

"Just tell me one thing. Was it John?"

"No. I've not seen John. I imagine he's had some company at his ranch this morning. I suspect you'll be seeing him shortly."

She was so not looking forward to that conversation. She walked down the front steps and then turned around. "Hey, isn't the church supposed to be a safe haven? Maybe I could just claim a pew as my own?"

Pastor Dan smiled and shook his head. "Face your fears with confidence," he said. "The reality is rarely as bad as the imagination."

He obviously didn't know John Beckett that well.

SARAH walked back to the hotel and found Freedom sitting on the bench outside the front door. She pulled money from her skirt pocket, enough to get food for her, for Suzanne, and for him, too. She hated giving money to the Brickstones. "This town needs a McDonald's," she said.

"What's that, Miss Sarah?"

"It's not important. Here. It might be better if Rosie doesn't know it's for us."

"Freedom don't have to explain why he's buying food. If Freedom's got money, that's all Freedom needs."

"Don't ask. Don't tell. It worked well for the military for years."

"What? Freedom don't understand."

"Never mind. Just hurry. I'm sure Suzanne is starving."

"Freedom thinks she's sleeping. She had a visitor last night." Freedom hitched up his pants and took a step.

"Wait a minute," Sarah said. "How'd you know that?"

"Freedom's got eyes, don't he? There ain't nothing that goes on in this hotel that Freedom don't know about."

She'd totally forgotten about Freedom. "Whatever you saw last night, you need to forget it."

"Don't you worry about Freedom. Like you said. Freedom don't ask. Freedom don't tell."

She resisted the urge to salute. She hugged the small black man instead. "You've been a big help, Freedom. I'll never forget you."

"Freedom ain't never going to forget you either, Miss Sarah."

She watched him, her eyes moist with tears, until he got to the end of the wooden sidewalk and stepped off onto the dirt road. When she turned, John Beckett stood behind her.

Her heart thumped and her stomach growled.

"I want to talk to you," he said. "Now."

She sat down on the bench, resigned to her fate. "Okay. Talk."

"I don't want to sit. And I don't want to talk where Turnip can stick his ugly face out the window and hear me. Let's walk."

He started off, walking toward the open country, not toward town. She skipped to catch up with him. They walked ten minutes in silence.

"Is the plan to walk all the way back to your ranch?" she asked, a little breathless. She had to take two steps for every one of John's long strides.

He stopped. "Look around," he said. "What do you see?"

That wasn't exactly how she'd expected the conversation to go. "John?"

"Just look around."

She turned, doing a full circle, taking the time to study the landscape. Cedarbrook stood off to her left and the Big Horn Mountains, rich and rugged, a soft green with their Scottish Pines, stretched out on her right. She and John stood on a dirt road bordered on both sides by new bright green grass, not yet bleached out by the summer sun. Tall trees, full of springtime bounty, waved in the morning wind. In the far distance, she could just make out a small herd of deer, ambling across the open fields.

"It's beautiful," she said.

"This is my home, Sarah."

"I know that." She still didn't understand.

"This is Fred Goodie's home. This is where he's chosen to raise his children."

Bingo. "Look, John. I'm not sure what you've heard but—"

"I've heard three versions. Each more detailed and disgusting than the previous one. The details don't matter."

Sarah cleared her throat. "Actually, the details can be kind of important."

John shook his head. "I can't believe that you almost had me fooled. Even after I saw with my own eyes how you ruined my brother's life, I had almost convinced myself that you'd changed. But you're the same selfish bitch that seduced my brother a year ago and now you've come back for Fred Goodie. God damn you, Sarah. I won't let you do it."

Sarah opened her mouth and gulped in air. She felt as if her throat had closed, that her lungs and her chest had tightened and all the air had been sucked from her body. His words, said with cold fury, slapped her, making her weak. *You're the same selfish bitch*. He hadn't even considered giving her a chance to explain.

He'd already judged her. He'd judged her by the woman he'd known, not the woman she was.

"The stage goes tomorrow," he said. "You're going to be on it. None of this pretending that you're staying to help Suzanne. I know better. Suzanne's just a convenient excuse."

He'd seen Suzanne. He'd seen the blood and the bruises. Did he think so little of her that he believed she'd profit from the other woman's misfortune? That somehow she encouraged Suzanne to languish in bed so that she could snag Fred Goodie? How he must hate her. Only hate could fuel those kinds of thoughts.

"Nothing to say, Sarah? Not going to try to talk your way out of this one? How much money will it take to get you to leave this time?"

She slapped him. Hard enough that the jolt went up through her arm. He balled his fist, pulled his arm back, and she waited, heart pounding furiously.

He stood perfectly still, his arm at the ready to swing

forward and knock her senseless. Then he took a step back
and slowly lowered his arm. His jaw was set and his eyes
were bleak. "Go back to where you came from, Sarah. You
don't belong here and all you do is cause heartache. Leave
us."

He turned and walked, heading back toward Cedarbrook. Sarah watched him, staring at the grassy hillside,
long after he'd vanished behind the hill. Then she sank to
her knees, wrapping her arms around her middle. She felt
cold and empty, as if he'd ripped her soul from her body.

WHEN John got back to Cedarbrook, he mounted his
horse and turned it toward Fred Goodie's ranch. He dug his
spurs into the horse's flesh, urging him to gallop. The faster
he got away from Cedarbrook, the better. Before he did
something stupid like apologize to Sarah.

Christ, she'd looked almost shocked. Just showed what
a fine actress she was. She'd been acting since she'd come
to Cedarbrook. Acting like she cared about him when he'd
been sick. Acting like she'd enjoyed his kisses, that they'd
meant as much to her as they'd meant to him. Acting like
things could be different.

The only thing different this time was that he'd gotten
smarter. He wouldn't sit back and watch, hoping that
everything would work out between Sarah and her man.
That had cost him his only brother. He wouldn't let it cost
him his best friend.

He raced down the lane to Fred's house, arriving just as
the sun reached its peak in the sky. Missy and Thomas
played on the tire swing and Helen sat off to the side, draw-
ing pictures in the soft dirt with a stick. "Hi, Uncle John,"
she said.

"Morning, Helen." He waved to the younger children.
"Where's your pa?"

"Inside. Taking a nap. He said he was tired."

John's gut churned. He knew exactly what had made his friend tired. "I've got something to say to him. Can you take your brother and sister for a short walk?"

Helen nodded and he patted her on the head as he walked past. Whatever their father had done, the children deserved to be protected from it. John walked in the house, pulling the door shut behind him with a sharp slam. Fred, on his side, lay on the floor, stretched across the round braided rug, so big that both his head and feet hung over the edges. His back faced the door.

"I'll be out in thirty minutes," he mumbled, without turning over. "I promise. Then we'll go down to the stream and catch some fish for lunch. Go back outside, now."

John quietly walked around the man's head. Then with one booted foot strategically positioned on Fred's shoulder, he pushed, flipping the man on his back. Fred's head hit the wooden floor with a thud.

"What the . . . ?" Fred sputtered, his eyes wide open. "What the hell is going on, John?"

"Get up," John said. "Get up so that I can kick your ass proper."

Fred sat up, then scrambled back on his hands and feet like a giant crab, until his back rammed up against the stone fireplace. "You're a crazy man," he said.

John took his hat off and carefully laid it on the table. "Get up," he repeated.

"No," Fred yelled back. "Not until I know why you're so intent on beating my brains in."

"You slept with Sarah."

Fred's mouth dropped open. "Who told you that?"

"It doesn't matter. By now, half the town knows. The other half will know by suppertime." John took three steps, leaned over Fred, and yanked up on the big man's shirt.

Fred didn't resist. Nor did he when John had him upright

and pushed him back against the wall, cracking his head again. "Damn you," John said. "Fight back."

Fred shook his head. John stared at him for a full minute, his hands full of Fred's shirt, holding the material tight up against Fred's windpipe. Fred didn't so much as blink. Without a word, John let go and walked away.

"You don't know what you're talking about," Fred said, sucking in air.

John raised an eyebrow. "Really? So you didn't ride into town last night and spend hours at the hotel? In Sarah's room?"

Fred let out a big sigh. "I did," he said.

"How could you?" With that simple question, John felt his emotions, the ones he'd kept so carefully controlled all morning, flood to the surface.

"It's not what you think."

"Funny. That's not what Sarah said."

Fred's face lost all its color. "You've already been to see Sarah?"

"Yes."

"Is she all right? You didn't hurt her, did you?" Fred accused, taking two steps toward John.

John held up a hand. "So you'll fight for her, will you? That's sweet."

"You're a fool, John Beckett."

"I'm a fool?" John could hardly believe his ears. "You're the one who slept with her."

"You're jealous," Fred said. "You're a jealous fool."

"Why would I be jealous?" John asked. The whole idea was ludicrous. "I don't even like her. I've never liked her."

Fred shook his head. "You might not have liked her once. But I saw you, remember. You want her."

"You're crazy."

"I'm not."

John paced around the room. "Well, I guess it doesn't

matter since you've already had her. How was it, by the way? She always was a little whore."

Fred hit him, his big fist slamming into John's cheekbone, sending him crashing into a chair.

John staggered to his feet and lunged at Fred. The two of them hit the floor in a tangle of arms and legs. They rolled over and over, fists flying, sending chairs skidding. Material ripped, bone cracked, and blood spilled.

"Uncle John? Father?"

Both men looked up. Helen, her small hand over her mouth, stood in the doorway. Missy and Thomas peeked around her skirt. "What are you doing?"

TWELVE

FRED and John jerked apart. John looked at Fred. Fred looked at the blood on his hands. He'd cracked the skin across the knuckles on his right hand. "Damn you, John," Fred said. "Do you have to have a face as hard as granite?"

Thomas pushed around his sister and walked up to the two men. "You broke a chair," he said, his voice filled with awe.

"I'm ashamed of both of you," Helen said, hands on her hips. John expected her to ask for the hickory switch to be brought forth.

Not that they both didn't deserve it. He didn't regret the fight but he'd have preferred not to have the children as an audience. John stood up, wincing a little. Fred had landed a couple of strong punches. He'd be very surprised if he didn't have a cracked rib. He picked up his hat and shoved it on his head. "I've got to be going," he said. "Goodbye, children."

Fred lifted his big frame off the wooden floor. "I'll walk out with you."

"No more fighting," Helen called after them.

They walked the first ten feet in silence. "I don't think she's going to let you forget this for a long time," John said, giving Fred a quick glance.

"Nope. I imagine the next time she and Thomas quarrel, it will come up."

"I'm sorry for that," John said.

Fred nodded, looking back over his shoulder, probably to verify that they remained without an audience. "There's something you need to know," he said.

John scratched his head. He didn't want to know. He didn't want to hear any details about Fred and Sarah. He didn't need that kind of pain. "I think we've said enough today."

"I haven't said nearly enough," Fred replied. "You're not getting on your horse until I do."

John picked up his horse's reins. "Fred, please don't tell me that you've fallen in love with her."

"I have."

A rush of emotions flooded John. He tried to sort them out. Disappointment. Rage. Jealousy. How could that be? How could he be jealous of Fred and Sarah?

"I'm in a hell of a mess," Fred said.

John's gut churned. How bad could it be? "You asked her to marry you?"

Fred shook his head.

What could be worse? She'd been in town for less than a week. That he knew of. Perhaps she and Fred had been together longer. "She's with child?" he asked, barely able to say the words.

Fred jerked his head back, looking visibly shaken. "I don't think so," he said. "She said she took care of those things."

He didn't want to hear about Fred and Sarah's conversations about such intimate topics. Words like that should be kept between a man and his woman.

"I've got to go," John said, grabbing his saddle horn.

Fred put his hand on John's arm. "Wait. Please?"

John gritted his teeth and nodded.

"I went to the hotel last night," Fred said. "I told myself that I should stay away but I just couldn't. It's not what you think, John. I went to see Suzanne. Not Sarah."

"Suzanne?"

"I've been seeing her for several months."

"Define seeing."

"Damn it man, you know exactly what I mean. I've been sharing her bed."

John rubbed his temples. "Let me get this straight," he said. "You spent several hours in that hotel room, not with Sarah, but with Suzanne. Where was Sarah during this?"

"Sleeping. On the steps. Before I left, I sat down with her for a few minutes. I wanted to thank her for taking such good care of Suzanne and for giving us some privacy. That's how Turnip found us. I knew what he thought and I still wasn't man enough to say the truth."

Every one of the angry words he uttered to Sarah echoed in John's head. He closed his eyes and he could see her face, the hurt, the pain he'd caused. She must hate him.

"Sarah knew about you and Suzanne?"

"When Sarah stayed with the children, Suzanne visited. They talked. Sarah figured it out pretty quickly. She asked me about it and I didn't deny it. It was a relief to finally tell someone. I asked her not to say anything to you."

"Why? Why couldn't you tell me?"

"I didn't want you to be disappointed in me. You're my best friend, John. I know you'd do about anything for me and I feel the same way about you. I care what you think."

"Why would I be disappointed?"

"That I'm not true to Franny's memory. That I'm weak. I didn't think you'd be as weak, John."

Weak? He'd be relieved to have such weakness. His sin loomed much greater. He coveted his dead brother's wife. John bent over his saddle, resting his pounding forehead on the hard leather. "You don't know what you're talking about."

"I had to tell you. I didn't want Sarah to leave with you thinking bad of her."

Sarah to leave? *The stage leaves tomorrow. You're going to be on it. You're a selfish bitch.* He'd all but run her out of town. She'd leave tomorrow and he'd never see her again.

How could he let that happen?

JOHN knocked on Sarah's hotel room door at just a few minutes after one.

"Who is it?"

Suzanne, not Sarah. "Suzanne, it's John Beckett. I'm looking for Sarah."

He heard footsteps and then the door opened. She looked better but it still made his heart hurt to see her battered face. "How are you?" he asked.

"Better," she said, her face solemn. "Thank you for asking."

"Is Sarah here?"

"No."

John swallowed. "I want to talk to her."

"I don't think she wants to talk to you. After the two of you conversed this morning, she spent the next hour curled up in a ball on the bed, sobbing."

John swallowed. He hadn't thought he could feel worse. He wanted to tell Suzanne that he'd been to Fred's and that he knew the truth. He couldn't. Those words needed to come from Fred.

"I won't upset her again," he said. "I promise. I just need to talk to her. Please."

Suzanne assessed him. "If you hurt her, I'll come find you, and make you regret it."

John had no doubt she meant it. This woman would be good for Fred.

"I won't. Where is she?"

"At Hooper's Mercantile. Said she needed a few things for tomorrow's trip."

"She's planning to go on tomorrow's stage?"

"I think so."

His chest hurt. "I'll see you later," he said.

"Remember what I said."

He nodded. Mostly all he could remember was the vile words he'd said to Sarah and the look in her eyes.

When he got to Hooper's, he slipped quietly in the door, ducking behind the sewing materials. A woman, a small baby in her arms, frowned at him. He nodded at her and then focused on Sarah.

She had her back to him. She had on Franny's skirt, rolled at the waist. She stood in front of the glass case where they kept the candy. She had one of Hooper's wicker shopping baskets looped over one arm. He watched as she leaned closer and looked at the red licorice. She straightened up, pulled her money out of her skirt pocket, counted it, and with a slight shake of her head, walked over to the front counter.

"I heard you were back." Alice Hooper stood behind the counter, her eyes narrowed, assessing Sarah, taking in her plain skirt and threadbare blouse. "Looks like you've fallen on hard times."

"You might say that. How are you, Alice?" Sarah pulled her purchases out of the basket. She had soap, tooth powder, a comb, a small towel, and a water canteen. "I'd like these, please."

Alice wrote down the prices on an invoice. "Turnip has coffee here every morning," she said, looking up at Sarah.

"Good for Turnip. He should put an extra lump or two of sugar in it. He's a little low on sweetness."

Alice Hooper smiled. "He's a snake. I don't see why my husband gives him the time of day. Men in this town think they can do whatever they want but women always pay the price with their reputations. It ain't fair."

Sarah chuckled. "You always were a forward thinker, Alice. A little ahead of your time."

"I don't know about that. You sticking around this time?"

"No. I'm leaving on tomorrow's stage."

"Where you going?"

"Home."

"Where's that?"

"California."

Alice's eyes widened. "Have you seen the ocean?"

"I have."

"Is it as beautiful as they say?"

"More beautiful than that even."

Alice Hooper nodded. "I bet they wear pretty dresses in California."

"About the same as here," Sarah said. "I took a look at the things on your rack. I can tell you're staying up on the fashions."

Alice Hooper beamed. "I try."

Sarah smiled in return.

"That will be three dollars and fifty-seven cents."

Sarah stopped smiling. "I'm a little short," she said. "I've got three dollars and twenty-five cents. I'll put the comb back."

John reached in his pocket.

"Don't worry about it," Alice Hooper said. "What you have is fine."

"Oh, no. I couldn't ask you to short yourself."

"It's no problem." Alice handed her the sack. "Take care, Sarah Beckett. Have a good journey."

John squatted down as Sarah walked past. The woman next to him cuddled her baby closer to her breast and edged away.

When Sarah got out the door, John made a beeline for

the counter. "Morning, Alice," he said. "I'd like a pound of that red licorice."

She nodded. "I thought maybe you planned to pick up a nice calico this morning."

John could feel the heat rise in his face. "It's complicated," he said.

"Always is. That will be twenty cents," she said, packaging up the candy.

He handed her a dollar. "Keep the change. Thanks for helping Sarah."

"She seems different."

"I know."

John left and caught up with Sarah, just outside the hotel. She had her hand on the doorknob. "Sarah," he called out.

She whirled around.

Her eyes and nose were pink, evidence of the tears Suzanne had witnessed. It made him sick to think he'd caused such heartache. To think that he'd hurt her so.

"What are you doing here?" she said.

Her voice was hoarse. He wanted to reach out, to hold her, to comfort her. He kept his arms stiff at his sides, afraid that she might run if he tried to touch her.

"I need to talk to you, Sarah."

"No." Tears filled her pretty blue eyes and he had to look away. "You surely must have said everything that you needed to say this morning," she said.

He'd said horrible things. He had to make her understand why. "Can we just walk a little?"

"No."

"Please?" he begged. "Two minutes. That's all I ask. Then I won't bother you again."

She sighed and nodded. He reached out, gently took her elbow, and guided her down the sidewalk. He could feel the stiffness in her body. "I went to see Fred today," he said.

She stumbled and he tightened his hold.

"I think he might have broken one of my ribs."

She stopped, turned toward him. "Are you all right?" she asked.

"Man's fist is as hard as an ax."

"Oh, John," she said, her voice filled with concern.

It gave him hope. "I'm fine," he said. "Looks like I'm an idiot, too."

"What?"

"He told me about Suzanne. He told me everything."

She started walking again and he moved quickly to catch up. "Stop, Sarah. Please."

She turned and looked at him.

"I'm sorry. I said hateful things, and if I could take the words back, I would. I can't. All I can do is ask for your forgiveness."

She stared at him. After a minute, she gave him a small smile. "It doesn't matter," she said. "None of it matters."

"How can you say that? It matters that I hurt you."

She shook her head. "I'm glad Fred told you the truth. Not for me, but for him. He's carrying a burden and he needs a friend to help him shoulder the weight."

"You paid the price for his silence," John said.

"It doesn't matter," she repeated. "I'll be gone tomorrow."

"Don't go."

She looked startled. As startled as he felt.

"What are you saying, John?" she asked.

What the hell was he saying? "I want you to stay."

"Why?"

What possible reason could he give her? "Suzanne still needs you," he said.

She shook her head. "I don't think so," she said. "She's much stronger today."

He could not let her go. Alice Hooper was right. Sarah seemed different. "What if she slips back?"

"She has Fred."

John resisted the urge to look over his shoulder, just to

make sure his friend with the rock-solid fists hadn't sneaked up behind him. "I'm not so sure of that," he said. "Fred can be kind of slippery."

"Fred? Your friend, Fred? Big guy? Lots of red hair?"

"You don't know him as well as I do." *Sorry, Fred.* "In any case, I don't believe he's thinking all that clearly right now. He might not mean to hurt Suzanne but there's no saying that he won't."

She looked even more distressed. "You've got to make sure that doesn't happen," she said.

"Fred won't listen to me. Not about this. I'm not saying he won't come around. I just think Suzanne might be too fragile to understand right now."

"I'll talk to her," she said.

Not if he had anything to say about it. "I just came from Hooper's. Alice asked me to send you back that way. She said it was important."

She glanced down the street toward Hooper's, as if she could tell by the air what it was that Alice Hooper needed to tell her. "I have to work tonight. I've only got a few hours to get packed."

He glanced at the items in her sack. "Besides that and the clothes you have on your back, what else is there?"

She shrugged. "I suppose I could take a few minutes and see what she needs."

Thank you, Jesus. "I'm sure she'd appreciate that."

Sarah stared at him. She looked very serious. "Thank you for telling me that you'd spoken to Fred."

"I'm truly sorry, Sarah."

"I am, too," she said. "More than you know."

What did she have to be sorry for? "I don't understand," he said.

She shook her head. Then she lifted her fingers to her lips, brushed them with a kiss, and gently placed them against his lips. He felt the warmth seep into his soul.

"Goodbye, John," she said. "I'll miss you."

No way was he letting her get on that stage. He watched her walk toward Hooper's, still feeling her burning touch. Then he walked into the hotel, bolted up the stairs, and pounded on Suzanne's door.

"What?" she asked, opening the door a crack.

"Let me in," he said. "Please. I don't have much time."

Suzanne whipped the door open and looked around him. "Where's Sarah?"

"I sent her back to Hooper's. Look, I need a favor."

"What kind of favor?"

"I need you to lie in bed and pretend you're sickly."

Suzanne frowned at him.

"Sarah's leaving on tomorrow's stage. The only thing that will keep her here is if she thinks you need her."

"I'm confused." Suzanne sat down on the edge of the bed. "Why is it so important for Sarah to stay? I always heard that you couldn't stand her."

"I couldn't," John admitted, pacing around the small room. "Before. I don't know what's happening now. All I know is I need time to figure it out. All I want is a week. Seven days."

"So I have to lie in bed for seven days?"

"No. Just a day or so. Then you can gradually start to bounce back. We don't want to make it obvious."

"This is crazy," Suzanne said. "She'll never believe it."

"She will. She's very concerned about you. A little nudge from you will make all the difference."

"I don't feel right about this," Suzanne said.

"She'll never know," John promised. "Please?"

She gave him a long, considering look before settling her stare on her hands. She had them clasped so tightly he could see white where she pinched her skin.

"You better not hurt her, John Beckett."

"I won't. I just want the chance to know her."

* * *

WHEN John walked into the saloon, Sarah lost her place. Confused, she stared at him, her fingers poised above the ivory keys. What the heck was he doing here? They'd said their farewells. She'd managed to do it without blubbering. Barely.

Nobody needed to know that. Least of all him.

"Evening, Sarah," he said, walking past her. The heels of his boots clicked against the wooden floor, echoing through the quiet room. He had on a long riding coat. The scratched and worn leather fell past his knees and made his broad shoulders look even broader. He took a seat at the bar, two stools away from George. When Thomas Jefferson poured him a whiskey, John pulled some coins from his coat pocket.

Thomas looked from Sarah to John and then back to Sarah. "You want to take a break?" he asked.

She took a breath. God, she was such a fool. "No," she said, forcing her eyes back to the music. She started the piece over.

And with every strike of a key, she resolved to ignore him, to pretend he wasn't there. It reminded her of a book she'd read as a child. Something about everyone trying to ignore an elephant in the corner of the room.

Twenty minutes later, she ended her first set. She pushed back her piano stool and walked outside. She stood there less than a minute before John joined her.

"Here," he said, handing her a glass of water.

She took a small sip, wondering what to say next.

"Drink it. If you need to take a trip to the privy," he said, "I'll go with you."

Was it really just twenty-four hours ago that he'd rescued her from Toby? It seemed like a lifetime. "I'll be fine," she mumbled, embarrassed to be talking to him about bodily functions.

He nodded. "You're really good," he said. "I had no idea. Where did you learn to play like that?"

"I took lessons as a child," she said.

"Did Peter know you could play?"

"No. I don't think so."

He fumbled with the edge of the blue bandanna he wore around his neck. "I miss him," he said.

The lump in her throat seemed a bit bigger, a bit harder to swallow around. "I'm sure you do," she said, thankful that Pastor Dan had filled in some of the blanks. At least she knew how Peter had died.

John leaned back against the building, one knee bent with the sole of his boot flat against the weathered wood. He tilted his head back and looked up at the quarter moon. "I wonder what he'd think if he saw the two of us standing here?"

"He'd be surprised." She figured that was a safe bet.

John chuckled. "All that and more. He'd be amazed."

Had Sarah One and John really hated each other that much? "Do you think so?"

"I'd like to think he might be happy," John said.

"Happy?"

"He wanted us to be friends."

Friends? Sounded nice. Unsatisfying, but nice. Kind of like taking second place in a two-person race.

"I'd like it if we could be friends, Sarah."

She didn't want to be his friend. She wanted more. "Have you noticed anything odd about Alice Hooper?" she asked, hoping to change the subject.

"No. Why?"

"It's the strangest thing. I went back to her store today, but when I asked her what she needed me for, she just looked at me, like she didn't understand. I explained that you'd sent me back. She sputtered a bit and then she walked over to the sewing section. She asked me to pick out the material I liked best."

"Material?"

"I was surprised, too. But she looked very serious. I didn't know what else to do so I pointed at a pretty pink cotton. She cut at least ten yards off and wrapped it up for me."

"Fascinating."

"When I asked her why, all she could say was that she expected I could use a new dress soon."

"Did she say why?"

"No. I tried to explain that I didn't have the money. She said it was a gift. I didn't want to offend her so I took it."

"Guess you got yourself a new dress."

Sarah shook her head. "I'll leave it for Suzanne."

He frowned at her. "So you're still planning on going tomorrow?"

She shrugged. She needed to leave. Every day she stayed, it would be that much harder to leave. "I have to."

"What about Suzanne?"

Sarah glanced in the saloon window. Her break was almost over. "When I got back from Hooper's, Suzanne had gone back to bed. She hardly said three words to me. She seemed so much better earlier in the day. I can't figure it out."

"Maybe she's not quite as strong as you think."

"She's strong. I don't have any doubts about that. I think she loves Fred, and after seeing him with her, I'm convinced that he loves her, too. If he comes back to town tonight, I'm going to try to convince him that he needs to make his feelings clear."

"I don't think you'll see Fred tonight," John said.

"Did he say that?"

John shook his head. "No. I just know Fred. He needs his sleep. If he doesn't get at least eight hours a night, he's useless. I'll bet he's already in bed. I wouldn't worry about him showing up."

That surprised her. "I guess I can't force him."

"No. Fred Goodie isn't the type to want someone meddling in his private life. He'd hate it if he knew we were even having this conversation. You know what I mean?"

"I understand. He won't hear it from me."

"Good."

No. There wasn't anything good about the situation. If only she knew why she'd been sent back. During the middle of the night, when she'd watched Suzanne sleep, she'd prayed for answers. There had to be a reason why she'd been whisked back more than a century. Was it to protect Suzanne? Had the stars somehow aligned so that she would be in the next room when Mitchell Dority tried to beat the hell out of Suzanne?

If so, how could she leave without finishing the job? How could she leave without making sure Suzanne was okay?

"I'll make my decision tomorrow," she said. "I need to talk to Suzanne first."

Thirteen

SARAH woke up the next morning with a stiff neck, cold toes, and a heavy heart. She tucked her feet back under the blanket, gently turned her head from side to side, and accepted that heartache would be harder to shake.

"Suzanne," she said, pulling herself into a sitting position, one vertebra at a time. The wooden floor hadn't gotten any softer over time. She rested her elbows on her friend's bed. "It's time to wake up."

Suzanne mumbled something in response but didn't turn over.

Sarah stood up, careful to keep the blanket wrapped around her. She walked over to the window and pulled back the curtain. Two wagons, each with two brown horses, were parked in front of Hooper's. Four other horses, their reins draped over a rail in front of the restaurant, patiently waited for their riders to return. Two women, holding up their long skirts to keep them from dragging in the dirt, crossed the street.

The town already bustled with activity. She'd slept later

than she'd planned. She had John to blame for that. He'd waited until she'd finished her last song and then walked her back to the hotel. His strong hand had cupped her elbow as he'd guided her across the street.

He'd walked her up the stairs, unlocked the door, and then ever so gently kissed her. It had been short, sweet, and it had kept her up for hours. Long after he'd given her one of his smiles, tipped his hat, and walked away.

It had been a friendly kiss. Just a peck between pals. Almost familial. Sort of like the kisses Uncle Salvador used to give her at Christmas.

However, Uncle Sal had never made her heart thump or her knees weak. John Beckett did both. Precontact. When he'd kissed her, when his lips had brushed against hers, she'd felt a rush of excitement, a spike of adrenaline.

Later, as she'd sat by the window and looked out at the moon and the star-filled sky, she remembered what it had reminded her of. The year before she'd driven two hours north to go downhill skiing. When she'd stood at the top of the slope and contemplated letting her body, supported only by two slim pieces of waxed lumber, fly down a two-thousand-foot ski run, she'd felt the same way. Like she couldn't quite get her breath.

Kissing John made her heart race just the same as a cup of double-chocolate mocha from the corner bakery.

Just a brush of his lips across hers. How could something so sweet, so innocent, leave her wanting, almost at the edge, ready to beg him to take her in his arms and satisfy her greed? How could something that clearly meant nothing to him mean so much to her?

Because she was an idiot.

She turned back toward Suzanne. "Come on, Suzanne. The stage leaves in an hour. Please see me off. It would mean so much to me."

"No." Suzanne rolled over in bed, giving Sarah her back. Sarah felt icy fingers of panic claw at her stomach. She couldn't leave Suzanne, but how could she stay? "You have got to get out of this bed." She walked around the edge of the bed so that Suzanne once again faced her. "Please," she said.

Suzanne opened one eye. "Why is that so important to you?"

"I can't leave if I don't know that you're going to be all right."

Suzanne opened both eyes and sat up in bed. "I've been thinking about something."

"Does it involve putting on a dress and walking down the stairs? If so, I'm interested."

"In due time."

"What's that mean?"

"I want to go with you," Suzanne said.

"What about Fred?"

Suzanne lowered her eyes and stared at her hands. She had the edge of the blanket clenched between her fingers. "It's time that I admit that nothing is ever going to change between Fred and me. I know that. Someday he is going to meet some fine lady who he'll take for his wife. I don't want to be here to watch that happen."

"I think Fred loves you."

"It doesn't matter. He's better off without me."

What was Suzanne going to think when Sarah disappeared into thin air? "I'm going to California. Are you planning to go the whole way?"

Suzanne shook her head. "No, I don't want to go further west. I'm far enough from my sister. I'll probably stay in Cheyenne. Maybe get me a job."

"A job like you have now?"

Suzanne shrugged. "I don't know. I can't think that far ahead. I just know I've got to leave."

Fred would be devastated. Sarah had to fight the urge to convince her friend to stay. This might be Suzanne's opportunity to leave this life behind. "Then get up. Stage leaves in an hour."

"I don't feel well enough to travel."

"Your face is much better—there's barely a bruise. You'll be sitting down. You don't have to do anything."

Suzanne shook her head. "I'm not up to it. I was hoping you might consider waiting a week. Then I could go with you. I know I'll have the strength by then."

A week? She'd already been in Cedarbrook for six days. "I have to go." Rosa and Miguel Lopez didn't have the luxury of time on their side.

"Please. I want to go with you. I really do. I need a chance to tell Fred goodbye. I just need a little more time."

Time. The great unknown. How much time did Miguel have? Was time constant? Would six days in 1888 Wyoming be six days in 2005 California? Was it possible it could be six minutes? Or six years?

There was no way to know. All she knew for sure was that Suzanne wanted a week. Was that too much time to save a friend? Was getting that ladder for Suzanne as simple as staying in Cedarbrook for another seven days? What was it that she'd wished that last night in California as she walked on the beach? That she would make a difference. Was this her chance?

Sarah stood up and yanked Suzanne's blankets off. "Here's the deal."

"The deal?" Suzanne asked, her arms wrapped around her shivering body.

"Get up. Get washed up and get dressed. We're going out."

"Out where?"

Sarah shrugged. "I don't know," she admitted. "It doesn't matter. You're not spending another minute in this room. You need to start building up your strength."

"If I do that, you'll stay?"

"Yes."

Suzanne's smile lit up the room. "Thank you, Sarah."

Sarah shook her head. "Don't thank me yet. You may hate me before the week is over."

JOHN pulled out his pocket watch and looked at it for the fourth time. He'd been standing outside Hooper's for the past hour, waiting for the stage. Waiting to see if Sarah got on. When he saw the hotel door open and Sarah step outside, his heart plummeted. She was leaving.

He was losing her. Before he'd really found her.

Damn it. Damn her.

When Suzanne joined Sarah on the sidewalk, he stopped cursing his fate and started hoping instead. He walked toward the women, his strides long and purposeful. Absolutely nobody needed to know that his legs were shaking with fear.

"Morning, ladies."

"Good morning, John," Suzanne said. Sarah didn't say a word. Lord, she looked beautiful this morning. Her pretty blond hair swung free on her shoulders, so different from the styles the other ladies wore. She looked fresh and young, and it made him want to be all those same things.

"Nice spring morning," he said.

"What are you doing in town?" Sarah asked.

She didn't sound all that happy to see him. Had Suzanne confessed his trickery? He gave her a quick glance and she responded with a slight shake of her head.

"I came to see you off on the stage."

"I'm not going."

"Why?" He hoped like Hell he could hide his smile.

"When I leave, Suzanne's going with me. She's not up to a long stage ride yet. We'll go next week. So, you wasted a trip."

He felt like dancing in the street. Singing too, maybe.

"No problem. I had a few things I needed to pick up in town anyway."

Sarah looked away. "Well, we don't want to keep you."

John stuck his hands in his pockets, terribly afraid he might do something stupid like reach out and grab her. "I suppose Thomas will let you keep working at the saloon for another week."

"I hope so. The money would help."

"He'd be a fool not to let you."

She smiled a little. "I'll tell him you said so."

"You do that. Where you ladies headed off to this morning?"

Sarah shrugged again.

"Have you had your breakfast?" John asked.

"No. I suppose we should try to find Freedom."

Suzanne gave her a long look. "They won't serve you at Brickstone's, will they?"

Sarah shook her head.

"I'm sorry," Suzanne said. "It's my fault."

"It's not your fault," Sarah said fiercely. "It's their problem."

Sarah was being shunned. How dare they? John wanted desperately to pound on somebody or something. "I'll go with you," he said.

Sarah shook her head. "That's not necessary. I'm sure you've already had breakfast. You've probably been up for hours."

He'd been up most of the night. He and his horse had spent the night down the road from Fred's house, knowing that the man would have to ride past him if he decided to take another midnight trip to town. John hadn't intended to let his friend ruin everything. Not after he'd worked so hard to get Sarah to stay.

Thankfully Fred had stayed home. John had breathed a sigh of relief, not relishing having to explain to his friend why he couldn't go see Suzanne. If Fred knew that John had suggested Fred was the love 'em and leave 'em type, he'd have more than a cracked rib to look forward to.

"I've been up for a spell. I imagine a cup of hot coffee and a slice of cake to go with it would hit the spot."

"You must have a thousand things to do," Sarah protested.

"Nothing that can't wait for fifteen minutes," John said.

"But . . ." Sarah looked to Suzanne, as if she expected her friend to have a reason why John shouldn't join them. John relaxed when Suzanne pressed a hand to her stomach and said, "I'm starving. Let's go."

"Oh, fine," Sarah said, looking at him. "Whatever."

Whatever? Sarah had picked up the strangest manner of speech.

They walked down the sidewalk in silence, the two women in front, him trailing a few feet behind. When Sarah and Suzanne stepped into Brickstone's, John stood close enough to hear the hiss of the startled customers. It reminded him of a sack of snakes, poised to strike, hoping to poison. He walked in and put a hand on each woman's shoulder.

"Table for three," he said.

Rosie Brickstone screwed up her face, looking like she'd stuck a thorn under her thumbnail. After a minute, she nodded her head toward the far corner. "Over there," she said.

Sarah didn't hesitate. She held her head high and gracefully walked across the room, not even hesitating when Morton Turnip scooted his chair away, as if he was afraid to let her skirt brush against him. Turnip sat across from Harry Pierce, who had his head down, reading some kind of book. Harry handled all the mail and telegrams that came into and out of Cedarbrook. He was known for keeping his mouth shut and his floors clean.

John gave Turnip a look that had him squirming in his seat. As he walked by, he leaned down and spoke quietly in the man's ear. "Mind your manners around the ladies. If you don't, you'll answer to me." He felt some satisfaction when the man turned green.

"Morning, John," Harry said, looking up. "Don't see you in town too often."

"That's right," he said.

"Got a letter for you sitting on my desk. Came by special post. I thought it might be important so I was going to bring it to you."

He'd sold some cattle a month before. It was no doubt the final part of the payment. "I'll stop by and save you a trip." He tipped his hat at Harry and ignored Turnip. He caught up with Sarah and Suzanne as they reached the table. He pulled back both their chairs and motioned for them to sit. They both looked surprised but then took their seats.

"Thank you for coming with us," Suzanne said, looking very troubled. "It's worse than I imagined. I had no idea Rosie would treat Sarah like this. I'm so sorry."

"It's no problem," Sarah said.

"It's not fair that you get treated poorly just because you helped me."

"What's Rosie got against you?"

Suzanne blushed. "I know her husband a bit better than I know her."

"I thought that might be the case," Sarah said, running her tongue across her lips. John felt the answering tug deep in his groin. He concentrated on inspecting his fork and knife.

"I imagine that's all it takes," Sarah whispered. She looked around the room. "Is he here?"

Suzanne nodded. "He's clearing the table over near the kitchen door. He saw me when I came in. He almost dropped his tray of glasses."

John watched Sarah pretend not to stare at Myron Brickstone. He didn't have to look. The man had bought a few horses from him over the years. He'd paid top dollar and treated his horses well. That's all John had been concerned about. Now, knowing that the man had stepped out on his wife, it made it harder to think of him in a kind manner.

John wasn't a fool. He understood why men went to see women like Suzanne. He understood the longing for a woman's body, a woman's heat. But when a man had taken marriage vows, he should keep his trousers buttoned around other women.

He looked up when the door opened again. Alice Hooper walked in. Rosie offered her a table but Alice shook her head. Rosie pulled an order pad from her pocket and started writing.

"Poor Alice," said Sarah. "She doesn't even have time to sit down for a meal." She pushed her chair back from the table. "I'm going to see if she has a minute to have a cup of coffee."

When Sarah reached Alice, the woman listened for a moment, then nodded. Both of them returned to the table. John stood up until both ladies had taken their chairs.

"Morning, Alice," he said. "Busy day?"

"Planting season is always like this. It'll be frantic for the next week or two with men needing tools and seed. Wish I had four hands instead of two."

"I'd be happy to help out."

Alice, Sarah, and John all stared at Suzanne. Her still slightly bruised cheeks were pink.

"I'm used to working," Suzanne said. "I can't just do nothing for the next week. I'll go crazy."

Alice narrowed her eyes at Suzanne. "I thought you had a job at the saloon. A night job."

Suzanne nodded. "I did. I quit."

"I heard about Mitchell Dority," Alice said. "Man should be beaten first and then castrated."

John could feel the blood drain out of his face. It wasn't that he didn't agree. He just didn't feel comfortable discussing castration in front of three women.

"You need to know," Suzanne said, "that I'm planning

on taking the stage next week. I'd be happy to help out for the next seven days. I understand, however, if having me work at the store would be uncomfortable for you."

At that moment, Rosie approached the table. She carefully set down full coffee cups in front of John, Sarah, and Alice. She slammed down Suzanne's cup, causing almost half of it to spill onto the table. She walked away without offering a towel.

John pulled his bandanna off and handed the blue cloth to her. Suzanne mopped up the mess.

"As you can see," Suzanne said, "not everyone feels all that kindly toward me."

Alice shook her head. "Rosie should be ashamed." She looked at Suzanne. "Can you add and minus your numbers?"

Suzanne nodded. "Yes."

"Ever handled money?"

John coughed into his hand.

"There were times," Suzanne said, "when I needed to make change for my customers."

Alice looked at Sarah, then John, before returning her gaze to Suzanne. "I don't see why this wouldn't work. After all, you got the time and I could sure use the help." She picked up her cup and drained it.

Suzanne looked as excited as a kid with her face pressed up against a candy counter. "Are you sure?"

"Positive. Eat your breakfast and then come on over. You can start today."

FRED almost dropped Missy when he opened the door of Hooper's Mercantile and saw Suzanne standing behind the counter. He juggled the small girl, bumping into Helen and Thomas, who walked at his side. Missy wrapped her arms tighter around his neck, almost strangling him. He patted her back to reassure her and she let go.

It didn't help his breathing one bit. It felt like he couldn't get enough air in his lungs.

She looked wonderful. She had her short hair pushed up, showing off her beautiful face, her long, perfect neck. She wore a green dress, one he'd never seen before. It covered parts that were usually uncovered when she wore her other dresses. It didn't matter. It wasn't like he'd ever forget her breasts and how they felt pushed up against his chest.

"Pa," Helen said, tugging on his coat. "Is that Miss Suzanne?"

He nodded.

"What's *she* doing here?" Helen asked.

"I don't know," Fred said.

"I'm going to ask her," Helen said.

"No," Fred said. They'd leave. They could shop another day. He couldn't talk to her in front of his children. They'd have all kinds of questions later.

Just then the bell at the front door opened. He could feel a rush of cold air hit his back. Knowing he blocked the entrance, he took two steps forward. Helen took six, reaching the wooden counter.

"Hello, Helen," Suzanne said, giving his daughter one of her sweet smiles.

"What are you doing here?" Helen asked.

"Mind your manners, young lady," Fred said, hurrying to the counter. He put Missy down.

Suzanne looked at him. "Hello, Fred."

He tried to swallow but his throat wouldn't work. "Suzanne," he said, his voice cracking like a young boy's.

Helen tapped her fingers on the wooden counter. Missy now stood next to her sister. She looked at Suzanne with the same suspicious look on her face that her sister had. Thomas hung back, staying close to Fred.

Suzanne returned her attention to his daughters. "How are you, girls?" She smiled at Missy.

"We didn't know you worked here," Helen said. "Tom

Turnip said that his father told him you lived and worked at the saloon. That you were a sinner."

Fred took a step forward but stopped when Suzanne gave him a quick shake of her head. "I used to work at the saloon. Now I work here."

"What about the sinner part?" Helen asked.

"I've sinned," Suzanne admitted. "I imagine most people have."

"How are you feeling?" Fred asked. "You look . . . good." He could feel the heat rush to his face. She looked good enough to eat. What kind of fool had those thoughts in front of his three young children?

Suzanne nodded. "I'm feeling much better." She glanced over her shoulders, as if she cared that no one overhear. "I'm leaving next week. I'm taking the stage with Sarah."

He felt his throat close up. "Where? Where are you going?"

She shrugged. "I'm not sure where I'll end up. Someplace where I can get a fresh start."

His arms felt heavy at his sides. He'd never hold her again. "That's probably a good idea," he said. He moved aside when a woman edged up to the counter, a bolt of material in her arms. He gently gripped both Helen's and Missy's shoulder and pulled them back.

"You look funny, Pa," Helen said. "Is something wrong?"

He shook his head.

"Aren't we going to get supplies?" Thomas asked. "You said we could get a treat."

"I want lemon drops," Helen said.

"I want peppermints," Thomas said, tugging on Fred's sleeve.

Missy stomped her feet and pointed at the candy counter.

He ignored them all. He'd loved two women in his life. One he'd lost to sickness and the other one was about to walk out of his life forever.

"Let's go," he said, pulling the children toward the door.

"But—"

He silenced Thomas with a look.

Helen rolled her eyes and Missy looked confused. He bent down, wrapped his arms around his younger daughter, and picked her up. He buried his nose in her sweet-smelling, baby-fine hair.

He couldn't let it matter. Franny would expect him to protect their children. He couldn't let her down.

JOHN walked Sarah back to her hotel, trying very hard to make it look like he had nothing better to do than walk around town with her.

"Nice day," he said.

"Beautiful," she said, raising her face to the sky.

She was. Absolutely. He took a breath. "Want to try it?"

"*It?*" She stopped walking.

Damn. He'd missed a step. He'd practiced it a hundred times and he'd still messed it up. "A picnic? You and me?"

"Oh. A picnic." She sighed. "I can't. If Thomas will have me, I intend to work tonight."

"What time do you start?"

"At seven."

"It's just a little after ten. That gives us plenty of time. We'll ride into the mountains, up Wolf Creek."

She looked confused. "I don't have a horse."

"We'll borrow one from Pappy at the livery stable. I'll get the restaurant to pack us a picnic lunch."

She narrowed her eyes at him. "You really want to go on a picnic with me?"

Damn. This wasn't going well. "Why not? You have to eat sometime, right?"

"I just had breakfast."

"Lunch. I meant lunch."

"I guess."

It was time to play dirty. He opened the bag he'd gotten from Hooper's the day before. "I've got licorice."

She peered inside the bag and licked her lips. Once again, he felt the answering response in his body. She needed to stop doing that.

"You've thought of everything, haven't you?" she asked.

If only she knew. He didn't have any notion what to do next.

Less than an hour later, Sarah's horse picked its way over the rocky terrain that bordered Wolf Creek. The mountains were breathtakingly beautiful. John, weaving around tall trees and full bushes, created a path as they went. He kept close to the creek. When she couldn't see the clear water flowing down the mountainside, she could still hear it, rushing over polished rocks.

"How are you doing?" he asked, turning in his saddle to look back at her.

"Wonderful." How could she not be? It was a warm, spring day in the mountains and she was with John Beckett. What could be better?

Staying forever.

But that wasn't going to happen. She'd have today. This afternoon. Then she'd leave Cedarbrook and John Beckett behind. There weren't other options.

That was the way it needed to be. She vowed not to waste a minute of the time she had worrying about what she could never have.

"I can literally see the fish jumping," she said.

"Brown trout. They make a nice supper, don't they?"

Right. She bought her fish shrink-wrapped or ordered it with a little butter and lemon at a restaurant.

"Here's where we cross. There's a clearing on the other side."

She leaned down and spoke into her horse's ear. "Please tell me you can swim."

She watched John pull on his horse's reins, turning him

to the right. In a matter of seconds, he dropped from sight. She saw his horse's rear end go up in the air as John guided the animal down the river embankment. She walked her horse to the edge and looked over.

No way. She couldn't do it. The creek didn't scare her. It wasn't that deep. She could see the rocky bottom through the two feet of clear water. She could handle that. It was the five-foot drop to get to the water that terrified her. John and his horse, already halfway across, ambled through the water as if they didn't have a care in the world.

She waited until he got to the other side before calling out to him. "John?"

He whipped his horse around. "What's wrong?"

"I can't do this. I'll fall off."

"No you won't. Remember when you, Peter, and I took the horses up to pasture last year? You did it then."

Maybe now would be a good time to tell him the truth. "I didn't realize this was the same spot," she said. She'd break her neck. She knew it.

She patted her horse and leaned down, once again putting her mouth close to his ear. "When I fall off," she whispered, "try not to step on me."

The horse raised his tail and pooped.

"I'll take that as a yes," she said.

"Don't lean forward," John yelled. "Lean backwards."

Sarah did as instructed, giving her horse a little nudge in the ribs. The horse started forward. Sarah closed her eyes as the earth fell away from under her horse's feet.

FOURTEEN

"SARAH," John yelled.

She opened her eyes. Her horse stood in the water, waiting patiently for her next command.

"I did it," she said. "I made it." She stood up in her stirrups and looked up and down Wolf Creek. She felt brave and powerful and very lucky. She reached down and hugged her horse.

John laughed at her. "What did you think was going to happen? Come on, let's go."

The climb out on the other side wasn't as steep. When they got over the edge, Sarah pulled on the reins of her horse, stopping to take in the sight. They were in a valley, surrounded by peaks of the Big Horn Mountains that glistened in the bright sun. Spring flowers, yellows and blues and purples, danced in the light wind. It was stunning.

She hadn't felt this alive in years.

"Hungry?" John asked.

She shouldn't be. She'd eaten barely two hours ago. But the gorgeous trip up the mountain had roused not only her appreciation for the pure beauty of nature but her appetite as well. "Starving," she answered.

He got off his horse and pulled a blanket from behind his saddle. Then he lifted off the tin pail that the restaurant had sent along with them.

She slid off and gave her horse another quick hug.

"You're going to spoil that horse," John said. "He's going to expect that from every rider." John reached into his saddlebag and his hand brushed against the still unopened letter that he'd picked up from Harry Pierce right after he'd picked up lunch. He left the letter where it was—today wasn't a day to worry about business. "Here," he said. "Give him a sugar cube. Then he'll know exactly how grateful you are."

"Give me two," she said. "He deserves it."

John tossed her a second one. He walked another thirty feet, stopping when he got close to a towering tree. He spread his blanket across the green grass. Then he sat down, his back up against the peeling bark.

She sat next to him, suddenly shy. "Should we tie up the horses?"

"No need. Just let the reins hang loose. The horses won't go anywhere. Do you like fried chicken?" John asked. He pulled out fried chicken, cabbage-slaw, rolls, and slices of chocolate cake. He unscrewed the lid of a canning jar and poured lemonade into two tin cups. He handed her a plate and a fork.

"You didn't tell them it was for me, did you?"

He shook his head. "No."

She filled her plate, making sure to leave room for the cake. "Wonderful. When I stop by tomorrow morning with cake crumbs still on my lips and tell them how much I enjoyed the lunch, Rosie will have a stroke."

John wiped his mouth with a napkin, suddenly looking very serious. "I won't stand for people being mean to you."

Her heart skipped a beat. No one had ever wanted to

slay any dragons for her. "In a week, these people will forget that they ever saw me again."

John put his lunch aside. "We never did get around to talking about why you came back. What happened that led you to my door that night?"

She could tell him. Right now. He'd be shocked and scared and his warm brown eyes would turn cold. Her perfect day in the mountains, the one and only perfect day she might ever have with him, would be ruined.

"I wanted to see you again," she said.

He looked surprised. "We didn't exactly part as friends."

"I know. I'm sorry about that. Peter's death was a difficult time for you and I don't think I appreciated how much you missed him. I could have handled things better."

"We all could have."

Sarah chewed her chicken and swallowed. She took a big drink of lemonade, hoping it would give her courage. "I hope you can forgive me. I never meant to hurt you or your family. If I had the money, I'd pay you back every cent."

"That's not necessary. Peter's share should have gone to you. You were his wife."

Wife. The word hung in the air. Then it floated down, surrounding them, almost choking Sarah. How could she go through with this deception? How could she not tell him the truth?

He stared at the blanket. "I'm glad you came back, Sarah."

She swallowed hard. "You are?"

"I feel differently about you than I did six months ago."

"Different?" She cringed when her voice creaked.

"We should talk about it."

No. What good would talking do? "John, I'm leaving in a week," she reminded him.

He nodded. "A week is not a long time."

"Not very long at all," she said.

He leaned forward. "Seven days."

His mouth, his delicious, delectable mouth, was just inches away.

"A hundred and sixty-eight hours," he whispered.

She wrapped her arms around his neck. "A bunch of minutes." Math had never been her strong suit.

He ran the tip of his finger across her jawbone, then traced her lips.

She licked his finger with the tip of her tongue, and when she closed her eyes, she felt his warm, sweet breath drift across her cheek.

"A million seconds," he said as he wrapped an arm behind her and gently pressed her back onto the blanket.

When he kissed her, he tasted like lemonade. Sweet with an edge.

She wanted to drink him in.

And when he moved his body so that he lay next to her on the blanket and his hardness pressed into her softness, she hoped that time would stand still—that they could capture all the seconds and hold them in their hands, in their hearts.

"I've wanted to do this for days," he said. "You're so beautiful."

For the first time ever, she felt it might be true. She parted her lips, brought him closer still, and drank of his goodness and strength. His lips were warm, and firm, and wonderful. When he swept his tongue into her mouth, she arched up against him.

"I want you," he said, his voice a murmur against her lips.

She wanted him, too. In a way she couldn't define, couldn't begin to put into words. She wanted like she'd never wanted before. Or ever would again.

She wanted to make love to John Beckett under the warm April sun. She wanted to touch him, to hold him in her arms, and take him into her body.

Wanting and not being able to take, hurt. More than she could have imagined.

"We can't," she said, turning her mouth away from his lips. If they didn't stop right now, she'd never be able to leave him—and staying wasn't an option.

His big body shuddered with emotion. He sat up in one jerky motion and pushed his hair back from his face. "Is it because of Peter?" he asked, looking miserable.

It would be easier to let him think so. But she just couldn't do that. "Your brother was a good man," she assured him. "But what I feel for you doesn't have anything to do with him. I just can't."

"I don't understand."

It would be wrong. For all kinds of reasons that he'd never know. "John, I'm leaving in a week."

"There's no talking you out of going?"

"No. I know I haven't explained it well. All I can say is that someone is counting on me to come back."

"To California?"

"Yes."

"I don't understand. Why did you come back to Cedarbrook if you knew you couldn't stay? Why did you come to my home?"

She shrugged miserably, not knowing what else she could say.

John rubbed a hand over his jaw and shook his head, as if he just couldn't believe it.

She'd hurt him. And she didn't know how to fix it.

When he stood up, his motions were abrupt as he threw the remains of their lunch back into the tin pail. He walked over to his horse. "I guess that's that," he said, his back to her. "We should go."

When Sarah stood up, her legs felt weak. It was nothing compared to her heart, which had cracked, leaving a row of jagged and frayed edges, offering no protection to either side.

* * *

"THANK you for letting me come and play again," Sarah said.

"No need for thanks." Thomas wiped the wooden bar clean. "Look around. Business hasn't been this good for months."

Sarah glanced over her shoulder. Four tables, six men each, played cards. Three more stood at the far end of the bar, and George had his customary spot.

"What would it take for you to stay?" Thomas asked. "With you at the piano and Miss Suzanne back upstairs, I'd spend less time worrying about paying my bills."

She'd worked at her school for six years and nobody had ever bothered to tell her they were glad she was around. "You know I'm only playing for another week," she said.

"I know. At least I still got Suzanne."

Sarah leaned over the bar. "Actually," she said, lowering her voice, "she's not coming back."

Thomas dropped his bar rag. "Miss Suzanne's going to quit whoring?"

"Shush," Sarah said, looking around. So much for her trying to be discreet. Thankfully most of the card players were too far into their game even to look up. Sarah would have thought the outburst had gone unnoticed if it hadn't been for George.

And only because she'd been watching him for the past week, she noticed the difference. His almost imperceptible slide forward on the bar stool and the slight cock of his head told her that they'd gotten his attention.

"What the hell did I do wrong?" Thomas asked. "Did that damn Justine give her a better deal? I thought she favored Chinese girls."

"There are more prostitutes in Cedarbrook?"

Thomas frowned on her. "They been there for two years or more. I don't know how you forgot about them. Seems to me I heard rumors that your husband visited there a time or two."

Oh. "We never talked about it."

"That ain't what I heard. I recall talk of the two of you having quite the discussion about it just outside of Hooper's. Peter left the next day for the silver mine."

"It was a long time ago," Sarah said.

"I suppose. I heard one of Justine's girls has never quite been the same. Missed him something fierce."

Thomas said it without malice, and for some reason, Sarah felt better. She was glad that Peter's death had been marked by someone other than his brother and his mother. She hadn't even known the man and she was sure he deserved better than to be forgotten by his wife.

"Well, Suzanne isn't going to Justine's. She's coming with me. We're leaving on next week's stage."

"That's a damn shame," Thomas said. "She's the best whore I've had in a long time."

"She's more than a whore," Sarah said, beginning to get irritated at Thomas's mercenary response.

Thomas shook his head, looking ashamed. "Hell, I know that. She's a fine woman, too. I like her. I do. You can't blame me for thinking about my business."

"I don't," Sarah assured him. "I'm sure she'll be in to tell you goodbye."

"She's a dandy," Thomas said.

Sarah smiled at him. "That she is," she said, walking back to her piano. "That she is."

Sarah played for another hour. The highlight of the evening came when two cowboys decided to dance to "Buffalo Gals." Their hearts may have been in it but whiskey had dulled their heads and their coordination. At one point, in the middle of a complicated series of steps and turns, they'd bumped into one another and sent each other sprawling on their butts.

Sarah laughed until she cried.

"Last song," she said, loud enough that the room could hear. "Any requests?"

"Yeah," said a man at the far table. "Play that one about the strawberry fields."

The Beatles would never forgive her.

Halfway through the song, George got up from his stool, gathered up his dirty coat, and left the bar. When he walked by the piano, he reached out and stuffed something in the tip jar.

Sarah finished her song. As was her custom, she went behind the bar, emptied out her tips, and counted them so that she could give Thomas his half. He looked over her shoulder. "Jesus," he said. "You got yourself a twenty-dollar silver certificate."

"George left it."

"Son of a bitch must have been drunker than I thought," Thomas said.

"It's got to be a mistake."

"His loss. Our gain," Thomas said, running his hands across the money.

"I can't take this," Sarah said. "*We* can't take this. The poor man doesn't even have a decent shirt or pants. He can't afford this."

"I ain't giving up my half."

"Oh, fine," Sarah said. "I'll give you the twenty. Give me ten dollars in return."

Thomas looked pained. "You're going to give him twenty back, aren't you? You're going to take the ten I give you and add another ten of your own."

Sarah shrugged. "So what if I do?"

"Well, don't that make me feel like a big, fat toad?"

Sarah smiled at him. "If the lily pad fits . . ."

Thomas shook his head and threw the twenty back at Sarah. "Go. You can probably catch him. He's got a room above Hooper's Mercantile. It's a good thing you're leaving soon. I'm getting a soft head."

Sarah leaned forward and brushed the man's cheek with a kiss. "I'll see you tomorrow night."

Sarah left the saloon. Instead of walking across the street, she walked with purposeful strides toward the general store. The moon had slipped behind a cloud, leaving eerie patches of smoky white light in the dark sky. It offered just enough light that she could easily see the wooden sidewalk. She wrapped her arms around her middle, wishing she'd put on a coat.

So intent was she on reaching Hooper's before her teeth started to chatter, she almost missed George. If the spark of a match, when he lit his cigarette, hadn't caught her eye, she'd have stumbled right into him and Mitchell Dority.

Sarah's heart started to race. *Dority*. The bastard.

Hate. Fear. Emotions warred, each more intense than the other.

She needed to warn Suzanne. She took a step backward but the terror, the absolute terror that she might be too late, paralyzed her, making it impossible for her to move. What if Dority had already finished what he'd started just a week ago? What if he'd already been to the hotel while she sat and played her stupid songs on the piano?

Freedom would have come and got her. He'd have seen Dority. Nothing happened in that hotel that Freedom didn't see.

She remembered Dority backing Freedom up against the banister and watching Freedom's mop drop onto the first floor. What if, this time, it had been Freedom's slim body plummeting over the railing, landing with a crash on the floor, his bones crushed? Sarah covered her mouth with her hand, afraid she might vomit.

She heard Dority laugh and resolve filled her. If he'd hurt Suzanne or Freedom, he'd answer to her. She turned and ran, staying as close to the buildings as possible, until she got to the hotel. She whipped open the door and breathed a little deeper when she saw the small lobby was empty. The lamps had been turned down and Morton

Turnip sat behind his counter, his eyes closed, his hands resting on his big stomach.

She ran up the stairs and opened the door.

Fred sat on the bed with Suzanne on his lap. She had her arms wrapped around his neck and he had one hand entwined in her hair and one hand on her breast. They were kissing. No. They were devouring each other, using their lips as utensils.

At least they both had their clothes on.

She cleared her throat. "Evening," she said.

Suzanne jerked back so fast that she lost her balance. Fred grabbed for her while at the same time trying to leap off the bed.

It was a tangle of arms and legs and it ended with Suzanne sitting primly on the bed, smoothing down her skirt with Fred, his face as red as his hair, standing next to the bed, his hands in his pockets.

"You two look ridiculous," Sarah said. She walked into the room, kissed Fred on the cheek, and hugged Suzanne.

Suzanne managed to hide her grin. "Your face is damp," she said.

"I jogged over from the hotel."

"Jogged?" Suzanne frowned.

Sarah intended to tell Suzanne about seeing Dority and George but she didn't intend to do it in front of Fred. She'd learned enough about men like Fred and John to know that neither would think twice about going after the men, not caring that the odds were two against one.

"I guess I better get going," Fred said.

"I can come back later," Sarah said.

Fred shook his head. "We . . . we were just saying goodbye."

"Goodbye? We're not leaving for a week."

"My sister's husband died a couple months ago. Doctor thought it might have been his heart. Anyway, she lives in

Kansas City and wants to come for a visit. I'm going to meet her train in Cheyenne. I'll be gone for a few days."

"Who is watching the children?"

"Mrs. Warner."

"The sourpuss?" Sarah asked.

Fred nodded. "It's only for a few days."

In a few days, Missy could retreat into a shell that would take them months to get her out of. "Let Suzanne and me watch them," Sarah said.

Fred looked shocked. "I couldn't do that. Why, you both have jobs. You're working at the saloon and Suzanne's working at Hooper's."

"I already offered," Suzanne said, with a pointed look in Fred's direction.

"Don't be a fool, Fred. Thomas Jefferson won't be happy about it but he'll understand. I was only going to play a couple more nights. Your children are more important. Let Suzanne and me help."

Fred shook his head. "I couldn't ask you to do that. Besides, three rambunctious children need space. They'd tear this room up within an hour."

"We'll stay at your house."

"Oh, no. That wouldn't be proper," Fred said. "Plus, it could be dangerous. You'd be out in the country, all by yourselves. What if Dority decided to come back to town?"

Yikes. He had a point. Dority had come back and who knew how long he planned to stay.

"Maybe we could stay at John's?" Suzanne said, looking hopeful. "It'd just be for a few days."

Stay at John's? How could they? She could still see the pain in John's eyes. It would haunt her forever. He'd been distantly polite on the trip down the mountain. When they'd reached the hotel, he'd tipped his hat, nudged his horse, and ridden away.

"I'm sure he wouldn't mind," Suzanne said. "He'd be

there in case anything happened. We'd be fine. Don't you agree, Sarah?"

No, she'd be miserable. Right up to the day they left town. But now she had bigger issues to worry about. She needed to make sure Suzanne had the chance to leave town. In one piece. Without bruises or busted teeth.

"That's fine," she said. She could deal with John for a couple days. After all, the children would be there. They'd keep them busy. "I know John won't mind. He'd do anything for your children."

"I don't know how to thank you," Fred said. "Both of you."

By the hungry look in his eyes, he wanted to do more than thank Suzanne. Sarah cleared her throat. She needed Fred out of the room and out of town. "Fred, I'm really tired. I'd be happy to step out into the hall for a minute but I'd really appreciate getting to sleep as soon as possible."

"I'll be right along," he said.

Sarah closed the door behind her and walked to the railing. She wasn't surprised when Freedom joined her.

"Freedom knows something," he said.

"What?"

"Dority's back in town."

"Did he come here?"

"If he had, he'd be a dead man right now. Freedom is ready for him this time. Freedom ain't going to let him harm Miss Suzanne or you. Freedom ain't never known two such delightful women."

She was delightful. How nice. "I saw him with George."

Freedom drew his eyebrows together. "That don't sound right."

"I saw it. Why do you say that?"

"George don't seem like Dority's type."

"How can you tell? He never says a word to anybody. Just acts like he'll bite your head off if you try to talk to him."

"George didn't bite Freedom's head off."

"What are you talking about?"

"Freedom don't sleep much. Freedom likes to walk at night. Quiet as a mouse. Nobody even knows he's there. One night, in the middle of the night, Freedom almost stumbles over George as he's coming out of the jail. An empty jail. Deputy Lewis wasn't even there. When George saw Freedom, he looked real surprised. He didn't try to explain or nothing. He just looked at Freedom for the longest spell and then walked past."

"What do you think he was doing there?"

"Maybe just trying to find a place to sleep. Freedom knows what that's like. Freedom never said a word to anybody about seeing him there. A couple days later, Freedom saw George walking down the street. George looked Freedom right in the eye and smiled. Not many people smile at Freedom. Definitely not men like Dority."

"Dority?" Fred stood just outside the room door, his head cocked to one side. "What's this about Dority? Is he back in town?"

"Heavens no," Sarah said, her heart rate jumping up again. "Do you think I'd be standing here talking to Freedom about hot water if Dority had returned?"

"I'm sure I heard Freedom say his name."

"No, sir. I said majority. The majority of the time Freedom don't have a fire going this late at night but I just knew Miss Sarah would want a bath."

She owed Freedom a really great lunch.

"Have a good trip, Fred," she said. "Don't worry about the children."

SARAH waited until Fred walked out the front door before slipping into the room. Suzanne sat on the bed. Traces of tears lingered on her cheeks.

"It's harder than I thought," she said, "to tell him good-bye."

"I'm sorry if I interrupted something tonight."

Suzanne shook her head. "I'm not going to bed him again. If I did, I might not get on that stage. A month from now I'd be in the same situation I'm in now."

"And what's that?"

"Loving him and knowing nothing can come of it. Closing my eyes every time another man lies on top of me so that I can pretend it's Fred."

Sarah sat down on the edge of the bed and reached for Suzanne's hand. "It didn't exactly look like the two of you were saying goodbye."

"I know. It seems like every good intention either one of us has goes up in smoke the minute we're alone."

"That's a problem. You're going to have to deal with it eventually. But tonight, we've got a more immediate problem. Dority's back in town."

Suzanne's eyes flicked to the door, as if she expected Dority to break it down. "He was at the saloon?"

"No. I saw him talking to George, near Hooper's Mercantile."

"Do you think," Suzanne asked, her eyes bigger than usual, "that he's coming for me?"

"I don't know," Sarah said.

"I'm glad you didn't say anything to Fred."

"He'd go after him. He's a big man but I can't help but think Dority and George would get the best of him."

"He's got those sweet children to think of. He needs to stay strong and healthy for them."

"Maybe we should go to Deputy Lewis," Sarah said.

Suzanne hissed. "He won't do anything. The man's afraid of his own shadow."

Sarah stood up, walked over to the window, and looked out into the dark night, lit only by the sporadic dirty yellow glow of hanging lanterns. "Then there's no one to help us," she said.

"There's John," Suzanne said.

Sarah felt the chill run down her spine. She couldn't shake the memory of John lying battered and bruised in his bed, a chunk out of his skull. She'd been half crazy with worry.

And that was before she loved him.

She would leave loving him. She'd accepted that. The least she could do was leave him whole.

She heard Suzanne get up off the bed. She wasn't startled when the woman wrapped her arm around Sarah's shoulder. Neither one of them said anything for a minute.

"I know," Suzanne said softly, "why it can never work out between Fred and me. I don't understand what's keeping you and John apart."

About a hundred years. "It's complicated," Sarah said.

"Everything is," Suzanne said. "I know you were married to his brother. He's dead. You and John are alive."

"It's not that easy." Sarah pulled away from Suzanne.

Suzanne lifted both hands in the air. "I'm sorry, Sarah. I have no right to judge."

Sarah smiled at her friend. "We're a pair, aren't we?"

"I'm grateful to you, Sarah. You've helped me so much. I want you to know something."

"What's that?"

"There's no need to be afraid. I won't let Dority win. I've spent most of my life letting men win, letting men take something from me. I'm not going to let it happen again."

FIFTEEN

SARAH woke up with gritty eyes and a throbbing headache, unhappy that the soft mattress and cool sheets hadn't brought her any comfort from the ugly vision of Dority and George enjoying a cigarette together.

Suzanne, saying she felt better, had insisted that they trade off sleeping on the floor. Sarah, after arguing about it for ten minutes, had reluctantly crawled into the narrow bed. When she had managed to doze off, she'd awakened hours later, only to find Suzanne not sleeping on the floor but rather, wide awake, sitting in the chair. Resting securely across her lap was the rifle that Freedom had brought them just before they'd turned down the light the previous night.

She looked every bit like a woman ready and able to kill.

"Good morning," Sarah said. She flexed her toes and stretched her body. "Did you sleep at all?"

"There will be time to sleep later," Suzanne said. "I'm going to get washed—"

A knock on the door interrupted her. With solid confidence, Suzanne raised her gun.

"Miss Suzanne. Miss Sarah. Freedom brung you some breakfast."

Suzanne lowered the gun.

"Thanks, Freedom," Sarah said. "Just a minute."

"No need to hurry. Freedom will leave it outside your door."

They heard the clink of a tray on the wooden floor. Sarah started to swing her legs over the bed.

"Let me," Suzanne said, standing up. "You've been waiting on me long enough."

Both women were quiet as they ate the bread and oatmeal Freedom had brought them. Then Suzanne left for Hooper's and Sarah walked to the livery stable and paid the man part of George's twenty dollars to rent a horse for the day.

The trip to John's took longer than she had expected. She had to walk her horse most of the way. When she tried to trot, it seemed like her teeth might shake loose. She'd been willing to risk a gallop, anything that might smooth out the ride, but the horse had other ideas, his days of galloping apparently over.

She heard Morton before she saw him. The dog barreled over the hill and proceeded to run circles around her horse, who didn't even seem to notice. When John poked his head out of the barn a minute later, she gave him a little wave.

He stared at her. Then he looked down, rubbed his forehead like he had a very bad headache, then looked up again.

What the heck? She got off her horse and stooped to pet Morton. The dog immediately stopped barking and flopped flat over onto his back, giving her free access to his white tummy. She rubbed, never taking her eyes off John, who hadn't moved an inch away from the barn door.

"Is this a bad time?" she called.

He didn't respond.

This was going to be worse than she had imagined. She gathered her nerve, stood up, and walked toward him. Morton fell into step next to her.

"You look a little pale," she said when she got close enough to get a good look at him.

He took his hat off and slapped it against his leg. "I thought I dreamed you," he said. His pale face took on a pink hue. "I was thinking about you," he said.

Oh, my goodness. She could feel the heat rise in her own face. "I don't understand," she said.

He shrugged. "I haven't stopped thinking about you since I left you at your hotel. I haven't stopped thinking about kissing you. It's that simple."

That wasn't simple at all. It was complicated and messy and it made her want to yell with joy and weep with despair. "John, please. Don't make more of this than what it is. I'm here to help Fred."

"Fred?" He frowned at her. "What happened to Fred?"

"Nothing has happened to him. Fred came to see Suzanne last night."

"You didn't say anything to him about our conversations about Suzanne?"

"Of course not," she said.

John nodded, looking satisfied. "He's a lovesick fool."

"You're right. Anyway, he left town early this morning to go meet his sister in Cheyenne. He's only planning to be gone a few days and he had intended to ask Mrs. Warner to watch the children."

"Sour-as-a-pickle Mrs. Warner?"

"The same. Suzanne and I didn't like the sound of that. So we volunteered. Fred's worried that the children will tear up our room at the hotel."

"He's probably right."

"I told him we could stay at his house."

John shook his head. "Not alone, you can't. It's not safe."

"That's what Fred said. So, I told him I thought you'd be willing to have the children, Suzanne, and me stay here. How do you feel about houseguests?"

"You're coming back here?"

He asked it casually enough. If she hadn't seen the pinched white of his fingers, where he clenched the brim of his cowboy hat, she'd have thought it didn't matter to him.

"Only if it's okay with you," she said.

"Fred knows he can ask anytime," John said.

"You don't mind?"

"I love those children like they were my own."

So, he didn't intend to answer the question. "He doesn't want to bother anyone."

"No bother. How are you going to get the children over here?"

Sarah looked at her horse. He'd barely been able to carry her. Three children would bring him to his knees. "I don't know," she said.

"I'll hitch up the wagon. That way they can bring a few things back."

He turned back toward the barn. She stopped him with a touch to his arm. "Thank you, John. I mean it. I know this is a surprise. I'm sure Fred will really appreciate this."

"I'm not doing this for Fred."

"Oh. Well, then the children."

"I'm not that noble, Sarah."

"What do you mean?"

"You don't get it, do you?"

A little voice, in the back of her head, told her to walk away. "Get what?"

He slapped his cowboy hat back on his head. "I'm not going to pretend that I'm not glad to see you. If that makes you uncomfortable, that's too bad."

It made her heart thump. That was pretty darn uncomfortable.

"So, if you see a smile on my face, you can tell yourself that I'm happy to help a friend and his children. Or you can tell yourself that it's because it's a sunny April day and spring flowers are everywhere. You go ahead. But in your heart, understand this. I'm smiling because you're here."

Her heart stopped thumping and started racing. "Oh," she said.

John cocked his head. "Oh? Is that the best you can do?"

She nodded. "Oh, boy."

Suddenly looking very young, he smiled at her.

"Oh, boy, I think I'm in trouble," she added.

He winked at her, grabbed her hand, and pulled her toward the barn. "Shut your mouth, Sarah. Flies are going to get in."

HELEN had already fed Thomas and Missy. She stood at the table, washing the dishes in a metal pan.

She looked at Sarah. "Pa told me you were coming. He didn't say anything about Mr. Beckett. I don't see the reason. We're not babies," she said.

She sounded tough and she had her upper lip curled up in a way no eight-year-old should have been able to manage. Sarah, however, didn't miss the look of pure relief in her eyes.

"I'm hoping," John said, not missing a beat, "that you'll leave tending the children to Sarah and help me in the barn. I've got some cows close to birthing and I know you're a big help to your pa at those times."

Helen's eyes lit up. "Did he tell you that?"

"You bet. How else would I know?"

Helen nodded. "I suppose we could go." She looked at Sarah. "Missy likes you well enough. She's been practicing those words."

John's head snapped up. "Words? Missy talked?"

Shoot. She'd made sure Fred wouldn't share her secret. She hadn't counted on Helen spilling the beans.

"Finger words," Helen said. "Sarah taught her some kind of secret code."

"It's sign language," Sarah said. "It's a way for the deaf to communicate with each other and with hearing people."

"Where'd you learn sign language?" John asked.

"In California."

"How come you never said anything?"

"The subject never came up. It's not that big of a deal."

John studied her. "Maybe not to you. Sounds like it might be a big deal to Missy. Where are your sister and brother, Helen?"

"Down at the creek."

Sarah walked over to the cabinet that held the children's clothes. "John, I'll pack a few things if you want to go get them."

"Fine. We'll be back in ten minutes. Helen, you want to stay here and help Sarah or come with me?"

"I'll stay."

John had barely closed the door behind him when Helen began her questioning. "So, are you and Mr. Beckett getting married?"

"Married?" Sarah almost shut her finger in the cabinet. "Whatever gave you that idea?"

"You look at each other like people do when they're getting married. You wouldn't even have to change your last name. It's already Beckett."

"That is convenient," Sarah said, wanting to talk about anything else. "Does Thomas have any other clean trousers?"

"Hanging on the line. Pa and me washed clothes last night before he left."

"Go out and grab them. And anything else that's out there. We'll take it with us."

"If you and Mr. Beckett get married, you could sleep in the same bed. Just like my ma and pa. Maybe even make a baby."

"That's true," Sarah said, making an effort to swallow. "Let's get those clothes packed."

"God sees a man and a woman lying together in a bed and he knows it's time to give them a baby."

Sarah licked her lips. She had no responsibility to set the record straight. "Is that how it works?"

"Yes. God puts a baby in the ma's stomach and she hollers like crazy for it to come out. And when it does, the baby hollers right back at its ma."

"Sounds about right," Sarah said. "Will Missy want her doll?"

"Tom Turnip said my pa and Miss Suzanne might get a baby."

"Oh."

"I told him he didn't know what he was talking about."

"I'd just forget about what he said," Sarah said. "Let's take this box out to the wagon."

Helen held the door. "It's not like I'd mind so much."

Sarah almost dropped her box. "Mind what?"

"If Pa and Miss Suzanne got married. I would have the most beautiful mother of all the girls in school."

Sarah knew she should leave well enough alone. "Have you ever," she asked, "told your pa that?"

Helen's eyes filled with tears. "No. Grandpa told me that Pa is sad sometimes because he misses my mother. I don't want to make him sad by talking about things like mothers. It's not like I have to have one. Even if I get one, she probably won't want a kid as old as me. She'll probably just want the baby that God brings."

Sarah wrapped her arms around the child. "It's okay," she said. "Someday you'll have a new mother and she's going to love you very much. She's going to appreciate having such a good helper, especially if there is a new baby."

Helen brushed the tears from her face. "Do you think it's bad to want a new mother? What if Ma is looking down from Heaven? I don't want her to think I've forgotten her."

Such a heavy load for an eight-year-old. "I'm sure she is

in Heaven. She's proud as can be of how you've helped your pa take care of Thomas and Missy, but she knows how important it is for a girl, especially a girl who is getting older like you, to have a mother. Somebody to talk to. Somebody to tell secrets to."

"Maybe you could be my mother? Since you and Mr. Beckett aren't getting married."

Sarah shook her head. "I'd be honored. Really. But I can't. I'm leaving Cedarbrook in less than a week."

"Why? Don't you like it here?"

"I love it here," Sarah said. It was true. She'd stopped thinking about showers and flush toilets and shopping malls. "I have to leave. If I don't, there's a little boy, about your age, that won't get the medical care he needs. He's dying. I have to help him."

"Help who?" John said, coming up behind them. He had Missy on his shoulders and Thomas at his side.

Sarah winked at Helen. "Help you. I need to help you get this wagon loaded so that we can get home. We don't want that cow having her baby without us."

"I get to help," Helen said, looking at Thomas.

He stuck out his tongue at her. "I saw Pa stick his arm up a cow's—"

"Never mind, Thomas," John said. "Get in the wagon."

Missy tugged on Sarah's dress. "Bee," she spelled. "Sting." She pointed at her arm, where Sarah could easily see the bright red skin.

Sarah made a face. "Hurt," she spelled. Then repeated it.

Missy nodded, looking proud. Sarah didn't know if she was proud of the sting or proud she'd remembered how to spell the words.

John stood there, a look of awe on his face.

Sarah smiled at him. "Shut your mouth, John. Flies are getting in."

*   *   *

BY the time Suzanne arrived late that afternoon, Missy had learned the entire alphabet, Helen had helped bring a calf into the world, and Thomas had fallen out of two trees. All in all, Sarah thought, stretching her back, it had been a great day.

Sarah got Suzanne and Missy settled at the table and went in search of John. He'd come back from checking fence an hour earlier and had gone to the barn to finish the evening chores.

She slid the heavy barn door open. "John," she called.

No response.

"John."

Nothing.

She walked farther into the barn, stopping at the stall where the mother cow nursed her newborn calf. "You're a good mommy," she said. "You've got a beauty there," she said, wondering how the calf's thin legs managed to hold up his body.

She took another six steps. The barn was dark and smelled like animals and hay. Earthy. Solid.

"John," she called again.

"What?" he whispered, grabbing her from behind.

She shrieked as he wrapped his arms around her middle, lifted her up off the ground, keeping her back to his front, and then turned in a circle, swinging her around and around.

"Put me down," she said, laughing.

"Not unless you do exactly what I tell you," he said.

"Anything. I'm getting dizzy."

He slowed down the turning and gently set her feet back on the ground. He held her steady when she swayed.

"I hate carnival rides," she said.

"What?"

"I'll explain later," she said, turning. He stood so close, just barely inches away. His big body held the same richness of the barn, the earthy smell of a hardworking man. He had straw in his hair and a smudge of dirt on his cheek. He looked adorable.

"Kiss me," he said.

She did. He pulled her closer still and his hot, moist mouth consumed her.

"I have to go," she said, after finally breaking away. They were both breathing hard.

"Stay," he said.

She shook her head. "That wouldn't be smart." The cows didn't need that kind of excitement.

"I need someone to help me with chores."

She shook her head at him. "The old *I need help* might work on Helen but I'm a lot older and a little wiser."

He kissed her again and she felt her resolve weaken.

"I came out to tell you supper would be ready in thirty minutes," she said, barely able to catch her breath.

"I'm hungry now," he whispered, and ran his fingers down her back, stopping when he reached the hollow of her spine. He looked her straight in the eye, all traces of teasing gone. "I want you. I want you with a fierceness that, until you came back, I'd only dreamed about."

She wanted to throw him down in the hay and keep him there for a couple weeks. "John," she said, brushing her fingers across his lips, "nothing has changed since yesterday. I'm still leaving on next Wednesday's stage."

"It doesn't have to be that way."

"It does. I can't really explain why. It just does."

"Yesterday, up on that mountain, I felt something when I kissed you. I think you felt it, too."

She nodded. It would be foolish to deny it.

"That doesn't make any difference to you? It doesn't matter? You can still walk away?"

She could hear the hurt in his voice and she felt her resolve weaken. She tried hard to remember Miguel Lopez and his desperate mother.

"It's difficult to explain," she said. "It's not easy for me to walk away. I thought it would be, but it's not."

He ran his fingers through his hair. "I don't want you to go, but I don't know what to say or do to keep you here."

She'd waited a lifetime for someone to say those kinds of words to her.

"I wish it was that easy, John. It's so much more complicated. Let's just say I don't belong here," she said.

"You belong in California?"

"I guess," she said.

"You guess? What kind of answer is that?"

"It's the best I can do. I work there. I guess that means I belong there."

"Work?" He raised an eyebrow.

Too late she remembered that women in 1888 rarely worked outside the home, and based on what she knew about Sarah One, it made it seem even more preposterous.

"I work with children. Kind of like a teacher."

"We've got a school in Cedarbrook. If it's so important for you to work, you could get a position there."

She shook her head.

His head fell forward. He took one tanned hand and massaged his temple. "You said there wasn't another man?"

He hadn't even looked up. As if he couldn't bear it if he was wrong. She took her hand, placed it under his chin, and gently lifted his face.

"There's no one," she said.

His big body shuddered. The electricity, the pent-up emotion, it shook her very soul, burning her, marking her.

She would never be the same.

"I need to finish up here," he said, pulling away.

"John," she said, reaching for his arm.

He took a step back. She slowly lowered her arm and let it hang next to her side. It felt cold, as if life had been stripped out of it. "Supper will be ready when you come in," she said.

"I'm not hungry." He turned away from her.

"It doesn't have to be this way," she said, speaking to his back. "You and I don't have to fight about this."

"I'm not fighting. I'm working, Sarah. That's what I do. I work."

"Fine," she said, tossing her head back. "Then you need to eat. I don't want you to go hungry because of me."

He let out a loud sigh. "Take it from me, Sarah. You don't always get what you want."

She silently counted to ten. "Just please come inside and eat. I feel bad enough about things. I don't want to feel bad that you're hungry."

He turned, his broad shoulders moving so fast that she felt the breeze on her face. His jaw was set and his eyes flashed fire. "I damn well can decide when and where I eat. Now get the hell out of my barn, Sarah."

She could smell his fury, the edgy, hot scent of an angry predator. She took a step back. Then another. She whirled, hiked up her skirt, and ran. She yanked open the heavy door.

"Sarah."

It sounded as if her name had been ripped from his soul.

"Sarah," he said, softer this time.

She looked over her shoulder.

"I'm sorry," he said.

He looked as if he'd lost his best friend. "It's my fault," she said.

"No." He shook his head. "I'm being an ass. Look, tell the children I'm busy with the stock. Send Thomas out with a sandwich later."

SARAH and Suzanne slept in the double bed and Helen and Missy curled up on the rug in front of the fireplace. Thomas slept in the barn with John.

Sarah, waking up first, slipped quietly out of bed. She added wood to the stove and lit it. She stood close, grateful for the immediate heat. Knowing it wouldn't be enough to warm the big room, she carefully stepped over Helen and Missy, added some kindling to the big log in the fireplace, and lit it.

At times like this, she really missed her microwave and her gas furnace.

She filled the coffeepot with fresh water from the bucket near the door. Then she added the coffee grounds and put it on the burner to brew. She slipped off her cotton nightgown and pulled on her skirt and blouse. Pushing her feet into Franny Goodie's worn shoes, she grabbed a basket from the table.

By the time the children woke up, she'd have a plate of scrambled eggs waiting.

When she opened the cabin door, the absolute perfection of the spring morning hit her. Birds chattered in the trees. Flowers waved in the light wind. The bright orange sun, almost over the horizon, bathed the land in a warm richness.

She took a deep breath and walked to the chicken coop. Within minutes, she had a basketful of light brown eggs. She walked back to the house, holding the basket with two hands.

"You're up early."

She juggled the basket, barely keeping it from turning upside down. She whirled to stare at John. "You scared me," she accused.

"I'm sorry," he said.

The dark circles under his eyes made him look tired. "Where's Thomas?" she asked.

"Still sleeping. He's a lot like his father. He snores."

"Did he keep you awake?"

"Some," he said. "How about you? How did you sleep?"

"Fine."

"That's good." He looked at her like he wanted to eat her up, then quickly looked down at the ground.

She lifted the basket, holding it out, as if it were some sort of prize. "I was going to make some breakfast."

"Good. Thanks." He rubbed a hand over his whiskered chin.

She set the basket on the ground. The way the two of them were dancing around each other, the eggs would surely get broken sooner or later. "Look, John. This is awkward for both of us. I shouldn't have come back to the ranch. I don't know what I was thinking. I'm sorry."

He shook his head. "Things got a little heated up last night. It's nobody's fault. It won't happen again."

"How do you know?" she asked, wondering if relief or disappointment caused the empty feeling in her stomach.

"I'm not going to let it," he said.

"Is it as simple as that?"

He shrugged. "I'm going to pack up some sandwiches. I'll be in the north pasture most of the day. If you need anything, use the gun I keep behind the door. Shoot it twice, quick-like, in the air. I can hear that from where I'll be."

"Will you be home for supper?"

"I'll need to come back for the night chores. I'll grab something quick. I've got some work to do in the barn. I'll take care of that after supper."

In other words, he intended to avoid her. It was probably for the best. "Sounds like a plan. If I don't see you again today, I'll catch you tomorrow. Fred thought he'd be back by noon. Suzanne and I'll leave for town after that."

"I imagine his sister might want to spend a few minutes with Suzanne."

"I'm not sure Fred will tell her about Suzanne."

"He won't need to. All she'll have to do is see how Fred looks at her and she's going to know he's smitten."

Did she look at John that way? Could just anyone see that she'd lost her heart to this man? "If Fred intends to pursue Suzanne, you might want to tell him not to wait too long. She intends to get on the stage with me on Wednesday."

"Wednesday," he repeated.

She could see the strong muscles in his neck move as he swallowed.

"Yeah, Wednesday."

John nodded. He looked over her shoulder, his eyes not focused. "I'm guessing he knows what day the stage leaves."

"I'm guessing so," she said.

He shifted his glance and looked her right in the eye. "If I think about it," he said, his tone deliberately casual, "I'll remind him. I expect I'll be pretty busy for the next couple days."

Busy breaking her heart.

"Yeah, me too," she said. She bent down and picked up her eggs. She needed to get back inside before she did something incredibly stupid like cry in front of him.

She got twenty feet before he stopped her.

"Sarah," he said.

She didn't turn around. "Yes."

"I'm sorry about the things I said last night. I had no right to be cruel."

She sucked in her breath and held it.

"Sarah, I'm glad you came back. I'm glad I got the chance to know you."

She couldn't stop the tears that ran down her cheeks.

"And, Sarah," he said. "I'm never going to forget you."

It was the last six words that broke her heart.

SIXTEEN

ON Sunday morning, Sarah arrived at the church before Pastor Dan had had a chance to put his robes on. He sat in the first pew, one leg crossed over the other, papers spread out around him.

She clenched her sheet music to her breast. "Pastor Dan?"

He looked up and smiled at her. "Morning, Sarah. You caught me making a few last-minute adjustments."

"From your mouth to God's ears," she said.

He laughed. "Something like that. You're here early. Church doesn't start for another hour."

"I know. I couldn't sleep."

"I understand Fred and his sister got in safely yesterday."

"Yes. They arrived by noon. She's a lovely woman. Very friendly."

"I'm sure. I look forward to meeting her today."

"I think Fred might have told her about Suzanne."

"Really?" He put down his pencil. "Why do you think that?"

"I could just tell by the way she looked at Suzanne."

"Like she was judging her?"

"Oh, no. She didn't look at her in a mean way. She just seemed curious."

"That's a good sign," Pastor Dan said, gathering up his papers. "If he can talk about it to someone he trusts, it means he's one step closer to coming to terms with it. How did Suzanne react?"

"She didn't say much about it, but I'm pretty sure she noticed it."

"Did you both return to the hotel last night?"

"Yes." She didn't elaborate. It probably wasn't necessary for him to know that Suzanne, with some feeble excuse about it being easier to sleep if they each had a bed, had asked Morton Turnip for two rooms. In the middle of the night, Sarah had heard a soft knock on Suzanne's door and the gentle murmur of Fred's voice. Later, when the unmistakable sounds of a woman's and a man's pleasure had seeped through the thin walls, she'd simply pulled the pillow over her head, burrowed under the blanket for good measure, and counted sheep.

"Nervous?" Pastor Dan asked.

"No. I think you should be, though. The good folks of Cedarbrook may run you out of town on a rail once they see me at the piano."

Pastor Dan rubbed his hands together. "I've told everyone I can think of that you're playing the piano."

"You must have a death wish."

He winked at her. "Preachers like to play to a full house." He spread his arms wide. "Welcome to my stage, Sarah."

"If this is going to be an opera, I'm a little worried about the inevitable death scene. It might be my own."

"Your God will not desert you, Sarah."

"Once again, from your lips to God's ears. What time should I start playing?"

"Church starts at ten. Perhaps twenty minutes before that. You've got plenty of time to join me for a cup of coffee."

"Thanks for the offer but I think I'll stick around here. Maybe send up a few prayers of my own."

"As you wish. I'll see you soon."

Sarah watched the small man with the big heart walk out the door. She sat in the first pew.

It's me again, God. I've had a busy couple of days since we last talked.

She got up and walked over to the stained glass window. She ran the tip of her index finger through the dust that had gathered at the edge. *A few days ago I told you that I had a thing for John Beckett. Well, against my better judgment, I've fallen in love with him.*

She drew a heart in the dust. Then she bent down, and with one quick puff of breath, she scattered the dust. Only the tip of the heart remained. *I have to go back. I don't have a choice.*

She walked over to the piano, sat on the bench, leaned forward, and rested her forehead against the polished wood. *Send him someone else, God. I don't want him to be alone.*

She wiped away the tear that leaked from her closed eyes. *I can't even believe I'm saying this. But he needs a wife and children. He'll be such a great dad.*

Sniffing, she sat up straight and ran her fingers across the ivory keys. *I've got just one more request. I'm going to hurt him when I go. I don't know how to avoid that. Heal him, God. Take away his pain.*

"Sarah?"

She jerked her hands off the keys. John stood in the back of the church.

"What are you doing here?" she asked.

He shrugged, looking too innocent. "It's Sunday. Isn't that the day people go to church?"

"When is the last time you've been inside a church?"

He tapped his chin. "When Missy got baptized. Fred and Franny wanted me there."

"You can't stay," Sarah said. Nobody would be baptized today unless Mrs. Beckett tried to drown her.

"Why not?"

"I . . . I get nervous playing the piano in front of people I know."

He shook his head at her. "I've been in the saloon when you played. You didn't get nervous."

"Church is different. Besides, there's no room," she said, grasping for straws. "Everyone has assigned seats. You'll be bumping somebody out of their prayerful place."

"I'll stand in the back."

Great. He'd have a bird's-eye view when his mother rushed the altar and strangled her.

She so did not want to come between John and his mother. She'd caused the man enough pain. "This is not a good idea."

He shrugged and leaned against the wall.

She swallowed. "Don't say I didn't warn you."

"Warn me about what?" Pastor Dan, his robe half unbuttoned, came around the corner. When he saw John in the back of the room, he stopped.

"John," he said, "I haven't seen you in church lately."

"It's been a while," John said.

Sarah had no doubt that Pastor Dan knew exactly how long it had been since John had been to church.

"What's the occasion today?" Pastor Dan asked.

John gave Pastor Dan a small smile. "Can't a man get close to his God without having to explain himself?"

Pastor Dan shook his head. "Not you. Not in my church."

John didn't say anything for a long minute. When he did, Sarah felt a sharp pain in her chest, as if the point of the tiny heart she'd left on the windowsill had poked her.

"I thought Sarah might need me."

He'd come because she might need him.

Oh, God. Forget what I said earlier. Don't send someone else for him. Find a way to let me stay.

"God will watch over Sarah," Pastor Dan said.

"I'll just be around in case He needs any help," John said.

"I'm sure He appreciates that." Pastor Dan, his long robe dragging on the ground, walked up the aisle. "Whatever the reason, I'm grateful to the good Lord for bringing you back."

The church door opened and a stream of cool April air whipped through the church, lifting the edges of Sarah's sheet music. Myron and Rosie Brickstone walked in. Myron looked at his shoes and Rosie frowned at Sarah.

"I guess it's show time," Sarah said.

Pastor Dan smiled wide, showing all his teeth. "Have a seat, John."

"I'll stand if it's all the same to you," John said, moving toward the back of the church.

Pastor Dan shrugged. "God's voice will reach you either way."

Myron and Rosie took the front pew on the right side of the aisle. Sarah resisted the urge to wave at them. She started playing "Amazing Grace."

Within minutes, Mrs. Beckett entered. Sarah thought the wind seemed positively warm in comparison to the look the older woman gave her. Sarah kept one eye focused on her music and, with the other, watched John's mother grab at her chest when she saw her son standing watch in the back corner of the room.

Mrs. Beckett looked from John to Sarah and back to John again. John gave his mother a guarded nod. In return, Mrs. Beckett stuck her nose in the air and took a seat behind the Brickstones.

Next came Deputy Lewis and his wife, Lana. They slid into the pew next to Mrs. Beckett. When Toby and Harietta Ryan came in, dragging their four children, each looking surlier than the last, Sarah wasn't surprised to see them take the next pew.

She sent up a prayer of thanks when Fred, his sister, and his three children came in. He parked his family on the left side of the aisle, directly across from the Brickstones. It took only minutes before Alice and Charles Hooper came in. Charles started to sit behind the Ryans but Alice tugged on his sleeve, guiding him into the pew behind Fred. Charles rolled his eyes but let himself be pulled.

Thomas Jefferson came next and slid in next to the Hoopers. When Freedom arrived, he took a place directly behind Thomas Jefferson.

The Hatfields and the McCoys. Everybody was choosing sides. If she hadn't been the chip they were fighting about, it would have been hilarious. Now it was just darn uncomfortable. She couldn't wait for the morning to end. *Talk fast, Pastor Dan.*

Within five minutes, others filtered in until the pews were all full. As Sarah played her last notes and Pastor Dan took his spot at the pulpit, she realized that the preacher had gotten his wish. He would play to a full house.

And when he said his first word, she knew the man had been born to be a star. He intended to enjoy every minute of the lead role.

"Sin. S. I. N. One word. One syllable. Three simple letters."

He stared at his flock, letting his glance settle on each wayward sheep. "Simple, yes. But nevertheless, a heavy burden. A burden on our hearts and our souls. A burden that prevents us from our ultimate glory, sitting at the right hand of our heavenly Father."

Mrs. Beckett plucked at the tight neckline of her white blouse. Fred bowed his head and stared at his big hands.

"To lessen our burden, we must admit our sin. Before God and before others."

Toby Ryan stared at Sarah, his eyes filled with hostility,

his fingers doing a nervous dance on the pew in front of him.

"Who wants to be first? Who wants to be the first to stand up and admit their sin before God and their neighbors, to ask forgiveness from both?"

Rosie Brickstone pulled out a handkerchief and started coughing into it. No one else moved, not even an inch.

Pastor Dan tapped a finger against his pursed lips. "I see. Well, perhaps it would be easiest if we start by separating the sinners from the nonsinners. Those of you without sin, take a step forward now."

Myron Brickstone's eye started to twitch and Toby Ryan's wife turned to stare at her husband. Fred turned a brilliant shade of pink.

"What? Surely there must be one of us without sin?" Pastor Dan stopped tapping on his mouth and started tapping his finger against his Bible. Sarah thought she saw John's mouth twitch, as if a smile threatened to break free at any moment.

"We can't all be sinners." Pastor Dan's indignation rang through the church. Mrs. Beckett took a sudden interest in the hem of her cloak.

"It must be true, then," Pastor Dan said in a sad voice. "We are all sinners. There is not one among us who is without sin." He rubbed his chin as if in deep contemplation. Sarah knew he was just timing his next line.

"But perhaps," his voice rose, "your sins are not as serious as your neighbor's sins. I imagine that's a great comfort to many of you."

Sarah didn't think anybody looked all that comfortable. With the exception of Freedom. He sat relaxed in the pew, his skinny legs extended in front of him and his arms folded across his chest, looking every bit like a man who intended to enjoy the show.

"I caution you," Pastor Dan said, his voice thundering in the quiet room, "do not take pleasure in comparing your sins to your neighbor's. When you judge another, do not rejoice. For you have committed the greatest sin of all. Only God has the right to judge."

Rosie let out a puff of breath, Thomas Jefferson wiped sweat off his brow with the back of his hand, and Fred sat absolutely still, his mouth hanging open. Sarah glanced at Pastor Dan. He stood a little straighter, his chin had a cocky tilt, and his eyes danced. He'd scored and he knew it.

"And He," Pastor Dan lowered his voice, almost to a whisper, "will judge us most kindly. Especially those of us brave enough to admit our sins and to ask for His forgiveness. Our God is a kind God."

Mrs. Beckett examined the buttons on her shoes. Lana Lewis had her eyes shut and one hand over her mouth.

"Our God is an understanding God, too." Pastor Dan, like any great actor who has taken command of the stage, eloquently waved his arms, making his robe billow. "He understands temptation. He understands weakness."

Sarah made the mistake of looking at John. He stared at her, the muscles in his strong neck flexing.

"He's an expecting God, too. He expects each and every one of us to examine our sin, to repent, and sink to our knees and to beg for His forgiveness. He expects us to beg forgiveness from those we've hurt."

From the set of Mrs. Beckett's mouth, Sarah thought Hell might freeze over first.

"As we ask God to forgive our sins, let us give thanks for our neighbors and our community. Let us give thanks that we are able to gather together as one. Let us commit our intentions and our resources to ensuring that we honor our God and maintain this most holy place of worship."

Men reached into their pockets and Mrs. Beckett snapped open the little purse in her lap.

Pastor Dan held up a hand. "Let us pray," he said, his voice loud and clear. The congregation bowed their heads. "Dear God, thank you for the many blessings you have given us. Guide us gently, yet firmly. Grant that our giving may be generous. This house of worship needs a new roof." He paused for effect. The dutiful parishioners kept their hands clasped and their eyes down.

"Please recognize that all we give, we give in Your name. Amen." Pastor Dan stepped from behind his altar, picked up the small round basket at the end of the first pew, and passed it to Mrs. Beckett.

After nodding at Sarah, Pastor Dan, looking as if he barely needed the cane at his side, fairly waltzed out of the church, as if he were walking on air. Sarah launched into "Shall We Gather at the River."

Thomas Jefferson, a sour look on his face, dug a little deeper in his pocket. Deputy Lewis squirmed in his pew, then nodded to his wife. She took her hand off her mouth, lifted up the hem of her skirt, and pulled some folded paper money out of her sock. When the collection basket reached Toby Ryan, he threw some coins in. His wife reached across two children and gave him a quick rap on the shoulder. He dropped another handful in.

Sarah's fingers flew across the keys as the basket made its way to the back of the church. When the last man had dropped his money in, he brought the basket back up to the front of the church and set it on top of the plain wooden altar.

As soon as his hand let go, people started gathering up their things and gently pushing their children toward the aisle.

Sarah played until the church cleared. Then she stopped for a minute before flipping a page and beginning a whole new song. When she finished that one, she let her hands rest of the ivory keys. Then she sorted through her music, making sure the pages were folded just so. She took a minute to blow some imaginary dust off the keys. Then she resorted the music, putting it in alphabetical order.

She was stalling. Knew it. Didn't like it, especially, but

she didn't think her nerves could handle one more meeting with John Beckett. If he could avoid her on his turf, then she sure as heck could avoid him on her turf.

Sorry, God. Your turf.

She waited another five minutes before walking down the short aisle and opening the heavy door.

John and his mother stood less than five feet from the door. Pastor Dan chatted with Rosie and Myron Brickstone. Fred talked to Thomas Jefferson while his children ran in circles around the small yard.

Everywhere she looked, fools lingered. Didn't these people have anywhere to go? That's what was wrong with the good old days. There was no damn rat race.

"Sarah," Pastor Dan called out. "Your music was lovely. Thank you for sharing your gift."

She nodded, uncomfortable that everyone had stopped socializing and turned toward her. What had been a big-screen action movie suddenly became a silent picture.

Darn it. Pastor Dan might be happy starring in his own drama series but she was the type who preferred to be backstage, painting scenery or arranging sound effects.

Pastor Dan waved her over. "Rosie and Myron have just extended to me a very kind invitation to join them for lunch at their restaurant. You've been such a help today. I couldn't imagine going without you. You will join us, won't you?"

Sarah thought Rosie might explode. Her cheeks puffed up, her face got red, and her eyes bulged, as if they might just pop out of her head.

For a brief second, Sarah thought about saying yes. It would serve Rosie, with her I'm-so-much-better-than-you attitude, right. Then she caught a glimpse of John's mother. The woman had gone completely white.

Pastor Dan's words confirmed her fear. "John and his mother," the preacher said, "are joining us. Come on, we'll have a party."

Sarah looked at John. He gave her one of his sleepy,

sexy smiles that left an answering ache in the core of her soul.

She forced her eyes back to Pastor Dan. "I have to be getting back to my room. I . . . I have things to do."

She took another three steps. Pastor Dan hooked his arm around her shoulders. "Nonsense. You need to eat anyway."

Mrs. Beckett stepped forward. "Pastor Dan," she said, her voice chilly, "I recall that Sarah never was much for eating a big dinner. Always a little too worried about her waistline."

Everyone turned to look at Sarah. She resisted the urge to suck in her stomach.

"I think," Mrs. Beckett said, "that we should just let Sarah go on about her business and the five of us can have dinner like we planned." She grabbed John's arm and tried to pull him forward.

It was sort of like trying to move a big rock with a very small shovel. He didn't budge.

John looked first at his mother, then at Sarah. "If Sarah's not going," John said, his voice quiet, "I'm not either."

Mrs. Beckett's hand shook as she grabbed at her son. "Don't be a fool," she said, her tone rising in decibels with each word.

John didn't answer. He gently removed his mother's fingers from his sleeve. "Sarah?"

"John," she said, wishing the earth would open and swallow her up, "it's fine. I'm not all that hungry. I made plans to meet Suzanne anyway. Go have a nice dinner."

He shook his head.

Pastor Dan looked expectantly at Mrs. Beckett. She had her lips pressed together so tightly that they had lost their color. Myron Brickstone drew circles in the dirt with the toe of his boot.

"Mother?" John urged.

Mrs. Beckett spun around, bringing her face to within

inches of Sarah's. "This is all your fault," she said. "I don't know why you had to come back."

"Mother." John's voice held a warning now.

Great. Just what she'd hoped to avoid. "Look," she said, taking a step back from the group. "I have to go. Suzanne's expecting me."

"I'll walk you back to the hotel," John said, falling into step beside her.

"Don't do it, John," Mrs. Beckett urged.

"Go have your dinner, Mother," John said, never breaking stride. They'd walked halfway to the hotel before he spoke again. "I'm sorry about that."

"You're not responsible for your mother."

"No. I suppose not. You know, she's not a bad person. I think she really misses Peter."

"So do you."

"Yes. Every day. But I was his brother, not his mother. She needs to have someone to blame for his death."

She stopped walking. What was he saying? "And you don't?"

He kept walking and she had to skip to catch up. "Peter was a grown man," John said. "He's the one who decided to make his fortune in that silver mine. You didn't hold a gun to his head."

She grabbed hold of his sleeve. "Wait. You can't drop a bombshell like that and expect me not to notice!"

"A bomb what?"

She massaged her forehead with her fingertips. "John, I'm starting to get behind. I can't keep up. Two nights ago you almost ran me out of your barn with a pitchfork. Today, you stood up for me when your mother wanted to pick a fight. What's going on?"

John opened the hotel door and held it for her. She walked in and saw Morton Turnip sitting behind the counter. John nodded at Morton and, with one hand on her back, gently pushed her up the stairs.

"Same room as before?" he asked, heading toward a door.

"That's Suzanne's room," Sarah said. "I'm next door."

John's eyes widened. "You have your own room?"

She nodded.

"Give me the key?" he said, his voice suddenly deep with need.

She dug it out of her purse with shaky fingers.

John opened the door, pulled her inside, kicked the door shut, took off his cowboy hat, and pushed her back up against the door.

He stepped into her body, wedging one thigh between her legs. With one hand behind her neck and the other high on her ribs, his thumb just resting underneath her breast, he bent his head and kissed her.

His lips were warm and wet and delicious, better than any Sunday dinner. She opened her mouth and his tongue slipped inside.

"Oh, John," she said. She felt the hunger, the bone-deep hunger for him, storm through her body. She pushed herself against his thigh, riding him. He pushed his leg even more intimately against her and she thought she might explode.

"I don't understand," she whispered against his lips.

"I don't either," he said and kissed her hard.

"We can't do this," she said, summoning all her strength to pull away.

"We can." In one smooth motion, he shifted his leg and pulled her body, her whole needy body, up against him. He was warm and solid and—oh my—hard as a rock. He cupped her bottom with one hand and pulled her tight against him.

"I want you," he moaned.

She'd never wanted anything more.

He pulled back, and with infinite care, he started to undo the buttons on her plain tan blouse. When he finished, he gently pushed the material aside.

He chuckled, a dry kind of laugh, when he saw the row of buttons on her borrowed camisole.

"I'll do them," she said. He was way too slow.

She got to the last button when there was a knock on the door.

"John, are you in there? It's Myron."

John's head jerked up. "What do you want, Myron?"

"You better come quick, John. It's your mother. We think it may be her heart."

"What?"

"She fainted at the restaurant. Pastor Dan sent me for you."

Sarah pulled the edges of her camisole together. "Go," she said. "She needs you."

"I can't leave you like this," he said, indecision in his dark eyes.

"I'll be fine. Go."

"You're sure?"

"Yes."

"I want to see you later," he said, already grabbing his hat from the floor.

"Tomorrow," she said, knowing her foolish heart was simply asking to be broken. "Come back tomorrow."

SEVENTEEN

WHEN John got to the café, they had his mother propped up in a chair. Pastor Dan, on his knees, held his mother's hand. The crowd, three deep, parted just far enough to allow him passage.

"Mother," he said, squatting in front of her chair. "Are you sickly?"

Her eyelids fluttered. "Thank you for coming."

John looked at Pastor Dan. "How is she?"

Pastor Dan shrugged. "I'm not sure. One minute she was talking, and the next minute, we were picking her up off the floor."

"Probably my heart," his mother said.

John reached out and laid a thumb over the pulse in her wrist. Her skin felt warm, not clammy like he might have expected. Her cheeks were pink and her pulse seemed strong.

"How are you feeling now?" he asked.

"Better now that you're here," she said. "Maybe I should just go home, John."

Rosie stepped forward. "You haven't had your dinner

yet. Why don't you just sit a spell with us and eat a little something?"

Pastor Dan stood up. "That's it. You're probably just hungry. Let's eat."

"Rosie," his mother said, ignoring Pastor Dan, "I'll feel much better if I can eat in my own house. Would you be so kind as to pack up a couple chicken dinners?"

Rosie nodded and walked toward the kitchen. "John," his mother said, "you will come along, won't you? I know I'll feel better if you're there with me."

John thought of Sarah, sweet Sarah with all her buttons, and indecision tore at his soul.

"Please, John. This has been terribly frightening. I really need to lie down and I just can't stand the thought of being alone. You know, in case my heart acts up again."

He licked his lips. Oh, no. He could still taste Sarah. He shifted, hoping his Sunday trousers hid his need. "Let's get going, then." He offered his mother his hand, and when she grabbed it, her grip was surprisingly strong. An ugly suspicion bloomed, poking awkward stems into his heart. Good color. Warm skin. Strong grip.

"So you fell right off your chair?" he asked.

"I don't remember," she said, shaking her head. "Terribly frightening. You just can't imagine."

"I suppose not. I think we better get you home." They left Brickstone's and began the half-mile walk back to his mother's house. He set the pace slow and steady and he noticed his mother didn't falter once. In fact, by the time they'd reached her door, her steps seemed almost spry.

"I'll probably feel a little better after we have our chicken," she said. "Maybe we could play a few hands of cards after that. You know, to relax me."

Cards? Hell, he didn't want to play cards. He wanted to bury himself inside Sarah. "I can't. I've got to go."

"You're going back to *her,* aren't you?" His mother turned toward him, her eyes wild. "That woman is wicked."

"You're wrong," John said, opening up his mother's front door. "You couldn't be more wrong. And please don't refer to her as *that woman*. Her name is Sarah."

"You couldn't be more blind," she yelled. "What's gotten into you?"

He gave his mother a gentle push and closed the door behind her. No need for all of Cedarbrook to hear them. "Sit down, Mother. You don't want to have another spell."

"I don't need to sit down," she said, waving her arms.

He felt the slow burn of disappointment in the pit of his stomach. "I didn't think so," he said. "You missed your calling, Mother. You should have been an actress. You put on quite a performance."

"What are you talking about?"

"You didn't have a fainting spell. You slipped out of that chair so that you could drag me away from Sarah."

His mother's face turned so pink that it looked like she'd spent the day in the fields. "That's crazy talk," she said.

"Is it, Mother?" He set the sack of food down on her table. "Have your dinner, Mother. I'll talk to you later."

She moved, faster than he would have thought possible, and blocked the front door. "You're not leaving. I won't let you go back to that whore."

"Whore?" The slow burn of disappointment turned into a raging fire of anger. "Did you just call Sarah a whore?"

"John," his mother said, running her hands through her hair. "You're always such a sensible boy. I don't understand what's happening here."

Sensible. That, more than anything, summed up his life. He got up, worked all day, and then went to bed. Only to do it all the same the next day. He didn't even go to town unexpectedly. He'd turned into an old man. A sensible, do-what's-expected, old man.

And why not? He'd taken on a man's role at the age of ten. The years had slipped by, and now, at thirty-two years of age, he could barely remember what it felt like to be young.

Except that Sarah made him feel young and very alive. He'd managed to find a way to have her stay for a week, and like a fool, he'd wasted days. Come hell, high water, or his mother's ugly accusations, he wanted his week with Sarah.

"I'm going now," he said, "and on Wednesday, I'm leaving on the stage."

"You're leaving?" All the pink drained from her face, leaving it a deadly white.

"I'm going to see Sarah safely back to California." Once the words were out of his mouth, he knew, with absolute certainty, that it was the right thing to do. "I'll ask Freedom to take care of my stock. I'll be back the week after next."

"No." The word exploded from his mother's mouth. "She can't ask you to do that."

"She didn't. I'm going to ask her."

His mother leaned against the door. "She's never going to let you come back. She's going to dig her evil claws into you and you'll never come back. You're going to leave me."

John tried to ignore the tears that ran down his mother's face. He was thirty-two years old and he couldn't remember ever having caused his mother to cry.

"I'll be back," he said. "I promise."

She sniffed and pointed a shaky finger at him. "I will not lose another son to that woman."

"She's different," John said, trying to make his mother see what he'd finally seen. "She's changed. I don't know what happened but she's not the same woman who married Peter."

"She is. People don't change," his mother said. "She's fooling you. She's trying to trap you."

"I don't think so," John said.

"You know what she did with Fred Goodie. Your best friend. Doesn't that make a difference to you?"

He really wanted to shake her. "You shouldn't listen to idle gossip. It's not true and I won't have you repeating it."

"You won't come back," his mother said, slumping down in the chair next to the door.

John rubbed his head. "I said I'd be back in two weeks and I will. I promise."

"Your brother promised me that he'd be back, too. He didn't keep his promise. He couldn't. I don't even have his body to pray over."

His brother rested in the cold earth, in the bowels of the silver mine, covered by hundreds of feet of dirt and water. The mine had collapsed, killing Peter and three others. They'd plummeted to their death and the ground had literally swallowed them up. "I'm sorry about that," John said. "I'm sorry he's dead."

"She made him do it." His mother sobbed the words. "She caused his death."

"No," John said. "I wanted to blame her, too. It was better than blaming Peter. But you know how Peter was. He didn't always make the best decisions. I'm probably to blame for that. After Father died, I tried to protect him. I protected him too much."

"No."

"Yes. Remember the time he got in trouble with the sheriff's wife in Carson City? I had to take off in the middle of the night to save him. He just expected it."

"You loved him."

"I loved him," John replied. "I miss him, too. Every day."

"It's her fault."

"I don't think so," John said. "It was his choice."

"She's bewitched you. With her pretty face and her charms. Just like your brother. She's made you forget everything else that's important."

Everything, including her. She didn't need to say the words. "I'm not doing this to hurt you, Mother. But I'm doing it. I wanted you to hear it from me. I'll ask Mr. Hooper and Pastor Dan to check in on you regularly."

He stood up. She grabbed his sleeve. "Don't go," she pleaded. "Don't leave me."

He gently removed her fingers. "I have to, Mother. I don't have a choice. I need to do this for Sarah. I need to do this for me."

WHEN Fred walked into the saloon that night, all the other men looked up, their glances ripe with speculation, obviously wanting to assess the accuracy of Morton Turnip's gossip. Fred, his head high, his big chest broad as the doorway, stared back, until each one had returned their gaze, if not their dirty thoughts, back to their card games. When he took his seat at the bar, Sarah smiled at him, her hands never missing a beat on the ivory keys.

Thomas Jefferson slid a glass of whiskey toward him. "She's packing them in," he said. "Twice as many customers tonight. She's something special."

Fred nodded, all too aware of how special she was. On his way to town, he'd stopped by John's ranch. His best friend hadn't been forthcoming with exact details but Fred could see that there was something different. John had said that he intended to ride into town tomorrow to see Sarah.

When Sarah took her first break, Fred followed her outside. He handed her a glass of water. "Here," he said. "Thomas gave it to me for you."

She took a deep drink.

"I saw John. What's going on between the two of you?"

"What makes you ask that?"

"Just two days ago, when my sister and I got to his ranch, the two of you weren't even looking at each other. Then I see him in church today. I don't mind telling you that scared the Hell out of me. He's not a man for public praying. Then this afternoon, when I stopped by on my way here, he said he intended to see you tomorrow. He looked like a man eager for the hours to pass."

Her stomach jumped. She only had until tomorrow to prepare all the reasons why it was crazy for him to kiss the breath out of her. "It's complicated," she said.

"Still planning on leaving on Wednesday's stage?"

"I have to."

He nodded. "I assume you've got good reasons."

She thought a dying eight-year-old seemed like a pretty good reason. "Have you seen Suzanne?"

"No. But I will yet tonight."

He didn't seem happy about it. Not like a man about to have really good sex. "Is something wrong, Fred?"

"I started thinking about Suzanne in church this morning and I haven't stopped since. She's a wonderful woman."

"She is," Sarah agreed. "Is that what's making you miserable?"

"In a way. You see, I've been enjoying her body and that makes me no better than the other men who've come before me or will come after me."

"Fred," Sarah said, putting her hand on the big man's arm. "Suzanne doesn't consider you to be the same. She knows you're different."

"I'm not. I'm not any different than the man who pays his two dollars and then goes home to share a bed with his wife. Just like that man pretends not to know her on the street when his wife walks beside him, I pretend not to know her when my children are at my side. It's a good thing that she's leaving on Wednesday's stage. She deserves something better."

Why did everything have to be so difficult? Why couldn't things just work out for somebody? "She could stay here and have something better."

"I don't understand."

"Yes, you do. Quit playing dumb, Fred. You love Suzanne

and she loves you. But neither of you will say the words. You both pretend it's just about sex."

Fred sucked in a loud breath. "You shouldn't be saying such things, Sarah. It's not ladylike."

She turned toward him and stabbed him in the chest with her finger. "Screw ladylike. You're being a fool and Suzanne's no better. I can't seem to talk any sense into her but I hoped I'd have better luck with you."

"I can't—"

"Yes, you can. That's what makes me crazy. There's nothing keeping you and Suzanne apart. Nothing but your stupid, foolish pride. You two don't even seem to understand how special what you have is. Do you know how rare that is? To find someone you love? To find someone you want to spend the rest of your life with? Do you?"

"You don't know what you're talking about," Fred denied.

"I do," Sarah insisted, wrapping her arms around her stomach. Loving John literally made her ache.

"Oh my," Fred said, sudden knowledge dawning in his eyes. "It's John, isn't it? You love him. Does he know?"

"No." The word exploded from her mouth. "And please don't tell him. It will only make it worse. It's not the same for us. There's a reason we can't be together. Something bigger than both of us."

"Don't you think he deserves to know?"

"It won't change anything." She moved the empty water glass from hand to hand. "Look, I've got to get back inside. Thomas will have a cow."

He brushed his big thumb across her cheek, wiping away a tear that had leaked. "We're a couple of losers when it comes to love, aren't we?"

"You're not going to change your mind about Suzanne, are you? You're not going to ask her to stay?"

Fred shook his head. "No. It'll be good for her to move on. She'll find somebody."

Sarah reached up and wiped Fred's own tear off his

cheek. "I'll miss you, Fred. You've been a good friend. You made being here easier."

"I can't figure out why you came back," Fred said. "I'm glad you did, mind you, but I can't figure out why you did it if you didn't plan to stay."

"If staying was an option," Sarah said, standing on her toes to give him a kiss on the cheek, "then I wouldn't be going. Good night, Fred."

He nodded, tipped his hat, and got on his horse. Sarah watched him ride out of town.

"Isn't that interesting?"

Sarah whirled around. John's mother stood twenty yards away, her arms crossed over her chest. "Evening, Mrs. Beckett," Sarah said. How much had the other woman heard?

"Were you giving poor Fred the brush-off so that you could focus on my son? My only living son?"

"I have to go inside," Sarah said. She didn't want to fight with this woman.

"Not yet," Mrs. Beckett said. "Come here."

Sarah looked up and down the dark street. She didn't really want to walk into an alley with John's mother.

"I won't harm you," Mrs. Beckett said. "I have a proposition for you."

Great. Sarah walked toward the woman.

"I want you to leave town," Mrs. Beckett said. "I want you to leave, and this time, I don't want you to come back."

Looked like Mrs. Beckett was going to get her wish. "I'll be on the Wednesday stage."

"That's not soon enough. I don't want you to spend any more time bewitching my son."

"Bewitching?"

"What else could it be? You've got him talking crazy. He plans to go with you on the Wednesday stage."

"What? That's not true."

"It is. I think he thinks he can convince you to stay if he has time alone with you."

She couldn't let John go with her. It would make it all the harder to say goodbye. She couldn't bear to hurt him like that. "You're his mother. He respects you. You need to convince him that would be a mistake."

"I tried. He won't listen. Says he's owes it to Peter."

Pain speared her tender heart. Did it always come back to Peter? "Owes it to Peter? What?"

"That's what he told me. Everything he does for you, he does for his brother. In a way, he's a lot like Fred. He can't say goodbye to the dead."

"That's not true."

"You know it's true. Through you, he touches Peter. That's what's important to him."

"You're lying."

Mrs. Beckett pulled an envelope out of skirt pocket. "Read this."

Sarah opened the envelope with shaking fingers. She pulled out a single sheet of paper.

Dear Mother,

   I'll be gone for several weeks. Need to clean up another one of Peter's messes. It's too late for him to appreciate it but it makes me feel like I'm doing something.

                                        Love, John

She recognized the bold, slanted writing. *She* was another one of Peter's messes.

Mrs. Beckett took the letter from her. "I have two hundred dollars in my purse. I'll consider it money well spent if you'll take it and leave. Tonight. You ride out of town tonight."

Two hundred dollars. Enough that she could get to California. Enough that Suzanne could get a fresh start in a new place. *It makes me feel like I'm doing something.*

She held out her hand and Mrs. Beckett slapped the envelope of money into it.

"I've arranged for Deputy Lewis to take you to Morgansville. It's on the way to Cheyenne and it's no more than a three-hour trip. You can spend the night there at the hotel. In the morning, it will be easy enough for you to find someone to take you to Cheyenne. Then I want you on the first train west to California."

She was going home. She should have been thrilled.

"What if I can't find someone to take me on to Cheyenne?"

Mrs. Beckett shrugged. "You're a smart woman, Sarah. I'm sure you'll figure it out. I imagine that for the right price, there's always someone willing to take a job. You'll have plenty of money to buy your way there."

"I'm not sure I like the sound of this," Sarah said.

"Listen, Sarah. Deputy Lewis and his wife are my good friends. He's doing it as a personal favor to me. He'll take care of it. Just be ready to leave in an hour."

An hour? "Ninety minutes," Sarah said. "I can't be ready before then. I've still got an hour's worth of work to do."

"Forget it. It doesn't matter. You're never going to see Thomas Jefferson again."

"It matters to me. I gave him my word."

Mrs. Beckett stared at her. "Fine. Just remember, you've given me your word, too. He'll bring the carriage around back of the hotel."

"Make sure there is room for two. I'm taking Suzanne with me."

DEPUTY Lewis drove, Suzanne cried, and Sarah simply stared out into the dark night, not seeing much, trying awfully hard not to feel much or to remember much.

Especially not the feel of John Beckett's strong arms or

his warm mouth. Every time her thoughts had the audacity to run in that direction, she concentrated on the cramps in her legs or how Suzanne's trunk, wedged up behind her in the back of the buggy, wore a shallow ridge into her spine.

Deputy Lewis had loaded them without ceremony. He'd pulled up behind the hotel, and within minutes, Suzanne, Sarah, and their respective luggage had been thrown in the back of the flat-bed buggy. Deputy Lewis sat up front, chewing and spitting tobacco like a crazy man, and had driven like the hounds of Hell were after him. He hadn't said a word the entire way.

Now, as they pulled into Morgansville, he shifted in his seat. "Get ready to get out," he said.

Suzanne sat up straighter and started to gather her bags. Sarah put a hand on her leg and looked around. Morgansville looked a lot like Cedarbrook. The hotel that Deputy Lewis had pulled in front of actually looked a little bigger, a little fancier. It looked pretty dark, however.

"Deputy, I hope you don't intend to just dump us in the middle of the street?"

"Damn mess," Deputy Lewis muttered. He jerked on the reins and the horses whined in response. The gas street-lights showed the sneer on the deputy's face.

"Pardon me." What did she have to lose? She'd already lost everything that mattered. "Were you talking to us?"

Deputy Lewis didn't answer. He shoved the wheel brake forward and the wagon jerked to a stop. "I'll go check on a room," he said, climbing down. "When I get back, you better both be off my wagon with your things next to you on the street. I'm sorry I ever agreed to this."

He spun around on his heel and walked up to the hotel door. Neither woman moved. Once he disappeared inside, Suzanne sighed. "You know," she said, "I'm not sure he likes us."

Sarah laughed and hugged her friend. "That's okay. I don't much like him either." She hiked up her skirt, climbed out of the wagon, then turned to help Suzanne. When Suzanne stood up, she swayed, and would have fallen if Sarah hadn't reached up and grabbed her waist, steadying her.

"Suzanne. What's wrong?"

"Nothing. I'm fine. Really."

Suzanne proceeded to get out of the wagon and stand next to it for about five seconds before she clapped her hand over her mouth. She turned and took seven steps before bending over and vomiting.

"Oh, sweetie," Sarah said, gently pulling her upright after Suzanne finished. She handed her the handkerchief from her skirt pocket. "Here. Wipe your mouth."

Suzanne dabbed. "Sorry about that," she said.

"You should have said something. Do you have the flu?"

"Flu?" Suzanne tilted her head.

"The . . . um . . . the influenza?"

Suzanne gave her a sweet smile. "If I do, then I've got the nine-month variety."

"Nine months?" Sarah put two fingers under Suzanne's chin and lifted her face. "You're pregnant?"

Suzanne nodded and her lower lip trembled. "I should have begun my monthly last week."

"Last week?" Sarah waved her free hand. "That's nothing. You've been under a lot of stress. You're probably just late."

"I've been having my monthly every twenty-eight days since I was thirteen years old. Not twenty-six and not thirty. Always twenty-eight."

"What day would today be exactly?"

"Thirty-six."

"Shit." Sarah looked up and down the dark street. "What we need is a Walgreens. A twenty-four-hour Walgreens."

"A wall what?"

Sarah threw her hands up in the air. "A drugstore. We need a damn drugstore and one of those tests. You get a little stick and you pee on it. It turns pink or blue or I'm not sure what color, but we need one."

Suzanne looked at her as if she'd lost her mind. "I already did my own test."

Sarah stopped pacing. "What?"

"I asked Freedom to bring me some fresh ground raw beef."

"And?"

"He got about three feet away and I had to stop him from coming closer. The smell made me sicker than a dog eating grass."

"That's your test?"

"That's how my sister knew."

Sarah resisted the urge to knock her head against the wooden sidewalk. "Okay. Let's assume you're right. Do you . . . do you know who the father is?"

Suzanne nodded, not looking offended. If anything, her face brightened and little twitch danced across her lips. "It's Fred's. I'm going to get to hold on to a little piece of Fred."

Sarah didn't know any other way to ask it. "How can you be sure?"

"Fred's the only one I've lain with the past month."

"But it's only been the last week or so that you haven't been working."

"I've had customers. I let them take their pleasure with my mouth. I swear, if a woman's good at that, I think a man actually prefers it over the other."

"Oh. Really?"

When Deputy Lewis approached the wagon several minutes later, both women stood in the same place, lost in their own thoughts. "What the hell are you doing just standing there? Get your things out of my rig."

"Do we have a room?" Sarah asked.

Deputy Lewis held out a key. "Here. Now get going."

Sarah took the key, being careful not to touch the deputy. "You're the reason," she said, "that police are called pigs. It's all your fault." Sarah picked up her bag and grabbed the handle of Suzanne's trunk. She walked, dragging the heavy case behind her.

"Let me help," Suzanne said.

"Just open the door," Sarah said. Suzanne ran a couple steps ahead and threw open the heavy brown door. Inside, the hotel looked much the same as the one in Cedarbrook with the exception that rather than fat Morton Turnip behind the desk, a pretty young woman, no more than eighteen, sat behind the counter.

"Evening, Ladies," she said. "Your room is number four. Up the stairs, to the left."

Sarah dragged the case another six steps. "Let me help you with that," the girl said, coming out from behind the desk. "I'm Mary Beth, by the way."

Sarah stopped to catch her breath. The girl, broad-shouldered and wide-hipped, wrapped her fingers around the handles on each end, and picked the case up. She took off for the stairs as if the case barely weighed anything.

Sarah smiled at Suzanne and skipped to catch up. "You always work the night shift?"

"My pa runs this hotel," the girl said. "I'm just filling in for him while he catches a nap. He's in the room right next door to you."

When they got to number four, Sarah unlocked the door and pushed it open. Mary Beth walked in first. "Let me get you ladies a light," she said. Within seconds, Sarah heard the sound of a match and the room was bathed in soft light from the oil lamp on the dresser. "There you go," she said, turning to look at both Sarah and Suzanne. "Pretty late to be traveling, isn't it?" the girl asked.

"Kind of a spur-of-the-moment trip," Sarah said.

"Your man just left you here?"

"He's not our man," Suzanne said. "He's nobody's man. He's a weasel dressed in trousers."

The big girl laughed, a deep, hearty sound. "We got some of them two-legged weasels in this town, too. You two fine ladies have a good night. Pa will have a pot of coffee made before the sun rises. Guests are welcome to help themselves to a cup and a warm muffin."

"How nice. A B and B. I love B and B's," Sarah said, sinking down on the bed. She flopped back, hitting the thin mattress with a thud. "Last summer I stayed in the nicest B and B in Napa Valley—practically had grape vines outside my window. Had the prettiest yellow comforter, too."

"What?" Suzanne asked.

Sarah opened one eye. A frowning Suzanne and an openly curious Mary Beth stared at her.

She needed to get some sleep before she did some real damage. She sat up. "Just listen to me rattle on. I suppose we better call it a night. I could use some sleep."

"Sleep cures most worries," Mary Beth said, moving toward the door. "That's what my pa always says. By the way, chamber pots are under the bed."

The girl closed the door behind her. Suzanne sat on one of the single beds, facing Sarah, who sat on the other. "You're acting odd, Sarah."

Sarah reached out for Suzanne's hand. "I'm sorry, Suzanne. It's just been a really long day. I'll be fine in the morning."

"Maybe she's right that sleep cures most worries."

"Great." Sarah smiled at her friend. "Maybe you'll wake up not pregnant."

Suzanne laughed but then looked very serious. "I'm glad I'm carrying Fred's baby."

"Really?"

"Oh, yes. I know it's going to be hard and I'm already worried about how I'll provide for my child. But I will. I will do everything in my power to be the best mother I can be. I'll do it for the baby. I'll do it for Fred."

Sarah hugged her friend. "I wish I could do more to help you," she said.

"More? You've already given me all that money. Are you sure you won't need it yourself?"

"I kept a little. I just need enough to pay someone to take me to Cheyenne. Once I'm there, I'll need train fare to California."

"What happens when you get back to California?"

"Everything. Nothing. It's hard to explain. Let's just say that I go back to my life."

"Like I said, you're sounding odd."

"Trust me. Not nearly as odd as I could." Sarah stood up next to the bed and unbuttoned her blouse and skirt. She took off her clothes, leaving just her camisole and petticoat. "Come on, let's get some sleep. Pregnant women need their rest. How are you feeling now?"

"Better. Just in case," Suzanne said, reaching over the side of the bed, "I'll keep this little pot handy."

Sarah rubbed the back of her neck. Lord, she was tired. "If you get sick," she said, "wake me up. I mean it."

Suzanne nodded and leaned closer to Sarah. "You don't look so good yourself. Are you terribly sorry about leaving John?"

John. Solid, sensible John Beckett. She would miss him forever. "I'm just tired," Sarah said. She didn't want to talk about John. Didn't want to think about him. Certainly didn't want to remember the look in his eyes when she'd unbuttoned her camisole, his gaze almost burning through the thin material.

"What's he going to think when he comes to town and you're gone?"

He'd think he was right about Sarah One. "He won't waste time thinking about it," she said. "He's got the ranch."

"A ranch don't keep a man warm at night."

She thought about his strong hands, his firm thighs, his tender lips. She squeezed her eyes shut, hoping to chase away the image. "He'll probably be glad I'm gone," she said.

Suzanne snorted. "Don't be a fool, Sarah. John Beckett had the eyes of a wanting man every time he looked at you. He's going to go crazy when he finds out that you sneaked out in the middle of the night."

EIGHTEEN

JOHN woke up when Morton started growling. Silently, he rolled out of bed and walked across the room, grabbing his rifle off the wall on his way. With just the tip of his finger, he edged the curtain aside.

Fog swept across the valley, obscuring his view. John listened. Horses approached. Two riders, he thought, working their horses hard, not even trying to be quiet. He opened the window and stuck the barrel of his rifle out.

"Quiet, Morton," he ordered, his voice low. The dog paced nervously in front of the door.

The pounding of hooves ceased. The animals were close enough that he could hear their labored breathing but he still couldn't see a thing. He put his finger on the trigger.

When he heard the footsteps, he pushed his gun out another inch. "That's far enough. I don't want to have to shoot you."

"Christ, don't do that."

Fred? "Fred, what's going on?"

"You're not going to believe it," Fred said just as he

came into full view, not more than three feet from the front door. "Let us in. We don't have time to waste."

John blinked his eyes. George, the stranger from the saloon, followed Fred. What the Hell was going on?

He strode over to the door and whipped it open. "This better be good," he said. He put his gun down, struck a match, and lit a lantern. He held it up, looking at the two men. It was the pure look of panic in Fred's eyes that scared him.

"What's wrong?" John asked. "Are the children—"

"They're fine," Fred said.

"What then?" John resisted the urge to shake his friend. "Why are you with—"

"We need to get going," George interrupted, nodding at the door.

Christ, he'd been wanting to rip something apart with his bare hands ever since he'd been dragged away from Sarah's nearly naked body. It might as well be George's face. "What the hell are you doing here?" John asked.

The man didn't answer.

John turned toward Fred. "What's he doing here?"

George took a step forward. "My name is George Tyler. I'm the sheriff of Bluemont, North Dakota." The man rubbed a hand across his chin. "My wife," he said, his voice softer, "was killed. Murdered. Almost six months ago. A neighbor saw three men riding away and described them. Still, it took me four months to track down the first one."

"Did you kill him?"

"I didn't have to. He was already dying. Had consumption. Before he died, he told me about the two other men. Guess he thought confession might help the soul. Anyway, he knew one of them. Mitchell Dority. He said Dority . . . he said the bastard forced himself on my wife before he killed her."

John felt his anger slip away, replaced by an over-whelming sadness for the woman who had suffered. And the husband who still suffered.

"I started tracking Dority. He managed to keep one step ahead of me. I asked around and it didn't take long to learn that he and Deputy Lewis had joined up to cheat the Indians."

"Lewis?" John asked, hardly able to believe it. No wonder the man had turned a blind eye and a deaf ear toward Suzanne's injuries. "Lewis is the third man?"

"No. I don't think so. The man I'm tracking is very thin, very blond, not much over thirty. I knew if I stuck close to Lewis, I'd get Dority. I intended to give Dority the chance to lead me to the third man."

"Then what?"

"Then I plan to kill them both."

John didn't doubt it one bit. George Tyler said it without emotion, without fear.

"I'd met Sheriff Armstrong years ago," George said. "I asked him to leave town, hoping that Lewis would get brave and careless. He was happy to do it. He don't think much of Lewis."

"No one does," Fred said.

"Well, I made sure that Lewis didn't have any reason to think much of me. In fact, I made sure he thought I'd go along with most any scheme. Just two days ago, Lewis and Dority approached me about taking liquor out to the reservation."

John felt the muscles in his stomach tighten up. "Dority is back in Cedarbrook?"

"Yes."

John looked at Fred. "We've got to warn Sarah and Suzanne."

"It's too late," George said.

John whirled toward the man. "What do you mean it's too late?"

Fred put a hand on his arm. "You're not going to like it, John."

John shook him off. "I need to see Sarah," he said, picking up his rifle.

"Pack for a long ride," George said.

"What?"

"Sarah and Suzanne left town earlier tonight," George said.

"What? Why?"

"I don't know why," Fred said. "I do know how. Deputy Lewis drove them."

"Lewis? I don't understand."

"John," Fred said, staring somewhere over John's head, "your mother asked him to."

John felt the tightness spread from his gut to his chest, like a wall of burning fire. "What's my mother got to do with this?"

"I don't know," George said. "I do know what I heard Lewis tell Dority."

"What?" John demanded.

"I saw Lewis drive his rig back to town about an hour ago. I was about to approach when Dority emerged from the darkness. I got close enough to overhear. Lewis told him that your mother had asked him to drive the women to Morgansville. Dority said something about finishing what he'd started and he rode out of town a half hour later."

John reached for his coat and hat, his mind whirling. He'd underestimated his mother, and now Sarah could pay the price.

"We need to get to Dority before he gets to the women," George said.

John reached for a box of bullets. "I'll kill the bastard myself if he touches Sarah."

"Get your horse," Fred said, opening the door. "We're going to need to ride hard."

* * *

SARAH woke up when the chamber pot skidded across the wooden floor. It hit the far wall with a thump. She turned over in bed and the moonlight shining in the window offered just enough light that she could see Mitchell Dority standing over Suzanne's bed.

"Well, well. Looks like my lucky night," Dority said. He reached down and splayed his hand across Suzanne's neck, effectively pinning her to the bed. He stared at Sarah. "Two for the price of one."

Sarah scrambled to sit up. Dority laughed, an ugly wicked sneer. "Don't bother," he said. "I like my women on their backs."

Sarah knew she'd die first. "Help! Help us!" she screamed.

"Scream all you want," Dority said. "There ain't nobody else staying in this place. I checked the guest register. Right before I took my pleasure with that sweet little thing sitting behind the desk."

"You bastard," Sarah cried. "She was just a girl."

Dority stood up, reached over, and slapped her so hard her head bounced off the headboard.

"Sarah." Suzanne tried to climb out of bed but Dority whirled, pulled a knife from his belt, and pressed the blade up against her throat.

"Get up," he said to Sarah. "Come over here."

She didn't move.

"Do it or I'll slit her throat."

Sarah pushed her legs over the side of the bed. She took five steps.

Dority grabbed the sheet off Suzanne's bed and, with the flick on his wrist, sliced it three times. He threw it at Sarah. "Rip it," he said.

Her hands shook so badly that she could barely hold the material.

"Do it," he yelled. He pressed the knife into Suzanne's throat.

Sarah ripped. When she had three strips, Dority motioned her toward the bed. "Tie her hands and feet. Tie them tight."

Sarah took a step forward. If she could get close enough to knock the knife out of his hand, they might have a chance. "Give me your wrists, Suzanne," she said. When Suzanne held out her arms, Sarah squeezed one hand before wrapping the sheet around.

"Tighter," Dority said, pushing the knife against Suzanne's throat. Sarah saw a thin line of fresh blood. She pulled the sheet tight and knotted it.

"Now her feet," Dority ordered.

When Sarah finished, Dority grabbed the remaining cloth, sliced a section off, wadded it up, and stuck it in Suzanne mouth. She gagged.

"She's choking," Sarah cried.

Dority laughed. He leaned close to Suzanne's face. "I should have killed you when I had the chance. Now, you lay back and watch while I have some fun with your friend."

JOHN rode his horse as he'd never ridden him before, crashing through the dense fog, sometimes barely able to see fifty feet ahead. He gave his horse plenty of rein, trusting in the animal's surefootedness. After an hour, the stifling white fog dissipated and the trio continued on, through the still, black night, lit only by a few stars and a quarter moon. Their horses flew across the rough ground, as if the animals, too, somehow realized that seconds counted and caution was a luxury they could ill afford.

John tried to stay focused. He couldn't think about Dority, couldn't let himself wonder at the damage and pain a man like Dority could cause. He certainly couldn't let himself remember how poor Suzanne's face had looked and how much worse it might have been had Sarah, foolish, sweet Sarah, not rushed in and saved her friend.

So he thought about Sarah's face. Her pretty skin, the light freckles on her pert little nose, the deep, clear blue of her eyes, and the sexy dimple next to her mouth. He thought about the softness of her hands, the hands that had washed his naked body. He thought about the silkiness of her hair when he'd run his hands through it, and he thought about the sweetness of her lips when he'd kissed her.

He could see her at the saloon, her hands flying over the piano keys, a smile dancing in her eyes. And as clear as if she sat in front of him, he could remember the pure joy on her face the day he'd taken her up in the mountains.

The day he'd realized he loved her.

He kicked his horse, urging the animal on. If Dority had touched her, had caused her even a moment of pain or fear, he would pay.

"There's the hotel," George said.

It was the first word any of the men had spoken for three hours.

"That's Dority's rig," Fred said.

John was out of his saddle before his horse had fully stopped. He took the two hotel steps in one leap and threw open the door.

He smelled the blood before he saw it.

George pushed past him and leaned over the counter. "Christ," he said.

Fred and John looked. A girl, no more than eighteen, naked from the waist down, blood smeared on the inside of her thighs, lay on her back, her eyes closed. George moved around the end of the counter and squatted down. He placed two fingers against the pulse in her neck.

"Is she dead?" Fred asked.

"No." George gently touched her face, turning her head to the side. "She's got a hell of a bump on her head. Probably knocked her out."

"Before or after?" Fred asked, his voice thick with disgust.

"I don't know," George said.

"We've got to find Sarah," John said, already moving. He didn't get more than two steps before he heard her scream.

"Upstairs," he said, taking off at a dead run. He made it halfway before he heard another half-scream and then the dull thud of weight hitting the floor.

He took the last eight steps, Fred and George on his heels, then kicked open the door. He saw Suzanne first, her ankles and wrists bound, lying on the bed. She looked scared to death but otherwise unharmed.

Then he saw Sarah. She lay on the floor, five feet away from Dority, her body, dressed in white undergarments, curled up into a ball. Dority stood over her, a knife in his hand.

"I've got Dority," George said, his gun pointed right at the man's heart.

Dority stood perfectly still, his mouth hanging open, as if he couldn't believe he'd been caught.

"Sarah?" John cried, praying that he wasn't too late, that she wasn't dead.

And then, miracle of miracles, she lifted her head, turned her face to him, and gave him a wobbly smile.

He crossed the room, knelt down, and gathered her in his arms. She buried her face into his chest. She felt warm and alive and he thought his heart might burst. Wrapping his arms around her, he rested his chin on her head, and breathed in the sweet scent of her hair.

"Oh, Sarah," he said. "Oh, sweetheart. Are you hurt? Did he hurt you?"

She shook her head but her body began to tremble. He could feel the moisture from her tears on his shirt. Not sure what else to do, he patted her back. He looked over at Fred. His friend had untied Suzanne and now he sat on the bed with Suzanne in his lap. Together, the two of them rocked back and forth, back and forth.

"It's over, Sarah," John said. "I won't let him hurt you. Ever again. Come on, sweetheart. Look at me."

He pulled back and cupped her face. That's when he saw the red welt on her cheek, the unmistakable mark of an angry man's palm against soft skin. He reeled away from her and raised his gun toward Dority. "You son of a bitch. I'm going to—"

"You hurt my little girl."

Everyone in the room, including Dority, whirled toward the door. A man, almost as big as Fred, stood there, wearing nothing but a nightgown and socks and holding a rifle in his arms. Before anyone could move, he fired. Dority staggered back, his hands clenched to his chest, before dropping awkwardly to his knees, then facedown on the wooden floor.

"Jesus Christ," Fred said.

Suzanne looked up, saw Dority and the blood pooling under his body, and clapped her hand over her mouth. Fred stared at her for just a second before reaching one long arm down and grabbing the chamber pot off the floor. Then he held it for her while she vomited.

John lowered his gun. He turned and grabbed Sarah, who stood absolutely still, as white as her undergarments. "Sweetheart, don't look at him. Look at me. Come on, Sarah."

George looked from Dority to the old man in the doorway and then back again to Dority. He bent down and felt Dority's neck. He stood up and shrugged. "It's over," he said.

The old man in the doorway hadn't moved. "He hurt my daughter," he said, his voice quiet.

"I know he did, sir." George reached into his vest pocket and pulled out his tin star. "I'm the sheriff of Bluemont, North Dakota. You need to put your gun down."

Sarah lifted her head. "Sheriff?"

John nodded.

"She was a good girl," the man said. "She insisted on helping me. Said I needed my sleep. She's only seventeen." A tear ran down the man's weathered face.

"She needs a doctor," George said, taking a step toward the man. "Is there one nearby?"

The man didn't act like he'd heard George. "I woke up when I heard someone screaming," he said. "I didn't know what was going on. I went downstairs and I"—the man's voice faltered—"I saw Mary Beth. I went to get my gun. I keep it in the kitchen. I heard another scream and then saw the three of you running up the stairs. I knew the bastard was still here. He had to pay for what he did. It's only right."

"I understand," George said. He was close enough now that he gently removed the gun from the man's hand. "More than you know. I understand."

"I've got to go tend to my daughter," the man said. "She ain't got no mother."

George nodded. "I'll help you."

"You going to arrest me?" the old man asked.

"I . . . I don't—"

"The way I saw it," John said, interrupting George, "it was self-defense. He was coming at you with his knife."

"That's what I saw, too," Fred said. He got up, walked over to the dressing table, poured water out of the pitcher onto a strip of sheet, returned to the bed, and carefully wiped Suzanne's face.

George looked from Fred to John, indecision clear on his face. Then he looked at the old man before raising his eyes to the sky. "This is for you, Hannah," he whispered. He brought his gaze back to the old man. "No doubt about it. Self-defense. You didn't have any choice but to shoot him. I'll talk to the sheriff for you."

Sarah let out a sigh and John hugged her tighter.

"What are you going to do with him?" the old man asked.

"We'll leave him right where he is until the sheriff can get here," George said.

"I'll go find him," Fred offered.

"That's fine," George said. "John, why don't you take the women somewhere else? They don't need to be seeing this."

"I'll take care of it," John said.

George wrapped an arm around the old man's shoulder. "Come on," he said. "Let's go."

John turned toward the women. "Get your things and wait for me down the hall."

"I want to help him," Sarah said, reaching for her skirt and blouse. "I want to help Mary Beth."

"Me, too," Suzanne said, already moving off the bed. "She'll need a woman to talk to."

AN hour later a remarkably calm Mary Beth had regained consciousness. Sarah and Suzanne had cleaned her up and sat with her until she'd fallen asleep.

"She's amazing," Sarah whispered as the two women walked out of the room. "I'd have been hysterical. When she said that Dority's badness didn't shame her, I thought I was going to lose it."

"Lose it?"

"You know, go crazy."

"I think she'll be fine," Suzanne said. "She'll have some bad days ahead but she's got a good head on her shoulders. She knows life goes on."

Sarah turned toward her friend. She remembered Suzanne admitting that she'd sold herself at thirteen, but her friend's knowing tone told her this was something else. "You say that," she said, carefully picking her words, "like you've had some experience with this."

Suzanne nodded. "Men can be bastards."

Sarah felt rage, pure burning rage, at the hurt both

Suzanne and Mary Beth had suffered. "How old were you?"

"Twelve. He was my mother's cousin."

"God." Sarah rested her head against the wide wooden trim around the doorway.

"Come on," Suzanne said, pulling at her arm. "I'm so tired I could fall asleep standing up. I need a bed."

They walked down the hall and ran into John Beckett. He held two keys in his hand. "How's she doing?" he asked.

"As well as can be expected," Suzanne said. "How is her father?"

"The sheriff wanted him to come down to his office. Before he left, he said you two could move to new rooms."

"Rooms with a bed?" Suzanne asked.

"Yes."

"Thank you," she said. "I thought I might have to sleep in the hall."

John handed her a key. "Fred's outside taking care of the horses. We rode them pretty hard. He should be back in a few minutes. I . . . I gave him your room number."

Suzanne blushed. "That was very thoughtful of you." She turned toward Sarah. "Will you be all right?"

"Dandy," Sarah said, hugging her friend. She waited until Suzanne had unlocked her door and gone inside before turning toward John.

"Separate rooms?" she asked.

John looked over her shoulder. "Fred's idea."

Maybe, just maybe, it was going to work out for one of them. "When he sat on that bed with Suzanne, he looked every bit like a man who didn't intend to let go."

"I thought the same thing."

"I'm happy for them," she said. She needed to concentrate on that. Not on how darn unhappy she was. And she most definitely needed to get inside before she did something incredibly stupid like ask John to come in. "May I?" she asked, holding out her hand.

John didn't answer. Instead he walked over and un-locked the door. "I'd like a few minutes of your time," he said.

A few minutes of her time. He sounded stiff and formal and not at all like the man who'd held her in his arms just an hour before. "Come in," she said.

This room looked identical to the one they'd left just an hour before—with the exception that there wasn't a dead man on the floor. Sarah took a seat on one bed, careful to keep her eyes off the spot where, two doors down, Dority probably still lay in a puddle of his own blood.

John took off his hat and hung it on the hook by the door. He remained standing, just staring at his boots. For a man who'd needed to talk to her, he seemed to have little to say.

Lord, but he looked tired. She desperately wanted to wrap her arms around him and hold him close. She wanted to comfort him, to console, to soothe. She wanted what she couldn't have.

She slipped her hands under her bottom. "John," she said, unable to stand the silence a moment longer, "I appreciate your help tonight."

He looked up, one eyebrow raised.

Great. Now she sounded like a tired hostess thanking a party guest who'd stayed around to pick up dirty dishes. Like a nervous hostess, she rattled on. "That's kind of surprising news about George. He's a sheriff?"

John nodded. "With a reason to hate Dority."

Dority. Would she ever hear the name and not feel the bone-chilling fear? "I never thought he'd follow me."

John pushed himself away from the wall. "Follow you? You knew he was in Cedarbrook?"

He asked it casually enough but she could hear the ten-sion in his tone. "I saw him smoking with George." She smiled at John but he didn't smile back. "I didn't realize that George was on our side."

"I suppose," he said, inspecting the nails on his right hand, "that you forgot to mention it to either Fred or me."

She wouldn't lie about it. "No, I didn't forget. I chose not to tell you."

His head jerked up and he had fire in his eyes. "I thought you were smarter than that."

Sarah took a deep breath and tried to remember that this man had, in all likelihood, saved her life earlier that night.

John began to pace around the small room, his steps short and jerky. He ran his hands through his glorious hair. "I thought you cared more about Suzanne."

That hurt more than most any insult he could have come up with. "I warned Suzanne," she said. "Freedom knew, too."

John threw one hand in the air. "No wonder you felt so safe."

Sarah stood up. She'd been awake for close to twenty-four hours and she couldn't handle this. "Look, John. I can tell that you're pissed."

He stopped pacing and stared at her.

"Yes, I said pissed. I'm not only stupid, I'm vulgar. Maybe I screwed up. Maybe I underestimated Dority."

"You think so?"

Damn him for acting so smug. "Everything I did, I did to protect Suzanne or Fred or you. I did the best I could. If it wasn't good enough for you, that's too freakin' bad."

"Protect me?" He threw out both hands, as if he couldn't believe it. "Who told you I needed to be protected?"

"Nobody. I figured it out all by myself."

John shook a finger at her. "Do you know? Do you have any idea how lucky you are? Do you know what Dority could have done if he'd had five more minutes?"

Did she know? It was her body the man's hands had crawled across. All the fear, all the shame, all the pent-up rage she'd felt for the last hour exploded. "Yes, damn you," she yelled. "I do. When he put his hands on my breasts and squeezed and groped, I knew. When he pushed himself up against me and I could feel him, I knew. And"—she could no longer hold back her tears—"when I thought about what he'd done to that young girl, I thought dying might be easier. I started to pray for that."

"Oh, sweetheart," he said, all traces of anger gone.

His concern made the dam break. She cried, her body heaving with sobs.

"Now, now," he said, wrapping his arms around her. "Don't cry. Please don't cry."

She cried harder.

He put one hand behind her neck and pressed her face into his shirt. He absorbed her cries, her pain, her utter desperation at having been at the mercy of Mitchell Dority. When she finally stopped, he had a big, wet spot on his blue shirt. "I'm sorry," she said. She lifted up the edge of the bedspread and dabbed at it.

"Forget it," he said, and captured both her hands in one of his. He took his free hand and brushed remaining tears off her cheeks. "You're a mess," he said, giving her one of his sweet smiles.

Mess. It reminded her of the note John had left for his mother. *Need to clean up another one of Peter's messes.* "John," she said, trying to scoot away. He held her tight. She squirmed but couldn't budge him. "Thank you," she said. "Even if you just did it for Peter, that's okay. You still came. I'm alive today because—"

John pushed her away. "What did you just say?"

"I'm alive—"

"No, before that."

Too late, she realized her mistake. John didn't know that his mother had shared his note. She doubted Mrs. Beckett would have offered that up.

"Sarah?"

In for a penny, in for a pound. "I saw the note you left for your mother."

"I left a note for my mother?"

"You need to know something. Your mother came to see me last night at the saloon. She offered me two hundred dollars to leave town."

"Two hundred dollars?"

"Yes. And I took it."

He sat down on the bed, looking dazed. He closed his eyes and rubbed the bridge of his nose. "I don't understand."

"It's pretty simple. Your mother believed that you intended to go with me on Wednesday's stage."

"I told her that," John said.

"You never said anything."

"I meant to. I hadn't had the chance."

"Why?"

"I . . . I don't know."

Sarah swallowed. John Beckett was a good man. Even when he did something for the wrong reasons. "I saw the note, John. You told your mother that you had to leave town for a couple days so that you could clean up another one of Peter's messes. After all that happened between us, that's all I was. Just another one of Peter's messes."

"No," he said, standing up.

"John, I saw the note."

"It's not what you think."

"It was pretty clear."

"No. What you saw wasn't clear, it was convenient. I know the note. I wrote that note when Peter got in trouble with a married woman. Three years ago."

"Three years?" Sarah put one hand over her mouth. "You wrote it three years ago?" She shook her head, trying to clear it. "How your mother must have hated Sarah One."

"Sarah One?"

With every word she said, she seemed to be digging a deeper hole. She couldn't even keep her stories straight anymore. Everything was so mixed up. And John was looking at her like he couldn't figure out if she was the lunatic or if he was. He deserved to know the truth. "John, I think you better sit down."

NINETEEN

"THERE'S more?" John asked.

She inclined her head toward the chair by the door. "Please, just sit." She couldn't bear to have him too close. Her resolve would weaken. When John sat on the edge of the chair, she jumped in.

"I'm not who you think I am."

He seemed to consider that. "Go on," he said.

"I'm not your sister-in-law and I was never married to Peter."

He shook his head. "That's nonsense. I saw the license myself."

"Before last week, I'd never been in Cedarbrook. I'd never even heard of it."

"Sarah," he said, his voice soft. "You've had a difficult night. You need some sleep."

"I was born in 1977."

He swallowed, the muscles of his strong neck visibly working.

"My name is Sarah Jane Tremont and I've lived my

whole life in California. I was walking on the beach and I got swallowed up by a big wave. The next thing I knew, I was flat on my back, about a mile from your house."

His face lost all color. When he stood, his movements were uncoordinated. "Sarah, if this is some kind of joke—"

"It's no joke. I'm telling you that on the seventeenth of April, I woke up in my own bed, went to work, had some chicken at lunch, and when I went to bed that night, I was sleeping on your mattress. I somehow traveled back in time. I don't know how and I don't know why. I just know that I did."

"It's impossible," he said, shaking his head.

"I would have thought so, too. I thought if I told you the truth, you'd think I was crazy."

He sat down hard on the chair. "Crazy? Why would I think that?" He laughed, a shaky, brittle chuckle.

"It's true. When I realized that you'd mixed me up with your sister-in-law, I didn't correct you. I was scared. So I pretended to be her."

"Her?"

"Sarah One. Or at least, that's what I call her."

He stood up and began to pace, taking five steps forward, then five back. Finally, he stopped and stared at her, his eyes dark with pain. "You've been in Cedarbrook for ten days. Why tell me this now?"

Because I love you. She shook her head. "I don't know. I guess because I'll be getting on a train in Cheyenne and I'll never see you again. I wanted you to know the truth."

John picked his hat up off the hook and slapped it against his leg. "The truth? None of this makes any sense. I don't know who the hell you are. Here's what I do know. You may not be Sarah Beckett but the two of you have a lot in common. She was a liar, too."

JOHN stepped off the wooden sidewalk and checked the saddle on his horse, making sure it was still cinched tight.

He couldn't stay in this town another minute. Knowing it would be foolish to travel without water, he lifted the flap of his saddlebag and yanked out his canteen. The envelope, the one he'd picked up from Harry Pierce and had been carrying around for days, fell in the dirt. He'd forgotten all about it.

He picked it up, dusted it off, and started to stuff it back in his saddlebag. Hell, maybe before he left, he'd take a few dollars of his cattle money and go have a big steak and a bottle of whiskey to go with it. Maybe then he'd quit acting like an ass. Sarah didn't want him. She'd resorted to making up wild stories to drive him away.

He ripped the envelope open, and when he unfolded the single sheet, paper money fell into his hand. Way more money than he was owed for the cattle. He sat down on the sidewalk and began to read.

Dear Mr. Beckett,

Please allow me to introduce myself. My name is Franklin Wimberly, and by profession, I am an attorney at law. It is in this capacity that I regret to inform you of the passing of your sister-in-law, Sarah Beckett. Mrs. Beckett became ill following a most serious accident with her horse. She passed from this life on the seventeenth of April.

Prior to Mrs. Beckett's unfortunate demise, she, being of sound mind and counsel, asked that following her death, the sum of three thousand and two hundred dollars be returned to you along with her gravest apologies for any injustice done or unhappiness brought upon your family.

Her last thought on earth was a wish that she could have returned to Cedarbrook and made amends somehow.

My most sincere regards,
Franklin Wimberly

John leaned his head against the hitching post and closed his eyes. After several deep breaths, he opened them and read the letter twice more.

The day she'd left, Peter's wife had taken with her thirty-two hundred dollars. It had to be true. She was dead. She'd passed from this life on the seventeenth of April.

What was it that Sarah had said? She'd woken up in her own bed on the seventeenth of April and ended up on his mattress.

Was it possible that Sarah, the woman upstairs who drove him to sheer madness, had somehow come back in time—perhaps at the exact time his sister-in-law had passed from this life? How could it be?

Somehow it was. He knew it. He could see the look in her eyes when he'd called her a liar. She hadn't been lying.

She'd forgiven him once for accusing her of something she was innocent of. Would she be so willing a second time? "Oh, God," he said.

"What do you have to 'Oh, God' about?"

John jerked his head up. George stood less than three feet away, his arms folded across his chest.

"I think I've made a terrible mistake," John said.

"Tell me," George said, sinking down next to John.

John shook his head. He couldn't tell anybody. He barely believed it himself.

"Humor me," George said. "After all, I did come get you last night. I could have ridden after Dority on my own. Anyway, I'd appreciate having something new to think about."

The man looked exhausted, like every bit of life had been drained out of him. John remembered what Dority had done to George's wife and knew that seeing the bastard had taken its toll on the lawman. "How is Mary Beth's father?" he asked, choosing his words carefully. George didn't seem like the type to want others to be overly concerned about him.

"I sent him home with Mary Beth. Hotel is officially closed for the day."

John could still see the look of pure disbelief on George's face when Mary Beth's father had fired his gun. "Dority died before you could question him," he said, stating the obvious.

"That's about all I've been thinking about for the last two hours. I'd been waiting for Dority to lead me to the third man. I could have killed the bastard weeks ago and none of this would have happened."

Would Sarah have gotten the chance to tell him that she wasn't really Peter's wife? Would he feel better or worse than he did right now? "I guess things work out the way they're supposed to," John said. "Now what happens?"

"I don't know." George scooted back on the sidewalk, far enough that he could rest his shoulders against the hotel wall. "Part of me wants to go on looking. But—this is going to sound odd—it's almost like I can hear Hannah talking to me."

"Talking to you?" John felt a shiver run down his spine. "What does she say?"

"That vengeance will not heal the pain."

"That's it?"

"No." George smiled and his eyes looked like he was far away. "She tells me she loves me and that I need to let go so that she doesn't have to worry about me."

"Was she right? You got your vengeance. You might not have fired the shot but that doesn't make Dority any less dead."

George shook his head. "Like always, Hannah is right. Seeing Dority bleed out didn't make me miss her any less."

George sounded old and weary. "You must have loved her very much," John said.

"I did. I suspect sort of like the way you love Sarah."

He wouldn't deny it. "How did you know?"

"Since Hannah's death, I've become a good watcher. I

see you when Sarah's in the room. You can't keep your
eyes off her. And then if some crazy fool is stupid enough
to even look her direction, you're like a snarling dog protecting his bone. You've got it bad."

He did have it bad. He loved a woman and he didn't even
know who she was. She'd lied to him. But what choice had
she had? If she'd told him the truth that first night, he
wouldn't have believed her. He'd have assumed it was another one of his sister-in-law's schemes and he'd have rid
himself of her at the first possible moment. She'd have been
alone, in a strange place, with no money, no hope.

"Well?" George prompted. "What are you doing down
here?"

"I said some things to Sarah that I'm not proud of. I hurt
her."

"So, you've chosen to hide down here rather than be upstairs, begging for her forgiveness."

"I can't face her."

George shook his head. "Do you know what I'd give to
have my Hannah back, to hold her, love her, talk to her? Do
you know what I'd do to have her for one more day?"

John ran his hands through his hair. "Christ, I don't
know what to make of all of this."

"Pastor Dan told me that peace comes to those who can
forgive, whether it's forgiving God or someone else."

"Pastor Dan?"

"I went to see him after I started hearing Hannah's
voice. I got kind of spooked."

"He's a good man."

"Seems like it. When I heard the rumors about Sarah
and Fred, I went to see him. Anybody with half a mind
would know it wasn't true. I'd overheard Sarah tell Thomas
Jefferson that she planned to play for Sunday services. I
didn't want Pastor Dan thinking poorly of her."

"What did he say?"

"He said that the Lord works in mysterious ways and

that, as hard as it might be to believe, even Turnip with his vicious lies could be God's instrument."

Hearing about Fred and Sarah had been what had pushed him to admit his feelings about Sarah. "Maybe Pastor Dan is right. It doesn't really matter now. She's leaving anyway."

"When?"

John shrugged. "I guess she plans to take the train from Cheyenne to California."

"Last time I checked, it was a two-day stage ride from here to Cheyenne."

"So?"

"Here's the thing. You don't ever know how much time you have. The morning Hannah was killed, I'd left early. I had a prisoner at the jail and I wanted to relieve my deputy. Hannah had been up late the night before. She was carrying our child and had been sick."

John swallowed hard. "Dority will burn in hell. I'm sorry, George. I'm sorry for your loss."

"I left that morning without waking her. I left without a kiss or a hug or telling her that I loved her."

"She knew."

"I think she did. I hope so. I tell her now, when she comes to talk to me."

Sarah would leave thinking he hated her. It wasn't true. Sarah Beckett? Sarah Jane Tremont? It didn't matter. She was his Sarah. Sarah who made him laugh, who made him want, who made him yearn.

"Don't let her go without saying goodbye. Don't make the same mistake I did."

SARAH opened the door and almost ran into John's fist.

"I was just about to knock," he said. "I didn't realize you were on your way out."

Sarah blinked and hoped she'd run out of tears. "I need to check on transportation to Cheyenne."

"May I come in for a few minutes?"

So he could step on her heart again? "That didn't work out so well the last time you asked that question. I think we've said everything that needs to be said."

He shook his head. "Please. Just a few minutes. That's all I'm asking."

Damn him. She didn't know how many more hurtful, hateful words she could endure. "Fine," she said and stepped back into the room.

He'd barely shut the door when he started talking. "Sarah, I acted like an ass earlier. You caught me a little short and I didn't handle it well." He brushed a hand across her cheek, his fingertips just grazing her lashes, which were still wet with tears. "I caused these tears. I'm sorry for that, more sorry than you'll ever know."

Sure that her legs could no longer hold her, she sank down on the bed. "It doesn't matter. I'm—"

"Sarah." He moved in front of her and grabbed her hands in his. "It matters. It matters very much. I'm begging you. Please forgive me."

"I lied to you. Can you forgive that?"

He put his finger under her chin and tilted her head up. "You're really from the future?"

"Yes."

"From California?"

"Yes."

His face got very serious and she expected him to bolt for the door. What she didn't expect was for him to calmly walk back over to the door, slip the hook into the latch, and hang his hat on the hook by the door.

"John?"

He turned toward her. "The last ten days have been the best ten days of my life. I got kicked in the head by a horse and even that was good. Because you were there. Only because of you."

He crossed the room and held out a hand to her. She took it and they stood together, just inches apart. She could feel his warm breath wash across her cheek.

"I know I should have a thousand questions for you. You could tell me about things that are beyond my imagination. But I've only got one question."

"Yes."

"Will you let me kiss you, Sarah?"

Sarah's body started to shake. Her knees, her silly bony knees, trembled against his strong legs. John looked down and smiled. "Is that a yes?"

She nodded, unable to speak.

He pulled her closer still. She could feel his heat and the pure, powerful strength of his body. He took his hands and cupped them around her face. "So beautiful."

She felt beautiful. For the first time ever, she felt perfect.

"I dream about you," he said. "I see your face, your adorable freckles, your mouth." He ran the tip of his finger across her lips and she felt the answering zing rip through her body.

Then, ever so lightly, with the pad of his thumb, he traced her collarbone. "So delicate. So womanly."

He ran his finger up her neck, tilting her chin up. He lowered his head until his lips just brushed hers. Then he ran the tip of his tongue across her lower lip. His hand, the one that remained on her shoulder, quivered.

When he pulled her close and pressed his lips to hers, she savored the warm, complex taste of his mouth. He kissed her for a very long time. When he pulled back, they were both breathless.

"Sarah," he said, his chest rapidly rising and falling. "I've got one more question."

"Yes?"

"Will you let me share your bed?"

Now it was her body that quaked. "I've never wanted anything more," she said.

He sighed, a deep, long release of air. Then, with excruciating slowness, he undid the buttons of her blouse. He smiled and shook his head when he saw the buttons of her camisole. Then, deliberately, careful not to touch her, he undid all seven.

He slipped one hand inside and cupped her bare breast. Her breath caught in her throat. She needed air, she needed strength, she needed him. When he flicked his finger across the nipple, her body jerked in response.

He grabbed the edges of the material and freed her arms. The cotton dropped to the floor and she stood before him, naked to the waist. She felt the cool air in the room brush against her heated skin.

"So full. So pretty." He bent his head down. "In my dreams," he said, "I take you in my mouth."

He ran his tongue across her.

"Your body is warm and soft," he said as his tongue darted across her one more time.

She felt it all the way to her toes.

"You taste rich and sweet and I am a greedy man," he said, and his mouth clamped down on her turgid nipple.

She thought she might just die, right then and there. When she swayed, she felt his strong arms hold her. He suckled harder and she felt the answering response deep in her core. She arched her back and pushed herself into him.

He lifted his head and gave her a sleepy smile.

He dipped his index finger inside the waistband of her skirt and skimmed the material until he came to rest on the button. "May I?"

She nodded, her head feeling heavy.

Within seconds, her skirt and petticoat pooled around her ankles. He stared at her blue bikini panties. He ran a finger under the elastic waist and her stomach muscles jerked in response.

"What do you call these?" he asked, his voice hoarse.

"Panties. They're popular in my day."

He studied her. "I like them. Very much." He traced them, from one hip to the other, brushing intimately against her. She pressed her legs together. My God, she was going to come and he'd barely touched her.

He laughed. "Sweet Sarah," he said. He gently pushed her back until her legs hit the bed. Then he lowered her on it and lay next to her, his head propped up on his bent arm. "In my dreams, you come to my bed, naked, and you slip between the sheets. I take you in my arms and you slide against my body."

Nothing else, she knew, would stem the wanting.

"Your skin is like sun-warmed silk and I want you desperately but I make myself wait. I pull back the sheets and the cool night air blows across your body."

She could practically feel the chill. Her nipples, wet from his kisses, strained upward.

"Every part of you is perfect. Even your toes." With the tip of his index finger, he traced from her heel to her toes.

Her foot arched in response.

Bold and brazen, she lifted her hips and he pulled her panties down. She kicked the silk free. He ran his hands up and down her thighs. "Beautiful," he said. "So delicate, yet so strong. In my dreams, you wrap your legs around me and I feel your strength."

She was going to explode.

"Your womanly scent fills my bed," he said, "making me want with an urgency I cannot describe."

He didn't need to describe it. She was on fire with it.

Then he laid his cheek against her blond curls and kissed the inside of her thigh.

Oh my God. "Take your clothes off," she said.

He lifted his head. "Not yet." He took his hands and gently spread her legs apart. Then he made love to her with his mouth.

And when she came, it was with such force that her body shook from the power of it. Afterward, he rested his head against her still-quivering stomach.

"Are you all right?" he asked.

She felt like purring. Like she was a big cat who'd gotten stroked.

"Thank you," he said. "For making my dream come true."

Her heart did a funny little pitter-pat. For a man who didn't talk much, he had a way with words. "You have too many clothes on," she said.

He lifted his head. "Are you sure?"

"Absolutely."

She could feel him gather his big, warm body up. He stood up, shrugged each shoulder, dropping his suspenders. He pulled his shirt from his pants and started to pull it off.

He got naked the same way he did everything else. Efficiently, with no wasted motion. He stood before her, in all his splendid glory. She couldn't tear her eyes away.

"Sarah?"

"Yes."

"Is something wrong?"

"No. No, I wouldn't exactly say that."

He tilted his chin up, looking unsure. "Well, then. What exactly would you say?"

"Wow."

He smiled. "I want to share your bed, Sarah."

She'd never wanted anything more. With one finger, she motioned him close. He stretched his long frame out next to her. She could feel the hair on his arms, his legs, brushing up against her body.

She turned on her side and faced him. She ran the tip of her index finger across his chest and smiled when his flat nipples hardened. "Like that?" she asked.

He nodded, looking very serious. "I want you to touch

me. Everywhere. Next time. And the time after. But Sarah"—his voice sounded strained—"I don't believe I can wait. I very much want to make you mine. Now."

She wrapped her arms around his neck. "I've been waiting for days."

"Days?" He blinked his dark brown eyes. "Oh, Sarah," he moaned. In one swift motion, he flipped her over onto her back. His hands raced over her, touching her breasts, her stomach, her thighs. He bent his head and suckled at her nipples, first one then the other.

With one knee, he nudged her thighs apart. She arched, wanting, needing, willing to beg. He pressed himself up against her and pushed.

And pushed.

She prayed.

"Relax," he murmured, his voice close to her ear.

She tried, she really tried.

He shoved into her and suddenly tore beyond her resistance. Pain, slices of it, ripped through her.

His head jerked up. "Oh, my Sarah."

With every bit of strength she had, she grabbed his bare hips and pulled him into her, bringing him to her core.

"Jesus Christ," he said.

She squeezed her inner muscles. He moved and each stroke was hot and wet and more intense than she could have imagined. Desperate for release, she pressed. Hard. And when he rocked against her, she exploded.

Wave after wave of pleasure wracked her body like surf crashing on a beach. It rolled over her, sweeping her up, tossing her, carrying her to places unknown. When finally the tide ebbed, it left her trembling.

"Oh, John," she said.

He cupped her face with his hands and very gently kissed her. Then he started to move. Slow at first, then faster, then faster still, until finally, she could not separate where he ended and she began. He pounded into her, slapping against her skin, taking her, making her his. With a sudden cry, he stiffened, and his body jerked in the spasms of completion.

He held himself still, the weight of his upper body braced on his forearms, his eyes closed. Then, slowly, gently, he left her. She squeezed her legs together and looked at him through one barely open eye.

He lay absolutely still. He stared at her, then at himself. She could see the smear of fresh blood on his skin. He didn't say a word. Finally, he walked across the room. He poured water from the pitcher onto a clean towel and folded it twice. He walked back to the bed and handed it to her.

"I imagine some cool water might help," he said, as if they'd just finished a brisk walk around the block rather than some bed-shaking, body-bruising sex.

Fine. Two could play this game. "Thank you." With as much grace as she could muster, she pressed the cool cloth to herself.

He nodded and reached for his shirt.

He was leaving? Just like that? She swallowed, hoping like heck she wouldn't cry in front of him.

He buttoned his pants and slipped his suspenders over his shoulders.

Damn him. Damn him for making her love him. Damn him for making her want to stay. Damn him for touching her, for changing her, for leaving her. She curled up on the bed, wanting to protect her naked body, her naked soul.

She waited. John walked to the door and took a seat in the chair that sat next to it. He held his hat in his hand.

"Get out," she said. "Go ahead and leave."

He shook his head, looking a little dazed. "I'm not planning on leaving, Sarah. I just thought it might be helpful if one of us had some clothes on."

He wasn't leaving. "I don't understand."

He shrugged. "Me neither. I know you told me you came from the future. I believed you. At least, I thought I

did." His face lost all color and she could see the strong
muscles of his throat working as he tried to swallow. "You
were untouched. No man has ever lain with you."

I think I was waiting for you. "John, we don't have to
talk about this."

He shook his head. "We do. You're not Peter's wife?"

"I'm not."

He nodded and stared straight ahead. She wondered
what he was seeing. The room was so quiet that she
could hear the early-morning birds chirping outside the
closed window.

"There's something you need to know," John said, his
voice soft. "Peter's wife, that Sarah, is dead."

"Dead! What?"

He turned toward her. "For almost a week, I've been
carrying around a letter. I hadn't opened it. I thought it was
something else. An attorney wrote it. Turns out he witnessed Sarah's death. On the seventeenth of April."

April seventeenth. She tried to swallow but her throat
was dry.

"She sent the money back. All of it. Her final wish was
to make amends."

Oh, my. "Do you feel differently about her now?"

"I think so," John said. His voice was filled with sadness.
"But I don't think it's because of the money. I think I feel
differently because I've finally let go of the hatred. You
know, it was easy to hate Sarah. It allowed me to focus on
the kind of woman I thought she was. Then I didn't have to
think about the kind of man I'd become."

"You're a good man, John Beckett," Sarah said, trying to
reassure him.

John shrugged his broad shoulders. "Earlier you said
that you didn't know how or why you came. I don't know
how but I know why. You came for me. To save me. To
make me whole. To make a difference in my life."

She'd made a difference.

She and Sarah One had both gotten their wishes.

"And Sarah, you were wrong," he added, his voice even softer. "You said I could never see you as anything besides Sarah Beckett. That I'd only be able to think of you as Peter's wife."

"John, you don't need to . . ."

He gave her a look that heated her blood. "There's only one way I can think of you now. You're my Sarah. My sweet Sarah."

She couldn't talk. She couldn't even think. It had been so wonderful, so absolutely right. It made it all that much harder to know that she had to leave him.

"John," she said, "you need to understand something. I still have to go. I can't stay."

"Will you tell me why?"

"There's a child who needs me."

"Not your child," he said knowingly, looking at the tangled sheets.

She could feel the warmth flood her face. After what they'd shared, how could she still blush? "Remember I told you that I work at a school? I'm a social worker."

He did his eyebrow thing again.

"I have special training to help children who have troubles. You know, trouble at home, trouble at school, trouble learning."

"I imagine you're very good at that," he said, his eyes warm with appreciation. "You've a gift with children."

"No," she denied, thinking her chest might burst. He thought she had a gift.

He smiled at her. "I've seen you with Fred's children."

Sarah shrugged. "Fred's children are easy. Some of the kids I'm trying to help have very serious problems."

"You do important work," he said.

"I used to think it was important," she said. "But the

truth is, that for every child I help, there are ten more waiting in line. I can't do enough, it's never enough."

He got up from his chair, walked over to the bed, and sat down. He reached out for her hand. "If you help one, even though there are more, then at least one child suffers less. That is more than most people will ever do. Now, tell me about the child that needs you."

His hand felt warm and strong and she thought that if she could just hold it forever, then everything might be okay. "His name is Miguel Lopez. He's eight and he's wonderful. Very polite. Very sweet. Good to his sisters and a joy to his mother."

"His father?"

"No father. He died just a few months before Miguel's mother left Mexico to bring Miguel and his two sisters to live in the United States."

"And what is Miguel's trouble?"

"He's dying."

John's arm jerked but he didn't release her hand. If anything, he held it a little tighter. "You can keep him from dying?"

I wish. "No. He has a brain tumor. It's hard to explain but his brain has something growing on it. Sometimes the doctor can operate and remove the growth, the tumor."

"But not always?"

"No. Not with this certain kind of tumor."

"Is he in pain?" John asked, his voice soft.

"Not so much now. But he will be. It will soon be difficult for him to walk or to talk or to even feed himself. Every day he will get a little worse. This is a horrible type of illness. He needs his mother," she said, swallowing hard.

"Of course," he said.

And if she hadn't loved him before, it would have been that simple comment, that simple understanding, that pushed her over the edge. "I have information that his mother needs." Thank God for that customer service representative who'd had the brains and compassion to actually pull the file, rather than simply read the computerized records. Rosa had applied for the home health rider and had been approved. The insurance company had failed to increase her premium, and when everyone had simply looked at the computerized record, they assumed Rosa Lopez, who didn't speak much English and wrote even less, didn't have a clue what she was talking about.

John reached up and tucked a piece of hair behind her ear.

"Maybe I'm a selfish bastard," he said, his voice husky with emotion, "but I have to ask. I have to know. Is there no one else who can help? Does it have to be you?"

She placed the palm of her hand against his cheek. His skin was warm and rough with a day's worth of whiskers. "There's no one else. That family needs me."

He drew in a deep breath and stroked her hair. "You said earlier that you could never do enough. You're wrong, Sarah. You will be *their* enough."

The tears she'd tried to hold back would not be denied. "I'd stay forever if I could."

He leaned forward and brushed her lips with a kiss. "And I would ask you to stay with me. For forever. But I learned something today."

"What?" she asked, sniffling.

He took the edge of the sheet and dabbed at her eyes and at her runny nose. Then he smiled at her. "A man, a much wiser man than me, told me that you never know how much time you get. You might get an hour, a day, or a lifetime." John stood up. "I'm not going to get a lifetime with you, am I, Sarah?"

She shook her head.

"But we could have an hour, a day, maybe even a couple. Would you like that?"

"Yes."

John started to unbutton his shirt.

"What are you doing?" she asked, her heart afraid to hope.

"We've wasted enough time."

TWENTY

WHEN the stage pulled in, John motioned for Sarah to wait. He stuck his head in, looked around, and then stepped back. "You can get in," he said.

"What were you looking for?" Sarah asked.

"We're going to be on that stage for three days. I don't especially want to make the trip with somebody who thinks bathing is an annual event."

She wrinkled her nose. "What's the verdict?"

"Lemon and Wintergreen, I believe. Two old ladies. We'll make George sit between them."

"You're terrible," Sarah teased.

"I'm not the one who asked him to come along."

She'd made the decision to tell George. He'd been reluctant to go with her and John on the stage until she'd blurted out the truth. He'd gone pale and hadn't said a word for two minutes. Then he'd laughed. For a very long time. Until he'd been short of breath and red in the face. She'd worried that she'd pushed him over the edge. The man had had enough heartache in the past six months. He deserved to have a breakdown.

"Why are you laughing?" she had asked.

"Hannah was right again," he'd said. And for the first time since she'd met George, he'd almost looked at peace.

"About what?" she'd asked.

"Just a couple nights ago, Hannah came to me. I woke up and she was sitting next to me, drinking a cup of tea. I could smell the tea. It was strong, just like she loved it. She said that I was going to meet someone, someone very different, and that this person would need my help."

"Different?"

"I thought she meant different from her. Now, I'm sure she must have meant you. Someone from another time. That's different. You're different."

Sarah hadn't known whether to be insulted or not. She didn't worry about it once George agreed to come with them.

"You know why I did it," she said, grabbing John's arm.

"I know," he said, gently removing her fingers. "You don't want me to be alone when you get on that train." He pulled her away from the stage and wrapped his arms around her. "I hate it. I hate it more every day."

"I'd stay if I could."

"I believe you. It doesn't make it easier."

She'd never, ever, find another man like John Beckett. "John, maybe we should part here. Maybe it would just be better."

"Remember what the wise man said. You never know how much time. We've got now. We've got right now and no one can take it away from us." He kissed her. With the same passion and intensity that he'd kissed her with for the last two days.

They'd practically barricaded themselves in the hotel room. Even when she'd thought her body could take no more, that she had no more to give, John had pushed her higher, pushed her to new limits. They'd surfaced last night. George had organized a pig roast in honor of Fred and Suzanne's marriage announcement. Mary Beth and her father had come. The celebration had gone late into the night but still, when they'd returned to the room, John had made love to her.

"So, my Sarah," John said, shaking her out of her reverie, "let's go. I've already loaded your bag in the back." He held out his hand and helped her into the stage. She sat on the empty bench and John slid in beside her.

Sarah looked at her traveling companions and delicately sniffed. "Good morning, ladies," she said.

"Morning, dear," Lemon said.

"Oh, good. Young people," added Wintergreen. "Where are you headed?"

"Cheyenne," Sarah said.

Lemon clapped her hands. "Us, too. Looks like we'll have plenty of time to get acquainted."

"Is this your wedding trip? You two act like newlyweds," Wintergreen said.

"Oh, we're not—"

"Newlyweds," John interrupted Sarah. He gave her a look that had her squirming in her seat. "We've been married almost six months."

"Oh, remember what it was like to be young." Wintergreen grinned and poked Lemon in the arm.

"Barely," she said, her faded blue eyes blinking furiously.

"I haven't had my Henry for four years and I can still remember his touch," Wintergreen said. She closed her eyes and a sad smile crossed her face.

John leaned close to Sarah's ear. "An hour. A day. You never know."

The stage door opened and George poked his head in.

"Isn't that right, George?" John asked.

"What?"

"Sit right here, young man." Lemon slid over and patted the seat between her and Wintergreen. "That way we can fight over you."

For a lawman, George looked downright scared.

"What's in that box?" Wintergreen asked.

"My camera." George squeezed between the two women. "I thought I might snap a picture or two along the way."

Sarah understood the significance of the statement. Last night, George had shared with John that he'd loved taking pictures of his wife but that he hadn't been able to use his camera since her death.

"Why you wanted a picture of that pig on a stick is beyond me," Sarah said, smiling at George.

"I took one of you, too."

"No you didn't."

"I most certainly did. You had your back to me, staring into the fire. I took it just as a gust of wind blew your hair ribbons. John saw me. I got him in it, too."

Sarah's heart leapt, and she put her hand over her mouth. The picture. The one she'd bought at the antique store. It had been of her and John.

"What's wrong?" John asked, sitting up straighter.

She smiled at him. "Nothing. Everything makes perfect sense." She closed her eyes.

Three hours later, when Sarah woke up, both of the old ladies looked a lot fresher than she felt. John had one arm around her and her head rested against his chest.

When she sat up, he gingerly removed his arm and wriggled his fingers. "What's wrong?" she asked.

He smiled at her. "My hand hasn't had any feeling for the past half hour."

She punched his shoulder. "You fool. You should have woken me up."

"I liked the feel of you in my arms."

"My, my," Wintergreen said. "You must have been tired."

Sarah looked across the stage and couldn't keep the grin off her face. George held a ball of yarn in his lap, and with each click of her knitting needles, Wintergreen pulled a string.

"I didn't know you could knit," Sarah said, looking at George.

George narrowed his eyes at her. "You sleep with your mouth open."

Sarah tossed her head. "Sticks and stones."

Lemon picked up the pretty ribbon that hung around her neck and looked at the timepiece that swung at the end. "We'll be stopping for lunch soon."

As if on cue, Sarah's stomach growled.

"Don't get too excited," John said. "The driver would have picked up sandwiches and cold drinks in Morgansville. We won't have a hot meal until we get to the changing station tonight. We'll spend the night there and get fresh horses for tomorrow's trip."

When the stage did stop fifteen minutes later, George got out first. Then he turned to help Lemon and Wintergreen. The trio moved away from the door. John got out and turned to help Sarah. He placed his hands around her waist and gently lifted her out of the stage. When he set her down, he slid her down his hard body. They were front to front, heat to heat, need to need.

"Why did you tell Wintergreen and Lemon that we're married?" she asked.

"I thought they might be the type to want to protect a young woman's honor. I could probably handle interference from one. I didn't know how I'd fare with the pair of 'em."

She kissed him. "I would protect you," she teased.

"Like this?" he asked, putting his hands on her bottom and pulling her close. She could feel every hard inch of his body. She squirmed and he groaned and bent his head to kiss her.

"Hey, you two, you know we're only stopping for ten minutes." The stage driver, a disapproving look on his weathered face, stood less than six feet away.

John released her and stepped away. She pursed her lips at him and he rolled his eyes.

Ten minutes. At the rate she was heating up, it would have been over long before that.

"There are some trees over there," the driver continued. "That's where the women take care of their needs."

Sarah shrugged. If Lemon and Wintergreen could squat to pee, so could she.

Late that night, John, Sarah, and George were the only ones awake inside the changing station. It was a simple place, no bigger than John's cabin. There were cots along one wall, a big round table for eating and playing cards, and a stove for cooking and heat. Wintergreen and Lemon had been asleep for an hour, snoring lightly in the corner. The stage driver paced outside, his boots a solid thud against the wooden porch.

"What's his problem?" Sarah asked. "After lunch he started acting strange."

"It's going to storm," George said. "These roads can be pretty dangerous if they get a good drenching."

Sarah was more thankful than ever to have shelter. She'd thought they might have to sleep outside. The changing station had been a nice surprise. The only problem was that it didn't provide any privacy for her and John.

He sat facing the stove. He'd thrown wood in earlier and now a nice fire warmed the room. The fire, along with two lanterns, provided all the light in the room.

George lay on the floor. "Tell me about your time, Sarah."

"Much about life is the same in my time. But we do," she said, rubbing her tailbone, "have better roads and cars."

"Cars?" George asked.

"Yes. Horse riding is purely for pleasure. A car is sort

of a box of plastic and metal that you sit in, that has four tires. It runs on fuel, not coal or oil, but gasoline."

"You have one of these cars?"

"I do. Almost everyone does. It's crazy. There are cars everywhere. Mine is parked at the beach. It needs a key and I lost mine somewhere between 2005 and 1888."

"What will you do?" John asked, sounding concerned.

"I have an extra key at my house. I live about two miles from the beach, in a little white two-story, right across the street from the park."

Sarah felt tears stinging behind her eyes and she tried to blink them away. "So I need to get back to the beach and find the footprints again, the ones that will take me back."

John stood up abruptly, setting his tin coffee cup down with a clank. "Let's take a walk," he said.

She leaned into him, loving the feel of his hard body. "I thought you said it was going to storm."

"We'll be fine." He grabbed two blankets off the cot and shoved one under an arm. He wrapped the other one around her.

When they opened the door, the air had an odd stillness about it. Knowing the storm was coming, Sarah had expected wind and rain. But the cool night air barely stirred.

The stagecoach driver sat on the porch, his boots propped up on the railing. "It's going to be a fierce one," he said. "I wouldn't go far."

"We won't," John said. He led her around the corner of the changing station and then up a hill, to a grove of pine trees. He spread the blankets out, one on top of the other, making a bed on the soft, fragrant pine needles. He sat down and pulled her down into his lap.

She laughed and kissed him. "We didn't say goodbye to George. What's he going to think?"

"If he's anywhere near as bright as I think he might be,

he's going to know that I brought you up to this stand of trees to ravish you."

She licked her lips. "Sounds interesting. What exactly does a man do when he ravishes a woman?"

John nuzzled her neck. "A little of this, a little of that."

Sarah shook her head. "Little? That doesn't sound so good to me. Maybe I'm not interested after all."

In one smooth motion, he moved her off his lap and onto her back. He knelt next to her. "Not interested?" he growled.

She could smell the earth, the coming rain, and his wanting. It was all mixed together and it seeped in, shaking her, bruising her, changing her. "Maybe you could convince me."

He kissed her. Hard. And when she opened her mouth, he pushed his tongue inside. His hands were everywhere, touching her face, her neck, her breasts. She lifted her hips, not able to pretend that she could wait.

He unbuttoned her blouse while she yanked it free of her skirt. When he undid the last button, her breasts sprang free, falling into his hands. "Your camisole?" he said, his mouth nipping at her neck.

She reared up and licked his ear. "I took my panties off, too," she whispered.

He froze. And then it was as if she'd unleashed a tiger. His hands were under her skirt, touching, finding, caressing, teasing. She arched into his hand, and his fingers probed, robbing her of breath, driving her high, making her beg.

"Oh, John," she said. "Oh, yes. Yes." And when she came, a million tiny sparks shot through her.

"Oh, God," she said. She looked at him, half sitting, half reclining, his eyes bright in the moonlight. And she heard the roar of thunder in the distance.

He took his hand away and she mourned the loss. John stood up. He shed his coat, his shirt, his pants, everything. Until he was absolutely, splendidly naked. She unbuttoned

her skirt and pulled it down, not wanting anything to separate them.

Lightning cracked above them. "John, it's going to
rain."

"I'm not stopping now," he said, his lips barely moving.
He knelt between her legs. "I want you, Sarah. I want to
feel your heat, your softness."

She pulled him toward her and they were one. He moved,
letting her adjust, letting her know his strength, his power.
He bent his head and caught her nipple in his mouth. When
he scraped his teeth across her, he pushed her over the edge
again.

The storm was closer now. Thunder rumbled and lightning flashed. He waited, letting the shudders subside. Then
he slipped his hands underneath her and lifted her closer,
his penetration deeper with each stroke. He rode her with a
desperation that had little to do with the impending storm
and everything to do with her leaving.

Deeper. Harder. Tempting. Leading. "Oh, God," she
said, her tired body rising up once again. She came, her inner muscles clamping down on him.

He surged, let out a hoarse cry, and emptied himself in
her. Then he collapsed. She couldn't breathe. She couldn't
move. She loved it.

It wasn't until he slipped out of her and moved to her
side that she realized it was raining.

He put one arm underneath her head and pulled her
close. Then he reached out, grabbed his coat, and covered
the two of them. That, along with the trees and the blanket
above them, protected them from the worst of the rain.

"We should go inside," she said.

He shook his head. "Not yet. I want to hold you."

She wished he could hold her forever. "John, we need to
talk about this," she said. "The stage will be in Cheyenne
tomorrow."

"I know that."

She knew as well as he did that they had made love for the last time. "I don't want to go, John. I love you. I'll always love you."

He started to cry. She could feel his big body silently quaking. She caught his hand in hers and brought it up between the two of them. She laid it on her breast. "I will keep you here, John Beckett. I will keep you in my heart until the end of time."

"I love you, Sarah. I know I said that I could be happy with an hour, a day, whatever we had. But I don't want to let you go."

She kissed him and she tasted salt. "I love you, too. I think I've loved you since you bandaged my foot that first night."

"I've loved you since you made me soup."

She kissed the tip of his nose. "It's true then. The way to a man's heart is through his stomach."

"Oh, Sarah. You are my heart. You are my love. My everything. I don't know what I'm going to do without you."

She knew she could not leave without loving him one more time. She pushed him onto his back, shedding his coat on the way.

"Sweetheart, you'll get wet," he said.

"I don't care." She took him in her mouth and delighted in the immediate response. When he was hard, his head thrashing from side to side, she gave him a final kiss before letting go. Then she sank down on him, taking him into her warmth.

"Christ, Sarah," he said, thrusting up inside her.

She rode him as thunder roared and lightning crashed, and wind whipped around them. Up. Down. Squeezing. Taking. And when he reared up, his hips coming off the ground, she hurtled over the edge and they flew into the storm, reckless, fearless, joyful.

Later, he helped her dress. "My skirt is wet," she said.

"It's going to get a lot wetter," he answered, peering out

of the trees. "I thought it might let up but it's getting worse. That wind is wicked, maybe the worst I've ever seen. I'm going to hang on to you. Don't let go of my hand."

They ran down the hill, the wind stealing their breath. They were halfway there when a bolt of lightning cracked and a tree, a huge, towering tree, no more than two hundred yards from them, split in half, making the ground literally shake. John grabbed her and swung her up into his arms, running the rest of the way. He kicked at the door and it flew open.

"Jesus," George said. "Get in here."

John shifted her and let her slide down his body. When Sarah looked around, she saw Lemon and Wintergreen, wide awake, sitting up, their arms wrapped around each other. They looked frightened to death.

The stage driver sat on the cot next to them, working his jaw around a wad of chewing tobacco. His hands were clasped and his eyes closed.

Funny. She hadn't figured him for a praying man.

When the thunder boomed, so loud it hurt their ears, Lemon shrieked and started to cry. Rain hit the tin roof and the noise vibrated through the small room.

The wind blew harder, the shrill cry of an angry woman, shaking the small building. John grabbed her and took her to the corner. He wrapped her in blankets and then sat next to her, cuddling her.

The stage driver pulled out a big bottle of whiskey, took a deep drink, then passed it to Wintergreen and Lemon. They didn't hesitate. The three of them kept rotating the bottle until they all passed out. Lemon had her head on the driver's shoulder and Wintergreen had her head in Lemon's lap.

It went on forever. The wind, the thunder, the lightning. A cacophony of noise and light and power. Sarah clapped her hands over her ears and John pulled her closer.

And then it ended. Almost as quickly as it had begun.

John and George looked at each other, then looked

around the small room, as if they couldn't believe the building had managed to stand up against the storm.

"I've never heard anything like that," George said.

"Me either," John said.

Sarah sat in the corner, too afraid to move. She had. Once.

John stood up and stretched. He smiled down at her but his smile quickly faded. "Sarah? Honey? What's wrong? You're pale as a ghost." John shook her gently. "It's over. We're okay."

Feeling stiff and old, she got up and walked to the door. She opened it, knowing what she would see. And they were there.

Footsteps. The ground was a swirling mass of mud with the exception of the footprints. They were clear. And leading away from the changing station.

John came up behind her. She heard his quick intake of breath and felt the tension in his body. She took another step toward the door and he yanked her back.

"No," he cried. "No. I'm not ready."

She'd never be ready. It would kill her to leave him. But she didn't have a choice. She turned to him. "An hour. A day. We had both. A lifetime was not ours to have."

He hung his head. Then with a courage she knew cost him dearly, he lifted his chin and met her eyes. "I love you. I will always love you. Forever. Until we meet again, my sweet Sarah."

Then he kissed her. And when the kiss ended, she clung to him, savoring his scent, memorizing his strong lines.

Then she turned and took the first step. The ground inside the footstep was firm and hard, so different from the swirling mud that surrounded them. She held her breath, knowing that at any minute she would be sucked up, taken from John.

She took another step. Then another. Until she reached the end.

It was nothing like before. The footsteps still stretched inches beyond her shoes. She turned to John. He stood in the doorway, his face absolutely white.

"Something's wrong," she cried.

"What should I do?" he asked.

"I don't know."

"Come back. Now. Sarah, come back."

She tried. She couldn't lift a foot. She tried, with every ounce of strength she had, but she was captured.

John stepped off the porch.

"No," she wailed. He'd be lost, too.

It took him just seconds to reach her. Then he lifted her up in his arms, held her to his chest, his face smothered in her neck. "I can't lose you," he said. "I can't survive it."

She shook in his arms. "Take me inside," she said. "Take me back."

When they got inside, they both collapsed on the floor, tears running freely down their faces.

George stood at the door, a strange look on his face. He looked at the footprints, then back at Sarah and John.

"I think it's time for me to go," he said, his voice soft.

Sarah peered over John's shoulder. "What?"

"It's time."

"What are you talking about, George?" John asked, his voice hoarse.

"The other night, I told you that Hannah came to me and told me that a woman needed my help."

"Yes."

"She told me something else. It didn't seem to make much sense so I didn't say anything. She said that I was going to take a long journey to a faraway place filled with strangers and strange things. But that I shouldn't be frightened."

Sarah jerked away from John and ran to George. She put her hand on his arm. "What are you saying?"

"Those footprints are for me."

"It's not possible," Sarah said.

George leaned down and kissed Sarah's cheek. "Don't worry. I'll make sure Miguel stays at home with his mother."

There was so much she needed to tell him. So much he needed to know. "Wait," she said.

"No. It has to be now." George walked over to the table, picked up his camera, and slung the strap of the brown case over his shoulder. He turned to John. "Good luck, my friend. Remember. An hour, a day, a lifetime."

John came to the door and wrapped his arms around George. "Thank you," he said. "For everything."

George winked and looked at Sarah. "Give my best to Lemon and Wintergreen. Tell them they'll have to find somebody new to hold their yarn."

George turned and took his first step. The ground rumbled. He took another. Red and green and purple balls of light appeared, then exploded, until the sky was a blaze of color.

He took his third step. Wisps of steam escaped the earth and Sarah smelled her ocean once again.

He took a fourth step and Sarah could hear the seagulls, swooping low, teasing, calling.

He took a fifth step and he was gone.

EPILOGUE

SARAH thought she might sweat to death before the wedding started. "Stand still," she mumbled, her mouth full of hairpins. She'd spent the last ten minutes cleaning dirt off Thomas's pants, and now Helen, half her hair up and the other half down, squirmed in front of her.

"Let's go," said the girl. "It's going to start without us."

"It can't. You're the bridesmaid and I'm providing the music. Nothing happens without us."

Helen turned and looked up, her eyes bright with tears. "It's really happening. I prayed and prayed."

Sarah let the pins drop to the floor. Who cared about hair at a time like this? She wrapped her arms around the girl's shoulders.

"I heard Father tell Grandfather that he was a lucky man to have loved two wonderful women." Helen leaned close to Sarah. "I'm the lucky one, to have two mothers."

Sarah looked down the aisle of the small church to where John Beckett sat. She watched as his mother entered the church, looking uncertain. She came to the end of John's pew and stood there.

When he looked up and smiled, the woman's shoulders lifted, as if a great weight had been removed. John patted the spot next to him.

It would be okay. Maybe she and Mrs. Beckett might even be friends one day.

Sarah straightened Helen's bow, catching John's eye. He winked at her, pulled out his pocket watch, and tapped on it.

An hour. A day. A lifetime.

They were going to have it all.

BERKLEY SENSATION
COMING IN FEBRUARY 2005

Depth Perception
by Linda Castillo
Nat Jennings nearly died the night her family was murdered. Now, three years later, she's teaming up with a sexy ex-con to hunt down the killer who destroyed both their lives.

0-425-20109-0

Vision in Blue
by Nicole Byrd
Orphan Gemma Smith is desperate to know who she really is. One day, a letter sends her to London where she meets the handsome Matthew Fallon. Both searching for loved ones, they are drawn together by their quest—and their passion.

0-425-20110-4

Nothing to Lose
by Kathryn Shay
Three years after the World Trade Center attacks, firefighter Ian Woodward struggles with his physical and emotional wounds—to become whole for a woman who loves him.

0-425-20111-1

I Spy
by Jacey Ford
The three beautiful FBI agents of *Dangerous Curves* return, risking their lives—and their hearts.

0-425-20112-0

Jane's Warlord

by Angela Knight

The sexy debut novel from
the author of
Master of the Night

The next target of a time travelling killer,
crime reporter Jane Colby finds herself in the
hands of a warlord from the future sent to
protect her—and in his hands is just where
she wants to be.

"CHILLS, THRILLS...[A] SEXY TALE."
—EMMA HOLLY

0-425-19684-4

Available wherever books are sold or at
www.penguin.com